CHARLAINE HARRIS

DEADLOCKED

GOLLANCZ
LONDON

First published in Great Britain in 2012 by Gollancz
An imprint of the Orion Publishing Group
Orion House, 5 Upper St Martin's Lane, London WC2H 9EA
An Hachette UK Company

A CIP catalogue record for this book is available from the British Library

ISBN 978 0 575 09657 8 (Cased)
ISBN 978 0 575 009658 5 (Export Trade Paperback)

1 3 5 7 9 10 8 6 4 2

Printed in Great Britain by
Clays Ltd, St Ives plc

www.charlaineharris.com
www.orionbooks.co.uk

Julia, this is for you.
I love you, honey.

ACKNOWLEDGMENTS

I appreciate the advice and encouragement given by my friends Dana Cameron and Toni L. P. Kelner. I couldn't do any of this without my husband, Hal. Paula Woldan (bffpaula) has made my life a cakewalk rather than an obstacle course. And heartfelt thanks to my agent, Joshua Bilmes of JABberwocky, who guards the entrance to my cave.

My sincere gratitude to Stefan Diamante of Body Roxx for his Male Strippers 101 course.

Chapter 1

It was hot as the six shades of Hell even this late in the evening, and I'd had a busy day at work. The last thing I wanted to do was to sit in a crowded bar to watch my cousin get naked. But it was Ladies Only night at Hooligans, we'd planned this excursion for days, and the bar was full of hooting and hollering women determined to have a good time.

My very pregnant friend Tara sat to my right, and Holly, who worked at Sam Merlotte's bar like me and Kennedy Keyes, sat on my left. Kennedy and Michele, my brother's girlfriend, sat on the other side of the table.

"The *Sook*-ee," Kennedy called, and grinned at me. Kennedy had been first runner-up to Miss Louisiana a few years ago, and despite her stint in prison she'd retained her spectacular looks and grooming, including teeth that could blind an oncoming bus.

"I'm glad you decided to come, Kennedy," I said. "Danny doesn't mind?" She'd been waffling the very afternoon before. I'd been sure she'd stay at home.

"Hey, I want to see some cute guys naked, don't you?" Kennedy said.

I glanced around at the other women. "Unless I missed a page, we all get to see guys naked, on a regular basis," I said. Though I hadn't been trying to be funny, my friends shrieked with laughter. They were just that giddy.

I'd only spoken the truth: I'd been dating Eric Northman for a while; Kennedy and Danny Prideaux had gotten pretty intense; Michele and Jason were practically living together; Tara was *married and pregnant*, for gosh sakes; and Holly was engaged to Hoyt Fortenberry, who barely stopped in at his own apartment any longer.

"You gotta at least be curious," Michele said, raising her voice to be heard over the clamor. "Even if you get to see Claude around the house all the time. With his clothes on, but still . . ."

"Yeah, when's his place gonna be ready for him to move back?" Tara asked. "How long can it take to put in new plumbing?"

Claude's Monroe house's plumbing was in fine shape as far as I knew. The plumbing fiction was simply better than saying, "My cousin's a fairy, and he needs the company of other fairies, since he's in exile. Also, my half-fairy great-uncle Dermot, a carbon copy of my brother, came along for the heck of it." The fae, unlike the vampires and the werewolves, wanted to keep their existence a deep secret.

Also, Michele's assumption that I'd never seen Claude naked was incorrect. Though the spectacularly handsome Claude was my cousin—and I certainly kept *my* clothes on around the house—the fairy attitude about nudity was totally casual. Claude, with his long black hair, brooding face, and rippling abs, was absolutely mouthwatering . . . until he opened his mouth. Dermot lived with me, too, but Dermot was more modest in his habits . . . maybe because I'd told him how I felt about bare-assed relatives.

I liked Dermot a lot better than I liked Claude. I had mixed feelings about Claude. None of those feelings were sexual. I'd very recently and reluctantly allowed him back into my house after we'd had an argument, in fact.

"I don't mind having him and Dermot around the house. They've helped me out a lot," I said weakly.

"What about Dermot? Does Dermot strip, too?" Kennedy asked hopefully.

"He does managerial stuff here. Him stripping would be weird for you, huh, Michele?" I said. Dermot's a ringer for my brother, who'd been tight with Michele for a long time—a long time in Jason terms.

"Yeah, I couldn't watch that," she said. "Except maybe for comparison purposes!" We all laughed.

While they continued to talk about men, I looked around the club. I'd never been in Hooligans when it was this busy, and I'd never been to a Ladies Only night. There was a lot to think about—the staff, for example.

We'd paid our cover charge to a very buxom young woman with webs between her fingers. She'd flashed me a smile when she caught me staring, but my friends hadn't given her a second glance. After we'd passed through the inner door, we were ushered to our seats by an elf named Bellenos, whom I'd last seen offering me the head of my enemy. Literally.

None of my friends seemed to notice anything different about Bellenos, either—but he didn't look like a regular man to me. His head of auburn hair was smooth and peltlike, his far-apart eyes were slanting and dark, his freckles were larger than human freckles, and the points of his needle-sharp inch-long teeth gleamed in the dim house lights. When I'd first met Bellenos, he'd been unable to mask himself as human. Now he could.

"Enjoy, ladies," Bellenos had told us in his deep voice. "We've had this table reserved for you." He'd given me a particular smile as he turned to go back to the entrance.

We were seated right by the stage. A hand-lettered sign in the middle of the tablecloth read, "Bon Temps Party."

"I hope I get to thank Claude real personally," Kennedy said, with a sultry leer. She was definitely fighting with Danny; I could tell. Michele giggled and poked Tara's shoulder.

Finally, knowing Claude was a perk.

"That redhead who showed us to the table thought you were cute, Sookie," Tara said uneasily. I could tell she was thinking of my full-time boyfriend and vampire husband, Eric Northman. She figured he wouldn't be too happy about a stranger ogling me.

"He was just being polite because I'm Claude's cousin," I said.

"Like hell! He was looking at you like you were chocolate-chip-cookie-dough ice cream," she said. "He wanted to eat you up."

I was pretty sure she was right, but maybe not in the sense she meant; not that I could read Bellenos's mind, any more than that of any other supernatural creature . . . but elves are what you'd call unrestricted in their diet. I hoped Claude was keeping a close watch on the mixed bag of fae he'd accumulated here at Hooligans.

Meanwhile, Tara was complaining that her hair had lost all its body during her pregnancy, and Kennedy said, "Have a conditioning session at Death by Fashion in Shreveport. Immanuel's the best."

"He cut my hair once," I said, and they all looked at me in astonishment. "You remember? When my hair got singed?"

"When the bar was bombed," Kennedy said. "That was Immanuel? Wow, Sookie, I didn't know you knew him."

"A little," I said. "I thought about getting some highlights, but he left town. The shop's still open." I shrugged.

"All the big talent leaves the state," Holly said, and while they talked that over, I tried to arrange my rump in a comfortable position on the folding metal chair wedged between Holly and Tara. I carefully bent down to tuck my purse between my feet.

As I looked around me at all the excited customers, I began to relax. Surely I could enjoy this a little bit? I'd known the club was full of displaced fae since my last visit here, after all. I was with my friends, and they were all ready to have a good time. Surely I could allow myself to have a good time with them? Claude and Dermot were my kin, and they wouldn't let anything bad happen to me. Right? I managed to smile at Bellenos when he came around to light the candle on our table, and I was laughing at a dirty joke of Michele's when a waitress hustled over to take our drink orders. My smile faded. I remembered her from my previous visit.

"I'm Gift, and I'll be your server tonight," she said, just as perky as you please. Her hair was a bright blond, and she was very pretty. But since I was part fae (due to a massive indiscretion of my grandmother's), I could see past the blonde's cute exterior. Her skin wasn't the honey tan everyone else was seeing. It was a pale, pale green. Her eyes had no pupils . . . or perhaps the pupils and irises were the same black? She fluttered her eyelids at me when no one else was looking. She might have two. Eyelids, that is. On each eye. I had time to notice because she bent so close to me.

"Welcome, Sister," she murmured in my ear, and then straightened to beam at the others. "What y'all having tonight?" she asked with a perfect Louisiana accent.

"Well, Gift, I want you to know up front that most of us are in the serving business, too, so we're not going to give you a hard time," Holly said.

Gift twinkled back at her. "I'm so glad to hear that! Not that you gals look like a hard time, anyway. I love Ladies Only night."

While my friends ordered their drinks and baskets of fried pickles or tortilla chips, I glanced around the club to confirm my impression. None of the servers were human. The only humans here were the customers.

When it was my turn, I told Gift I wanted a Bud Light. She bent closer again to say, "How's the vampire cutie, girlfriend?"

"He's fine," I said stiffly, though that was far from true.

Gift said, "You're so cute!" and tapped me on the shoulder as if I'd said something witty. "Ladies, you doing all right? I'm going to go put your food orders in and get your drinks." Her bright head gleamed like a lighthouse as she maneuvered expertly through the crowd.

"I didn't know you knew all the staff here. How *is* Eric? I haven't seen him since the fire at Merlotte's," Kennedy said. She'd clearly overheard Gift's query. "Eric is one fine hunk of man." She nodded wisely.

There was a chorus of agreement from my friends. Truly, Eric's hunkiness was undeniable. The fact that he was dead weighed against him, especially in Tara's eyes. She'd met Claude, and she hadn't picked up on the fact that there was something different about him; but Eric, who never tried to pass for human, would always be on her blacklist. Tara had had a bad experience with a vampire, and it had left an indelible mark on her.

"He has a hard time getting away from Shreveport. He's pretty busy with work," I said. I stopped there. Talking about Eric's business was always unwise.

"He's not mad you're going to watch another guy take off his clothes? You sure you told him?" Kennedy asked, her smile hard and bright. There was definitely trouble in Kennedy-and-Danny land. Oh, I didn't want to know about it.

"I think Eric is so confident he looks good naked that he doesn't worry about me seeing someone else that way," I said. I'd told Eric I was going to Hooligans. I hadn't asked his permission; as Kennedy had said about Danny, he was not the boss of me. But I *had* sort of floated the idea by him to see how he reacted. Things between us hadn't been comfortable for a few weeks. I didn't want to upset our fragile boat—not for such a frivolous reason.

As I'd expected, Eric had not taken our proposed girls' night out very seriously. For one thing, he thought modern American attitudes about nudity were amusing. He'd seen a thousand years of long nights, and he'd lost his own inhibitions somewhere along the way. I suspected he'd never had that many.

My honey not only was calm about my viewing other men's naked bodies; he wasn't concerned about our destination. He didn't seem to imagine there'd be any danger in the Monroe strip club. Even Pam, his second-in-command, had only shrugged when Eric had told her what we human females were going to do for entertainment. "Won't be any vampires there," she'd said, and after a token jab at Eric about my wanting to see other men in the buff, she'd dismissed the subject.

My cousin Claude had been welcoming all sorts of displaced fae to Hooligans since the portals to Faery had been shut by my great-grandfather Niall. He'd shut the portals on an impulse, a sudden reversal of his previous policy that human and fae should mix freely. Not all the fairies and other fae living in our world had had time to get on the Faery side before the portals closed. A very small one, located in the woods behind my house, remained open a crack. From time to time, news passed through.

When they'd thought they were alone, Claude and my great-uncle Dermot had come to my house to take comfort in my company because of my dab of fairy blood. Being in exile was terrible for them. As much as they had previously enjoyed the human world, they now yearned for home.

Gradually, other fae had begun showing up at Hooligans. Dermot and Claude, especially Claude, didn't stay with me as regularly. That solved a lot of problems for me—Eric couldn't stay over if the two fairies were in the house because the smell of fairy is simply intoxicating to vampires—but I did occasionally miss Great-Uncle Dermot, who'd always been comfortable company for me.

As I was thinking of him, I spotted Dermot behind the bar. Though he was my fairy grandfather's brother, he looked no older than his late twenties.

"Sookie, there's your cousin," Holly said. "I haven't seen him since Tara's shower. Oh my God, he looks so much like Jason!"

"The family resemblance is real strong," I agreed. I glanced over at Jason's girlfriend, who was not any kind of pleased at seeing Dermot. She'd met Dermot before when he'd been cursed with insanity. Though she knew he was in his right mind these days, she wasn't going to warm up to him in any kind of hurry.

"I never have figured out how you're kin to them," Holly said. In Bon Temps everybody knew who your people were and who you were connected to.

"Someone was illegitimate," I said delicately. "Not saying any more. I didn't find out until after Gran passed, from some old family papers."

Holly looked wise, which was kind of a stretch for her.

"Does having an 'in' with the management mean we're going to get a freebie drink or something?" Kennedy asked. "Maybe a lap dance on the house?"

"Girl, you don't want a lap dance from a stripper!" Tara said. "You don't know where that thing has been!"

"You're just all sour-grapey because you don't have a lap anymore," Kennedy muttered, and I gave her a meaningful glare. Tara was super-sensitive about losing her figure.

I said, "Hey, we already got a reserved table right by the stage. Let's not push it by asking for anything else."

Luckily, our drinks arrived then. We tipped Gift lavishly.

"Yum," Kennedy said after a big sip. "That is one wicked appletini."

As if that had been a signal, the house lights went down, the stage lights popped on, music began to play, and Claude came prancing out in spangled silver tights and boots, and nothing else.

"Good God, Sookie, he looks edible!" Holly said, and her words flew straight to Claude's sharp fairy ears. (He'd had the points surgically removed so he wouldn't have to expend energy looking human, but the procedure hadn't affected his hearing.) Claude looked over at our table, and when he spotted me, he grinned. He twitched his butt so that his spangles flew out and caught the light, and the women crammed into the club began clapping, full of anticipation.

"Ladies," Claude said into the microphone, "Are you ready to enjoy Hooligans? Are you ready to watch some amazing men show you what they're made of?" He let his hand stroke his admirable abs and raised one eyebrow, managing to look incredibly sexy and incredibly suggestive in two simple moves.

The music escalated, and the crowd shrieked. Even the heavily pregnant Tara joined in the chorus of enthusiasm as a line of men danced out on the stage behind Claude. One of them was wearing a policeman's uniform (if cops ever decided to put glitter on their pants), one was wearing a leather outfit, one was dressed as an angel—yes, with wings! And the last one in the row was . . .

There was a sudden and total silence at our table. All of us sat with our eyes straight ahead, not daring to steal a look at Tara.

The last stripper was her husband, JB du Rone. He was dressed as a construction worker. He wore a hard hat, a safety vest, fake blue jeans, and a heavy tool belt. Instead of wrenches and screwdrivers, the belt loops held handy items like a cocktail shaker, a pair of furry handcuffs, and a few things I simply couldn't identify.

It was painfully obvious that Tara had had no clue.

Of all the "oh shit" moments in my life, this was OSM Number One.

The whole party from Bon Temps sat frozen as Claude introduced the performers by their stripper names (JB was "Randy"). One of us had to break the silence. Suddenly, I saw a light at the end of the conversational tunnel.

"Oh, Tara," I said, as earnestly as anyone ever could speak. "This is *so sweet.*"

The other women turned to me simultaneously, their faces desperate with hope that I might show them how to spackle over this awful moment. Though I could *hear* Tara thinking she would like to take JB to the deer processing plant and tell the butcher to make him into ground meat, I plunged in.

"You know he's doing this for you and the babies," I said, injecting my voice with every drop of sincerity I could muster. I leaned closer and took her hand. I wanted to be sure she heard me over the booming music. "You *know* he meant the extra money as a big surprise for you."

"Well," she said through stiff lips, "I'm plenty surprised."

Out of the corner of my eye, I caught Kennedy closing her eyes in gratitude for the cue. I could feel the relief pouring from Holly's mind. Michele relaxed visibly. Now that the other women had a path to follow, they all fell into step. Kennedy told a very credible story about JB's last visit to Merlotte's, a visit in which he'd told her how worried he was about paying the medical bills.

"With twins coming, he was scared that might mean more time in the hospital," Kennedy said. She was making up most of this, but it sounded good. During her career as a beauty queen (and before her career as a convicted felon), Kennedy had mastered sincerity.

Tara finally seemed to relax just a smidgen, but I monitored her thoughts so we could stay on top of the situation. She didn't want to draw any more attention to our table by demanding we all walk out, which had been her first impulse. When Holly hesitantly mentioned leaving if Tara was too uncomfortable to stay, Tara fixed us all in turn with a grim stare. "Hell, no," she said.

Thank God drink refills came then, and the baskets of food soon after. We all tried hard to pretend that nothing out of the ordinary had happened, and we were doing pretty well by the time the music started pumping "Touch My Nightstick" to announce the arrival of the "policeman."

The performer was a full-blooded fairy; a little too thin for my taste, but he was real good-looking. You won't find an ugly fairy. And he could actually dance, and he really enjoyed the exercise. Every inch of gradually revealed flesh was just as toned and tempting as it could be. "Dirk" had a fantastic sense of rhythm, and he seemed to be enjoying himself. He was basking in the lust, the excitement of being the focus of attention. Were all the fae as vain as Claude, as conscious of their own beauty?

"Dirk" gyrated his sexy way around the stage, and a shocking number of dollar bills were stuffed into the little man-thong that had gradually become his only garment. It was clear that Dirk was generously endowed by nature and that he was enjoying the attention. Every now and then someone bold would give him a little rub, but Dirk would pull back and shake his finger at the miscreant.

"Eww," Kennedy said the first time that happened, and I had to echo her sentiment. But Dirk was tolerant if not encouraging. He gave an especially generous donor a quick kiss, which made the hollering rise to a crescendo. I'm good at estimating tips, but I could not even begin to guess how much Dirk had made by the time he left the stage—especially since he'd been handing off handfuls of bills to Dermot at intervals. The routine came to an end perfectly in time with the music, and Dirk took his bow and ran off the stage.

In a very short time, the stripper pulled on his glittery policeman pants (though nothing else) and came out to wander through the crowd, smiling and nodding as women offered him drinks, phone numbers, and yet more cash. Dirk took only a sip of the drinks, accepted the phone numbers with a charming smile, and tucked the money in his waistband until he seemed to be wearing a green belt.

Though this kind of entertainment wasn't something I'd want to experience on a regular basis, I honestly couldn't see the harm. Women were getting to shout and scream and get rowdy in a controlled environment. They were obviously having a great time. Even if some of these women were enthralled enough to come every week (a lot of brains were telling me a lot of things), well, it was only one night. The ladies weren't aware they were cheering for elves and fairies, true; but I was sure they were happier not knowing that (besides JB's) the flesh and skill they were so admiring wasn't human.

The other performers were more of the same. The angel, "Gabriel," was anything but angelic, and fluttering white feathers drifted through the air as he apparently divested himself of his wings (I was sure they were still there but invisible), and nearly every other stitch he'd worn, to "Your Heavenly Body." Like the policeman, he was in wonderful shape and apparently well endowed. He was also shaved smooth as a baby's bottom, though it was hard to think of him in the same sentence as the word "baby." Women grabbed for the floating feathers and the creature who'd worn them.

When Gabriel came out into the audience—wings again apparent, sporting only a white monokini—Kennedy seized him when he happened by our table. Kennedy was losing what few inhibitions she had as her drinks kept vanishing. The angel gazed at Kennedy with glowing golden eyes—at least, that was what I saw. Kennedy gave him her business card and a lopsided leer, running her palm down his abs. As he turned away from her, I gently inserted a five-dollar bill in his fingers, taking Kennedy's card away as I did so. The golden eyes met mine.

"Sister," he said. Even through the noise of the next performer's entrance, I could hear his voice.

He smiled and drifted away, to my great relief. I hastily concealed Kennedy's card in my purse. I gave a mental eye-roll at the concept of a part-time bartender having a business card; that was so Kennedy.

Tara had at least not been having a horrible time during the evening, but as the moment approached when JB would certainly be taking the stage, the tension inevitably ratcheted up at our table. From the moment he leaped to center stage and began dancing to "Nail-Gun Ned," it was obvious that he didn't know his wife was in the audience. (JB's mind is like an open book with maybe two words per page.) His dance routine was surprisingly polished. I sure hadn't known how flexible JB could be. We Bon Temps ladies tried hard not to let our eyes meet.

"Randy" was simply having a great time. By the time he stripped down to his man-thong, everyone—almost everyone—was sharing his elation, as the number of bills he collected bore witness. I could read directly from JB's head that this adulation was feeding a great need. His wife, tired and pregnant, no longer glowed with pleasure every time she saw him naked. JB was so used to receiving approval that he craved it—however he could get it.

Tara had muttered something and left the table just as her husband came on, so he didn't see her when he danced across the stage close to us. The moment he was near enough to realize who we were, a shade of concern passed over his handsome face. He was entertainer enough to keep on going, to my relief. I actually felt a bit proud of JB. Even in the arctic air-conditioning, he was sweating with his gyrations. He was vigorous, athletic, and sexy. We all watched anxiously to make sure he was getting just as many tips as the other performers, though we felt a bit delicate about contributing ourselves.

After JB left the stage, Tara returned to the table. She sat down and looked at us with the strangest expression on her face. "I was watching from the back of the room," she admitted, as we all waited in suspense. "He did pretty good."

We exhaled, practically in unison.

"Honey, he was really, *really* good," Kennedy said, nodding emphatically enough to make her chestnut hair swing back and forth.

"You're a lucky woman," Michele chimed in. "And your babies are going to be so gorgeous and coordinated."

We didn't know how much was too much to say, and we were all relieved when a loud chorus of "Born to Ride Rough" announced the performance of the guy in leather. He was at least part demon, of a stock I hadn't encountered before; his skin was reddish, which my companions interpreted as Native American. (It didn't look anything like that to my eyes, but I wasn't going to say any different.) He did have black, straight hair and dark eyes, and he knew how to shake his tomahawk. His nipples were pierced, which was not my special turn-on, but it was a popular touch with many members of the audience.

I clapped and I smiled, but in truth I was beginning to feel a little bored. Though Eric had I had not been on the same emotional wavelength lately, we had been operating very well with regard to sex (don't ask me how this could be so). I began to think I was spoiled. There was no such thing as boring sex with Eric.

I wondered if he'd dance for me, if I asked him nicely. I was having a very pleasant fantasy about that when Claude reemerged on the stage, still in his spangled tights and boots.

Claude was completely confident that the whole room could hardly wait to see more of him, and that kind of confidence pays off. He was also incredibly limber and flexible.

"Oh my God!" Michele said, her husky voice almost breaking. "Well! He hardly needs a partner, does he?"

"Wow." Holly's mouth was hanging open.

Even I, who had already seen the whole package and knew how

disagreeable Claude could be—even I was feeling a little jolt of excitement down where I shouldn't. Claude's pleasure in receiving all this attention and admiration was almost blissful in its purity.

For the grand finale of the evening, Claude leaped off the stage and danced through the crowd in his man-thong. Everyone seemed determined to unload all their remaining dollar bills—and their fives and a few tens. Claude distributed kisses with abandon, but he dodged more personal touches with an agility that almost betrayed him as other-than-human. When he approached our table, Michele tucked a five under his G-string, saying, "You earned this, buddy," and Claude's smile glinted back at hers. Then Claude paused beside me and bent to kiss me on the cheek. I jumped. The women at the surrounding tables shrieked and demanded their own kisses. I was left with the glow in his dark eyes and the unexpected chill left by the touch of his lips.

I was ready to leave a big tip for Gift and get out of there.

Tara drove back, since Michele said she was too tipsy. I knew Tara was glad to have an excuse to be silent. The other women were providing cover chatter about the fun they'd had, trying to give Tara space to come to terms with the events of the evening.

"I hope I didn't enjoy it too much," Holly was saying. "I'd hate it if Hoyt went to a strip club all the time."

"Would you mind it if he went once?" I asked.

"Well, I wouldn't like it," she said honestly. "But if he was going because he was invited to a stag party or something, I wouldn't kick up a fuss about it."

"I would hate it if Jason went," Michele said.

"Do you think he'd cheat on you with a stripper?" Kennedy asked. I was sure it was the liquor talking.

"If he did, he'd be out the door with a black eye," Michele said with a derisive snort. After a moment she said in a milder voice, "I'm a little older than Jason, and maybe my body isn't quite what it used to be. I look great naked, don't get me wrong. But probably not as great as the younger strippers."

"Men are never happy with what they've got, no matter how good it is," Kennedy muttered.

"What's up with you, girl? You and Danny have a fight over another woman?" Tara asked bluntly.

Kennedy turned a bright, hard look on Tara, and for a minute I thought she'd say something cutting. Then we'd have an open quarrel. But Kennedy said, "He's doing something secret, and he won't tell me what. He says he's gonna be gone on Monday/Wednesday/Friday mornings and evenings. He won't say where he's going or why."

Since the fact that Danny was totally smitten with Kennedy was obvious to the dimmest bulb, we were all struck silent with astonishment at her blindness.

"Did you ask him?" Michele said, in her forthright way.

"Hell, no!" Kennedy was too proud (and too scared, but only I knew that) to ask Danny directly.

"Well, I don't know who to ask or what to ask, but if I hear anything, I'll tell you. I really don't think you need to worry about Danny stepping out on you," I said. How such massive insecurity could lurk behind such a pretty face was amazing to me.

"Thanks, Sookie." There was a little sob in her voice. Oh, Lord. All the fun of the evening was draining away in a hurry.

We pulled up at the front of my house none too soon. I said my good-byes and my thank-yous in my brightest and most cheerful voice, and then I was hurrying to my front door. Of course the big security light was on, and of course Tara didn't back out until I'd reached my front door, unlocked it, and stepped inside. I locked the door behind me instantly. Though there were magical wards around the house to keep supernatural enemies away, locks and keys never hurt.

Not only had I worked today, I'd endured the raucous crowd and the pulse-pounding music, and there was all the drama with my friends, too. If you're telepathic, your brain gets exhausted. But in a contradictory way, I felt too twitchy and restless to head directly to my bedroom. I decided to check my e-mail.

It had been a couple of days since I'd had a chance to sit down at the computer. I had ten messages. Two were from Kennedy and Holly, setting a time to pick me up. Since that was a done deal, I tapped the Delete button. The next three were ads. Those were gone in a flash. There was a note from Amelia with an attachment, which proved to be a picture of her and her boyfriend, Bob, sitting at a café in Paris. "We're having a good time," she wrote. "The community over here is very welcoming. Think my little problem with my NO community has been forgiven. What about you and me?"

"Community" was Amelia's code word for "coven." Amelia's little problem had arisen when she'd accidentally turned Bob into a cat. Now that he was a man again, they'd resumed their relationship. Go figure. And now Paris! "Some people just lead charmed lives," I said out loud. As for Amelia and me being "okay"—she'd offended me deeply by trying to shove Alcide Herveaux into my sex life. I'd expected better from her. No, I hadn't entirely forgiven her, but I was trying.

At that moment there was a quiet knock on the front door. I jumped and spun around in the swivel chair. I hadn't heard a vehicle, or footsteps. Normally, that would mean a vampire had come calling; but when I cast out my extra sense, the brain it encountered was not the blank of a vampire's, but something else entirely.

There was another discreet knock. I edged to the window and looked out. Then I unlocked the door and flung it open.

"Great-grandfather," I said, and leaped up and into his embrace. "I thought I'd never see you again! How are you? Come in!"

Niall smelled wonderful—fairies do. To some extra-sensitive vampire noses, I have a faint trace of the same odor, though I can't detect it myself.

My ex-boyfriend Bill had told me once that to him the fae smelled like his memory of the taste of apples.

Enveloped in my great-grandfather's overwhelming presence, I experienced the rush of affection and amazement I always did when I was with him. Tall and regal, clad in an immaculate black suit, white shirt, and black tie, Niall was both beautiful and ancient.

He was also a dab unreliable when it came to facts. Tradition says fairies can't lie, and the fairies themselves will tell you so—but they sure skirt the truth when it suits them. Sometimes I thought that Niall had lived for so long that his memory simply skipped a beat or two. It was a struggle to remember this when I was with him, but I forced myself to keep it in my mind.

"I'm well, as you see." He gestured at his magnificence, though to do him credit I believe he simply intended to draw my attention to his unwounded state. "And you are beautiful, as always."

Fairies are also somewhat flowery in their speech—unless they've been living among humans for a long time, like Claude.

"I thought you were sealed off."

"I widened the portal in your woods," he said, as if the action had been a casual whim of his. After the big deal he'd made about sealing the fae in for the protection of humanity, severing all his business ties with the human world, and so on, he'd enlarged an opening and come through . . . because he wanted to check on my well-being? Even the fondest great-granddaughter could smell a rat.

"I knew that portal was there," I said, because I couldn't think of anything else to say.

He cocked his head. His white-blond hair moved like a satin curtain. "Was it you who put the body in?"

"I'm sorry. I couldn't think of anywhere else to put it." Corpse disposal was not one of my talents.

"It was consumed entirely, if that was your purpose. Please abstain in the future. We don't want there to be crowding around the portal," he said in gentle admonishment, rather as though I'd been feeding pets from the dinner table.

"Sorry," I said. "So—why are you here?" I heard the bluntness of my words and felt myself turning red. "I mean, to what do I owe the honor of your visit? Can I get you a drink or something to eat?"

"No thank you, dearest. Where have you been this evening? You smell of the fae and humans and many other things."

I took a deep breath and tried to explain Ladies Only night at Hooligans. With every sentence, I felt more of a fool. You should have seen Niall's face when I told him that one night a week, human women paid to watch men take their clothes off. He sure didn't get it.

"Do men do this also?" he asked. "Go in groups to special buildings, pay to watch women undress?"

I said, "Yes, men *much* more often than women. The other nights, that's what happens at Hooligans."

"And Claude makes money this way," Niall said wonderingly. "Why don't the men just ask the women to take their clothes off, if they want to see their bodies?"

I took another deep breath but let it out without attempting further explanation. Some topics were just too complicated to tackle, especially with a fairy who'd never lived in our world. Niall was a tourist, not a resident. "Can we bypass this whole discussion until another time, or maybe until never? Surely there's something more important you want to talk about?" I said.

"Of course. May I sit?"

"Be my guest." We sat on the couch, angled forward so we were looking into each other's faces. There's nothing like having a fairy examine you to make you acutely aware of your every flaw.

"You've recovered well," he said, to my surprise.

"I have," I said, trying not to glance down, as if my scarred thigh would show through my clothing. "It took a while." Niall meant I looked good for someone who'd been tortured. Two notorious fairies who'd had their teeth sharpened like the elves' had left me with some permanent physical damage. Niall and Bill had arrived in time to save my body parts and my sanity, if not all of my actual flesh. "Thanks for coming in time," I said, forcing a smile on my face. "I'll never forget how glad I was to see you-all."

Niall waved away my gratitude. "You are my blood," he said. That was reason enough for him. I thought about my great-uncle Dermot, Niall's half-human son, who believed Niall had cast a crazy spell on him. Kind of contradictory, huh? I almost pointed that out to Great-Grandfather, but I did want to keep the peace since I hadn't seen him in so long.

"When I came through the portal tonight, I smelled blood in the ground around your house," he said abruptly. "Human blood, fae blood. Now I can tell there is fae blood upstairs in your attic, recently spilled. And fairies are living here now. Who?" Niall's smooth hands took mine, and I felt a flush of well-being.

"Claude and Dermot have been living here, kind of off and on," I said. "When Eric stays over, they spend the night in Claude's house in Monroe."

Niall looked very, very thoughtful. "What reason did Claude give you for wanting to be in your house? Why did you permit this? Have you had sex with him?" He didn't sound angry or distressed, but the questions themselves had a certain edge.

"I don't have sex with relatives, first off," I said, an edge to my own voice. My boss, Sam Merlotte, had told me that the fae didn't necessarily consider such relationships taboo, but I sure did. I took yet another deep breath. I would hyperventilate if Niall stayed very long.

I tried again, this time making an effort to modify my indignation. "Sex between relatives is not something humans condone," I told him, making myself stop right there before adding any codicils. "I have slept in the same bed with Dermot and Claude, because they told me that would make them feel better. And I admit it helped me, too. They both seem kind of lost, since they're not able to enter Faery. A bunch of the fae got left outside, and they're pretty miserable." I did my best not to sound reproachful, but Hooligans was like Ellis Island in lockdown.

Niall was not going to be diverted. "Of course Claude would want to be close to you," he said. "The company of others with fairy blood is always desirable. Did you suspect . . . he had any other reason?"

Was this a hint, or just a simple hesitation in Niall's speech? As a matter of fact, I *did* think the two fairies had another reason for their attraction to me and my house, but I thought—I hoped—this reason was quite unconscious. This was a chance to unburden myself of a great secret and gain more information about an object I had in my possession. I opened my mouth to tell Niall about what I'd found in a secret compartment in an old desk.

But the sense of caution I'd developed in my life as a telepath . . . well, that sense jumped up and down, screaming, "Shut up!"

I said, "Do *you* think they had another reason?"

I noticed Niall had mentioned only his full-fairy grandson, Claude, not his half-human son Dermot. Since Niall had always acted very lovingly toward me, and my blood had only a trace of fairy, I couldn't understand why he wasn't equally loving toward Dermot. Dermot had done some bad things, but he'd been under a spell. Niall wasn't cutting him any slack for that. Just at the moment, Niall was looking at me doubtfully, his head cocked to one side.

My cheeks yanked up in my brightest smile. I felt increasingly uneasy. "Claude and Dermot have been real helpers. They carried down all the old stuff in the attic. I sold it to an antiques dealer in Shreveport." Niall smiled back at me and stood. Before I could say Jack Robinson, he'd glided up the stairs. He came back down them a couple of minutes later. I spent the time sitting there with my mouth hanging open. Even for a fairy, this was odd behavior. "I guess you were up there sniffing Dermot's blood?" I said warily.

"I can tell I have irritated you, dearest." Niall smiled at me, and his beauty warmed me. "Why was there bleeding in the attic?"

Niall didn't even use the pronoun "he." I said, "A human came in looking for me. Dermot was working and didn't hear him coming. The human clocked him one. Hit him on the head," I explained, when Niall looked confused.

"Is that the human whose blood I smelled outside in the ground?"

There'd been so many. Vampires and humans, Weres and fairies.

I actually had to think a minute. "Could be," I said at last. "Bellenos healed Dermot, and they caught the guys . . ." I fell silent. At the mention of Bellenos's name, Niall's eyes flashed, and not with joy.

"Bellenos, the elf," he said.

"Yes."

His head turned sharply, and I knew he'd heard something I hadn't.

We'd been too involved in our conversation to hear a car on the driveway, apparently; but Niall had heard the key in the lock.

"Cousin, did you enjoy the show?" Claude called from the kitchen, and I had time to think, *Another OSM*, before Claude and Dermot walked into the living room.

There was a frozen silence. The three fairies were looking back and forth like gunfighters at the OK Corral. Each one waited for the other to make some decisive gesture that would determine whether they fought or talked.

"My house, my rules," I said, and shot up from the couch like someone had lit my ass on fire. "No brawling! Not! Any!"

There was another beat of the tense silence, and then Claude said, "Of course not, Sookie. Prince Niall—Grandfather—I had feared I'd never see you again."

"Claude," Niall said, nodding at his grandson.

"Hello, Father," said Dermot very quietly.

Niall didn't look at his child.

Awkward.

Chapter 2

Fairies. Never simple. My grandmother Adele would definitely have agreed. She'd had a long affair with Dermot's fraternal twin, Fintan, and my aunt Linda and my father, Corbett, (both dead for years now) had been the results.

"Maybe it's time for some plain speaking," I said, trying to look confident. "Niall, maybe you could tell us why you're pretending Dermot isn't standing right here. And why you put that crazy spell on him." Dr. Phil to the fae—that was me.

Or not. Niall gave me his most lordly look.

"This one defied me," he said, tilting his head at his son.

Dermot bowed his head. I didn't know if he was keeping his eyes down so he wouldn't provoke Niall or if he was concealing rage or if he just couldn't think of where to begin.

Being related to Niall, even at two removes, was not easy. I couldn't imagine having a closer tie. If Niall's beauty and power had been united with a coherent course of action and a nobleness of purpose, he would have been very like an angel.

This conviction could not have popped into my head at a more inconvenient moment.

"You're looking at me strangely," Niall said. "What's wrong, dearest one?"

"In the time he's spent here," I said, "my great-uncle has been kind, hardworking, and smart. The only thing that's been wrong with Dermot is a bit of mental fragility, a direct result of being made crazy for years. So, why'd you do that? 'He defied me' isn't really an answer."

"You haven't got the right to question me," Niall said, in his most royal voice. "I am the only living prince of Faery."

"I don't know why that means I can't ask you questions. I'm an *American*," I said, standing tall.

The beautiful eyes examined me coldly. "I love you," he said very unlovingly, "but you're presuming too much."

"If you love me, or even if you just respect me a little, you need to answer my question. I love Dermot, too."

Claude was standing absolutely still, doing a great imitation of Switzerland. I knew he wasn't going to chime in on my side or Dermot's side or even Niall's side. To Claude, the only side was his.

"You allied yourself with the water fairies," Niall said to Dermot.

"After you cursed me," Dermot protested, looking up at his father briefly.

"You helped them kill Sookie's father," Niall said. "Your nephew."

"I did not," Dermot said quietly. "And I'm not mistaken in this. Even Sookie believes this, and she lets me stay here."

"You weren't in your right mind. I know you would never do that if you hadn't been cursed," I said.

"You see her kindness, and yet you have none for me," Dermot told Niall. "Why did you curse me? Why?" He was looking directly at his father, his distress written all over his face.

"But I didn't," Niall said. He sounded genuinely surprised. Finally, he was addressing Dermot directly. "I wouldn't addle the brains of my own son, half-human or not."

"Claude told me it was you who bespelled me." Dermot looked at Claude, who was still waiting to see which way the frog would jump.

"Claude," Niall said, the power in his voice making my head pound, "who told you this?"

"It's common knowledge among the fae," Claude said. He'd been preparing himself for this, was braced to make his answer.

"According to whom?" Niall was not going to give up.

"Murry told me this."

"Murry told you I had cursed my son? Murry, the friend of my enemy Breandan?" Niall's elegant face was incredulous.

The Murry I killed with Gran's trowel? I thought, but I knew it was better not to interrupt.

"Murry told me this before he switched his allegiance," Claude said defensively.

"And who had told Murry?" Niall said, an edge of exasperation in his voice.

"I don't know." Claude shrugged. "He sounded so certain, I never questioned him."

"Claude, come with me," Niall said, after a moment's fraught silence. "We will talk to your father and to the rest of our people. We'll discover who spread this rumor about me. And we'll know who actually cursed Dermot, made him behave so."

I would have thought Claude would be ecstatic, since he'd been ready to return to Faery ever since entrance had been denied him. But he looked absolutely vexed, just for a moment.

"What about Dermot?" I asked.

"It's too dangerous for him now," Niall said. "The one who cursed him may be waiting to take further action against him. I'll take Claude with me . . . and, Claude, if you cause any trouble with your human ways . . ."

"I understand. Dermot, will you take over at the club until I return?"

"I will," said Dermot, but he looked so dazed by the sudden turn of events that I wasn't sure he knew what he was saying.

Niall bent to kiss me on the mouth, and the subtle smell of fairy filled my nose. Then he and Claude flowed out the back door and into the woods. "Walked" is simply too jerky a word to describe their progress.

Dermot and I were left alone in my shabby living room. To my consternation, my great-uncle (who looked a tiny bit younger than me) began to weep. His knees crumpled, his whole body shook, and he pressed the heels of his hands to his eyes.

I covered the few feet between us and sank to the floor beside him. I put my arm around him and said, "I sure didn't expect any of *that*." I surprised a laugh out of him. He hiccupped, raising reddened eyes to meet mine. I stretched my free arm to reach the box of tissues on the table by the recliner. I extracted one and used it to pat Dermot's wet cheeks.

"I can't believe you're being so nice to me," he said. "It's seemed incredible to me from the beginning, considering what Claude told you."

I had been a little surprised myself, to tell you the truth.

I spoke from my heart. "I'm not convinced you were even there the night my parents died. If you were, I think you were under a compulsion. In my experience of you, you've been a total sweetie."

He leaned against me like a tired child. By now, a human guy would have made a huge effort to pull himself together. He'd be embarrassed at displaying vulnerability. Dermot seemed quite willing to let me comfort him.

"Are you feeling better now?" I asked, after a couple of minutes.

He inhaled deeply. I knew he was drawing in my fairy scent and that it would help him. "Yes," he said. "Yes."

"You probably need to get a shower and have a good night's sleep," I advised him, floundering for something to say that wouldn't sound totally lame, like I was coddling a toddler. "I bet Niall and Claude'll be back in no time, and you'll get to . . ." Then I had to trail off, since I didn't know what it was Dermot truly wanted. Claude, who'd been desperate to find a way to enter Faery, had gotten his wish. I'd assumed that had been Dermot's goal, too. After Claude and I had broken the spell on Dermot, I'd never asked him.

As Dermot trudged off to the bathroom, I went around the house checking all the windows and doors, part of my nightly ritual. I washed and dried a couple of dishes while I tried to imagine what Claude and Niall might be doing at this moment. What could Faery look like? Like Oz, in the movie?

"Sookie," said Dermot, and I jerked myself into the here and now. He was standing in the kitchen wearing plaid sleep pants, his normal night gear. His golden hair was still damp from the shower.

"Feeling better?" I smiled at him.

"Yes. Could we sleep together tonight?"

It was as though he'd asked, "Can we catch a camel and keep it as a pet?" Because of Niall's questions about Claude and me, Dermot's request struck me kind of weird. I just wasn't in a fairy-loving mood, no matter how innocently he intended it. And truthfully, I wasn't sure he hadn't meant we should do more than sleep. "Ahhhhh . . . no."

Dermot looked so disappointed that I caught myself feeling guilty. I couldn't stand it; I had to explain.

"Listen, I understand that you don't intend that we have sex together, and I know that a couple of times in the past we've all slept in the same bed and we all slept like rocks. . . . It was a good thing, a healing thing. But there are maybe ten reasons I don't want to do that again. Number one, it's just really peculiar, to a human. Two, I love Eric and I should only bunk down with him. Three, you're related to me, so sleeping in the same bed should make me feel really squicky inside. *Also*, you look enough like my brother to pass for him, which makes any kind of vaguely sexual situation double squicky. I know that's not ten, but I think that's enough."

"You don't find me attractive?"

"Completely beside the point!" My voice was rising, and I paused to give myself a second. I continued in a quieter tone. "It doesn't make any difference how attractive I find you. Of course you're handsome. Just like my brother. But I have *no* sex feelings about you, and I kind of feel the sleeping-together thing is just odd. So we're not doing the fairy sleep-athon of comfort anymore."

"I'm sorry I've upset you," he said, even more miserably.

I felt guilty again. But I made myself suppress the twinge. "I don't think anyone in the world has a great-uncle like you," I said, but my voice was fond.

"I'll never bring it up again. I only sought comfort." He gave me Big Eyes. There was a hint of laughter turning up the corners of his mouth.

"You'll just have to comfort yourself," I said tartly.

He was smiling as he left the kitchen.

That night, for the first time in forever, I locked my bedroom door. I felt bad when I turned the latch, like I was dishonoring Dermot with my suspicions. But the last few years had taught me that one of my grandmother's favorite sayings was true. An ounce of prevention *was* worth a pound of cure.

If Dermot turned my doorknob during the night, I was too soundly asleep to hear it. And maybe my ability to drop off that deeply meant that on a basic level I trusted my great-uncle. Or trusted the lock. When I woke the next day, I could hear him working upstairs in the attic. His footsteps sounded right above my head.

"I made some coffee," I called up the stairs. He was down in a minute. Somewhere he'd acquired a pair of denim overalls, and since he wasn't wearing a shirt underneath, he looked like he was about to take his place in the stripper lineup from the night before as the Sexy Farmer with the Big Pitchfork. I asked Sexy Farmer with a silent gesture if he wanted any toast, and he nodded, happy as a kid. Dermot loved plum jam, and I had a jar made by Maxine Fortenberry, Holly's future mother-in-law. His smile widened when he saw it.

"I was trying to get as much work finished as I could while it wasn't so hot," he explained. "I hope I didn't wake you up."

"Nope. I slept like a rock. What are you doing up there today?" Dermot had been inspired by HGTV to hang some doors in the walk-in attic to block off a part of the big room for storage, and he was turning the rest of the floored space into a bedroom for himself. He and Claude had been more or less bunking together in the small bedroom and sitting room on the second floor. When we'd cleared out the attic, Dermot had decided to "repurpose" the space. He'd already painted the walls and refinished and resealed the plank floor. I believe he'd recaulked the windows, too.

"The floor is dry now, so I built the new walls. Now I'm actually putting in the hardware to hang the doors. I'm hoping to get that done today and tomorrow. So if you have anything you want to store, the space will be ready."

When Dermot and Claude had helped me carry everything down from the packed attic, I'd gotten rid of the accumulated Stackhouse debris—generations of discarded trash and treasures. I was practical enough to know that moldering things untouched for decades really weren't doing anyone any good, and the trash had gone in a large burn pile. The nice items had gone to an antiques store in Shreveport. When I'd dropped by Splendide the week before, Brenda Hesterman and Donald Callaway had told me a few of the smaller pieces had sold.

While the two dealers were at the house looking through the possibilities, Donald had discovered a secret drawer in one of the old pieces of furniture, a desk. In it, I'd found a treasure: a letter from my gran to me and a unique keepsake.

Dermot's head turned at some noise I couldn't yet hear. "Motorcycle coming," he said around a mouthful of toast and jelly, sounding almost eerily like Jason. I snapped myself back to reality.

I knew only one person who regularly traveled by motorcycle.

A moment after I heard the motor cut off, there was a knock at the front door. I sighed, reminding myself to remember days like this the next time I felt lonely. I was wearing sleep shorts and a big old T-shirt, and I was a mess, but that would have to be the problem of my uninvited guest.

Mustapha Khan, Eric's daytime guy, was standing on the front porch. Since it was way too hot to wear leather, his "Blade" impersonation had suffered. But he managed to look plenty tough in a sleeveless denim shirt and jeans and his ever-present shades. He wore his hair in a geometric burr, à la the Wesley Snipes look in the movies, and I was sure he would have strapped huge weapons to his legs if the gun laws had let him.

"Good morning," I said, with moderate sincerity. "You want a cup of coffee? Or some lemonade?" I tacked on the lemonade because he was looking at me like I was crazy.

He shook his head in disgust. "I don't take stimulants," he said, and I remembered—too late—that he'd told me that before. "Some people just sleep their lives away," he remarked after glancing at the clock on the mantel. We walked back to the kitchen.

"Some people were out late last night," I said, as Mustapha—who was a werewolf—stiffened at the sight and scent of Farmer Dermot.

"I see what kind of work you been doing late," Mustapha said.

I'd been about to explain that Dermot had been the one who'd worked late, while I'd only watched him work, but at Mustapha's tone I canceled that plan. He didn't deserve an explanation. "Oh, don't be an idiot. You know this is my great-uncle," I said. "Dermot, you've met Mustapha Khan before. Eric's daytime guy." I thought it more tactful not to bring up the fact that Mustapha's real name was KeShawn Johnson.

"He doesn't look like anyone's *great-uncle*," Mustapha snarled.

"But he is, and it's none of your business, anyway."

Dermot hiked a blond eyebrow. "Do you want to make my presence an issue?" he asked. "I'm sitting here eating breakfast with my great-niece. I have no problem with you."

Mustapha seemed to gather up his stoic Zen-like impassivity, an important part of his image, and within a few seconds he was his cool self. "If Eric don't have a problem with it, why should I?" he said. (It would have been nice if he had realized that earlier.) "I'm here to tell you a few things, Sookie."

"Sure. Have a seat."

"No, thanks. Won't be here long enough."

"Warren didn't come with you?" Warren was most often on the back of Mustapha's motorcycle. Warren was a skinny little ex-con with pale skin and straggly blond hair and some gaps in his teeth, but he was a great shooter and a great friend of Mustapha's.

"Didn't figure I'd need a gun here." Mustapha looked away. He seemed really jangled. Odd. Werewolves were hard to read, but it didn't take a telepath to know that something was up with Mustapha Khan.

"Let's hope no one needs a gun. What's happening in Shreveport that you couldn't tell me over the phone?"

I sat down myself and waited for Mustapha to deliver his message. Eric could have left one on my answering machine or even sent me an e-mail, rather than sending Mustapha—but like most vamps, he didn't really have a rock-solid trust in electronics, especially if the news was important.

"You want him to hear this?" Mustapha tilted his head toward Dermot.

"You might be better off not knowing," I told Dermot. He gave the daytime man a level blue stare that warned Mustapha to be on his best behavior and rose, taking his mug with him. We heard the stairs creak as he mounted them. When Mustapha's Were hearing told him Dermot was out of earshot, he sat down opposite me and placed his hands side by side on the table very precisely. Style and attitude.

"Okay, I'm waiting," I said.

"Felipe de Castro is coming to Shreveport to talk about the disappearance of his buddy Victor."

"Oh, shit," I said.

"Say it, Sookie. We're in for it now." He smiled.

"That's it? That's the message?"

"Eric would like you to come to Shreveport tomorrow night to greet Felipe."

"I won't see Eric till then?" I could feel my face narrow in a suspicious squint. That didn't suit me at all. The thin cracks in our relationship would only spread wider if we didn't get to spend time together.

"He has to get ready," Mustapha said, shrugging. "I don't know if he got to clean out his bathroom cabinets or change the sheets or what. 'Has to get ready' is what he told me."

"Right," I said. "And that's it? That's the whole message?"

Mustapha hesitated. "I got some other things to tell you, not from Eric. Two things." He took off his sunglasses. His chocolate-chip eyes were downcast; Mustapha was not a happy camper.

"Okay, I'm ready." I was biting the inside of my mouth. If Mustapha could be stoical about Felipe's impending visit, I could, too. We were at great risk. We had both participated in the plan to trap Victor Madden, regent of the state of Louisiana, put in place by King Felipe of Nevada, and we had helped to kill Victor and his entourage. What was more, I was pretty sure Felipe de Castro suspected all this with a high degree of certainty.

"First thing, from Pam."

Blond and sardonic, Eric's child Pam was as close to a friend as I had among the vamps. I nodded, signaling Mustapha to deliver the message.

"She says, 'Tell Sookie that this is the hard time that will show what she is made of.' "

I cocked my head. "No advice other than that? Not too helpful. I figured as much." I'd pretty much assumed Felipe's post-Victor visit would be a very touchy one. But that Pam would warn me . . . seemed a bit odd.

"Harder than you know," Mustapha said intently.

I stared at him, waiting for more.

Maddeningly, he did not elaborate. I knew better than to ask him to. "The other thing is from me," he continued.

Only the fact that I'd had to control my face all my life kept me from giving him major Doubtful. Mustapha? Giving me advice?

"I'm a lone wolf," he said, by way of preamble.

I nodded. He hadn't affiliated with the Shreveport werewolves, all members of the Long Tooth pack.

"When I first blew into Shreveport, I looked into joining. I even went to a pack gathering," Mustapha said.

It was the first chink I'd seen in his "I'm badass and I don't need anyone" armor. I was startled that he'd even tried. Alcide Herveaux, the packleader in Shreveport, would have been glad to gain a strong wolf like Mustapha.

"The reason I didn't even consider it is because of Jannalynn," he said. Jannalynn Hopper was Alcide's enforcer. She was about as big as a wasp, and she had the same nature.

"Because Jannalynn's really tough and she would challenge someone as alpha as you?" I said.

He inclined his head. "She wouldn't leave me standing. She would push and push until we fought."

"You think she could win? Over you." I made it not quite a question. With Mustapha's size advantage and his greater experience, I could not fathom why Mustapha had a doubt he would be the victor.

He inclined his head again. "I do. Her spirit is big."

"She likes to feel in charge? She has to be the baddest bitch in the fight?"

"I was in Hair of the Dog yesterday, early evening. Just to spend some time with the other Weres after I got through working for the vamps, get the smell of Eric's house out of my nose . . . though we got a deader hanging around at the Hair, lately. Anyway, Jannalynn was talking to Alcide while she was serving him a drink. She knows you loaned Merlotte some money to keep his bar afloat."

I shifted in my chair, suddenly uneasy. "I'm a little surprised Sam told her, but I didn't ask him to keep it a secret."

"I'm not so sure he did tell her. Jannalynn's not above snooping when she thinks she ought to know something, and she doesn't even think of it as snooping. She thinks of it as fact-gathering. Here's the bottom line: Don't cross that bitch. You're on the borderline with her."

"Because I helped Sam? That doesn't make any sense." Though my sinking heart told me it did.

"Doesn't need to. You helped him when she couldn't. And that galls her. You ever seen her when she's got a mad on?"

"I've seen her in action." Sam always liked such challenging women. I could only conclude that she saved her softer, gentler side for him.

"Then you know how she treats people she sees as a threat."

"I wonder why Alcide hasn't picked Jannalynn as his first lady, or whatever the term is," I said, just to veer away from the subject for a moment. "He made her pack enforcer, but I would have thought he would pick the strongest female wolf as his mate."

"She'd love that," Mustapha said. "I can smell that on her. He can smell that on her. But she don't love Alcide, and he don't love her. She's not the kind of woman he likes. He likes women his own age, women with a little curve to 'em. Women like you."

"But she told Alcide . . ." I had to stop, because I was hopelessly confused. "A few weeks ago, she advised Alcide he should try to seduce me," I said awkwardly. "She thought I would be an asset to the pack."

"If you're confused, think how Jannalynn's feeling." Mustapha's face might have been carved in stone. "She's got a relationship with Sam, but you were able to save him when she wasn't. She halfway wants Alcide, but she knows he wanted you, too. She's big in the pack, and she knows you have pack protection. You know what she can do to people who don't."

I shuddered. "She does enjoy the enforcement," I said. "I've watched her. Thanks for the heads-up, Mustapha. If you'd like a drink or something to eat, the offer still stands."

"I'll take a glass of water," he said, and I got it in short order. I could hear one of Dermot's rented power tools going above our heads in the attic, and though Mustapha cocked an eye toward the ceiling, he didn't comment until he'd finished his drink. "Too bad he can't come with you to Shreveport," he said then. "Fairies are good fighters." Mustapha handed me his empty glass. "Thanks," he said. And then he was out the door.

I mounted the stairs to the second floor as the motorcycle roared its way back to Hummingbird Road. I stood in the attic doorway. Dermot was shaving the bottom off one of the doors. He knew I was there, but he kept on working, casting a quick smile over his shoulder to acknowledge my presence. I considered telling him what Mustapha had just told me, simply to share my worries.

But as I watched my great-uncle work, I reconsidered. Dermot had his own problems. Claude had left with Niall, and there was no way of knowing when he'd return or in what condition. Until Claude's return, Dermot was supposed to make sure all was running smoothly at Hooligans. What would that motley crew be capable of, without Claude's control? I had no idea if Dermot could keep them in line or if they'd ignore his authority.

I started to launch a boatful of worry about that, but I gave myself a reality check. I couldn't assume responsibility for Hooligans. It was none of my business. For all I knew, Claude had a system in place and all Dermot had to do was follow it. I could only worry about one bar, and that was Merlotte's. Kind of alternating with Fangtasia. Okay, two bars.

Speaking of which, my cell phone buzzed me to remind me we were getting a beer delivery that morning. It was time for me to hustle in to work.

"If you need me, you call me," I told Dermot.

With a proud air, as if he'd learned a clever phrase in a foreign language, Dermot said, "You have a nice day, you hear?"

I took a hasty shower and pulled on some shorts and a Merlotte's T-shirt. I didn't have time to blow-dry my hair completely, but at least I put on some eye makeup before I hustled out the door. It felt excellent to shed my supernatural worries and to fall back on thinking about what I had to do at Merlotte's, especially now that I'd bought into it.

The rival bar opened by the now-deceased Victor, Vic's Redneck Roadhouse, had taken a lot of customers away. To our relief, the newness of our rival was wearing off, and some of our regulars were returning to the fold. At the same time, the protests against patronizing a bar owned by a shapeshifter had stopped since Sam had started attending the church that had supplied most of the protesters.

It had been a surprisingly effective countermove, and I am proud to say I thought of it. Sam had blown me off at first, but he'd reconsidered when he'd cooled off. Sam had been pretty nervous the first Sunday, and only a handful of people talked to him. But he'd kept it going, if irregularly, and the members were getting to know him as a person first, a shapeshifter second.

I'd loaned Sam some money to float the bar through the worst time. Instead of repaying me bit by bit as I'd imagined he would, Sam now regarded me as a part owner. After a long and cautious conversation, he'd upped my paycheck and added to my responsibilities. I'd never had something that was kind of my own before. There was no other word for it but "awesome."

Now that I handled some of the administrative work at the bar and Kennedy could come in as bartender, Sam was enjoying a little more well-earned time off. He spent some of it with Jannalynn. He went fishing, a pastime he'd enjoyed with his dad and mom when he was a kid. Sam also worked on his double-wide inside and out, trimming his hedge and raking his yard, planting flowers and tomatoes in season, to the amusement of the rest of the staff.

I didn't think it was funny. I thought it was real nice that Sam liked to take care of his home, even if it was parked behind the bar.

What gave me the most pleasure was seeing the tension ease out of his shoulders now that Merlotte's was on an even keel again.

I was a little early. I had the time to make some measurements in the storeroom. I figured if I had the right to accept beer shipments,

I had the right to institute a few changes, too—subject to Sam's approval and consent, of course.

The guy who drove the truck, Duff McClure, knew exactly where to put the beer. I counted the cases as he unloaded them. I'd offered to help the first time we'd dealt together, and Duff had made it clear it would be a cold day in Hell before a woman helped him do physical work. "You been selling more Michelob lately," he remarked.

"Yeah, we got a few guys who've decided that's all they're gonna drink," I said. "They'll be back to Bud Light before too long."

"You need any TrueBlood?"

"Yeah, the usual case."

"You got a regular vamp clientele."

"Small but regular," I agreed, my mind on writing the check for the shipment. We had a few days to pay it, but Sam had always paid on delivery. I thought that was a good policy.

"They take three, four cases at Vic's," Duff said conversationally.

"Bigger bar." I began writing the check.

"I guess vamps are everywhere now."

"Um-hum," I muttered, filling it out carefully. I was serious about my check-writing privileges. I signed with a flourish.

"Even that bar in Shreveport, that one that turned out to be for werewolves, they take some blood drinks now."

"Hair of the Dog?" Hadn't Mustapha mentioned a vamp who was hanging out at the Were bar?

"Yeah. I delivered there this morning."

"Huh." This news was unsettling, but husky Duff was a huge gossip, and I didn't want him to know he'd shaken me. "Well, everybody's got to drink," I said easily. "Here's your check, Duff. How's Dorothy?" Duff tucked the check into the zippered pouch he kept in a locked box in the passenger floorboard. "She's good," he said with a grin. "We're having another young'un, she says."

"Oh my gosh, how many does that make?"

"This'll be number three," Duff said, shaking his head with a rueful grin. "They gonna have to take out some college loans, do it themselves."

"It'll be fine," I said, which meant almost nothing except that I felt goodwill toward the McClure family.

"Sure thing," he said. "Catch you next time, Sookie. I see Sam's got his fishing pole out. Tell him I said to catch some crappie for me."

When the truck had gone, Sam came out of the trailer and came over to the bar.

"You did that on purpose," I said. "You just don't like Duff."

"Duff's okay," Sam said. "He just talks too much. Always has."

I hesitated a moment. "He says they're stocking TrueBlood at the Hair of the Dog." I was treading on shaky ground.

"Really? That's pretty weird."

I may not be able to read two-natured minds as easily as I can human minds, but I could tell Sam was genuinely surprised. Jannalynn hadn't told him a vampire was coming into her bar, a Were bar. I relaxed. "Come on in and let me show you something," I said. "I've been in there measuring."

"Uh-oh, you want to move the furniture?" Sam was half-smiling as he followed me into the bar.

"No, I want to buy some," I said over my shoulder. "See here?" I paced off a modest area just outside the storeroom. "Look, right here by the back door. This is where we need us some lockers."

"What for?" Sam didn't sound indignant, but like he genuinely wanted to know.

"So we women won't have to put our purses in a drawer in your desk," I said. "So Antoine and D'Eriq can keep a change of clothes here. So each employee will have their own little space to store stuff."

"You think we need this?" Sam looked startled.

"*So* bad," I said. "Now, I looked in a few catalogs and checked online, and the best price I found . . ." We continued talking lockers for a few minutes, Sam protesting at the expense, me giving him all kinds of grief, but in a friendly way.

After a token fuss, Sam agreed. I'd been pretty sure he would.

Then it was thirty minutes till opening time, and Sam went behind the bar to start slicing lemons for the tea. I tied on my apron and began to check the salt and pepper shakers on the tables. Terry had come in very early that morning to clean the bar, and he'd done his usual good job. I straightened a few chairs.

"How long has it been since Terry had a raise?" I asked Sam, since the other waitress hadn't come in yet and Antoine was in the walk-in refrigerator.

"Two years," Sam said. "He's due. But I couldn't go giving raises until things got better. I still think we better wait until we're sure we're level."

I nodded, accepting his judgment. Now that I'd gone over the books, I could see how careful Sam had been in the good times, saving money up for the bad.

India, Sam's newest hire, came in ten minutes early, ready to hustle. I liked her more and more as I worked with her. She was clever at handling difficult customers. Since the only person who came in (when we unlocked the front door at eleven) was our most consistent alcoholic, Jane Bodehouse, India went back to the kitchen to help Antoine, who'd turned on the fryers and heated up the griddle. India was glad to find things to do while she was at work, which was a refreshing change.

Kenya, one of our patrol officers, came and looked around inquiringly. "You need something, Kenya?" I asked. "Kevin's not here." Kevin, another patrolman, was deeply in love with Kenya, and she with him. They ate lunch here at least once or twice a week.

"My sister here? She told me she was going to be working today," Kenya asked.

"Is India your sister?" Kenya was a good ten years older than India, so I hadn't put them together.

"Half sister. Yeah, our mother would get out the map when we were born," Kenya said, kind of daring me to find that amusing. "She named us after places she wanted to go. My big brother's name is Spain. I got a younger one named Cairo."

"She didn't stick to countries."

"No, she threw in a few cities for good measure. She thought the word 'Egypt' was 'too chewy.' That's a direct quote." Kenya was walking as she talked, following my pointed finger in the direction of the kitchen. "Thanks, Sookie."

The foreign names were kind of cool. Kenya's mom sounded like fun to me. My mom hadn't been a fun person; but then, she'd had a lot to worry about, after she'd had me. I sighed to myself. I tried not to regret things I couldn't change. I listened to Kenya's voice coming through the serving hatch, brisk and warm and clear, greeting Antoine, telling India that Cairo had fixed India's car and she should come by to pick it up when she got off work. I brightened when my own brother walked in just as Kenya was leaving. Instead of sitting at the bar or taking a table, he came up to me.

"You think I look like a Holland?" I asked him, and Jason gave me one of his blankest stares.

"Naw, you look like a Sookie," he said. "Listen, Sook, I'm gonna do it."

"Gonna do what?"

He looked at me impatiently. I could tell this wasn't how he'd expected the conversation to go. "I'm gonna ask Michele to marry me."

"Oh, that's great!" I said, with genuine enthusiasm. "Really, Jason, I'm happy for you. I sure hope she says yes."

"This time I'm going to do everything right," he said, almost to himself.

His first marriage had been a mistake from the start, and it had ended even worse than it had begun.

"Michele's got a good head on her shoulders," I said.

"She's no kid," he agreed. "In fact, she's a little older than me, but she don't like me to bring that up."

"You won't, then, right? No jokes," I warned him.

He grinned at me. "No jokes. And she's not pregnant, and she's got her own job and her own money." None of these facts had been true of his first wife.

"Go for it, Brother." I gave him a quick hug.

He flashed the grin at me, the one that had hooked scores of women. "I'm asking her today when she gets off work. I was gonna eat lunch here, but I'm too nervous."

"Let me know what she says, Jason. I'll be praying for you." I beamed at his back as he left the bar. He was as happy and nervous as I'd ever seen him.

Merlotte's began to fill up after that, and I was too busy to think much. I love being at work, because I get to be around people and I know what's going on in Bon Temps. On the other hand, most of the time I know *too* much. It's a feathery balance between listening to people with my ears and not listening to them in my head, and it's not too surprising that I have a big rep for being eccentric. At least most people are too nice to call me Crazy Sookie anymore. I like to think I've proved myself to the community.

Tara came in with her assistant, McKenna, to order an early lunch. Tara looked even bigger with her pregnancy than she had at Hooligans the night before.

Since she'd brought McKenna along, I couldn't ask Tara what I really wanted to know. What had happened when she talked to JB about his second job at Hooligans? Even if he hadn't seen Tara in the crowd, he'd have to know we were going to tell her.

But Tara was thinking about the shop with great determination, and when she wasn't planning to restock the lingerie counter, she was concentrating on the Merlotte's menu—the very limited menu that she knew back and forth—trying to figure out what she could digest, and how many more calories she could ingest, without actually exploding. McKenna's brain wasn't any help; though McKenna loved to know every little snippet of information about Bon Temps happenings, she didn't know about JB's moonlighting. She would have been vastly interested if I'd told her. McKenna would have *loved* to be a telepath, for about twenty-four hours.

But after she'd heard stuff like *I can't take it anymore, I'm going to wait till he's asleep and slash him* or *I'd like to take her and bend her over the bar and drive my . . .* Well, after a day or two of that, she wouldn't love it so much.

Tara didn't even go to the ladies' room by herself. She towed McKenna along. I looked questioningly at Tara. She glared at me. Not ready to talk, not yet.

When the lunch rush was over, only two tables remained in use, and they were in India's section. I went back to Sam's office to work on the endless paperwork. Trees had died to make these forms, and that seemed a great pity to me. I tried to fill out anything I could online, though I was very slow at it. Sam came back to his office to retrieve a screw-driver from his desk, so I asked him a question about an employee tax form. He was leaning over me to look at it when Jannalynn walked in.

"Hey, Jannalynn," I said. I didn't even look at her because I'd identified her mental signature before she'd entered, and I was trying real hard to complete the form while Sam's instructions were still fresh in my mind.

"Oh, hey, Jan," Sam said. I could feel his smile in his voice.

Instead of a response, there was an ominous silence.

"What?" I said, filling in one more figure.

I finally looked up to see that Jannalynn was in high offensive mode, her eyes round and wide, her nostrils dilated, her whole slim body tense with aggression.

"What?" I asked again, alarmed. "Are we being attacked?"

Sam remained silent. I swung around in the swivel chair to look up at him, and he was in a posture that was tense, too. But his face was one big warning.

"You two want to be alone?" I scrambled to get up and out from between them.

"I would have thought so before I walked in," Jannalynn said, her fists like little hammers.

"What . . . wait! You thinking Sam and I are fooling around in the office?" Despite Mustapha's warning, I was genuinely astonished. "Honey, we are filling out tax forms. If you think there's anything sexy about that, you should get a job with the IRS!"

There was a long moment when I wondered if I was going to get my ass kicked, but gradually the suspense ratcheted down. I did notice that Sam didn't say anything, not a word, until Jannalynn's stance had completely relaxed. I took a deep breath.

"Excuse us for a minute, Sookie," Sam said, and I could tell he was really angry.

"Certainly." I was out of that room as fast as a greased pig. I would rather have cleaned the men's room after a Saturday night than have stayed in Sam's office.

India was helping D'Eriq clear off a table. She glanced at me and half smiled. "What lit your tail on fire?" she asked. "Sam's scary girlfriend?"

I nodded. "I'm just going to find something to do out here," I said. This was a very good opportunity to dust the bottles and shelves behind the bar, and I moved them all carefully, cleaning a bit of shelf and moving on to another one.

Though I couldn't help but wonder what was going on in Sam's office, I reminded myself repeatedly that it wasn't my business. I had the bar as clean as a whistle by the time Jannalynn and Sam emerged.

"Sorry," she said to me, with no particular sincerity.

I nodded in acknowledgment.

Jannalynn thought, *She'll get Sam if she can.*

Oh, please! I thought, *She'd be real happy if I died.*

And then she left the bar, Sam following her to say good-bye. Or to make sure she actually got in her car. Or both.

By the time he returned, I was so desperate for something to do I was about to start counting the toothpicks in the clear plastic dispenser. "We can get back on that paperwork tomorrow," Sam said in passing, and continued walking. He avoided my eyes. He was surely embarrassed. It's always good to give people time to recover from that, especially guys, so I cut Sam some slack.

A work crew from Norcross came in, their shift over and some celebration in progress. India and I began putting tables together to accommodate all of them. While I worked, I thought about young shifter women. I'd encountered more than one who was very aggressive, but there were very few female packleaders in the United States, especially in the South. An outstanding few of the female Weres I'd met were extremely vicious. I wondered if this exaggerated aggression was due to the established male power structure in the packs.

Jannalynn wasn't psychotic, as the Pelt sisters and Marnie Stonebrook had been; but she was uber-conscious of her own toughness and ability.

I had to abandon theoretical thinking to get the drink orders right for the Norcross men and women. Sam emerged to work behind the bar, India and I began moving at a faster pace, and gradually everything settled back to normal.

Just as I was about to get off work, Michele and Jason came in together. They were holding hands. From Jason's smile, it was easy to see what her answer had been.

"Seems like we're going to be sisters," Michele said in her husky voice, and I gave her a heartfelt hug. I gave Jason an even happier one. I could feel his delight pouring out of his head, and his thoughts weren't so much coherent as a jumble of pleasure.

"Have you two had time to think about when it'll be?"

"Nothing stopping us from having it soon," Jason said. "We've both been married already, and we don't go to church much, so there's no reason to have a church wedding."

I thought that was a pity, but I kept my mouth shut. There was nothing to gain and everything to lose by adding my two cents. They were grown-ups.

"I might need to prepare Cork a little bit," Michele said, smiling. "I don't think he'll kick up a fuss over me remarrying, but I do want to break it to him gentle." Michele still worked for her former father-in-law, who seemed to have more regard for Michele than he had for his lazy son.

"So it'll be soon. I hope that it's okay if I come?"

"Oh, sure, Sook," Jason said, and hugged me. "We ain't eloping or anything. We just don't want a big church thing. We'll have a party out at the house afterward. Right, honey?" He deferred to Michele.

"Sure," she said. "We'll fire up our grill, maybe Hoyt can bring his over, too, and we'll cook whatever anybody brings. And other guests can bring drinks or whatever, vegetables and desserts. That way no one will worry and we'll all have a good time."

A potluck wedding. That was very practical and low-key. I asked them to let me know what I could bring that would be most helpful. After lots of mutual goodwill had been exchanged, they left, still holding hands and smiling.

India said, "Another one bites the dust. How you feeling about this, Sookie?"

"I like Michele real well. I'm so happy!"

Sam called, "They engaged?"

"Yeah," I called back, a few happy tears in my eyes. Sam was making an effort to sound upbeat, though he was still a little worried about his own romantic situation. Any irritation I'd felt about the Jannalynn episode simply melted away. Sam had been my friend for years, while significant others came and went. I went up to the bar and leaned against it. "Second time around for both of 'em. They're real good together."

He nodded, accepting my tacit reassurance that I wasn't going to bring up Jannalynn's little outburst of jealousy. "Crystal was all wrong for your brother; Michele is all right."

"In a nutshell," I agreed.

Since Holly called in to say her car wouldn't start but Hoyt was working on it, I was still at Merlotte's when JB came in about ten minutes later. My friend, the secret stripper, was looking handsome and hearty as always. There's something about JB, something warm and simple that's really appealing, especially when added to his nonthreatening good looks. He's like a great loaf of homemade bread.

"Hey, friend," I said. "What can I get for you?"

"Sookie, I saw you last night." He waited for my big reaction.

"I saw you, too." Just about every inch of him.

"Tara was there," JB told me, as though that would be news. "I saw her as she was leaving."

"Uh-huh," I agreed. "She was."

"Was she mad?"

"She was real surprised," I said cautiously. "Are you seriously telling me you-all have not talked about last night?"

"I got in pretty late," he said. "I slept out on the couch. When I got up this morning, she'd already gone to the store."

"Oh, JB." I shook my head. "Honey, you *got* to talk to her."

"What can I say? I know I should have told her." He made a hopeless gesture with his hands. "I just couldn't think of any other way to earn some extra money. Her shop's not doing so great right now, and I don't make a lot. We don't have good insurance. Twins! That's gonna be a big hospital bill. What if one of 'em's sick?"

It was so tempting to tell him not to worry about it—but there was every reason for him to be concerned, and it would be patronizing to tell him he didn't need to be. JB had made a clever move, for JB; he had found a way to use his assets to make extra money. His downfall had been in not informing his wife he was taking off his clothes in front of many other women on a weekly basis.

We talked off and on while JB nursed a beer at the bar. Tactfully, Sam pretended to be so busy that he was deaf to our intermittent conversation. I urged JB to cook something special for Tara that night or to stop off at Wal-Mart and buy her a little bouquet. Maybe he could give her a foot rub and a back massage, anything to make her feel loved and special. "And don't tell her how big she is!" I said, poking a finger into his chest. "Don't you dare! You tell her she's more beautiful than ever now that she's carrying your children!"

JB looked exactly as though he were going to say, "But that's not true." He was sure thinking it. He met my eyes and clamped his lips shut.

"Doesn't make any difference what the truth is, you say she looks great!" I told him. "I know you love her."

JB looked sideways for a minute, testing that statement for its truth value, and then he nodded. "I do love her," he said. Then he smiled. "She completes me," he said proudly. JB loved movies.

"Well, you just complete her right back," I said. "She needs to feel pretty and adored, because she feels big and clumsy and uncomfortable. It's not easy being pregnant, I hear."

"I'll try, Sookie. Can I call you if she doesn't soften up?"

"Yeah, but I know you can work this out, JB. Just be loving and sincere, and she'll come around."

"I like stripping," he said suddenly, as I was turning away.

"Yeah, I know," I said.

"I knew you would understand." He took a last sip of beer, left Sam a tip, and went to work at the gym in Clarice.

"This must be couples day," India said. "Sam and Jannalynn, Jason and Michele, JB and Tara." The thought didn't seem to make her particularly happy.

"You still dating Lola?" Though I knew the answer, it was always better to ask.

"Naw. It didn't work out."

"I'm sorry," I said. "Maybe some day soon the right woman will just walk in the door of the bar, and you'll be all fixed up."

"I hope so." India looked depressed. "I'm not a fan of the wedding industry, but I sure would like a steady someone. Dating makes me all confused."

"I never was any good at dating."

"That why you go with the vamp? To scare off everyone else?"

"I love him," I said steadily. "That's why I go with him." I didn't point out that human guys were simply impossible for me. You can imagine reading your date's mind every minute. No, it really wouldn't be any fun, would it?

"No need to get all defensive," India said.

I thought I'd been matter-of-fact. "He's fun," I said mildly, "and he treats me nice."

"They're . . . I don't know how to ask this, but they're cold, right?"

India wasn't the first person who'd tried to find a delicate way to ask me that. There wasn't any delicate way.

"Not room temperature," I said. I left it at that, because any more was none of anyone else's business.

"Damn," she said, after a moment. After a longer moment, she said, "Ew."

I shrugged. She opened her mouth, looked as though she wanted to ask me something else, and then she closed it.

Fortunately for both of us, her table gestured that they wanted their bill, and one of Jane Bodehouse's buddies came in drunk off her ass, so we both had things to do. Holly finally arrived to relieve me, complaining about her no-good car. India was working a double shift, so she kept her apron on. I waved a casual good-bye to Sam, glad to be walking out the door.

I just made it to the library before it closed, and then I stopped by the post office to buy some stamps from the machine in the lobby. Halleigh Bellefleur was there on the same errand, and we greeted each other with real pleasure. You know how sometimes you just like someone, though you don't hang around with them? Halleigh and I don't have much of anything in common, from our background to our educational level to our interests, but we like each other, anyway. Halleigh's baby bump was pronounced, and she looked as rosy as Tara looked wrecked.

"How's Andy doing?" I asked.

"He's not sleeping well, he's so excited about this baby," she said. "He calls me from work to ask how I am and to find out how many times the baby kicked."

"Sticking with 'Caroline'?"

"Yeah, he was real pleased when I suggested that. His grandma brought him up, and she was a fine woman, if a little on the scary side." Halleigh smiled.

Caroline Bellefleur had been more than a little on the scary side. She'd been the last great lady of Bon Temps. She had also been my friend Bill Compton's great-granddaughter. Halleigh's baby would be three more greats away.

I told Halleigh about Jason's engagement, and she said all the right things. She was as polite as Andy's grandmother—and a hell of a lot warmer.

Though it was good to see Halleigh, when I got back into the car with my stamps I was feeling a little blue. I turned the key in the ignition, but I didn't put the car in reverse.

I knew I was a lucky woman in many respects. But there was life being created all around me, and I wasn't . . .

I shut down that line of thought with a sharp command to myself. I would *not* start down the self-pity path. Just because I wasn't pregnant and wasn't married to someone who could make me that way, that was no reason to feel like an island in the stream. I shook myself briskly and set off to complete the rest of my errands. When I caught a glimpse of Faye de Leon coming out of Grabbit Kwik, my attitude adjusted. Faye had been pregnant six times, and she was around my age. She'd told Maxine Fortenberry that she hadn't wanted the last three. But her husband loved to see her pregnant, and he loved kids, and Faye allowed herself to be used "like a puppy mill," as Maxine put it.

Yes, attitude adjustment, indeed.

I had my evening meal and watched television and read one of my new library books that night, and I felt just fine, all by myself, every time I thought about Faye.

Chapter 3

There were no great revelations at work the next day, and not a single outstanding incident. I actually enjoyed that. I just took orders and delivered drinks and food, pocketing my tips. Kennedy Keyes was at the bar. I worried that she and Danny were still quarreling, though he might be at his other job at the home builders' supply place. Kennedy was subdued and dull, and I was sorry; but I didn't want to find out any more about her relationship problems—*anybody's* relationship problems. I had enough of my own.

It's a conscious effort to block out the thoughts of other people. Though I've gotten better at it, it's still work. I don't have to try as hard with the two-natured, because their thoughts are not as clear as human thoughts; I catch only a sentence or emotion, here and there. Even among humans, some are clearer broadcasters than others. But before

I learned how to shield my brain, it was like listening to ten radio stations at a time. Hard to act normal when all that's going on in your brain and you're still trying to listen to what people actually say with their mouths.

So during that little period of normality, I achieved a measure of peace. I convinced myself that the meeting with Felipe would go well, that he would believe either that we hadn't killed Victor or that Victor's death was justifiable. I was in no hurry to face him to find out.

I stayed gossiping at the bar for a few minutes, and on the way home I filled up the car with gas. I got a chicken sandwich from the Sonic and drove home slowly.

Sunset was so late in the summer that the vamps wouldn't be up for a couple of hours yet. I hadn't heard a word from anyone at Fangtasia. I didn't even know when I was supposed to get there. I just knew I had to look nice, because Eric would expect it in front of visitors.

Dermot wasn't in the house. I'd hoped Claude might have returned from his mysterious trip to Faery, but if he had, there was no sign. I couldn't spare any more concern for the fae tonight. I had vampire problems on my mind.

I was too anxious to eat more than half my sandwich. I sorted through the mail I'd picked up at the end of the driveway, throwing most of it into the trash can. I had to fish my electric bill out after I tossed it along with a furniture-sale flyer. I opened it to check the amount. Claude had *better* return from Faery; he was a reckless energy user, and my bill was almost double its normal size. I wanted Claude to pay his share. My water heater was gas, and that bill was way up, too. I put the Shreveport newspaper on the kitchen table to read later. It was sure to be full of bad news.

I showered and redid my hair and makeup. It was so hot that

I didn't want to wear slacks, and shorts would not suit Eric's sense of formality. I sighed, resigned to the inevitable. I began looking through my summer dresses. Luckily, I'd taken the time to shave my legs, a habit Eric found both fascinating and bizarre. My skin was nice and brown this far into the tanning season, and my hair was a few shades lighter and still looked good from the remedial trim the hairdresser Immanuel had given it a few weeks previously. I put on a white skirt, a bright blue sleeveless blouse, and a real broad black leather belt that had gotten too tight for Tara. My good black sandals were still in pretty fair shape. My hand paused over the drawer of my dressing table. Within it, camouflaged with a light dusting of face powder, lay a powerful fairy magical object called a cluviel dor.

I'd never thought of carrying it around on my person. Part of me was afraid of wasting the power of the cluviel dor. If I used it recklessly, it would amount to using a nuclear device to kill a fly.

The cluviel dor was a rare and ancient fairy love gift. I guess it was the fae equivalent of a Fabergé Easter egg, but magical. My grandfather—not my human one, but my half-human, half-fairy grandfather, Fintan, Dermot's twin—had given it to my grandmother Adele, who had hidden it away. She had never told me she had it, and I had only just discovered it during the attic clean-out. It had taken me longer to identify it and to learn more about its properties. Only the part-demon lawyer Desmond Cataliades knew I had it . . . though perhaps my friend Amelia suspected, since I'd asked her to teach me about what it could do.

Up until now, I'd hidden it just like my grandmother had. You can't go through life carrying a gun in your hand just in case someone wants to attack you, right? Though the cluviel dor was a love gift, not a weapon, its use might have results just as dramatic. Possession of the cluviel dor granted the possessor a wish. That wish had to be a personal one, to benefit the possessor or someone the possessor loved. But there were some awful scenarios I'd imagined: What if I wished an oncoming car wouldn't hit me, and instead it hit another car and killed a whole family? What if I wished that my gran were alive again, and instead of my living grandmother, her corpse appeared?

So I understood why Gran had hidden it away from casual discovery. I understood that it had frightened her with its potential, and maybe she hadn't believed that a Christian should use magic to change her own history.

On the other hand, the cluviel dor could have saved Gran's life if she'd had it at the moment she was attacked; but it had been in a secret drawer in an old desk up in the attic, and she had died. It was like paying for a Life Alert and then leaving it up in the kitchen cabinet out of reach. No one could take it, and it couldn't be used for ill; but then again, it couldn't be used for good, either.

If making one's wish might lead to catastrophic results, it was almost as perilous to simply possess the cluviel dor. If anyone—any supernatural—learned I had this amazing object, I would be in even more danger than my normal allotment.

I opened the drawer and looked at my grandmother's love gift. The cluviel dor was a creamy green and looked not unlike a slightly thick powder compact, which was why I kept it in my makeup drawer. The lid was circled with a band of gold. It would not open; it had never opened. I didn't know how to trigger it. In my hand, the cluviel dor radiated the same warmth I felt when I was close to Niall . . . the same warmth times a hundred.

I was so tempted to put it in my purse. My hand hovered over it.

I took it out of the drawer and turned it over and over in my hands. As I held the smooth object, feeling intense pleasure in its nearness, I weighed the value of taking it with me against the risk.

In the end, I put it back in the drawer with a powder puff on top of it.

The phone rang.

Pam said, "Our meeting is at Eric's house at nine o'clock."

"I thought I'd be coming to Fangtasia," I said, a little surprised. "Okay, I'll be on my way in a jiffy."

Without answering, Pam hung up. Vampires are not experts on phone manners. I leaned over to look in the mirror while I applied my lipstick.

In two minutes, the phone rang again.

"Hello?"

"Sookie," said Mustapha's gruff voice. "You don't need to be here till ten."

"Oh? Well . . . okay." That would give me a more reasonable amount of time; I wouldn't have to risk getting a ticket, and there were a few more little things I'd wanted to do before I left.

I said a prayer, and I turned down my bed as a sign of faith that I would return home to sleep in it. I watered my plants, just in case. I quickly checked my e-mail, found nothing of interest. After looking at myself one more time in the full-length mirror on the bathroom door, I decided to leave. I had a comfortable amount of time.

I listened to dance music on the way over to Shreveport, and I sang along with songs from *Saturday Night Fever*. I loved to watch the young John Travolta dance, and that was something I was good at. I could sing only when I was by myself. I belted out "Stayin' Alive," aware that might be my own theme song. By the time I stopped at the guardhouse at the entrance to Eric's gated community, I was a fraction less worried about the evening.

I wondered where Dan Shelley was. The new night guard, a muscular human whose nametag read "Vince," waved me through without getting up. "Enjoy the party," he called.

A little surprised, I smiled and waved back at him. I'd thought I was going to a serious council, but evidently this visit by the Grand Poobah was starting off on a social note.

Though Eric's fancy neighbors on the circle raised their eyebrows at cars parked on the street, I did just that because I didn't want to be blocked in. The broad driveway to the left of the yard, running slightly uphill to Eric's garage, was packed solid. I'd never seen so many cars there. I could hear music coming from the house, though it was faint. Vampires didn't need to turn the volume up like humans did; they could hear all too well.

I turned off the motor and sat behind the wheel, trying to get my head together before walking into the lion's den. Why hadn't I just said no when Mustapha told me to come? Until this moment, I literally hadn't considered the option of staying home. Was I here because I loved Eric? Or because I was in so deep in the vampire world that it hadn't occurred to me to refuse?

Maybe a little of both.

I turned to open the Malibu door, and Bill was standing *right there.* I gave a little yip of shock. "You know better than to do that!" I snarled, glad to vent some of my fear in the guise of anger. I shot out of the driver's seat and slammed the door behind me.

"Turn around and go back to Bon Temps, sweetheart," Bill said. In the harsh streetlight, my first vampire lover looked horribly white except for his eyes, which were shadowed pits. His dark thick hair and his dark clothing provided even more contrast, so much so that he looked as though he were enameled with luminescent paint, like a house sign.

"I've been sitting in my car thinking about it," I admitted. "But it's too late."

"You should go." He meant it.

"Ah . . . that would be kind of leaving Eric in the lurch," I said, and there might have been a bit of a question in my voice.

"He can manage without you tonight. Please, go home." Bill's cool hand took mine, and he applied very gentle pressure.

"You'd better tell me what's happening."

"Felipe has brought some of his vampires with him. They swept through a bar or two to pick up some humans to drink with—and from. Their behavior is . . . well, you remember how much Diane, Liam, and Malcolm disgusted you?"

The three vampires, now finally dead, had not had any qualms about having sex with humans in front of me, and it hadn't ended there.

"Yes, I remember."

"Felipe's ordinarily more discreet than that, but he's in a party mood tonight."

I swallowed. "I told Eric I'd come," I said. "Felipe might take it bad if I'm not here, since I'm Eric's human wife." Eric had coerced me into the title because it gave me a certain amount of protection.

"Eric will survive your absence," Bill said. If he'd extended that sentence, I was pretty sure the ending would have been, "But you may not survive your presence." He continued, "I'm stuck out here on guard duty. I'm not allowed inside. I can't protect you."

Leaving the cluviel dor at home had been a mistake.

"Bill, I do pretty good taking care of myself," I said. "You wish me well, you hear?"

"Sookie . . ."

"I have to go in."

“Then I do wish you well.” His voice was wooden, but his eyes were not.

I had a choice. I could be formal and go to the front door; a path of stepping stones branched off from the driveway and meandered up the yard to the massive front door. This path was prettily bordered by crepe myrtles, now in full bloom. My other option was to continue up the driveway, swing right into the garage, and enter through the kitchen. That was the one I chose. After all, I was more at home here than any of the Nevada visitors. I strode briskly up the driveway, my heels making a *tittup* sound in the quiet night.

The kitchen door was unlocked, which was also unusual. I looked around the large and useless kitchen. Someone should be guarding this door, surely, with guests in the house.

I finally realized Mustapha Khan was standing at the French windows at the back of the kitchen, past the breakfast table where no one ever ate breakfast. He was looking out into the night.

“Mustapha?” I said.

The daytime man swung around. His very posture was tense. He jerked his chin at me by way of greeting. Despite the hour, Mustapha was wearing his dark glasses.

I looked around for his shadow, but there was no Warren in sight.

For the first time, I wished I knew what Mustapha was thinking—but his thoughts were as opaque as those of any Were I'd ever encountered.

My skin crawled, but I didn't know why.

“How's it going out there?” I asked, keeping my voice quiet.

After a pause he answered me, his own voice just as hushed. “Maybe I shoulda gotten a job with some freakin' goblins. Or joined the pack and let Alcide boss me around. That would have been better than this. If I was you, I'd get my ass back in the car and go home. If Eric wasn't paying me so good, that's what I'd do."

This was beginning to sound more and more like the beginning of a fairy tale:

FIRST MAN: Don't cross the bridge; it's perilous.

HEROINE: But I must cross the bridge.

SECOND MAN: Upon your life, don't cross the bridge!

HEROINE: But I have to cross the bridge.

In a fairy tale, there'd be a third encounter; there are always three. And maybe I would have another one, yet. But I'd gotten the idea.

Anxiety trickled down my spine like sweat. I sure didn't want to cross that bridge. Maybe I should just ease on down the road?

But Pam entered the kitchen, and my opportunity was gone. "Thank God you're here," she said, her faint British accent more apparent than usual. "I was afraid you weren't going to come. Felipe has noticed you haven't put in an appearance."

"But you changed the time," I replied, puzzled. "Mustapha told me to be here . . ." I glanced at the clock on the microwave. "Just now."

Pam shook her head, then gave Mustapha a look that seemed more puzzled than irritated. "We'll talk later," she told him. She made an impatient beckoning gesture to me.

I took a second to stow my purse in one of the kitchen cabinets, simply because a kitchen is the safest storage place in a vampire house. Before I followed Pam into the large open living room/dining room area, I fixed a smile on my face. I couldn't help casting a glance over my shoulder at Mustapha, but all I saw was the blankness of the lenses of his dark glasses.

I looked ahead of me, after that. When you're around vampires, it's always better to have your eye on what's coming.

Though Eric's bold decorating had been featured in *Louisiana Interiors*, the photographer would hardly have recognized the room tonight. The striped drapes across the front windows were firmly drawn. There were no fresh flowers. A mixed group of humans and vampires were strewn around the large space.

A hugely muscular man with dyed blond hair was dancing with a young woman to my far left, close to the dining table, which Eric used for business conferences. As I approached, they stopped dancing and started kissing, noisily and with much tongue. A square-jawed male vampire was taking blood from a well-endowed human female on the loveseat, and he was making a messy job of it. There were blood drips on the upholstery.

Right then, I was pissed off. It added fuel to the flame when I absorbed the fact that a red-haired vamp I didn't know was standing on Eric's coffee table (in high heels!) dancing to an old Rolling Stones CD. Another vampire with thick black hair was watching her with casual appreciation, as if he'd seen her do the same thing many times but still enjoyed the sight. Her stiletto heels were digging, digging into the wood of the table, one of Eric's favorite acquisitions.

I could feel my lips draw in like purse strings. A sideways glance at Pam showed me she was keeping her face as smooth and empty as a pretty bowl. With a huge effort, I wiped my own expression clean. Dammit, we'd *just* replaced all the carpeting and had the walls repainted after the Alexei Romanov debacle! Now the upholstery would need to be cleaned again, and I'd have to find someone to refinish the table.

I reminded myself I had bigger problems than a few stains and gouges.

Bill had been right. Mustapha had been right. This was not a place I should be. Despite what Pam had said, I couldn't believe any of the vampires would have missed me. They were all too busy.

But then the man watching the dancer turned his head to look at me. I realized that he was a fully clothed (thank you, God) Felipe de Castro. He smiled at me, his sharp white fangs glistening in the overhead light. Yes, he'd been enjoying the dancing.

"Miss Stackhouse!" he said lazily. "I'd been afraid you wouldn't come tonight. It's been too long since I've had the pleasure of seeing you." Since Felipe had a thick accent, my name sounded more like "Meees Stekhuss!" The first time I'd met him, the king had been wearing an honest-to-God cape. Tonight he'd dressed conservatively in a gray shirt, silver vest, and black pants.

"It's been a while, Your Majesty," I said, which was simply all I could think of to say. "I'm so sorry I'm a bit late to greet you. Where is Eric?"

"He's in one of the bedrooms," Felipe said, still smiling. His mustache and chin strip were perfectly black and perfectly groomed. The King of Nevada, Arkansas, and Louisiana was not a tall man. He was strikingly handsome. He possessed a vitality that was hugely attractive—though not to me, and not tonight. Felipe was also quite the politician, I'd heard, and he was certainly a businessman. No telling how much money he'd amassed in his long life.

I smiled back at the king in a frozen way. I was mighty put out. The Nevada visitors weren't acting any better than, say, small-town firemen attending a convention in New Orleans. That these visitors were from Las Vegas and yet felt it necessary to misbehave in Shreveport . . . well, it didn't speak well for them.

"In one of the bedrooms" didn't sound good, but of course that was what Felipe had intended. "I'd better tell him I'm here," I said, and turned to Pam. "Let's go, girlfriend."

Pam took my hand, and it was a measure of the evening that I actually found that comforting. Her face was still as wax.

As we navigated through the room (the muscular man wasn't actually having sex with his companion, but it wasn't far in the future), Pam hissed, "Did you see that? The blood will *never* come out of the upholstery."

"It won't be as hard to clean up as the night Alexei went nuts here," I said, trying to get perspective. "Or the club, after we did—that thing." I didn't want to say "killed Victor" out loud.

"But that was *fun*." Pam was practically pouting.

"This isn't, for you?"

"No, I like my pleasures more personal and private."

"Oh, me, *too*," I said. "Why is Eric back here instead of out there?"

"I don't know. I just came back from a liquor run," she said briefly. "Mustapha insisted we needed some more rum."

She was doing Mustapha's bidding now? But I pressed my lips shut. It was no business of mine.

By that time we'd reached the door of the bedroom I used at Eric's, since I didn't want to be shut downstairs with him all day in his light-tight sleeping room. Pam, a step ahead of me, pushed open the door and stiffened. Eric was there, and he was sitting on the bed, but he was feeding off someone—a dark-haired woman. She was sprawled across his lap, her bright summer dress twisted around her body, one hand gripping his shoulder and kneading it while he sucked from her neck. Her other hand was . . . she was pleasuring herself.

"You *asshole*," I said, and I reversed on the spot. Getting the hell out of there was my all-consuming desire. Eric raised his head, his mouth bloody, and his eyes met mine. He was . . . drunk.

"You can't go," Pam said. She gripped my arm now, and I could tell it would break before she'd release me. "If you run out now, we'll look weak, and Felipe will react. We'll all suffer. Something's wrong with Eric."

"I really don't give a damn," I told her. My head felt oddly light and distant from the shock. I wondered if I would faint or throw up or leap on Eric and choke him.

"You need to leave," Eric told the woman. His words were slurred. What the *hell*?

"But we were just getting around to the good part," she said, in what she thought was a seductive voice. "Don't make me go, baby, before the big payoff. If you want her to join in, that's all right with me, sugar." It took all her effort to get the words out. She was white as a sheet. She'd lost a lot of blood.

"You must go," Eric said, a bit more clearly. His voice had the shove in it vampires use to get humans moving.

Though I refused to look at the brunette, I knew when she got off the bed, and Eric. I knew when she staggered and almost fell. *Now I can keep my car,* she thought.

I was so startled to hear this that I turned to look at her. She was younger than me, and she was skinny. Somehow that made Eric's offense worse. After a second I could glimpse, past my agitation, that she had a lot of sickness in her head. The stuff churning around in her mind was both awful and confusing. Self-loathing made her thoughts all tinged with gray, as if she were rotting from her core out. The surface still looked pretty, but it wouldn't be for long.

The girl also had twoey blood, though I couldn't tell what kind . . .

maybe werewolf. One of her parents was the real deal. That made sense, given Eric's condition. Twoey blood packed a punch for vampires, and she'd amped it up somehow to make herself more intoxicating.

Pam said, "I don't know who you are or how you got in here, girl, but you must leave now."

The girl laughed, which neither Pam nor I had expected. Pam jerked, and I felt a solar flare go off in my head. I'd added rage to disgust. Laughing! My eyes met the girl's. The smirk vanished from her lips, and she blanched.

I was no vampire, but I guess I looked pretty threatening.

"All right, all right, I'm going. I'll be out of Shreveport by dawn." She was *lying*. She decided to make one last attempt to . . . what? She sneered at me and said deliberately, "It ain't my fault that your man was hungry . . ." Before I could move, Pam backhanded her. The girl lurched against the wall, then slid to the ground.

"Get up," Pam said, her voice deadly.

With visible effort, the girl rose to her feet. There were no more smiles or provocative statements. She passed close to me as she left the room, and I smelled her; not only a trace of twoey, but another scent, blood with a sweet undertone. She made her way down the hall and out to the living room, supporting herself with one hand against the wall.

After she'd cleared the door, Pam shut it. The room was oddly quiet.

My brain was running in a hundred different directions. From my late arrival, to the new guard at the gate, to the strange thoughts I'd read from the girl, the odd scent I'd caught when she was near . . . and then my whole focus fell on a different subject.

My "husband."

Eric still remained sitting on the side of the bed.

The bed I thought of as mine. The bed where we had sex. The bed where I slept.

He spoke directly to me. "You know I take blood . . ." he began, but I held up a hand.

"Don't speak," I said. He looked indignant, and his mouth opened, and I said again, *"Don't. Speak."*

Seriously, if I could have gotten away by myself for thirty minutes (or thirty hours or thirty days), I could have dealt with the situation. As it was, I had to do a speed speech in my head.

I knew I wasn't Eric's only drinking fountain. (One person could not be the sole food source for a vampire; or rather, not for a vampire who doesn't supplement with synthetic.)

Not his fault he needed food, blah blah.

When it's freely offered, why not take it, blah blah.

But.

He knew I was due to arrive.

He knew I would let him drink.

He knew the fact that he chose to drink from another woman would hurt me deeply. And he did it, anyway. Unless there was something I didn't know about this woman, or something she'd done to Eric that had triggered this reaction, this signaled that he didn't care about me as deeply as I'd always thought.

I could only think, *Thank God I broke the blood bond. If I'd felt his enjoyment while he was sucking on her, I'd have wanted to kill him.*

Eric said, "If you hadn't broken our blood bond, this would never have happened."

I had another solar flare in my head. "This is why I don't carry a stake," I muttered, and swore long and fluently to myself.

I hadn't told *Pam* not to speak. After eyeing me intently to assess my mood, she said, "You know that in a while, you'll adjust. This was a question of timing, not of unfaithfulness."

After I took a long moment to resent the hell out of her conviction that I was going to accommodate Eric's behavior, I had to nod. I wasn't necessarily agreeing with the premise behind her words—that when I'd calmed down I wouldn't mind what Eric had done. I was simply acknowledging the fact that she had a point. Though it made me scream inside, I pushed aside all the things I wanted to say to Eric, because something more urgent was happening here. Even I could see that.

"Listen, here's the important stuff," I said, and Pam nodded. Eric looked surprised, and his back stiffened. He looked more like himself, more alert and intelligent.

"That girl didn't just wander in here out of the blue; she was sent," I said.

The vampires looked at each other. They shrugged simultaneously. "I'd never seen her before," Eric said.

"I thought she came in with Felipe's pickups," Pam said.

"There's a new guy at the gate." I looked from one to the other. "Where'd Dan Shelley go, tonight of all nights? And after Pam called me and told me to be here at nine, Mustapha called me right back and told me to be here an hour later. Eric, I'm sure that girl tasted different to you?"

"Yes," he said, nodding slowly. "I'm still feeling the effects. She was extra . . ."

"Like she'd had some kind of supplement?" I suppressed another surge of hurt and anger.

"Yes," he agreed. He got up, but I could see that standing wasn't easy. "Yes, as if she'd had a Were-and-fairy cocktail." His eyes closed. "Delicious."

Pam said, "Eric, if you hadn't been hungry, you would have questioned such an opportune arrival."

"Yes," he agreed. "My mind isn't yet clear, but I see the sense of your words."

"Sookie, what did you get from her thoughts?" Pam asked.

"She was earning money. But she was excited that she might die." I shrugged.

"But she didn't."

"No, I got here in time to interrupt what would have been a fatal feeding. Right, Eric? Could you have stopped?"

He looked profoundly embarrassed. "Maybe not. My control was almost gone. It was her smell. When she came up to me, she seemed so ordinary. Well, attractive because of the Were blood, but nothing really special. And I certainly didn't offer her money. Then, suddenly . . ." He shook his head and gulped.

"Why did her attraction suddenly increase?" Pam was nothing if not pragmatic. "Wait. I apologize. We don't have time to get lost in the whys and wherefores. We must get through this tonight, us three," she said, looking at me and at Eric in turn. I nodded again. Eric gave a jerk of his head. "Good," she said. "Sookie, you got here just in time. She wasn't here by accident. She didn't smell and taste that way by accident. A lot of things happened here tonight that reek of a plot. My friend, I'm going to repeat myself—you have to put aside personal pain for tonight."

I gave Pam a very direct look. If I hadn't gone into the bedroom, Eric might have drained the woman, and the woman herself had considered that result. I had a hunch something had been set in motion to catch Eric red-handed—red-fanged, more appropriately.

"Go brush your teeth," I told him. "Really scrub. Wash your face; rinse out the sink with lots and lots of water."

Eric didn't like being told what to do, but he understood expediency very well. He went into the bathroom, leaving the door open. Pam said, "Let me go check on what's happening with our special guests," and disappeared down the hall into the living room, where the low music had continued without a break.

Eric stepped back into the bedroom, drying his face with a towel. He looked more alert, more present. He hesitated when he saw I was by myself. Eric was pretty much a stranger to relationship problems. From little clues and reminiscences he'd let drop, I'd gotten the picture that during literally centuries of sexual adventures he'd called the shots and the women had said, "Whatever you want, you big handsome Viking." He'd had a fling or two with other vampires. Those had been more balanced connections, but brief. That was all I knew. Eric was not one to brag; he simply took sexual relationships for granted.

I was already feeling calmer. That was all to the good, since I was alone in a room with a man I'd wanted to shoot a few minutes before. Though we weren't bonded anymore, Eric knew me well enough to realize that he could now speak.

"It was only blood," he said. "I was anxious and hungry, you were late, and I didn't want to just bite into you the moment I saw you. She came in while I was waiting, and I thought I'd have a quick drink. She smelled so intoxicating."

"So you were trying to *spare* me," I said, letting sarcasm drip off my words. "I see." Then I made myself shut up.

"I acted impulsively." And his mouth compressed into a straight line.

I considered him. I acted on impulse sometimes, myself. For example, the few previous times I'd been this angry or this hurt, I'd walked out of the situation—not because I wanted the last word or because I wanted to make a dramatic statement, but because I needed alone time to cool off. I took a deep breath. I looked Eric in the eye. I realized we both had to make a huge effort to move past this, at least for tonight. Without conscious thought, I had identified the subtle scent that must have screamed out at Eric's senses.

"She's already part Were, and she was doused in the scent of fairy blood to make you want her more," I said. "I believe you'd have had better sense, if not for that. She was a trap. She came here because she expected to make a lot of money if you fed from her, and maybe to flirt with her death wish."

"Can you manage to carry on with the evening as if we were in harmony?" Eric asked.

"I'll do my best," I said, trying not to sound bitter.

"That's all I can ask."

"You don't seem to have any doubt that you can cope," I observed. But then I closed my eyes for a moment, and I used every bit of my self-control to pull myself together into a coherent person. "So if I'm here to officially greet Felipe and he's supposed to be talking to us about the 'disappearance' of Victor, when's all the whoopee out in the great room going to stop? And just so you know, I'm seriously mad about the table."

"Me, too," he said, with unmistakable relief. "I'll tell Felipe that we must talk tonight. Now." He looked down at me. "My lover, don't let your pride get the better of you."

"Well, me and my pride would be delighted to get back in my car and go home," I said, struggling to keep my voice quiet. "But I guess *me and my pride* will make the effort to stay here and get through this evening, if you could get everyone to stop screwing around long enough to get down to business. Or you can kiss me and my pride good-bye."

With that, I went into the bathroom and shut the door, very quietly and deliberately. I locked it. I was through talking, at least for a while. I had to have a few seconds when no one was looking at me.

From outside the door, there was silence. I sat down on the toilet lid. I felt so full of conflicting emotions that it was like walking through a minefield in my high-heeled black sandals with the silly flowers on them. I looked down at my bright toenails.

"Okay," I said to those toes. "Okay." I took a deep breath. "You knew he took blood from other people. And you knew 'other people' might mean other women. And you knew that some women are younger and prettier and skinnier than you." If I kept repeating that, it would sink in.

Good God—are "knowing" and "seeing" ever two different things!

"You also know," I continued, "that he loves you. And you love him." *When I don't want to yank off one of these heels and stick it . . .* "You love him," I repeated sternly. "You've been through so much with him, and he's proved over and over that he'll go the extra mile for you."

He had. He had!

I told myself that about twenty times.

"So," I said in a very reasonable voice, "Here's a chance to rise above circumstances, to prove what you're made of, and to help save both our lives. And that's what I'll do, because Gran raised me right. But when this is over . . ." *I'll rip his damn head off.* "No, I won't," I admonished myself. "We'll *talk* about it."

THEN I'll rip his head off.

"Maybe," I said, and I could feel myself smiling.

"Sookie," Pam said from the other side of the door, "I can hear you talking to yourself. Are you ready to do this thing?"

"I am," I said sweetly. I stood, shook myself, and practiced a smile in the mirror. It was ghastly. I unlocked the door. I tried the smile out on Pam. Eric was standing right behind her, I guess thinking Pam would absorb the first blast if I came out shooting. "Is Felipe ready to talk?" I said.

For the first time since I'd met her, Pam looked a little uneasy as she looked at me. "Uh, yes," she said. "He is ready for our discussion."

"Great, let's get going." I maintained the smile.

Eric eyed me cautiously but didn't say anything. Good.

"The king and his aide are out here," Pam said. "The others have moved the party into the room across the hall." Sure enough, I could hear squeals coming from behind the closed door.

Felipe and the square-jawed vamp—the one I'd last seen drinking from a woman—were sitting together on the couch. Eric and I took the (stained) loveseat arranged at right angles to the couch, and Pam took an armchair. The large, low coffee table (freshly gouged) that normally held only a few objets d'art was cluttered with bottles of synthetic blood and glasses of mixed drinks, an ashtray, a cell phone, some crumpled napkins. Instead of its normally attractive and orderly formality, the living room looked more like it belonged in a low dive.

I'd been conditioned for so many years that it was all I could do not to spring up, tie on an apron, and fetch a tray to clear away the clutter.

"Sookie, I don't believe you've met Horst Friedman," Felipe said.

I yanked my eyes away from the mess to look at the visiting vampire. Horst had narrow eyes, and he was tall and angular. His short hair was a light brown and closely cut. He did not look as if he knew how to smile. His lips were pink and his eyes pale blue; so his coloring was oddly dainty, while his features were anything but.

"Pleased to meet you, Horst," I said, making a huge effort to pronounce his name clearly. Horst's nod was barely perceptible. After all, I was a human.

"Eric, I have come to your territory to discuss the disappearance of Victor, my regent," Felipe said briskly. "He was last seen in this city, if you can call Shreveport a city. I suspect that you had something to do with his disappearance. He was never seen after he left for a private party at your club."

So much for any elaborate story Eric had thought of spinning for Felipe.

"I admit nothing," Eric said calmly.

Felipe looked mildly surprised. "But you don't deny the charge, either."

"If I did kill him, Your Majesty," Eric said, as if he were admitting to swatting a mosquito, "there would be not a trace of evidence against me. I regret that several of Victor's entourage also vanished when the regent did."

Not that Eric had given Victor and his cohorts any opportunity to surrender. The only one who'd been offered the chance to escape death was Victor's new bodyguard, Akiro, and he'd turned the offer down. The fight in Fangtasia had been a no-debate full-frontal assault, involving gallons of blood and a lot of dismemberment and death. I tried not to remember it too vividly. I smiled and waited for Felipe's response.

"Why did you do this? Are you not sworn to me?" For the first time, Felipe appeared less than casual. In fact, he looked downright stern. "I appointed Victor my regent here in Louisiana. *I* appointed him . . . and I am your king." At the escalation in tone, I noticed Horst was tensed for action. So was Pam.

There was a long silence. It was what I imagine is the definition of the word "fraught."

"Your Majesty, if I did this thing, it might have been for several reasons," Eric said, and I began to breathe again. "I am sworn to you, and I'm loyal to you, but I can't stand still while someone is trying to kill my people for no good reason—and without previous discussion with me. Victor sent two of his best vampires to kill Pam and my wife." Eric rested a cold hand on my shoulder, and I did my best to look shaken. (That wasn't too hard.)

"Only because Pam is a great fighter, and my wife can hold her own, did they escape," Eric said solemnly.

He gave us all a moment to contemplate that. Horst was looking skeptical, but Felipe had only raised his dark eyebrows. Felipe nodded, bidding Eric to continue.

"Though I don't admit to being guilty of his death, Victor was also attacking me—and therefore you, my king—economically. Victor put new clubs in my territory—but he kept the management, jobs, and revenue from these clubs exclusively for himself, which is against all precedent. I doubted he was passing along your share of the profits. I also believed he was trying to undercut me, to turn me from one of your best earners into an unnecessary hanger-on. I heard many rumors from the sheriffs in other areas—including some you brought in from Nevada—that Victor was neglecting all other business in Louisiana in this strange vendetta against me and mine."

I couldn't read anything in Felipe's face. "Why didn't you bring your complaints to me?" the king said.

"I did," Eric said calmly. "I called your offices twice and talked to Horst, asking him to bring these issues to your attention."

Horst sat up a little straighter. "This is true, Felipe. As I—"

"And why didn't you pass along Eric's concerns?" Felipe interrupted, turning his eyes on Horst.

I anticipated watching Horst wriggle. Instead, Horst looked stunned.

Maybe I'm just getting cynical from hanging around with vampires for so long, but I felt a near certainty that Horst *had* passed along Eric's complaints, but that Felipe had decided Eric would have to solve his issues with Victor in his own way. Now Felipe was throwing Horst under the bus without a qualm so he could maintain deniability.

"Your Majesty," I said, "we're awful sorry about Victor's disappearance, but maybe you haven't considered that Victor was a huge liability for you, too." I gazed at him. Sadly. Regretfully.

There was a moment of silence. All four vampires looked at me as if I'd offered them a bucket of pig guts. I did my best to look simple and sincere.

"He was not my favorite vampire," Felipe said, after what seemed like about five hours. "But he was very useful."

"I'm sure you've noticed," I said, "that in Victor's case, 'useful' was a synonym for 'money pit.' Cause I've heard from people who serve at Vic's Redneck Roadhouse, for example, that they were underpaid and overworked, so there's a big staff turnover. That's never good for business. And some of the vendors haven't been paid. And Vic's is behind with the distributor." (Duff had shared that with me two deliveries ago.) "So, though Vic's started out great and pulled business from every bar around, they're not getting the repeat customers they need to sustain such a big place, and I know that revenue's fallen off." I was only guessing, but I was accurate, I could tell by Horst's face. "Same thing for his vampire bar. Why pull customers away from the established vampire tourist spot, Fangtasia? Dividing doesn't mean multiplying."

"You're giving *me* a lesson in economics?" Felipe leaned forward, picked up one of the opened TrueBlood bottles, and drank from it, his eyes never leaving my face.

"No, sir, I would never do such a thing. But I know what's happening on the local level, because people talk to me, or I hear it in their heads. Of course, observing all this about Victor doesn't mean I know what happened to him." I smiled at him gently. *You lying sack of shit.*

"Eric, did you enjoy the young woman? When she came through this room, she said she'd been called to service you," Felipe said, not taking his eyes off me. "I was surprised, since I was under the impression you were married to Miss Stackhouse. But the young woman seemed like a nice change of pace for you. She had such an interesting odor. If she hadn't been earmarked for you, I might have taken her for myself."

"You would have been welcome to her," Eric said in a completely empty voice.

"She told you she'd been called?" I was puzzled.

"That's what she said," Felipe said. His eyes were fixed on my face as though he were a hawk and I were a mouse he was considering for supper.

On one level of my brain, I puzzled over this. I'd been delayed, the young woman had said she'd been called specifically for Eric . . . but on another level, I was busy regretting I'd saved Felipe's life when one of Sophie-Anne's bodyguards had been well on the way to killing him. I regretted this *intensely*. Of course, I'd been saving Eric, too, and Felipe had been a by-product, but still . . . back to level one, and I realized that none of this was adding up. I smiled at Felipe more brightly.

"Are you simple?" Horst asked incredulously.

I'm simply sick of you, I thought, not trusting myself to speak.

Felipe said, "Horst, don't mistake Miss Stackhouse's cheerful looks for any mental deficiency."

"Yes, Your Majesty." Horst tried to look chastened, but he didn't quite make it.

Felipe looked at him sharply. "I must remind you—unless I'm much mistaken—Miss Stackhouse took out either Bruno or Corinna. Even Pam couldn't have handled both of them at the same time."

I kept on smiling.

"Which one was it, Miss Stackhouse?"

There was *another* fraught silence. I wished we had background music. Anything would be better than this dead air.

Pam stirred, looked at me almost apologetically. "Bruno," Pam said. "Sookie killed Bruno, while I took care of Corinna."

"How did you do that, Miss Stackhouse?" Felipe said. Even Horst looked interested and impressed, which was not a good thing.

"It was kind of an accident."

"You are too modest," the king murmured skeptically.

"Really, it was." I remembered the driving rain and the cold, the cars parked on the shoulders of the interstate on a terrible dark night. "It was sure pouring buckets that night," I said quietly. Tumbling over and over down into the ditch running with chilly water, a desperate pawing to find the silver knife, sliding it into Bruno.

"Was this the same kind of accident you had when you killed Lorena? Or Sigebert? Or the Were woman?"

Wow, how'd he know about Debbie? Or maybe he meant Sandra? And his list was by no means complete. "Yeah. That kind of accident."

"Though I can hardly complain about Sigebert, since he would have killed me very shortly," Felipe observed, with an air of being absolutely fair.

Finally! "I wondered if you remembered that part," I muttered. I may have sounded a wee tad sardonic.

"You did do me a great service," he said. "I'm just trying to decide how much of a thorn you are in my side now."

"Oh, come *on*!" I was really put out. "I haven't done anything to you that you couldn't have taken care of before it even happened."

Pam and Horst blinked, but I saw that Felipe understood me. "You maintain that if I had been more . . . proactive, you would have been in no danger from Bruno and Corinna? That Victor would have stayed down in New Orleans, where the regent should be, and that, therefore, Eric could have run Area Five the way he has always run it?"

He had it in a nutshell, as my grandmother would have said. But (at least this time) I kept my mouth shut.

Eric, by my side, was rigid as a statue.

I'm not sure what would have happened next, but Bill appeared suddenly from the kitchen. He looked as excited as Bill ever looked.

"There's a dead girl on the front lawn," he said, "and the police are here."

A variety of reactions passed on Felipe's face in a few seconds.

"Then Eric, as the homeowner, must go out and talk to the good officers," he said. "We'll set things to rights in here. Eric, be sure to invite them in."

Eric was already on his feet. He called to Mustapha, who didn't appear. He and Pam exchanged a worried glance. Without looking at me, Eric reached back, and I stood to slide my hand into his. Time to close the ranks.

"Who is the dead woman?" he asked Bill.

"A skinny brunette," he said. "A human."

"Fang marks in her neck? Bright dress, mostly green and pink?" I asked, my heart sinking.

"I didn't get that close," Bill said.

"How did the police find out there was a body?" Pam said. "Who called them?" We moved toward the front door. Now I could hear the noise outside. With the drapes shut, we hadn't been able to see the flashing lights. Through the gap in the heavy fabric, I could see them.

"I never heard a scream or any other alarm," Bill said. "So I don't know why a neighbor would have called . . . but someone did."

"You wouldn't have summoned the police yourself, for any reason?" Eric said, and there was the smell of danger in the room.

Bill looked surprised—which is to say, his eyebrows twitched and he frowned. "I can't think of a reason I would do such a thing. On the contrary—since I was outside patrolling, I'll obviously be a suspect."

"Where is Mustapha?" Eric said.

Bill stared at Eric. "I have no idea," he answered. "He was patrolling the perimeter, as he put it, earlier in the evening. I haven't seen him since Sookie came in here."

"I saw him in the kitchen," I said. "We talked." A presence caught my attention. "Brain at the front door," I said.

Eric strode to the little-used front door, and since I was in tow, I trotted along. Eric threw the door open, and the woman standing on the porch was left standing foolishly poised to knock.

She looked up at Eric, and I could read her thoughts. To this woman, he was beautiful, disgusting, repellent, and oddly fascinating. She didn't like the "beautiful" and "fascinating" parts. She also didn't like being caught on the wrong foot.

"Mr. Northman?" she said, her hand dropping to her side like a stone. "I'm Detective Cara Ambroselli."

"Detective Ambroselli, you seem to know who I am already. This is my dearest one, Sookie Stackhouse."

"Is there really a dead person on the lawn?" I asked. "Who is she?" I didn't have to make up the curiosity and anxiety in my voice. I really, really wanted to know.

"We were hoping you could help us with that," the detective said. "We're pretty sure the dead woman was leaving your house, Mr. Northman."

"Why do you think so? You're sure it was this house?" Eric said.

"Vampire bites on her neck, party clothes, your front yard. Yeah, we're pretty sure," Ambroselli said drily. "If you could just step over here, keeping your feet on the stepping-stones . . ."

The stones, set at regular intervals in the grass, curved around to the driveway. The dark green and deep pink of the crepe myrtles coordinated with the pink and green of the dress worn by the dead woman. She was lying at their base, a little inclined to her left side, in a position disturbingly similar to the way she'd lain across Eric's lap when I'd first seen her. Her dark hair had fallen across her neck.

"That's the woman no one knew," I said. "At least, I think so. I only saw her for a minute. She didn't tell me her name."

"What was she doing when you saw her?"

"She was donating some blood to my boyfriend, here," I said.

"Donating blood?"

"Yeah, she told us she'd done it before and she was happy to give," I said, my voice calm and matter-of-fact. "She definitely volunteered."

There was a moment of silence.

"You're kidding me," Cara Ambroselli said, but not as if she were at all amused. "You just stood there and let your boyfriend suck the neck of another woman? While you did . . . what?"

"It's about food, not about sex," I said, more or less lying. It was about food, but quite often it was also definitely about sex. "Pam and I talked about girl stuff." I smiled at Pam. I was aiming for "winsome."

Pam gave me a very level look in reply. I could imagine her looking at dead kittens that way. She said, "I love the color of Sookie's toenails. We talked about pedicures."

"So you two talked about your toenails while Mr. Northman fed off this woman, in the same room. Cozy! And then, what, Mr. Northman? After you had your little snack, you just gave her some money and sent her on her way? Did you get Mr. Compton to escort her to her car?"

"Money?" Eric asked. "Detective, are you calling this poor woman a whore? Of course I didn't give her any money. She arrived, she volunteered, she said she had to go, and she left."

"So what did she get out of your little transaction?"

"Excuse me, Detective, I can answer that," I said. "When you're giving blood, it's really very pleasurable. Usually." Of course, that was at the will of the vamp doing the biting. I shot a quick glance at Eric. He'd bitten me before without bothering to make it fun, and it had hurt like hell.

"Then why weren't you the donor, Ms. Stackhouse? Why did you let the dead girl have all the fun of feeding him?"

Geez! Persistent. "I can't give blood as often as Eric needs it," I said. I stopped there. I was in danger of overexplaining.

Ambroselli's neck whipped around as she sprung the next question on Eric.

"But you could survive just fine on a synthetic blood drink, Mr. Northman. Why'd you bite the girl?"

"It tastes better," Eric said, and one of the uniforms spit on the ground.

"Did you decide you'd like a taste, Mr. Compton? Seeing as how she'd already been tapped?"

Bill looked mildly disgusted. "No, ma'am. That wouldn't have been safe for the young lady."

"As it turns out, she wasn't safe, anyway. And none of you knows her name, or how she got here? Why she came to this house? You didn't call some kind of *I need a drink* hotline . . . like a vampire escort service?"

We all shook our heads simultaneously, saying no to all these questions at once. "I thought she came with my other guests, the ones from out of town," Eric said. "They brought some new friends they met at a bar."

"These guests are inside?"

"Yes," Eric said, and I thought, *Oh, gosh, I hope Felipe got them out of the bedroom.* But of course, the police would have to talk to them.

"Then let's take this inside and meet these guests," Detective Ambroselli said. "Do you have any objection to us coming inside, Mr. Northman?"

"Not the least in the world," Eric said courteously.

So I traipsed back into the house with Bill, Eric, and Pam. The detective led the way as if the house were hers. Eric permitted it. By now the Las Vegas contingent would have cleaned up, I hoped, since they'd certainly heard what Ambroselli had said when Eric went to the door.

To my relief, the living room looked much more orderly. There were a few bottles of synthetic blood, but they were all positioned adjacent to a seated vampire. The big windows in the back were open and the air quality was much better. Even the ashtray was out of sight, and someone had positioned a large bowl over the worst gouge marks on the coffee table.

All the vamps and the humans, fully clothed, had assembled in the living room. They wore serious expressions.

Mustapha was not among them.

Where was he? Had he simply decided he didn't want to talk to the police, so he'd departed? Or had someone entered through the French windows in the kitchen doors and done something terrible to the Blade wannabe?

Maybe Mustapha had heard something suspicious outside and had gone to investigate. Maybe the killer or killers had jumped him once he got outside, and that was why no one had heard anything. But Mustapha was so tough that I simply couldn't imagine anyone ambushing him and getting away with it.

Though "Mustapha" might not fear anything, in actuality he was the former KeShawn Johnson, and he was an ex-con. I didn't know why he'd been incarcerated, but I knew it was for something he'd been ashamed of. That was why he'd adopted a new name and a new profession after he'd served his term. The police wouldn't know him as Mustapha Khan . . . but they'd know he was KeShawn Johnson as soon as they took his fingerprints, and he was scared of prison.

Oh, how I wished I could communicate all this to Eric.

I didn't believe Mustapha had killed the woman on the lawn. On the other hand, I'd never been completely inside his head, since he was a Were. But I'd never heard senseless aggression or random violence, either. Rather, Mustapha's top priority had always registered as control.

I believe most of us are capable of moments of rage, moments when our button's been pressed to the point where we lash out to stop the pressure. But I was sure that Mustapha was used to much worse treatment than anything that girl could have handed out.

While I was worrying about Mustapha, Eric was introducing the remaining newcomers to Detective Ambroselli. "Felipe de Castro," he said, and Felipe nodded regally. "His assistant, Horst Friedman." To my surprise, Horst rose and shook her hand. Not a vampire thing, handshaking. Eric continued, "This is Felipe's consort, Angie Weatherspoon." She was the third Nevada vampire, the redhead.

"Pleased to meetcha," Angie said, nodding.

The last time I'd seen her, Angie Weatherspoon had been dancing on the low table, enjoying Felipe's regard. Now the redhead was wearing a gray pencil skirt, a sleeveless green button-up blouse with tiny ruffles on the deep V neckline, and three-inch heels. Her legs went on forever. She looked great.

When Eric turned to the humans for their introductions, he paused. Eric clearly didn't know the hugely muscular man's name, but before the moment could become awkward, the man extended a bulging arm and shook the detective's hand very delicately. "I'm Thad Rexford," he said, and Ambroselli's mouth dropped open.

The uniform who'd come in behind her said, "Oh, wow! T-Rex!" with sheer delight.

"Wow," Ambroselli echoed, forgetting her stern expression.

All the vampires looked blank, but another human present, a plump and perky twenty-year-old with a light brown mane of hair of which Kennedy Keyes would have approved, looked proud, as if being at the same party with him raised her status. "I'm Cherie Dodson," she said, in a voice that was surprisingly babyish. "This is my friend Viveca Bates. What's going on out front, guys?" Cherie was the woman who'd been making out with T-Rex. Viveca, just as curvaceous but with slightly darker hair, had been the one giving Felipe the "donation."

Detective Ambroselli quickly recovered from the surprise of meeting a famous wrestler at a vampire's house, and she was twice as pugnacious since she'd shown a moment of starstruck awe. "There's a dead woman outside, Ms. Dodson. That's what's going on. You-all need to stay here to be ready for questioning. First off, did you ladies bring a third woman here with you?" The detective was clearly talking to the humans; that is, all the humans except me.

"These two lovely ladies were with me at the casino," T-Rex said.

"Which one?" Ambroselli was all about the details.

"The Trifecta. We met Felipe and Horst at the bar there, struck up a conversation over drinks. Felipe here kindly invited us to Mr. Northman's beautiful home." The wrestler seemed completely at ease. "We was just out on the town, having some fun. We didn't bring nobody else with us."

Cherie and Viveca shook their heads. "Just us," Viveca said, and gave Horst a coy sideways look.

"The victim came into the house, Mr. Northman says, but he doesn't seem to know who she was." Cara Ambroselli's flat tone made it clear what she thought of men who took blood from women they'd never met, while at the same time casting doubt on Eric's assertion that he hadn't known her. That was a lot to convey in one sentence, but she managed.

I was standing right behind her, and I was getting a good reading on her. Cara Ambroselli was both ambitious and tough—necessary attributes to get ahead in the law enforcement world, especially for a woman. She'd been a patrol officer, distinguished herself by her courage in rescuing a woman from a burning house, sustained a broken arm in the course of subduing a robbery suspect, kept her head low and her social life secret. Now that she was a detective, she wanted to shine.

She was simply packed full of information.

I kind of admired her. I hoped we wouldn't be enemies.

Cherie Dodson said, "Tell me she doesn't have on a green and pink dress." All the flirty fun had drained from her voice.

"That's what she's wearing," the detective said. "Do you know her?"

"I met her this evening," Cherie said. "Her name's Kym. Kym-with-a-y, she said. Her last name was Rowe, I think. T-Rex, you remember her?"

He looked down as though he were working hard at recovering the recollection, his dyed platinum hair showing a quarter-inch of dark root. T-Rex's cheeks sported reddish-brown bristles, and his tight black T-shirt revealed that he'd shaved his chest. I thought that he had some ambivalence about his hair growth, but I was kind of fascinated by his musculature, I have to admit. He just bulged muscles everywhere, even in his neck. I glanced up to find Eric giving me a frosty look. Well, big whoop, considering.

"I had quite a bit to drink tonight, Miz Ambroselli," the wrestler said, with a charming ruefulness. "But I remember the name, so I must have met her. Cherie, honey, was she at the bar?"

"No, baby. Here. While we were dancing, she walked through the living room. She asked where Mr. Northman was."

"How did this Kym arrive here?" Ambroselli asked. She looked at me first. I don't know why.

I shrugged. "She was already here when I came in this evening," I said.

"Where was she?"

"She was giving Eric blood back in the first room on the left past the bathroom."

"And you invited her?" Ambroselli asked Eric.

"To my house? No, as I said, I'd never met her—that I can recall. I'm sure you know I own Fangtasia, and many people come in and out of the bar, of course. I had gone to Sookie's room because I wanted to have a private word with her before the . . . before we entertained our guests. This woman, this Kym, came back to the room. She said that Felipe had sent her to me as a present."

The detective didn't even ask Felipe. She just switched her dark gaze to him. The king spread his hands charmingly. "She seemed at loose ends," he said, with a smile. "She asked me if I knew Eric. I told her where Eric might be found. I suggested she go back to Eric and ask him if he wanted a drink. I thought he might be lonely without Sookie."

"Did you see the dead girl arrive? Do you know how she got here, or why she came?" Ambroselli asked Pam.

"Our other guests entered through the front door, properly. I suppose this Kym entered through the kitchen," Pam said, shrugging elegantly. "Eric sent me on an errand, and I didn't see her arrive."

"No, I didn't," Eric said. "What errand?"

"Mustapha told me you wanted me to go buy some more rum," Pam said. "Was this not the case?"

Eric shook his head. "I wouldn't send you on an errand if Mustapha was here at the house," he said. "You're better protection, any day."

"I'll check from now on," Pam promised. Her voice was cold. "I assumed the order came from you, and of course I set off for the store. When I got back, I checked the living room to make sure all was well, and I heard Sookie enter. Since I knew you were anxious to see her, and I knew you were in the bedroom, I took her back there."

I was in a group of multi-projectors. Ambroselli's brain was the busiest, naturally. T-Rex was thinking he was glad his publicist was on speed dial, and wondering whether or not this incident would help his image. Viveca and Cherie were terribly excited. They didn't have the imagination to be relieved that the body on the lawn wasn't one of them. My own head was whirling with the excitement pouring from so many heads.

"Mr. Compton, same questions for you," Ambroselli said. "Did you see the victim arrive?"

"I did not," Bill said very positively. "I should have. I was in charge of watching the front of the house. But I didn't see her get out of a car or approach by foot. She must have come through the back gate and up the hill to creep around the corner of the house and enter through the garage, or perhaps she came in through the French windows that open onto the kitchen and the living room. Though I'm sure some of our guests would have noticed if she'd entered there."

There was a round of headshakes. No one had seen her come in that way.

"And you didn't know her? Had never seen her?" Ambroselli said to Pam.

"As Eric pointed out, she may have been to Fangtasia. I don't remember meeting her or seeing her there."

"Are there security cameras in Fangtasia?"

There was a moment of silence. "We don't permit any sort of camera in Fangtasia while the club is open," Eric said smoothly. "If patrons want pictures, there is a club photographer who is happy to take snapshots."

"So let me see if I've got this right," Ambroselli said. "This house belongs to you, Mr. Northman." She pointed from the floor to Eric. "And you're the proprietor of Fangtasia. Ms. . . . Ravenscroft works there with you as the club manager. Ms. Ravenscroft does not live here in this house. Ms. Stackhouse, from Bon Temps, is your girlfriend. She doesn't live here, either. Mr. Compton—who sometimes works for you?—also lives in Bon Temps."

Eric nodded. "Exactly so, Detective." Bill looked approving. Pam looked bored.

"If you-all would go sit over at the dining table"—and the cop's eyes expressed sardonic pleasure that a vampire had a dining table—"I'll talk to these nice people." She smiled unpleasantly at the visiting vamps.

Pam, Eric, Bill, and I went to sit at the table. The darkness pressing at the windows loomed at my back in a very nerve-racking fashion.

"Mr. de Castro, Mr. Friedman, Ms. Witherspoon," Ambroselli said. "You're all three visiting from—Vegas, is that right?" The three vampires, wearing identical approving smiles, nodded in chorus. "Mr. de Castro, you have a business in Las Vegas . . . Mr. Friedman is your assistant . . . and Ms. Witherspoon is your girlfriend." Her eyes went from Eric, Pam, and me to the Las Vegas trio, drawing a definite parallel.

"Right," Felipe said, as if he were encouraging a backward child.

Ambroselli gave him a look that told Felipe he was permanently on her shit list. She turned to the next trio.

"So, Mr. Rexford, Ms. Dodson, Ms. Bates. Tell me again how you came to be here? You met up with Mr. de Castro and his party in the bar of the Trifecta?"

"I been dating T-Rex here for a while," Cherie said. The massive wrestler put an arm around her. "And Viveca is my best buddy. We three were having a drink, and we met up with Felipe and his friends in the bar. We got to talking." She smiled to show off her dimples. "Felipe said they were coming over to visit Eric, here, and they invited us to come along."

"But the dead woman wasn't with you at the bar at the casino."

"No," said T-Rex, now grave. "We never seen her at the Trifecta, or anywhere else, before we came in this house."

"Was anyone else inside when they got here?" Detective Ambroselli asked Eric directly.

"Yes," Eric said. "My daytime man, Mustapha Khan." I fidgeted at his side, and he cast me a quick glance.

Ambroselli blinked "What's a daytime man?"

"It's sort of like having another assistant," I said, leaping into the conversation. "Mustapha does the things that Eric can't, things that require going out in the daylight. He goes to the post office; he picks up stuff from the printer; he goes to the dry cleaner; he gets supplies for this house; he gets the cars serviced and inspected."

"Do all vampires have a daytime man?"

"The lucky ones," Eric said with his most charming smile.

"Mr. de Castro, do you have a daytime man?" Ambroselli asked him.

"I do, and I hope he is hard at work in Nevada," Felipe said, radiating bonhomie.

"What about you, Mr. Compton?"

"I've been fortunate enough to have a kind neighbor who will help me out with daytime errands," Bill said. (That would be me.) "I'm hiring someone so I won't tax her goodwill."

The detective turned to the patrol officer behind her and issued some commands that the vampires could surely hear, but I could not. However, I could read her mind, and I knew that she was telling the officer to also search for a man named Mustapha Khan who seemed to be missing, and that the victim's name was probably Kym Rowe and he should check the missing-persons list to see if she was on it. A plainclothes guy—another detective, I guessed—came in and took Ambroselli out on the front porch.

While he whispered in her ear, I was sure all the vampires were trying hard to hear what he was telling her. But I could hear it in her brain. Pam touched my arm, and I turned to face her. She raised her eyebrows in a question. I nodded. I knew what they were talking about.

"I need to talk to all of you separately," Ambroselli said, turning back to us. "The crime-scene team needs to go through the house, so if you could come down to headquarters with me?"

Eric looked angry. "I don't want people going through my house. Why would they?" he asked. "The woman died outside. I didn't even know her."

"Well, you took her blood quick enough," Ambroselli said.

Valid point, I thought, tempted to smile for just a nanosecond.

"We won't know where she died until we look at your house, sir," Ambroselli continued. "For all I know, you're all covering up a crime that took place inside this very room." I had to repress an impulse to glance around in a guilty way.

"Eric, Sookie, and I were together from the time this Rowe woman left the bedroom until we came out here to talk to Felipe and his friends," Pam said.

"And *we* were all together until Eric and Pam and Sookie came out here from the bedroom," Horst said promptly, which was simply not true. Any of the Nevada vampires or their human pickups could have slipped outside and disposed of Kym.

At least Pam was telling the truth.

Then I remembered that I'd been shut in the bathroom. By myself. For at least ten minutes.

I'd assumed that Pam had remained outside the bathroom door; I'd assumed Eric had gone into the living room to tell Felipe and his crowd that it was time to get down to business. He would have suggested that the human guests go into the other bedroom while we had our discussion.

That's what I'd assumed.

But I had no way to know for sure.

Chapter 4

Down at the police station, we covered the same conversational ground, but this time on an individual basis. It was both boring and tense. When I'm dealing with the police, I'm always thinking what I could be guilty of. I always imagine there are laws I don't know about, laws that I've broken. And of course, I've broken a few major laws that haunt me, some more than others.

After the individual interviews, conducted by several policemen, we were deposited back in our little groups and stowed separately around the big room. The Nevada vampires were finishing up talking to a detective several yards away, while I could see Cherie in a glass-walled cubicle with yet another interviewer. T-Rex and Viveca waited for her on a bench against the wall.

I was more than ready to leave this building. This late at night, even on a Saturday, the traffic on Texas Boulevard would be light. If I had my car, I could be home in an hour, maybe less. Unfortunately, the police had suggested we all pile into Felipe's Suburban for the trip to the station. Since my car had been parked at the curb, it was temporarily part of the crime scene.

Simply for want of something else to do while she waited to hear from the crime-scene people, Cara Ambroselli was walking us through the evening one more time.

"Yes," an obviously bored Eric was saying. "My friend Bill Compton came in from Bon Temps. Since the other vampires who work for me were busy at the club, I asked Bill to help out at my house because I was having company, though I confess I wasn't expecting quite so much of it. Bill was . . . tasked . . . with patrolling the front grounds. Though I live in a gated community, from time to time curiosity seekers try to make my acquaintance, especially during a party. So Bill was doing a circuit of the front yard and the area around it, every few minutes. Right, Bill?"

Bill nodded agreeably. He and Eric were such buddies. "That's what I did," he said. "I surprised one old man who came down to the end of his driveway to get his newspaper, and I saw one woman out walking her dog. I talked to Sookie when she arrived."

It was my turn to do the smiling and nodding. We were all friends, here! *And if I'd followed Bill's advice,* I thought, *I would never have seen Eric sucking on Kym Rowe's neck, and I would never have seen her dead body, and I would be sound asleep in bed.* I looked at Bill thoughtfully. He raised his brows at me—*What?* I shook my head, a tiny motion.

"And you had asked this missing man, Mustapha, to help Mr. Compton keep intruders away. Though his employment is as your daytime man." Detective Ambroselli was talking to Eric.

"I think we've already covered that."

"Where do you think Mr. Khan is?"

"Last time I saw him, he was in the kitchen," I said, figuring it was my turn. "As I told you, we spoke when I came inside."

"What was he doing?"

"Nothing in particular. We didn't talk long. I was . . ." *I was in a hurry to see Eric, but he was busy with the dead woman.* "I was anxious to apologize to our guests for being a bit late," I said. Mustapha had made me late on purpose—but what that purpose had been, I couldn't fathom.

"And you came upon Mr. Northman in your bedroom, or at least the bedroom you customarily use, taking blood from another woman."

There was really nothing to say to that.

"Didn't that make you really angry, Ms. Stackhouse?"

"No," I said. "I get anemic if he drinks from me too often." At least that part was the truth.

"So you're not mad, even though he could get the same nourishment from a bottle?"

She just wasn't going to stop. That was what you wanted in a cop, unless you had stuff to hide.

"I wasn't happy," I said simply. "But I accepted it, like death and taxes. Comes with the territory when you're dating a vampire." I shrugged, trying to imitate nonchalance.

"You were unhappy, and now she's dead," Ambroselli said. She looked down at her notepad for dramatic effect. She thought we were all a bunch of lousy liars. "According to Ms. Dodson, she heard Ms. Ravenscroft threaten the victim."

Eric turned a dark blue gaze on Cherie Dodson, clearly visible through the glass of the enclosure. At the same moment, her wrestler friend, T-Rex, was looking at Cherie almost as unhappily as Eric. Though I had to stretch a little, I could get the gist of his thoughts. T-Rex knew what his girlfriend was saying to the police. Cherie's disclosure didn't accord with T-Rex's code of ethics. Thad Rexford had a very interesting mind, and I would have liked to wander around in it a little longer, but Eric gripped my hand to give it what he thought was a gentle squeeze. I turned to look up at him with narrowed eyes. He could tell I was distracted, and he didn't think my mind should be wandering.

"I advised the woman that she should leave town, yes," Pam said imperturbably. "I don't think that was threatening her. If I'd wanted to threaten her, I'd have said, 'I'll rip your head from its neck.' "

Ambroselli took a deep breath. "Why did you tell her to leave town?"

"She had been insulting and insolent to Sookie, who is my friend, and Eric, who is my boss."

"What did she say that was so insulting?"

Probably I should answer this one. It would sound haughty coming from Pam. Of course, Pam was haughty. "She was pretty excited that Eric had taken blood from her." I shrugged. "She seemed to think that made her special. She wasn't happy Eric told her to leave after I showed up. I guess she'd assumed that Eric's taking blood from her meant he wanted to have sex with her, and she thought I would, you know, participate in that." This was hard to say, and it must have been unpleasant to hear, from the face the detective made.

"You didn't feel that way, too?"

"Honestly, it was the equivalent of being insulted by a pork chop my boyfriend was eating," I said. And then I was smart enough to shut my mouth.

Eric smiled down at me. I would have given a lot to wipe that smile off his face. I took advantage of Ambroselli being distracted by her cell phone to smile back at Eric. He understood my expression well enough. His mouth straightened out. Over his shoulder, I could see that Bill looked unmistakably pleased.

"So, Ms. Ravenscroft, you told Kym Rowe to go, she left, and she died," Ambroselli said, by way of resuming the questioning. But she didn't seem focused on Pam the way she had been, and I could see that she was preparing to move out.

"Yes, that's right," Pam said. She'd read Ambroselli's body language the same way I had, and she was eyeing the detective thoughtfully.

"Please stay where you are. I have to return to Mr. Northman's place to check something out," Ambroselli said. She was on her feet, gathering up her shoulder bag. "Givens, make sure everyone stays here until I say they can go."

And just like that, she left.

Givens, a man with a starved, concave face, looked very unhappy. He called a few more people in—all men, I noticed—and assigned one to each batch of us. "If they need to go to the restroom, send someone with 'em, don't let 'em go alone," he instructed the heavy guy in charge of our little group. "She's the only one who should need to go," he added, pointing at me.

Bored, I turned my chair around to watch the Nevada vamps for a while. Felipe, Horst, and Angie seemed to have had a lot of experience with the police. They sat together in silence, though a little downturn to one corner of Felipe's lips told me he was mighty displeased. As a king, he probably hadn't been treated like an ordinary vampire in a long time—not that humans knew who or what he was, but ordinarily Felipe would have several layers of insulation between him and the regular pitfalls of the vampire world. If I had to pick a word to describe the king of Arkansas, Nevada, and Louisiana, that word would be "miffed."

He could hardly blame Eric for this turn of events. He might, anyway.

I switched my gaze to the human group in the glass-enclosed office. T-Rex was signing autographs for some of the uniforms. Cherie and Viveca were preening themselves, proud to be in such illustrious company. Under his air of just-a-good-ole-boy, T-Rex was bored. He would have been glad to be somewhere else. When the little cluster of cops dispersed, he pulled out his cell phone and called his manager. I couldn't tell what they were talking about, but from his thoughts I could read that T-Rex couldn't think of anyone else to call in the middle of the night. He was tired of conversation with his female companions, especially Cherie, who could not keep her mouth shut.

I spotted a familiar face among the cops going to and fro in the big room. "Hey, Detective Coughlin!" I said, oddly happy to see someone I knew. The middle-aged detective swung himself around, using his belly as a fixed point. His hair was shorter than ever, and a bit grayer.

"Miss Stackhouse," he said, coming over to us. "You found any more bodies?"

"No, sir," I said. "But a woman was found dead in the front yard of Eric's place, and I was in the house." I jerked my head toward Eric, in case Coughlin didn't know who he was. Pretty unlikely that a police officer in Shreveport wouldn't know the city's most prominent vampire, but it could happen.

"So, who you going with now, young lady?" Coughlin didn't approve of me, but he didn't hate me, either.

"Eric Northman," I said, and I realized I didn't sound at all happy about that.

"Out with the furries and in with the coldies, huh?"

Eric had been talking to Pam in a very low voice, but now he turned to stare at me.

"I guess so." The first time I'd seen Detective Coughlin, I'd been with Alcide Herveaux. The second time, I'd been with Quinn the weretiger. They had been in their human forms then, and he hadn't known their second identity since the two-natured hadn't revealed their existence. By now he'd figured it out. Mike Coughlin might be slow and unimpressive, but he wasn't stupid.

"So you're with the party that came in with T-Rex?" he asked.

I wasn't used to the humans being more interesting than the vampires. I smiled. "Yes, I met him tonight at Eric's."

"You ever see him wrestle?"

"No. He's a big guy, huh?"

"Yeah, and he does a lot for the community, too. He takes toys to the kids in the hospital at Christmas and Easter."

So, though T-Rex was not a wereanimal, he was two-faced. One side of him did community service and helped area charities raise money. The other side of him hit opponents upside the head with chairs and made out with women on other people's dining room tables.

Mike Coughlin said, "If they rope me in to help question, I'll ask for you."

"Thanks," I said, wondering if that was really anything to smile about. "But I hope I'm through with questions."

He went off to have a closer look at Thad Rexford. Pam, Eric, Bill, and I sat together without exchanging a word.

Vampires are super at silence. They just go into motionless vampire mode. You would swear they were statues, they get so still. I don't know what they think about when they do this; maybe they don't think at all, but just switch themselves off. It's almost impossible for a human to do this. I guess deep meditation would be the closest state a breather could achieve, and I am no practitioner of meditation, deep or shallow.

After a while, during which nothing much happened at all, Detective Coughlin came over to tell us we could go. He gave no explanation. Eric didn't request one. I had been on the point of asking if I could curl up under someone's desk. I was too tired to summon the energy to be resentful at our treatment.

Pam whipped out her cell phone to call Fangtasia so someone would pick us up. Dawn wasn't far away; Felipe and his party wanted to go directly to their vampire-safe rooms at the Trifecta, and the Shreveport vamps didn't want to wait on a human cab.

While we were standing outside waiting on our ride, the three vampires turned to me. "What was it the man on the telephone was telling Cara Ambroselli?" Pam asked. "What did they find?"

"They found a little glass vial, like florists stick individual flowers in?"

The vampires looked puzzled. I measured one off with my fingers. "Just big enough for one flower stem to soak in water," I said. "The vial may have had a stopper on it, but they didn't find that. The vial was on the ground underneath her. They think it had been tucked in her bra. It had traces of blood."

They all considered that. "I'll bet you a demon's dick that she had a bit of fairy blood in it," Pam said. "She came into the house somehow, and when she got close to Eric, she uncorked the little vial and made herself irresistible."

"Except he could have resisted," I muttered, but they all ignored me. "And if that's what happened, where is the stopper?"

We were all too tired to talk about this interesting development any further; at least, I was, and the other three didn't.

In five minutes, Palomino showed up in a candy-apple-red Mustang. She was wearing the uniform the female waitstaff wore at the Trifecta, and there wasn't much to it. I was too sleepy to ask her when she'd begun working at the casino. I climbed into the backseat with Bill, while Pam sat in Eric's lap in the passenger front seat. We didn't even discuss the seating.

Eric broke the silence by asking Palomino if anyone had heard from Mustapha.

The young vamp glanced over at him. Her hair was like corn silk and her skin was like milky caramel. The unusual combination had earned her the nickname, and that was the only thing I knew to call her. I had no idea what had been written on her birth certificate.

"No, Master. No one has seen or heard from Mustapha."

Bill silently took my hand. I silently let him. In the heat, his hand felt pleasantly cool.

"Everything all right at the club?" Eric said. "At least, as far as you know."

"Yes, Master. I heard there was one disagreement, but Thalia settled it."

"How big was the bill for this settling?"

"A broken arm, a broken leg."

Thalia was ancient, incredibly strong, and notoriously short on patience.

"No furniture?"

"Not this time."

"Indira and Maxwell Lee kept an eye on things?"

"Maxwell Lee says so," Palomino said cautiously.

Eric laughed; not a big laugh, but something in the chuckle range. "Damned with faint praise," he said.

Indira and Maxwell, who lived and worked in Eric's sheriffdom, Area Five, were required to put in so many hours a month at the bar so Fangtasia could boast that every night there were real vampires in the club. That was the big draw for the tourists. While Indira and Maxwell (and most of the other Area Five vamps) were dutiful about their bar appearances, they were not enthusiastic.

Palomino and Eric might have solved the mysteries of the universe during the rest of their conversation, but I didn't hear their conclusions. I fell asleep. When we arrived at Eric's, Bill had to help me scramble out of the backseat. Palomino pulled away the instant Bill slammed the door. Pam quickly got into her own car for the short drive to her house, casting an anxious glance at the sky as she backed out of the driveway.

If a crime-scene team had been at the house, its job was finished. We had to enter through the garage door, since there was tape around the place where Kym had lain. I trudged into the house, so groggy I was only partly aware of what was going on around me.

Bill didn't have time to get back to Bon Temps, so he was going to take one of the fiberglass "guest" pods that Eric kept in the second upstairs bedroom. He headed toward the back of the house immediately, leaving Eric and me by ourselves. I looked around me in a dazed way. The kitchen had an array of dirty bottles and glasses by the sink, but I noticed that the garbage bag was gone. The police must have taken it.

I told Eric, "Mustapha had that door open when I came in," and I pointed to the door onto the backyard patio. Without a word, Eric went over to the door. It was unlocked. He took care of that while

I started across the living room. It wasn't too disordered since Felipe, Horst, and Angie had neatened it, but still its disheveled state disturbed me. I began straightening chairs and gathering up the few remaining bottles and glasses to take to the kitchen.

"Leave it be, Sookie," Eric said.

I froze. "I know this isn't my house," I said, "but this mess just looks so nasty. I'd hate to get up to face this."

"The issue is not ownership of the house. The issue is that you are exhausted and yet you feel compelled to do the maids' job. I hope you're spending the rest of the night? I would feel uneasy if you drove back, as tired as you must be."

"I guess I'll stay," I said, though I was still far from satisfied with the way things stood between us. If I'd been strong enough, I would have left. But it would be very foolish to start driving home and risk having a wreck.

Eric was suddenly right in front of me, and he put his arms around me. I started to pull away. "Sookie," he said. "Let's make this right. I have enemies on every side, and I don't want to have one here at home." I made myself hold still. I reviewed everything I'd told myself while I'd been taking my time-out in the bathroom. That seemed to have been a week ago, instead of hours.

"Okay," I said slowly. "Okay. I know that I should be totally all right with what you did with that woman. I know if people are willing, there's no reason you shouldn't take a sip from them, especially since she was actually booby-trapped. I think you could have held out if you'd really wanted to. I know my reaction is emotional, not logical. But it's the reaction I'm having. I also know, in my head, that I love you. I'm just not feeling it at this moment. Oh, by the way, I have something to confess to you, too, regarding another man."

Ha! That sharpened him up. Eric's eyebrows flew up and he stepped back a little, looking down at me and very nearly scowling. "What?" he said, biting the word out as if it tasted bad. I felt more cheerful.

"Remember, I told you I was going to Hooligans to see Claude strip?" I said. "There were other guys, too, mostly fae, who did, well, almost the full monty." I raised one eyebrow and tried to look inscrutable.

Eric's mouth quirked in what was very nearly a smile. "Claude is a beautiful man. How do I stack up against the fairy?" he asked.

"Hmmm. The fairy was stacked all right," I said, looking off in another direction ostentatiously.

Eric squeezed me. "Sookie?"

"Eric! You know that you look pretty good naked."

"Pretty good?"

"That's right, fish for compliments," I said.

"That's not all I'm fishing for," he whispered. He picked me up by sliding his hands under my rear, and suddenly I was at just the right height to kiss him.

So an evening that had held so much that was bad ended in something good, after all, and for fifteen minutes I utterly forgot that I was in the same bed he'd sat on while he took blood from someone else . . . which may have been the target Eric was aiming for. He hit it, dead center.

He got downstairs in the nick of time.

Chapter 5

I didn't roll out of bed until noon. I had slept very heavily, and I'd had bad dreams. I woke up groggy, and I didn't feel refreshed at all. It didn't occur to me to check my cell phone until I heard it buzzing in my purse—but that wasn't until I'd drunk some coffee, showered and put on the change of clothes I kept in the closet, and (no matter what Eric had said) gathered up all the dirty "service items," as flight attendants call them.

By the time I'd dropped my hairbrush, opened my purse, and groped inside to extricate the phone, my caller had hung up. Frustrating. I checked the number, and to my astonishment I found that Mustapha Khan had been trying to get in touch with me. I called the number back as quickly as I could press the right buttons, but no one answered.

Crap. Well, if he wasn't picking up, there wasn't anything I could do about it. But I had other messages: one from Dermot, one from Alcide, and one from Tara.

Dermot's voice said, "Sookie? Where are you? You didn't come home last night. Everything okay?"

Alcide Herveaux said, "Sookie, we need to talk. Call me when you can."

Tara said, "Sookie, I think the babies are going to come pretty soon. I'm effacing and I'm starting to dilate. Get ready to become an aunt!" She sounded giddy with excitement.

I called her back first, but she didn't pick up.

Then I called Dermot, who actually answered. I gave him a condensed version of the night before. He asked me to come home immediately, but he didn't offer an explanation. I told him I'd start back within the hour unless the police arrived to delay me. What if they wanted to come into Eric's house? They couldn't just come in, right? They had to have a warrant. But the house was a crime scene. I was worried about them trying to get into Eric's downstairs bedroom, and I remembered that Bill was in the bedroom across the hall in a guest pod. What if the cops decided to open it? I needed a set of those "DO NOT ENTER VAMPIRE AT REST" coffin hangers I'd seen advertised in Eric's copy of *American Vampire.*

"I'll be there as soon as I can," I told Dermot. I hung up feeling a bit worried about Dermot's insistence that I return. What was happening at my house?

With great reluctance, I returned Alcide's call. He'd only try to get in touch about something pretty important, since we weren't exactly buddies anymore. We weren't exactly enemies, either. But we could never seem to be happy with each other at the same time.

"Sookie," Alcide said in his deep voice. "How you doing?"

"I'm okay. I don't know if you've heard what happened here at Eric's last night . . ."

"Yeah, I heard something about it."

No surprise there. Who needed the Internet, when you had the supes around? "Then you know Mustapha is missing."

"Too bad he's not pack. We'd find him."

Pointed, much? "After all, he's a werewolf," I said briskly. "And the police do want him. I know he could explain everything if he'd just come in to talk to them. So maybe if someone in the pack sees him somewhere, you could let me know? He called me—or at least someone using his phone did. I missed the call, and I'm really worried about him."

"I'll let you know if I find out anything," Alcide promised. "I need to talk to you about something else, though."

I waited to hear what he had in mind.

"Sookie, you still there?"

"Yes, I'm just waiting."

"I'm hearing a complete lack of enthusiasm."

"Well, considering last time." I didn't even need to finish the sentence. Finding Alcide naked in my bed had not endeared him to me. There was a lot to like about the werewolf, but his timing had never matched mine and he'd taken some bad advice.

"Okay, I was wrong there. We had a good result from you acting as our shaman, but I was wrong to ask you to do it, and I freely acknowledge that." Alcide said that kind of proudly.

Had he joined Werewolf Manipulators Anonymous? I looked at myself in the mirror and widened my eyes, to let my reflection know what I thought about the conversation.

"Good to hear that," I said. "What's up?"

Rueful chuckle. *Charming* rueful chuckle. "Well, you're right, Sookie, I do have a favor to ask you."

I showed myself Amazed in the mirror. "Do tell," I said politely.

"You know my pack enforcer has been going out with your boss for a while."

"I know that." Cut to the chase.

"Well, she wants you to help her out with something, and since you two have had your differences . . . for whatever reason . . . she asked me if I'd call you."

Sneaky Jannalynn. This was like a double . . . fake something. It was true I liked Jannalynn much less than I did Alcide. It was also true (though perhaps Alcide didn't know this) that Jannalynn suspected my relationship with Sam was far more than it should be between an employee and her boss. If this were the fifties, she'd be checking Sam's collars for lipstick stains. (Did people do that anymore? Why did women kiss collars, anyway? Besides, Sam almost always wore T-shirts.)

"What does she want me to help her with?" I asked, hoping my voice was suitably neutral.

"She's going to propose to Sam, and she wants you to help her set the stage."

I sat down on the end of the bed. I didn't want to make faces in the mirror anymore. "She wants *me* to help *her* ask Sam to marry her?" I said slowly. I'd helped Andy Bellefleur propose to Halleigh, but I couldn't imagine Jannalynn wanting me to hide an engagement ring in a basket of French fries.

"She wants you to get Sam to drive down to Mimosa Lake," Alcide said. "She's borrowed a cottage down there, and she wants to surprise

Sam with a dinner, kind of romantic, you know. I guess she'd spring the question there." Alcide sounded oddly unenthusiastic or perhaps unconvinced that he should be relaying this request.

"No," I said immediately. "I won't do it. She'll have to get Sam there on her own." I could just envision Sam imagining that I wanted him to go out to the lake with me, only to be confronted by Jannalynn and whatever she thought of as a romantic dinner—live rabbits they could chase together, maybe. The whole scenario made me acutely uncomfortable. I could feel a flush of anger creeping up my neck.

Alcide said, "Sookie, that's not . . ."

"Not helpful or obliging? I don't want to be, Alcide. There's just too much room for disaster in that plan. Plus, I don't think you understand Jannalynn too well." What I wanted to say was, "I think she's trying to get me somewhere alone to kill me, or to stage some scene to make me look guilty." But I didn't.

There was a long silence.

"I guess Jannalynn was right," he said, letting his dismay into his voice. "You do have it in for her. What, you don't think she's good enough for Sam?"

"No. As a matter of fact, I don't. Tell her I . . ." I automatically started to say I was sorry I couldn't oblige her, and then I realized that would be a big fat lie. "I'm just . . . unable to be of assistance. She can do her own proposing. Good-bye, Alcide." Without waiting to hear his response, I hung up.

Had his enforcer wrapped Alcide around her little finger, or what?

"Fool me once, shame on you. Fool me twice, shame on me," I said. I wasn't sure if I meant Alcide or Jannalynn or both of them.

I fumed as I gathered my few things together. Help that bitch propose to Sam? When Hell froze over. When pigs flew! Plus, as I'd told Alcide, if I'd been fool enough to go out to Mimosa Lake, she'd have staged some drama, for sure.

As I locked Eric's kitchen door behind me and stomped out to my car in my now-painful high heels, I said words that had seldom crossed my lips before. I slammed my car door shut behind me, earning a sharp look from a sleek, well-groomed neighbor of Eric's who was weeding the flower bed around her mailbox.

"Next people will be asking me to be a surrogate mom for their babies, cause it would be *inconvenient* for them to carry their own," I said, sneering in an unattractive way into my rearview mirror. That reminded me of Tara, and I tried her number again, but with no better result.

I pulled in behind my house about two o'clock. Dermot's car was still there. When I saw home, it was like I gave myself permission to run into a wall of weariness. It felt good that my great-uncle would be waiting for me. I grabbed my little bag of dirty clothes and my purse and trudged to the back door.

Tossing the clothes bag on the top of the washer on the back porch, I put my hand on the knob of the kitchen door, registering as I did so that two people were waiting inside.

Maybe Claude was back? Maybe all the problems in Faery had been solved, and everyone at Hooligans would be returning to the wonderful world of the fae. How many problems would that leave me with? Maybe only three or four big ones.

I was feeling honestly optimistic when I pushed the door open and registered the identity of the two men seated at the table.

Definitely an OSM. One man was Dermot, whom I'd expected. The other was Mustapha, whom I hadn't.

"Geez Louise, where have you been?" I thought I was going to yell, but it came out as a startled wheeze.

"Sookie," he said, in his deep voice.

"We thought you were dead! We were scared sick about you! What happened?"

"Take a deep breath," Mustapha said. "Sit down and just . . . take a breath. I got some things to tell you. I can't give you a full answer. It's not that I don't want to. It's really a life or a death."

His statement cut off the next seven questions poised to pour off my tongue. Tossing my purse on the counter, I pulled out a chair, sat, and took a deep breath as he'd advised me. I gave him all my attention. For the first time, I absorbed his ragged appearance. Mustapha's grooming had always been meticulous. It was a shock to see him rumpled, his precise haircut uneven, his boots scuffed. "Did you see who killed that girl?" I asked. I had to.

He looked at me, looked hard. He didn't answer.

"Did you kill that girl?" I tried again.

"I did not."

"And because of this situation you referred to, you can't tell me who did."

Silence.

I was sickeningly afraid that Mustapha was trying to tell me, without spelling it out, that Eric had killed her—had ducked out of the house after I'd shut myself in the bathroom. Eric could have lost his temper, projected his anger with himself onto Kym Rowe, and tried to make things right between him and me by snapping her neck. No matter how many times during the previous night I'd told myself such a premise was ridiculous—Eric had great control and was very intelligent, he was simply too aware of his neighbors and the police to do such a lawless thing, and such an act would simply be irrational—I'd never been able to tell myself that Eric wouldn't have killed her simply because doing so was wrong.

This afternoon, all those bad thoughts I had entertained came crashing back as I stared at Mustapha.

If Mustapha had not been a Were, I would have sat on his chest until I read the answer in his brain. As it was, I could only get an impression of the turmoil in his head, and his grim resolution that he would survive no matter what. And he was consumed with worry for someone else. A name crossed his mind.

"Where's Warren, Mustapha?" I asked. I leaned forward, trying to get a clearer read. I even reached toward him, but he flinched back.

Mustapha shook his head angrily. "Don't even try, Sookie Stackhouse. That's one of the things I can't talk about. I didn't have to come here at all. But I think you're getting a raw deal, and you're caught up in the middle of stuff you don't know about."

Like that was a new situation for me.

Dermot was looking back and forth between us. He couldn't decide how to act or what I wanted him to do.

Join the club, Dermot.

"You tell me what's going on, and then I'd know what to be careful of," I suggested.

"This was a mistake," he said, looking down and shaking his head. "I'm going to find somewhere to hide while I look for Warren."

I thought of calling Eric, leaving a message telling him his day man was here. I'd keep Mustapha a prisoner until Eric could come fetch him. Or I could phone the police and tell them a material witness to a murder was sitting in my kitchen.

These plans passed through my head with great rapidity, and I considered each of them for a second. Then I thought, *Who am I kidding? I'm not going to do any of those things.* "You should go to Alcide," I said. "He'll keep you safe if you pledge to the pack."

"But I'd have to face . . ."

"Jannalynn. I know. But that'll be later. Alcide'll keep you safe for now. I can call him." I held up my little phone.

"You got his cell number?"

"I do."

"You call him, Sookie. You tell him I'm trying to meet with him. You give him my cell number, and you tell him to call me when he's by himself. And that's a big thing. He has to be by himself."

"Why can't you call him?"

"It'd be better if it came from you," he said, and that was all I could get him to say. "You got my cell number, right?"

"Sure."

"I'm leaving now."

"Tell me who killed that girl!" If I could have yanked the answer out of him with tweezers, I would have.

"You'd just be in more danger than you are now," he said, and then he was out of the room and onto his bike, and then he was gone.

This had all occurred with such speed that I felt as though the room were shivering after he left. Dermot and I stared at each other.

"I have no idea why he was here instead of in Shreveport where he belongs. I could have held him," Dermot said. "I was just waiting for a signal from you, Great-Niece."

"I appreciate that, Great-Uncle. I guess I felt like that just wasn't the right thing to do," I muttered.

We sat there in silence for a moment. But I had to explain to Dermot about the night before.

"You want to know why Mustapha showed up here?" I asked, and he nodded, looking much more cheerful now that he was going to get some background. I launched into my narrative.

"No one knew her, and she hadn't come with anyone?" He looked thoughtful.

"That's what they all said."

"Then someone sent her, someone who knew there would be a party at Eric's. Someone ensured she could walk in and not be challenged because there were strangers at the house. How did she get past the guard at the gate?"

These were all pertinent questions, and I added another one. "How could anyone know in advance that Eric wouldn't be able to resist taking blood from her?" I sounded forlorn, and I could only hope I didn't come across as self-pitying. Unhappiness will do that to you.

"Obviously she was selected because she had two-natured blood of some variety, and then she enhanced that with the smell of fairy. We know too well it's enticing to the deaders. Since Mustapha's phone call made you late and, therefore, Eric was more willing to yield to temptation," Dermot said, "Mustapha must have had some hand in what happened."

"Yeah. I figured that out." I wasn't happy about this conclusion, but it fit the evidence.

"He may not have known what would happen as a result, but he must have gotten instructions from someone to make you late."

"But who? He's a lone wolf. He doesn't answer to Alcide."

"*Someone* has power over him," Dermot said reasonably. "Only someone with power over him could make a man like Mustapha betray

Eric's trust. He's looking for his friend Warren. Would Warren have some reason to want Eric behind bars?"

Dermot was really operating on fully charged batteries today. I was having a hard time flogging my tired brain into keeping up with him.

"That's the key, of course," I said. "His friend Warren. Warren himself would have no reason I can think of to want to harm Eric, who, after all, provides Mustapha's livelihood. But I think Warren's being used as a lever. Someone's taken Warren, I think. They're holding him to ensure they have Mustapha's cooperation. I need to think about all this," I said, yawning with a jaw-cracking noise. "But right now I just have to sleep some more. You going over to Hooligans?"

"Later," he said.

I looked at him, thinking of all the questions he'd never answered about the strange accumulation of the fae at a remote strip club in Louisiana. Claude had always told me it was because they'd all been left out when Niall closed the portals. But how had they known where to come, and what was their purpose in remaining in Monroe? Now was not the time to ask, since I was too exhausted to process his answers—if he would give me any. "Okay then, I'm taking a nap," I said. It was Sunday, and Merlotte's was closed. "Just let the answering machine take the calls, if you don't mind." I switched the ringer volume down even further on the kitchen phone and would do the same in the bedroom.

I took my cell phone into my bedroom and called Alcide. He didn't answer, but I left him a message. Then I plugged in my cell phone to charge. I dragged my weary body into my bedroom. I didn't even take off my clothes. I fell over the bed and fell asleep.

I woke two hours later feeling like something a cat spit up. I rolled onto my side to look out the window. The light had changed. The air conditioner was fighting the afternoon's worst heat, which shimmered in the air outside. I sat up to look out the window at the dry grass. We needed rain.

More random thoughts floated through my muzzy head. I wondered how Tara was doing. I didn't know what "effaced" meant. I wondered what had happened to Mr. Cataliades. He was my "sponsor," apparently the otherworldly equivalent of a godparent. I'd last seen the (mostly) demon lawyer running through my yard being chased by gray streaks from Hell.

Had Amelia gotten back from France yet? What were Claude and Niall up to in Faery? What did it look like there? Maybe the trees looked like peacock feathers and everyone wore sequins.

I checked my phone. I hadn't heard from Alcide. I called again, but it went right to voice mail. I left a message on Bill's cell to tell him that Mustapha had made an appearance. After all, he was the Area Five investigator.

Though I'd showered at Eric's that morning, that seemed like a week ago, so I got under the water again. Then I pulled on old denim shorts and a white T-shirt and flip-flops and went out in the yard with my wet hair hanging down my back. I positioned the chaise perfectly to keep my body in the shadow of the house while my hair was trailing over the end in the light because I liked the way it smelled when I let it dry in the sun. Dermot's car was gone. The yard and house were empty. The only background noises were the ever-present sounds of nature going about its business: birds, bugs, and an occasional breeze fluttering the leaves in a lazy way.

It was peaceful.

I tried to think of mundane things: a possible date for Jason and Michele's wedding, what I needed to do at Merlotte's tomorrow, how low on propane my tank might be. Things I could actually solve with a phone call or a pad and pencil. Since my car was in my line of sight, I noticed that one of my tires looked a little soft. I should get Wardell at the tire place to check my pressure. It had been wonderful to shower without worrying about having enough hot water; that was the upside to Claude's absence.

It was good to think about things that weren't supernatural.

In fact, it was blissful.

Chapter 6

When it was dark, my phone rang. Of course, that wasn't until after eight, this far into the summer. I'd had a very pleasant few hours all by myself. "Pleasant" didn't mean a positive good to me anymore: It meant an absence of bad. I had done a little straightening in the kitchen, read a little, turned on the television just to have voices in the background. Nice. Not exciting. I'd had enough exciting.

I hadn't checked my e-mail all day, and I'd considered giving it a pass for a couple more days. I found I didn't really want to answer the phone, either. But I'd left messages for both Alcide and Bill. On the third ring, I yielded to habit and picked it up. "Yes?" I said.

"Sookie, I'm on my way over to see you," Eric said.

See, I knew there'd been a good reason for not answering. "No,"

I said. "I don't think so." There was a little silence. Eric was as surprised as I was.

"Is this a punishment for last night?" he asked.

"For drinking from another woman when I was present? No, I think I have that issue squared away."

"Then . . . what? You really don't want to see me?"

"Not tonight. I do want to say a couple of things to you, though."

"By all means." He sounded stiff and offended, which wasn't any surprise. He could deal with it.

"If Bill is still the Area Five investigator . . ."

"He is." Cautious.

"Then he needs to get to work, don't you think? He could take Heidi with him, since she's supposed to be such a great tracker. How did Kym Rowe get past the guard? Unless someone bribed the guard—and it was a guy I didn't know—it's possible Kym came up from the gate at the back of your yard, right? Maybe Bill and Heidi could discover how she got there. Plus, I need to talk to Bill about something."

"That's a good idea." He was thawing out. Or at least he wasn't dwelling on the offense he'd taken.

"I'm full of 'em," I said, feeling anything but clever. "Also. How did Felipe know all about the death of Victor?"

"None of my vampires would say a word," Eric said with absolute certainty. "Colton is still in the area, but Immanuel has gone to the West Coast. You would not tell anyone. Mustapha's friend Warren, who acted as our cleanup man . . ."

"None of them would speak. Warren wouldn't say boo to a goose if Mustapha didn't tell him to." I thought so, anyway. I didn't really know much about Warren, who wasn't big on talking. I was just about to tell Eric that Mustapha had appeared in my kitchen when he continued, "We should have taken care of Colton and Immanuel."

Did Eric mean the vampires should have killed the human survivors of that vicious brawl, even if they'd fought on Eric's side? Or was he simply implying he should have done a preemptive glamour, erasing their memories? I closed my eyes. I thought of my own humanity and vulnerability, though glamouring had never worked on me.

Time to move on to another subject before I lost my temper. "Do you know why Felipe is really here? Cause you *know* it's not because of Victor, or at least only partly because of Victor."

"Don't discount his need to discipline me for Victor's death," Eric said. "But you're right, he's got another agenda. I realized that last night." Eric grew more guarded. "Or at least, I became surer of it."

"So you already know this secret agenda, and you're not telling me."

"We'll talk about it later."

Of course I should have told him about Mustapha's visit, but I lost my remaining patience. "Uh-huh. Right." I hung up. I looked down at my hand, a bit stunned at my own action.

I spotted the little bundle of mail and the newspaper on the counter. Earlier in the day, I had walked down the driveway in the bright sunshine to retrieve the previous day's mail and the daily Shreveport newspaper from their respective boxes on Hummingbird Road. Now I sat down to read the paper. On the front page I discovered that Kym Rowe had been twenty-four, she had been from Minden, and (after looking at the picture of her accompanying the main article) I wasn't surprised to read she'd recently been fired from her job as an exotic dancer for assaulting a customer.

That must have been a hell of a night at that strip club.

The cause of Kym's death, according to the paper, had been a broken neck. Quick, quiet, requiring only strength and the element of surprise. That was why, even in that quiet neighborhood, no one had heard her scream . . . not even Bill, with his vampire hearing. Or so he said. Kym Rowe, I discovered, had good reason to have a short temper.

"Rowe was desperate for money. 'She was behind on her car payments, and her landlord was about to evict her,' Oscar Rowe, the victim's father, said. 'She was doing crazy things to earn money.'" That was the short and sad story of the life of Kym Rowe. One thing stood out: She'd had nothing to lose.

Of course, much was made of the fact that she'd been found on the lawn of a "prominent vampire businessman and his party guests." Eric and his uninvited company were in for a hard time with the publicity machine. There was at least one picture of T-Rex in his wrestling costume. The words "bulging" and "manic" came to mind. I turned to the inside page where the article continued. Kym's grieving parents were posed clutching a Bible and a bouquet of daisies, which they said had been Kym's favorite flower. Though I chided myself for my snobbishness, they didn't look like much.

Before I could finish the article, the phone rang. I jumped about a foot. I'd been wondering if Eric would call back after he'd had enough time to get really angry with me, but the caller ID let me know my caller was Sam.

"Hey," I said.

"What happened last night?" he asked. "I just watched the Shreveport news."

"I went over to Eric's because of the out-of-town vamp visitors," I said, condensing. "This Kym Rowe left the house right after I got there. Eric had taken blood from her." I had to pause to collect myself.

"Then Bill found her dead on the lawn. They might have hushed it up. . . . Oh, hell, of course they'd have hushed it up. Moved her body, or something. But the police had gotten an anonymous call that there was a body at Eric's, so the police were there before he even knew her body was on the lawn."

"Do you know who did it?"

"No," I said. "If I knew who'd killed her, I'd have told the cops last night."

"Even if the killer was Eric?"

That stopped me dead. "It would depend on the circumstances. Would you turn in Jannalynn?"

There was a long silence. "It would depend on the circumstances," he said.

"Sam, sometimes I think we're just dumb," I said, and then I heard myself. "Wait, not speaking for you! Just for me!"

"But I agree," he said. "Jannalynn . . . she's great, but I feel like I've bitten off more than I can chew some days."

"Do you tell her everything, Sam?" How much did other couples share? I needed some feedback. I'd had so few relationships.

He hesitated. "No," he said, finally. "I don't. We haven't gotten to the 'I love you' stage yet, but even if we had . . . no."

My mental focus took a U-turn. Wait a minute. According to Alcide, Jannalynn had told him she was going to propose. Sure didn't sound like Sam was ready for that, if they hadn't even told each other they loved each other. That couldn't be right. Someone was lying or deluded. Then Sam said, "Sookie?" and I knew I'd been letting silence fill the air while I thought all this.

"So it's not just me and Eric," I said hastily. "Between us, Sam, I feel like Eric's not telling me some pretty important stuff."

"What about the things you aren't telling him? Are those things important?"

"Yeah, they are. Important, but not . . . personal." I hadn't told Eric about Hunter, my little second cousin, being telepathic like me. I hadn't told Eric how worried I was about the concentration of the fae in Monroe. I'd tried filling Eric in on the fae situation, but it had been easy to tell that the politics of his own kind were at the top of his list these days. I couldn't blame him for that.

"Sookie, you're okay, right? I don't know what you mean by 'not personal.' Everything that happens to you is personal."

"By personal stuff . . . things that are only about me and him. Like if I wasn't happy with the way he treated me, or if I thought he needed to be around more, or if he'd go with me to Jason and Michele's wedding. If I needed to talk about any of those things, I would. But I know pieces of information that affect other people, and I don't always tell him those things, because he has such a different perspective."

"You know you can tell me, if you need to talk about something. You know I'll listen and I won't tell anyone."

"I know that, Sam. You're the best friend I've got. And I hope you know I'm always ready to listen to anything you need to talk about. I'm sure Eric and I will get back to normal when Felipe leaves . . . when the boat stops rocking."

"Maybe you will," he said. "But you know that if you get nervous out there, I got an extra bedroom here."

"Jannalynn would kill me," I said. I'd spoken the first thought that went through my head, and I could have slapped myself. I'd spoken the truth—but I was talking about Sam's girlfriend. "Sorry, Sam! I'm afraid Jannalynn believes you and I have a—a lurid past. I guess she's not there tonight?"

"She's working tonight, at Hair of the Dog. She's watching the phones and the bar traffic while Alcide's having meetings in the back room. You're right, she's a little possessive," he admitted. "It was kind of flattering at first, you know? But then I began to wonder if that means she doesn't have any faith in my integrity."

"Sam, if she has a grain of sense she can't possibly doubt you." (I was pretty sure Jannalynn blamed it all on me.) "You're an honest guy."

"Thanks," he said gruffly. "Well . . . I've kept you talking long enough. Call me if you need me. By the way, as long as we're talking about relationship stuff, do you know why Kennedy's mad at Danny? She's been snapping at everyone."

"Danny's keeping some kind of secret from her, and she's afraid it's about another woman."

"It's not?" Sam knew all about my telepathic ability.

"No, it isn't. I don't know what it is. At least he isn't stripping at Hooligans." One of us had talked, which was inevitable, and the story of JB's second job had gotten a lot of comment in Bon Temps.

"She didn't think about just asking Danny what he was doing?"

"I don't think so."

"Children, children," Sam said, as if he were in his sixties instead of in his thirties.

I laughed. I was in a better mood when we hung up.

Dermot came in about half an hour later. Normally, my great-uncle was at least content in a low-keyed way. Tonight he wasn't even approaching happiness; he was actively worried.

"What's up?"

"Claude's absence is making them restless."

"Because he has such charisma that he keeps them all in line." Claude had as much personality as a turnip.

"Yes," Dermot said simply. "I know you don't feel Claude's charm. But when he's among his own people, they can see his strength and purpose."

"We're talking about the guy who chose to stay among humans rather than go into Faery when it was closing." I just didn't get it.

"Claude's told me two things about that," Dermot said, going to the refrigerator and pouring a glass of milk. "He said he knew the portals were closing, but he felt he couldn't leave without tying up his business affairs here, and he never imagined that Niall would really stick to his decision. On the whole, the gamble of staying here appealed to him more. But he told the others, all the assortment of fae at Hooligans, that Niall denied him entry."

I noticed that Dermot was admitting, though not explicitly, that he didn't have the high opinion of Claude that the other fae did. "Why'd he tell two stories? Which do you believe?"

Dermot shrugged. "Maybe both are true, more or less," he said. "I think Claude was reluctant to leave this human world. He's amassing money that could be working for him here while he's in Faery. He's been talking with lawyers about setting up a trust, or something like that. It would continue to earn him money even if he vanishes. That way if he wants to return to this world, he will be a rich man and able to live as he wants. And there are advantages, even when you live in Faery, to having financial assets here."

"Like what?"

Dermot looked surprised. "Like having the ability to buy things that aren't available in Faery," he said. "Like having the wherewithal to make trips out here occasionally, to indulge in things that aren't . . . acceptable in our own world."

"Like what?" I asked again.

"Some of us like human drugs and sex," Dermot said. "And some of us like human music very much. And human scientists have thought of some wonderful products that are very useful in our world."

I was tempted to say "Like what?" a third time, but I didn't want to sound like a parrot. The more I heard, the more curious it seemed.

"Why do you think Claude went with Niall?" I asked instead.

"I think he wants to become secure in Niall's affection," Dermot said promptly. "And I think he wants to remind the rest of the fae world what an enticing option they have cut off, since Niall closed the portals and guards them so rigorously. But I don't know." He shrugged. "I'm his kinsman, so he has to shelter me and defend me. But he doesn't have to confide in me."

"So he's still trying to have it both ways," I said.

"Yes," Dermot said simply. "That's Claude."

Just then there was a knock at the back door. Dermot raised his head and sniffed. "There's one of the troubles," he said, and went to answer it. Our caller was Bellenos the elf, whose needlelike inch-long teeth were terrifying when he smiled. I remember how he'd grinned when he'd presented me with the head of my enemy.

Our new visitor had bloody hands. "What you been doing, Bellenos?" I asked, proud that my voice was so even.

"I've been hunting, my fair one," he said, and gave me that scary grin. "I was complaining of being restless, and Dermot gave me leave to hunt in your woods. I had a wonderful time."

"What did you catch?"

"A deer," he said. "A full-grown doe."

It wasn't hunting season, but I didn't think anyone from the Department of Wildlife and Fisheries was going to fine Bellenos. One look at his true face, and they'd run screaming. "Then I'm glad you took the opportunity," I said, but I resolved to have a private word with Dermot about granting hunting privileges on my land without consulting me.

"Some of the rest of us would like to hunt here, too," the elf suggested.

"I'll think about it," I said, none too pleased at the idea. "Long as that hunting was restricted to deer, and you stayed on my land . . . I'll let you know soon."

"My kindred are getting restless," Bellenos said, in what was not quite a warning. "We would all like to get out of the club. We would all like to visit your woods, experience the peacefulness of your house."

I shoved my deep uneasiness down into a little pocket inside me. I could fish it out later and have a good look at it after Bellenos left. "I understand," I said, and offered him water. When he nodded, I poured a glass full of cold water from the pitcher in the refrigerator. He gulped it all down. Hunting deer in the dark with your bare hands was apparently thirsty work. After the water was gone, Bellenos asked if he could clean up, and I pointed out the hall bathroom and put out a towel.

When the door was safely shut, I gave Dermot a look.

"I know you have reason to be angry, Sookie," he said. He came closer and dropped his voice. "Bellenos is the most dangerous. If he gets tense and bored, bad things will happen. It seemed wisest to give him a safety valve. I hope you'll forgive me for granting him permission, since we're family." Dermot's big blue eyes, so like my brother's, looked at me imploringly.

I wasn't too pleased, but Dermot's reasoning made all kinds of sense. The image of a repressed elf finally cutting loose on the people of Monroe was a picture I didn't want in my head. "I get what you're saying," I told him. "But if you ever want to let someone run free on my land again, check with me first." And I gave him a very level look to let him know I meant it.

"I will," he said. I wasn't convinced. Dermot was a lot of good things, but I couldn't see him as a strong or decisive leader. "They're tired of waiting," he said hopelessly. "I guess I am, too."

"Would you leave for Faery?" I asked. I tried a smile. "Can you live without your HGTV and your Cheetos?" I wanted to ask my great-uncle if he could live without *me*, but that would be too pitiful. We'd gotten along without each other just fine for most of our lives—but there was no denying I was fond of him.

"I love you," he said unexpectedly. "The happiest I've been in years is the time I've spent here with you, in this house. It's so peaceful."

This was the second time in a few minutes that a fae had said my house was peaceful. My conscience stirred inside me. I suspected very strongly that it was not me or the house that attracted creatures with fae blood; it was the hidden presence of the cluviel dor.

Bellenos came out wrapped in a towel, holding out his bloody clothes. His pallor—and his freckles—extended all over. "Sister, can you wash these in your machine? I had only planned to scrub my face and arms, but I thought how good it would feel to be completely clean."

As I took the stained clothes to the washer on the back porch, I was glad I'd taken Mr. Cataliades's warning to heart. If the cluviel dor had such influence when they couldn't even see it, didn't even know it was present, how much more would they want to touch it if they could? What would they do if I wouldn't give it up?

After I'd started Bellenos's clothes on the cold cycle, I remained on the back porch looking out through the screen door at the night. The bugs were in full symphony. It was almost noisy enough to be annoying. I was glad all over again for the blessed invention of air-conditioning, even if the house was cooled by window units instead of central heat and air. I could close and lock my windows at night and keep the drone of the insects at bay . . . and feel safe against the appearance of other things. One of those other things was strolling out of the trees right now.

"Hey, Bill," I said quietly.

"Sookie." He moved closer. Even when I knew he was there, I couldn't hear him. Vampires can be so quiet.

"I guess you heard my visitor?" I said.

"Yes. Found what was left of the deer. Elf?"

"Bellenos. You've met him."

"The guy who took the heads? Yeah. Dermot is home?"

"He's here."

"You really shouldn't be alone with Bellenos." Bill, a serious guy, sounded very grim indeed when he said this.

"I don't intend to be. Dermot will take him back to Monroe, either tonight or tomorrow morning. Eric call you tonight?"

"Yeah. I'm going to Shreveport in an hour. I'm meeting Heidi there." He hesitated for a moment. "I understand she still has a living relative."

"Her son in Nevada. He's a drug addict, I believe."

"To have living flesh of your flesh. It must be a very strange feeling to be able to talk to your immediate kin. This age of vampires is so much different from that when I was turned. I can hardly believe that I now know my great-great-great-grandchildren."

Bill's maker had ordered him out of Bon Temps and even out of the state for a long time, so he wouldn't be recognized by his wife and children or his local acquaintances. That was the old way.

I noted the wistfulness in his voice. "I don't think it's been very healthy for Heidi to keep in touch with her son," I said. "She's younger than he is, now, and . . ." Then I shut up. The rest of the sad story was Heidi's to tell.

"Several days ago, Danny Prideaux came to me to ask if he can be my daytime man," Bill said suddenly, and after a moment I understood that Bill was thinking of human connections.

So that was Danny's big secret. "Huh. He already has a part-time job at the lumberyard."

"With two jobs, he thinks he can ask his young woman to marry him."

"Oh, wow! Danny's gonna ask Kennedy to marry him? That's wonderful. You know who he's dating? Kennedy, who works behind the bar at Merlotte's?"

"The one who killed her boyfriend." Bill seemed displeased by this bit of information.

"Bill, the guy was beating her. And she served her jail time. Not that you have any room to talk. You hired him?"

Bill looked a little abashed. "I agreed to a trial period. I don't have enough work for a full-time person, but it would be very pleasant to have a part-time helper. I wouldn't have to ask you for help all the time, which I'm sure is inconvenient for you."

"I haven't minded making the occasional phone call," I said. "But I know you'd like to have someone you don't have to keep thanking. I wish Danny'd tell Kennedy what he's up to. Not knowing is making her have all kinds of bad thoughts about him."

"If they're going to have a real relationship, she has to learn to trust him." Bill gave me an enigmatic look and melted back into the trees.

"I trust people when they've proved they're trustworthy," I muttered, and went back in the house. The kitchen was empty. Sounded like Bellenos and Dermot had gone upstairs to watch television; I caught the faint sound of a laugh track. I climbed halfway up the stairs, intending to suggest that Bellenos move his own clothes from the washer to the dryer, but I paused when I heard them talking during a commercial break.

"It's called *Two and a Half Men*," Dermot was telling his guest.

"I understand," Bellenos said. "Because the two brothers are grown, and the son isn't."

"I think so," Dermot said. "Don't you think the son is useless?"

"The half? Yes. At home, we'd eat him," Bellenos said.

I turned right around, sure I could put the clothes into the dryer myself. "Sookie, did you need us?" Dermot called. I might have known he'd hear me.

"Just tell Bellenos that I'm putting his clothes in the dryer, but he's responsible for getting them out. I think they'll be dry in . . ." I made some hasty calculations. "Probably forty-five minutes. I'm going to bed now." Though I'd had the nap, I was beginning to drag.

I barely waited to hear Dermot say, "He'll get them," before I hurried to the back porch to toss the wet clothes into the dryer. Then I went into my bedroom, shut the door, and locked it.

If the rest of the fae were as casual about cannibalism as the elf, Claude couldn't come back soon enough to suit me.

Chapter 7

Cara Ambroselli called me first thing Monday morning, which was not a great way to start the week.

"I need you to come to the station so I can ask a few more questions," she said, and she sounded so brisk and awake that I could easily dislike her.

"I've told you everything I know," I said, trying to sound alert.

"We're going over everything again," she said. "I know you're as anxious as we all are to find out who caused this poor woman's death."

There was only one possible response. "I'll be there in a couple of hours," I said, trying not to sound sullen. "I'll have to ask my boss if I can be late to work."

That really wasn't going to be an issue since I was scheduled to work the later shift, but I was grumpy enough to drag my heels. I did call

Jason to tell him where I was going, because I think someone always needs to know where you are if you're going into a police station.

"That's no good, Sis," he said. "You need a lawyer?"

"No, but I'm taking a number with me just in case," I said. I looked at the front of the refrigerator until I spotted the "Osiecki and Hilburn" business card. I made sure my cell phone was charged. Just to cover all kinds of crises, I put the cluviel dor into my purse.

I drove to Shreveport without noticing the blue skies, the shimmering heat, the big mowers, the eighteen-wheelers. I was in a grim mood, and I wondered how career criminals managed. I was not cut out for a life of crime, I decided, though the past few years had held enough mayhem to last me till I was using a walker. I hadn't had anything to do with the death of Kym Rowe, but I'd been involved in sufficient bad stuff to make me nervous when I came under official scrutiny.

Police stations are not happy places at the best of times. If you're a telepath with a guilty conscience, this unhappiness is just about doubled.

The heavy woman on the bench in the waiting room was thinking about her son, who was in a cell in the building. He'd been arrested for rape. It wasn't the first time. The man ahead of me was picking up a police report about an accident he'd been in; his arm was in a sling, and he was in a fair amount of pain. Two men sat silently side by side, their elbows on their knees, their heads hung. Their sons had been arrested for beating another boy to death.

It was a positive treat to see T-Rex come out of a door, apparently leaving the building. He glanced my way, kept moving, but did a double take.

"Sookie, right?" Under the harsh light, his dyed platinum hair looked garish but also cheerful, simply because he was such a vital person.

"Yeah," I said, shaking his hand. *Pretty, vamp's girl, from Bon Temps?* He was having his own little stream of consciousness about me. "They call you in, too?"

"Yeah, I'm doing my civic duty," he said with a very small smile. "Cherie and Viv already came in."

I tried to smile in a carefree way. I didn't think I was very successful. "I guess we all got to help them find out who killed that girl," I offered.

"We don't have to enjoy it."

I was able to give him a genuine smile. "That's very true. Did they wring a confession out of you?"

"I can't keep secrets," he said. "That's my biggest confession. Seriously, I'd've told them anything after we were here a couple hours the night it happened. T-Rex is not one for secrets."

T-Rex was one for talking about himself in the third person, apparently. But he was so vivid, so full of life, that to my surprise I found I liked him.

"I have to go tell them I'm here," I said apologetically, and took a step toward the window.

"Sure," he said. "Listen, give me a call if you ever want to come to a wrestling match. I get the feeling you ain't been to many, if at all, and you might have a good time. I can get you a ringside seat!"

"That's real nice of you," I said. "I don't know how much time I'll have, between my job and my boyfriend, but I do appreciate the offer."

"I never hung around with vampires before. That Felipe, he's pretty damn funny, and Horst is okay." T-Rex hesitated. "On the other hand, your boyfriend is pretty damn scary."

"He is," I agreed. "But he didn't murder Kym Rowe."

Our conversation ended when Detective Ambroselli called me to her desk.

Cara Ambroselli was a little dynamo. She asked me the same questions she'd asked me Saturday night, and I answered them the same way. She asked me a few new questions. "How long have you been dating Eric?" (He was no longer Mr. Northman, I noticed.) "Did you ever work in a strip club?" (That was an easy one.) "What about the men you live with?"

"What about them?"

"Doesn't Claude Crane own a strip club?"

"Yeah," I said warily. "He does."

"Did Kym Rowe ever work there?"

I was taken aback. "I don't know," I said. "I never thought about that. I guess she might have."

"You call Crane your cousin."

"Yeah, he is."

"We got no record of him being related to you."

It would be interesting to know what records they could possibly have about Claude, since he wasn't human. "He comes from an illegitimate birth," I said. "It's private family business."

No matter how many times she asked questions about Claude, I stuck to my guns. She eventually gave in to my determination, since there was really no way she could link Kym to Claude to me. At least, I hoped that was the case. This was something else I needed to talk to Claude about, when I had the chance.

I'd nodded to Mike Coughlin, who was sitting a few desks away. He'd been doing some paperwork, but now he was talking to a young man who sat with his back to me. It was the guy who'd watched the gate to Eric's community on Saturday night.

Ambroselli had been called away by another police officer, one in uniform, so I felt free to listen. And there was nothing wrong with my hearing.

Evidently, Coughlin had asked—and I had a hard time remembering the name he'd had on his shirt—Vince, that was it. Coughlin had asked Vince why he'd been substituting for Dan Shelley the night of Eric's party.

"Dan was sick," Vince said instantly. I could tell his mind was full of agitation, and I wondered what was so scary. "He asked me to sit in for him. Said it was easy work. I needed the money, so I said sure."

"Did Dan tell you what was wrong with him?" Mike Coughlin was persistent and thorough, if not brilliant.

"Sure, he said he'd had too much to drink. I'd keep that to myself, normally, but we're talking about murder here, and I don't want to get into trouble."

Coughlin gave Vince a level stare. "I'm betting it was you called us to the scene," he said. "Why didn't you own up to it?"

"We're not supposed to call the cops," Vince said. "Dan said the vamp tips him big to keep his mouth shut about his doings. The vamp, that is."

"He's seen other girls in trouble?" There was an ominous undertone to Coughlin's voice.

"No, no! Dan woulda called that in. No, the extra money was just to keep Dan quiet about the goings and the comings from the house. There are reporters and just plain snoopy people who'd pay to know who visits a vampire. This vampire, Eric whatever, he didn't want his girlfriend to catch grief about staying over at his place."

I hadn't known that.

"But when I stood up to stretch, I could see the front of his yard, and I saw the body lying there. I didn't know who it was, but she wasn't moving. That's definitely the kind of thing I need to report to the police." Vince was practically glowing with virtue by the time he finished his account.

The detective was regarding Vince with open skepticism, and Vince's glow of civic virtue diminished with every second of Coughlin's stare. "Yeah, buddy," Coughlin said finally, "I find that real interesting, since you couldn't possibly see the girl's body from the guard shack. Unless you did that big stretch while you were hovering over the ground."

I tried to remember the lay of the land in the little gated community, while Vince goggled at the detective. Coughlin was right: Eric's house was higher than the guard shack, and furthermore, the row of crepe myrtles by the walkway would prevent an easy sight line.

I sure wanted to hold Vince's hand. It would make it so much easier to find out what was going on in his head. I sighed. There was simply no casual way to touch flesh with a virtual stranger. Cara Ambroselli returned, looking impatient.

The interview staggered on for thirty more minutes. I gradually understood that Ambroselli had assembled a lot of facts about each of the people present at the scene, but that all these facts might not add up to anything. She appeared to be homing in on the stripper part of Kym Rowe's life, rather than the desperate-and-reckless part . . . or the part-Were part.

I had no idea how to make that add up to clues about why Kym Rowe had shown up at Eric's house, or who'd paid her to do so. But to me, it seemed obvious that the girl had been bribed to do her best to seduce Eric. Who'd paid for this and what they hoped to gain . . . I was as far from discovering the guilty party as Ambroselli.

While I worked that night, I went over and over the events of

Saturday at Eric's house. I served beers on autopilot. By the time I fell into bed, I found I couldn't remember any of the conversations I'd had with customers and co-workers.

Tuesday was another black hole. Dermot came in and out without saying much. He didn't look happy; in fact, he looked anxious. When I asked him a question or two, he said, "The fae at the club, they're worried. They wonder why Claude left, when he'll return, what will happen to them when he does. They wish they had seen Niall."

"I'm sorry about Niall's attitude," I said hesitantly. I didn't know if I should broach the subject or not. It had to be a painful one for Dermot, Niall's son, to be so pushed aside and disregarded.

Dermot looked at me, his eyes as pathetic as a puppy's.

"What's Faery like?" I asked, in a clumsy attempt to change the subject.

"It's beautiful," he said immediately. "The forests are green, and they stretch for miles and miles. Not as far as they used to . . . but still they're green and deep and full of life. The shoreline is stony; no white sand beaches! But the ocean is green and clear. . . ." He stood, lost in dreaming of his homeland. I wanted to ask a thousand questions: How did the fae pass their time? Did creatures like Bellenos mix with the fairies? Did they get married? What was childbirth like? Were there rich and poor?

But when I saw the grief in my great-uncle's face, I kept my curiosity to myself. He shook himself, gave me a bleak look. Then he turned to go upstairs, probably to seek consolation in *House Hunters International*.

That night was notable only for what didn't happen. Eric didn't call me. I understood that his out-of-town company had the biggest claim on his time, but I felt almost as shoved aside and disregarded as Dermot. As far as I was concerned, the vampires of Shreveport weren't speaking to me, consulting me, or visiting me. Even Bill was conspicuously absent. Mustapha was presumably still searching for Warren. Ambroselli was presumably searching for the killer of Kym Rowe.

Normally, I was a pretty cheerful person. But I wasn't seeing an end to this complicated situation, and I began to think there might never be one.

I made a creditable effort to leap out of bed with enthusiasm the next morning. I was rested, and I had to go to work, no matter what was happening in the supernatural world.

Not a creature was stirring, not even an elf. I ate some yogurt and granola and strawberries, drank some coffee, and put on some extra makeup since I was still feeling unhappy in general. I took a few minutes to paint my fingernails. A girl's gotta have a little color in her life.

At the bustling post office, I used my key to empty the Merlotte's mailbox, which served Sam for both business and personal use. Sam had gotten three envelopes from his duplex tenants. I riffled through the flyers that had been stuffed in the box and saw that the only bill worth worrying about was the electric bill. It soared in the summer, of course, since we had to keep the bar cool. I was almost scared to open it. I bit the bullet and slit the envelope. The total was bad, but not more than I expected.

Terry Bellefleur pushed open the glass door while I was tossing unwanted mail into the trash. He looked good: more alert, not as skinny, maybe. There was a woman with him. When Terry stopped to speak to me, she smiled. She needed some dental work, but it was a good smile.

"Sook, this here's Jimmie Kearney from Clarice," Terry said. "She raises Catahoulas, too." Terry loved his dogs, and he seemed to have overcome his bad luck with them. His latest bitch, Annie, had had her second litter of puppies. This time they'd been purebred. I'd heard Terry talk about Jimmie when he'd found a match for Annie, but I'd assumed Jimmie was a guy. She very much wasn't.

"I'm pleased to meet you," I said. Jimmie was younger than Terry. I put her at about forty. There were streaks of gray in her long brown hair, which hung nearly down to her waist. She wore baggy khaki shorts with a ruffled white peasant blouse and huaraches.

"I heard a lot about you," Jimmie said shyly. "You should come by Terry's and see the puppies. My Tombo is the daddy. They're just as cute as they can be. And we've got them all sold! We had to check out the homes they would go to, of course."

"Good job," I said. I was getting the information from Jimmie's head that she was over at Terry's a lot of the time. A *lot*. Just in my little peek, Jimmie seemed like an okay person. Terry deserved someone really nice; he needed someone really, really stable. I hoped she was both. "Well, maybe I'll get a chance to see those puppies before they go to their new homes. I'm glad I got to meet you, Jimmie. Terry, talk to you later."

Before I headed to the bar, I needed to check on Tara, who hadn't returned my calls. Maybe she'd gone to work today, too? Sure enough, her car was parked beside Tara's Togs.

Inside, she was sitting at the wedding table, the one where brides sat to order their invitations and their napkins and anything else a bride could want.

"Tara?" I said, because the expression on her face was very peculiar. "How come you didn't call me back? What's 'effaced' mean? Does that mean you're gonna have the babies soon?"

"Um-hum," she said, but it was clear her attention was on something else entirely.

"Where's McKenna?" Tara's assistant had been working more and more hours as Tara grew more and more great with child. Well, great with children.

"She's at home. She's been run off her feet. I told her to stay home today, that I'd work. Today's my last day."

"You don't look like you can work a whole eight hours," I said cautiously. Tara had gotten pretty snappish during her pregnancy, and the bigger she got, the more likely she'd become to give you her unvarnished opinion on almost anything—but especially if you said something about her stamina or appearance.

"I can't," she said, and my mouth fell open.

"How come?" I said.

"I'm having the babies today."

I felt a thread of panic rise up out of my stomach. "Does . . . who all knows this, Tara?"

"You."

"You haven't called anyone else?"

"No. I'm just trying to deal. Having a little moment, here." She tried to smile. "But I guess you better call McKenna and tell her to come in to work, and you better call JB and tell him to get to the hospital in Clarice, and you could call his mama. Oh, and maybe the ambulance."

"Oh my God! You're hurting?" Oh, Shepherd of Judea!

She glared at me, but I don't think she knew she was looking at me like she hoped I'd turn green. "It's not too bad yet," she said with an air of great restraint. "But my water broke just now, and since it's twins . . ."

I was already punching in 911. I described the situation to the dispatcher, and she said, "Sookie, we'll be right over to get Tara. You tell her not to worry. Oh, and she can't eat or drink anything, you hear?"

"Yes," I said. I hung up. "Tara, they're coming. Nothing to eat or drink!"

"You see any food around here?" she said. "Not a damn thing. I've been trying to keep my weight gain to a minimum, so Mr. Bare-Naked Booty will have something to keep him home when I get over having his children."

"He loves you! And I'm calling him right now!" Which I did.

After a frozen moment, JB said, "I'm coming! Wait, if you called the ambulance, I'll meet it at the hospital! Have you called the doctor?"

"She didn't put him on my list." I was waving my hands in agitation. I'd made a mistake.

"I'll do it," JB said, and I hung up.

Since there didn't seem to be anything I could do to help Tara (she was sitting absolutely still with an expression of great concentration on her face), I called Mrs. du Rone. Who said very calmly, "All right, if you're going to stay there with Tara, I'll drive straight to the hospital. Thank you, Sookie." Then, without hanging up, she shrieked, "Donnell! Go start the car! It's time!"

I hung up. I called McKenna, who said, "Oh my God! I just got out of bed! Lock up and I'll get there within an hour. Tell her I said good luck!"

Not knowing what else to do, I went to stand by Tara, who said, "Give me your hand." I took her hand, and she got a death grip on mine. She began to pant in a rhythm, and her face turned red. Her whole body tensed. This close to her, I could smell something unusual. It wasn't exactly a bad smell, but it was certainly one I'd never associated with Tara.

Amniotic fluid, I guessed.

I thought all the bones in my hand would snap before Tara finished puffing. We rested a moment, Tara and I, and her eyes remained fixed on some far-distant shore. After a short time, she said, "Okay," as if I'd know what that signaled. I figured it out when we started again with the huffing and puffing. This time Tara turned white. I was incredibly relieved to hear the ambulance approaching, though Tara didn't seem to notice.

I recognized the two EMTs, though I couldn't recall their names. They'd graduated with Jason, or maybe a year ahead of him. As far as I was concerned, they had haloes.

"Hey, lady," the taller woman said to Tara. "You ready to take a ride with us?"

Tara nodded without losing her focus on that invisible spot.

"How close are the contractions, darlin'?" asked the second, a small, stocky woman with wire-rimmed glasses. She was asking me, but I just gaped at her.

"Three or four minutes," Tara said in a monotone, as if she thought she'd pop if she spoke emphatically.

"Well, I guess we better hustle, then," the taller woman said calmly. While she took Tara's blood pressure, Wire Rims set up the gurney, and then they helped Tara up from the chair (which was soaking wet), and they got Tara onto the gurney and into the ambulance very quickly, without seeming to hurry in the least.

I was left standing in the middle of the store. I stared at the wet chair. Finally I wrote a note to McKenna. "You will need to clean the chair," it said. I stuck it to the back door, where McKenna would enter. I locked up and departed.

It was one of those days I regretted having a job. I could have gone to Clarice and waited for the birth of the babies, sitting in the waiting room with the other people Tara cared for.

I went into Merlotte's feeling ridiculously happy. I just had time to put the mail on Sam's desk when Kennedy came in the employee door, and India was hard on her heels. Both of them looked pretty down in the mouth, but I wasn't having any of that. "Ladies," I said. "We are gonna have us a good day here."

"Sookie, I'd like to oblige, but my heart is breaking," Kennedy said pathetically.

"Oh, bullshit, Kennedy! It is not. You just ask Danny to share with you, you tell him what a man he is and how you love his hot body, and he'll tell his heap big secret. You got no reason to be insecure. He thinks you're fabulous. He likes you more than his LeBaron."

Kennedy looked stunned, but after a moment a small smile flickered across her face.

"India, you'll meet a woman who's worthy of you any day now, I just know it," I told India, who said, "Sookie, you are as full of bullshit as a cow is of milk."

"Speaking of milk," I said, "we're going to hold hands and say a prayer for Tara, cause she's having her babies right now."

And that was what we did.

It wasn't until I was halfway through my shift that I realized how much more enjoyable work was when you had a light heart. How long had it been since I'd let go of my worries and simply allowed myself to enjoy the happiness of another person?

It had been way too long.

Today, everything seemed easy. Kennedy was pouring beers and tea and water with lemon, and all the food was ready on time. Antoine was singing in the kitchen. He had a fine voice, so we all enjoyed that.

The customers tipped well, and everyone had a good word for me. Danny Prideaux came in to moon longingly at Kennedy, and his face when she gave him a smile—well, it was all lit up.

Just when I was thinking I might glide through this day with happiness all around, Alcide came in. He'd clearly been working; there was a hard hat impression in his thick black hair, and he was sweaty and dirty like most of the men who came in at midday in the summer. Another Were was with him, a man who was just as glad to be in the air-conditioning. They breathed simultaneous sighs of relief when they sank into the chairs at a table in my section.

Truthfully, I was surprised to see Alcide in Merlotte's. There were plenty of places to eat in the area besides our bar. Our last conversation hadn't been exactly pleasant, and he'd never responded to the message I'd left on his cell phone.

Maybe his presence constituted an olive branch. I went over with menus and a tentative smile. "You must have a job close to here," I said, by way of greeting. Alcide had been a partner in his dad's surveying company, and now he owned the whole thing. He was running it well, I heard. I'd also heard there'd been big personnel changes.

"We're getting ready for the new high school gym in Clarice," Alcide said. "We just finished. Sookie, this is Roy Hornby."

I nodded politely. "Roy, nice to meet you. What can I get for you-all to drink?"

"Could we have a whole pitcher of sweet tea?" Roy asked. He gave off the strong mental signature of a werewolf.

I said, "Sure, I'll just go get that." While I carried a cold pitcher and two glasses filled with ice over to the table, I wondered if the new people at AAA Accurate Surveys were all two-natured. I poured the first round of tea. It was gone in a few seconds. I refilled.

"*Damn*, it's hot out there," Roy said. "You saved my life." Roy was medium: hair a medium brown, eyes a medium blue, height a moderate five foot ten, slim build. He did have great teeth and a winning smile, which he flashed at me now. "I think you know my girlfriend, Ms. Stackhouse."

"Who would that be? Call me Sookie, by the way."

"I date Palomino."

I was so startled that I couldn't think of what to say. Then I had to scramble to get some words out. "She's sure a pretty young woman. I haven't gotten to know her real well, but I see her around."

"Yeah, she works for your boyfriend, and she moonlights at the Trifecta."

For a vampire and a Were to date was very unusual, practically a Romeo and Juliet situation. Roy must be a tolerant kind of guy. Funny, that wasn't the vibe he was giving off. Roy seemed like a conventional Were to me: tough, macho, strong-willed.

There weren't many "granola" Weres. But Alcide, though not exactly beaming at Roy, wasn't scowling, either.

I wondered what Roy thought of Palomino's nestmates, Rubio and Parker. I wondered if Roy knew Palomino had been part of the massacre at Fangtasia. Since Roy was a bit clearer to read than some Weres, I could tell he was thinking of Palomino going to a bar with him. Something clicked inside me, and I knew I'd gotten an idea, but I wasn't sure what it was. There was a connection I should be drawing, but I'd have to wait for it to pop to the top of my brain. Isn't that the most irritating feeling in the world?

The next time I passed Alcide's table, Roy had gone to the men's room. Alcide reached out to ask me to pause. "Sookie," he said quietly,

"I got your message. Nobody's seen Mustapha yet, and nobody's heard from him. Or his buddy Warren. What did he say to you?"

"He gave me a message for you," I said. "You want to come outside for a second?"

"Well, all right." Alcide rose and walked to the door, and I trailed after him. There was no one lingering in the parking lot on a day this hot.

"I know you won't want to hear this, but he said Jannalynn was out to get me, and not to trust her," I said.

Alcide's green eyes widened. "Jannalynn. He says she's untrustworthy."

I raised my shoulders, let them drop.

"I don't know how to take that, Sookie. Though she hasn't been herself for a few weeks, she's more than proved herself as my enforcer." Alcide looked both bewildered and irritated. "I'll think on what you've told me. In the meantime, I'm keeping my eyes and ears open, and you'll hear soon's I know something."

"He wants you to call him," I said. "When you're alone. He put a lot of weight on that."

"Thanks for passing along the message."

Though that wasn't the same thing as telling me he'd place the call, I made myself smile at him as we went back inside. He resumed his seat as Roy returned to the table. "And now, what can I get you hungry guys for lunch?"

Alcide and Roy ordered a basket of fried pickles and two hamburgers apiece. I turned in their order and made the rounds of my other tables. I had my cell phone in my pocket, and I checked it from time to time. I was very anxious to hear about Tara, but I wasn't going to bug JB. I figured he was nervous enough as it was, and there was a good chance he'd have turned off his cell phone since he was in the hospital.

I was more worried about JB than I was Tara. For the past two weeks, he'd been coming in to parade his worries to me. He hadn't been sure he could handle being in the delivery room, especially if Tara had to have a C-section. He hadn't been sure he could remember his coaching lessons. I figured it was good he was presenting a strong face to his wife and saving the worries for a friend, but maybe he should have been sharing his qualms with Tara or her doctor.

Maybe he was passed out on the hospital floor. Tara . . . she was made of stronger stuff.

Alcide and Roy ate with the hearty appetites of men who've been working outside all morning—men who also happen to be werewolves—and they drank the whole pitcher of tea. They both looked happier when they were full, and Alcide made a big effort to catch my eye. I dodged it as long as I could, but he nailed me fair and square, so I went over, smiling. "Can I get you-all anything else? Some dessert today?" I said.

"I'm tight as a tick," Roy said. "Those were great hamburgers."

"I'll tell Antoine you said so," I assured him.

"Sam not here today?" Alcide said.

I almost asked him if he saw Sam anywhere in the room, but I realized that would just be rude. It was not a real question. He was trying to segue into another topic.

"No, Kennedy is on the bar today."

"I bet Sam's with Jannalynn," Roy said, grinning significantly at me.

I shrugged, tried to look politely indifferent.

Alcide was looking off into the distance as if he were thinking about something else, but I knew he was thinking about me. Alcide was feeling kind of lucky that he'd never managed to clinch our relationship, because he figured there was something fishy going on between Jannalynn and me. Alcide didn't consider that he himself could be the bone of contention, since Jannalynn had told him she was going to propose to Sam, and I was Eric's girlfriend. But we two women clearly had issues, and he had to wonder how that would affect the pack, which had become the most important thing in the world to Alcide.

He was thinking this all so clearly that I wondered if he was trying to let me know his concerns, projecting them on purpose.

"Apparently we do have issues," I told him. "At least, she does." Alcide looked startled, and half turned. Before Roy could begin asking questions I said, "How's the bar doing?" Hair of the Dog, the only Were bar in Shreveport, wasn't a tourist bar like Fangtasia. It was not exclusively for Weres, but for all the twoeys in the Shreveport area. "We seem to be pulling out of our slump, here."

"It's doing good. Jannalynn is doing a great job of managing it," Alcide said. He hesitated for a moment. "I heard that those new bars were falling off some, the ones the new guy opened."

"Yeah, I heard that, too," I said, trying not to sound too smug.

"Whatever happened to that new guy?" Alcide said, keeping his words guarded. "That Victor?" Though the world knew about the existence of vampires and the two-natured, their infrastructure was not common knowledge. It would remain a secret if the supes had their way. Alcide took an elaborately casual sip of the remaining tea. "I haven't seen him around."

"Me, either, for weeks," I said. I gave Alcide a very direct look. "Maybe he went back to Nevada." Roy's mind was empty of Victor-thoughts, and I was glad that Palomino had kept her mouth shut. Palomino . . . who hung out in a Were bar. Now I made the connection. That was why the distributor was leaving TrueBlood at Hair of the Dog . . . it was for Palomino. Just Palomino? Was another vamp visiting the Were bar, too?

"Your boyfriend doing well?" Alcide asked.

I came back to the here and now. "Eric's always well."

"Find out how that girl got into the house? The gal that got killed?"

"You-all don't want any dessert? Let me get your check." Of course I had it ready, but I needed to create a little bustle in the air, get them moving. Sure enough, Alcide had pulled his wallet out of his pocket by the time I got back. Roy had gone to the bar to talk to one of the men who worked at the lumber mill. Apparently they'd gone to high school together.

When I bent over to put the check by Alcide, I inhaled his scent. It was a little sad to remember how attractive I'd found him when I first met him, how I'd allowed myself to daydream that this handsome and hardworking man might be my soul mate.

But it hadn't worked out then, and now it never would. Too much water had passed under that particular bridge. Alcide was getting deeper and deeper into his Were culture, and further and further away from the fairly normal human life he'd managed to live until his father's disastrous attempt to become packmaster.

He was scenting me, too. Our eyes met. We both looked a little sad.

I wanted to say something to him, something sincere and meaningful, but under the circumstances I really couldn't imagine what to say.

And the moment slid by. He handed me some bills and told me he didn't need any change, and Roy slapped his buddy on the back and returned to the table, and they prepared to go back out into the heat of the day to drive to another job in Minden on their way back to the home office in Shreveport.

After they left, I began to bus their table because I didn't have anything else to do. There were hardly any customers, and I figured D'Eriq was taking the opportunity to slip out back to have a smoke or listen to his iPod.

My cell phone vibrated in my apron pocket, and I whipped it out, hoping that it was news about Tara. But it was Sam, calling from his cell.

"What's up, boss?" I asked. "Everything's fine, here."

"Good to know, but not why I called," he said. "Sookie, this morning Jannalynn and I went down to Splendide to make a payment on a table she's buying." Sam had been the one who'd recommended Splendide to me when I'd cleaned out the attic. It still seemed strange to me that the young Jannalynn was an antiques fan.

"Okay," I said when Sam paused. "So, what's going on at Splendide?" *That I need to know?*

"It got broken into last night," he said, sounding oddly hesitant.

"Sorry to hear that," I said, still not getting the importance to me of this situation. "Ah . . . her table okay?"

"The things you sold to Brenda and Donald . . . those things were dismantled on the spot, or taken."

I pulled out a chair and sat down in it abruptly.

It was lucky no one was waiting for service for the next few minutes while Sam told me everything he knew about the break-in. Nothing he told me was illuminating. A few little items that had been in the display cases had been grabbed, too. "I don't know if you sold them anything small or not," Sam said.

"Was other stuff taken? Or just mine?"

"I think enough else was gone to kind of camouflage that the targeted stuff had come from your attic," he said, very quietly. I knew other people were around him. "I just noticed because Brenda and Donald pointed out your pieces to show me how they'd cleaned them."

"Thanks for letting me know," I said, strictly on autopilot. "I'll talk to you later, Sam." I shut my phone and kept to my seat for a moment, thinking furiously.

Danny was talking so earnestly to Kennedy that I could tell he'd finally told her why he'd been out of her sight lately. She leaned across the bar and kissed him. I made myself get up to carry the bin of dirty dishes back to the kitchen. Behind me, the door swung open. I looked over my shoulder to check on the size of the party and got yet another unpleasant surprise.

Bellenos was standing in the doorway. I glanced around quickly, but no one—not that there were more than five people in the big room—seemed to be paying the elf any attention. They were not seeing the same creature I was seeing.

Bellenos, who looked very strange in regular human clothes (when he was being himself, I'd seen him in a sort of kilt and a one-shouldered T-shirt), looked around Merlotte's, slowly and warily. When he didn't spot anything threatening, he glided over to me, his slanting dark eyes full of mischief. "Sister," he said. "How are you today?" He showed his needle teeth in a big smile.

"I'm good," I said. I had to be very wary. "How're you?"

"Happy to be out of that building in Monroe," he said. "I see you are not busy. Can we sit and talk?"

"Yes," I said. "Let me clear this table." I was sorry that didn't take longer to do. By the time I sat down with the elf warrior, I was no closer to having a good idea about how to handle this visit than I had been the moment Bellenos walked in. I pulled out a chair to his right. I wanted to talk in a low voice, because I certainly didn't want anyone to overhear our conversation, but I also wanted to keep an eye on the few people in the room.

In the fae way, Bellenos took my hand. I wanted to snatch it back, but there wasn't any point in offending him. The bones stood out so much that his hand hardly looked human—which, of course, it wasn't. It was pale, freckled, and very strong.

Past his shoulder, I saw Kennedy glance our way. She shook a playful finger at me. She thought I was flirting with someone besides Eric. I gave her a stiff smile. Ha. Ha.

"There are too many of us crowded under one roof at Hooligans," Bellenos said.

I nodded.

"Claude is a leader. Dermot is not."

I nodded again, just to show I was following his conversation. He wasn't voicing any new ideas, so far.

"If you have any means of reaching Niall, now is the time to make use of it."

"I would if I could. I don't have any such secret." His slanting eyes were a bit disturbing close up.

"Is that the truth?" An auburn eyebrow rose.

"The truthful answer is that I really don't have any certain means of contacting Niall," I said flatly. "I'm not completely sure I would get in touch with him, if I had the ability."

Bellenos nodded thoughtfully. "The fairy prince is capricious," he said.

"That's for damn sure." Finally, we were in agreement.

"I'm sorry that you can't help," Bellenos said. "I hope nothing worse happens."

"Like what?" Did I really want to know?

"Like more fights breaking out." He shrugged. "Like one of us leaving the bar to have some fun amongst the humans."

That sounded like a threat.

I suddenly remembered that Claude had brought me a letter from Niall, one he said he'd received through the portal in the woods. That was what he'd told me when he'd delivered the letter, if I was remembering correctly. "I could write a letter," I offered. "I don't know if it would reach him, but I can try."

I was sure Bellenos would press me for details, but to my relief he said, "You had better try anything you can think of. You don't know me well, but I'm telling the truth in this matter."

"I don't doubt you," I said. "I'll do my best. And I have a question to ask you."

He looked politely attentive.

"A young woman, a woman at least part Were, came to my boyfriend's home a few nights ago," I said. "She was irresistible to him."

"Did he kill her?"

"No, but he drank from her, though normally he has very good self-control. I think this young woman was carrying a vial of fairy blood. She opened it when she got close to Eric to make herself attractive to him. She may even have drunk it herself so the blood would permeate her. Do you have any ideas about where the blood might have come from?" I regarded him steadily.

"You want to know if she got the blood from one of us?"

"I do."

Bellenos said, "It's possible a fairy sold blood without knowing what it would be used for."

I thought that was bullshit, but in the interests of getting an answer, I said, "Certainly."

"I'll inquire," he said. "And you send the letter."

Without further ado, he rose and glided out of the bar, receiving only a casual glance or two. I went back to the calendar to check, the one posted behind the bar. Danny had finally left to return to work, and Kennedy was actually singing to herself as she aimlessly shifted bottles and glasses around. She grinned at me as she "worked."

I was just bending closer to look at the June page when my cell rang. I whipped it out of my pocket. JB!

"What happened?" I asked.

"We got a boy and a girl!" he yelled. "They're fine! Tara's fine! They got all their fingers and toes! They're big enough! They're perfect!"

"Oh, I'm so happy! You give Tara a hug for me. I'll try to get over to the hospital to see those little ones. The minute you're home I'll bring supper over, you hear?"

"I'll tell her," he said, but he was in such a daze I knew he'd forget the minute he hung up. That was okay.

Grinning like a baboon, I told Kennedy the good news. I called Jason, because I wanted to share the happiness.

"That's good," he said absently. "I'm real glad for 'em. Listen, Sook, we may be closing in on a wedding date. There any day you just couldn't be there?"

"Probably not. If you pick a weekday, I might have to change my work schedule, but I can usually swing that." Especially now that I owned a piece of the bar, though I'd kept that to myself. As far as

I knew, Jannalynn was the only person Sam had told, and even that had surprised me a little.

"Great! We're going to pin it down tonight. We're thinking in a couple of weeks."

"Wow, that's quick. Sure, just let me know."

There were so many happy events going on. After Bellenos's unexpected visit, it was impossible to forget that I had worries . . . but it was fairly easy to put them on the back burner and revel in the good things.

The hot afternoon drew to an end. In the summer, fewer people came in to drink after work. They headed home to mow their yards, hop in the aboveground pool, and take their kids to sports events.

One of our alcoholics, Jane Bodehouse, showed up around five o'clock. When she'd gotten cut from flying glass during the firebombing a few weeks before, Jane had gotten sewed up and had returned to the bar within twenty-four hours. For a few days, she got to enjoy painkillers *and* alcohol. I'd wondered if Jane's son might be angry that his mom had gotten hurt at Merlotte's, but as far as I could tell, the poor guy had only a mild regret that she'd survived. After the bombing, Jane had abandoned her barstool in favor of the table by the window where she'd been sitting when the bottle came through the window. It was like she'd enjoyed the excitement and was ready for another Molotov cocktail. When I went over to give her a bowl of snack mix or replenish her drink, she always had a plaintive murmur about the heat or the boredom.

Since the bar was still almost empty, I sat down to have a conversation with Jane when I served her the first drink of the day. Maybe. Kennedy joined us after she'd made sure the two guys at the bar had full glasses. To make them even happier, she turned the TV to ESPN.

Any conversation with Jane was rambling and tended to bounce back and forth between decades with no warning. When Kennedy mentioned her own pageant days, Jane said, "I was Miss Red River Valley and Miss Razorback and Miss Renard Parish when I was in my teens."

So we had a pleasant reminiscence about those days, and it was good to see Jane perk up and share some common ground with Kennedy. On the other hand, Kennedy was a little freaked out at the idea someone who'd started out like her had ended up a barfly. She was thinking some anxious thoughts.

After a few minutes, Kennedy had to get back behind the bar, and I rose to greet my replacement, Holly. I'd opened my mouth to tell Jane good-bye when she said, "Do you think it'll happen again?"

She was looking out the smoky glass of the big front window.

I started to ask her what she meant, but then from her addled brain, I got it. "I hope not, Jane," I said. "I hope no one ever decides to attack the bar again."

"I did pretty good that day," she told me. "I moved real fast, and Sam got me going down that hall at a pretty good clip. Those EMTs were real nice to me." She was smiling.

"Yes, Jane, you did real good. We all thought so," I told her. I patted her shoulder and walked away.

The firebombing of Merlotte's, which was a terrible night in my memory, had turned into a pleasurable reminiscence for Jane. I shook my head as I collected my purse and left the bar. My gran had always told me it was an ill wind that blew nobody good. Once again, she was proved right.

Even the break-in at Splendide had served a purpose. Now I knew for sure that someone, almost certainly one of the fae, knew my grandmother had had possession of the cluviel dor.

Chapter 8

An hour later, having come home to a blessedly cool and empty house, I was sitting at my kitchen table with my best stationery and a black pen. I was trying to decide how to begin the letter, the one I'd promised Bellenos I'd attempt to send to Faery. I had doubts about how well this was going to go.

The last time I'd fed something into the portal, it had been eaten. Granted, it had been a human body.

My first attempt had run on for five handwritten pages. It was now in the kitchen trash can. I had to condense what I needed to convey. Urgency! That was the message.

Dear Great-Grandfather, I began. I hesitated. *And Claude,* I added. *Bellenos and Dermot are worried that the fae at Hooligans are getting too restless to stay confined to the building. They miss Claude and his leadership.*

We are all afraid something bad will happen if this situation doesn't change soon. Please let us know what's going on. Can you send a return letter through this portal? Or send Claude back? Love, Sookie

I read it over, decided it was as close as I was going to get to what I wanted to say (*Claude, get your butt back here now!*). I wrote both Niall's and Claude's names on the envelope, which was real pretty—cream with pink and red roses on the border. I almost put a stamp on the upper right corner before I realized it would be a ridiculous waste.

Between the heat, the bugs, and the burgeoning undergrowth, my jaunt into the woods to "mail" my letter was not as pleasant as my previous rambles had been. Sweat poured down my face, and my hair was sticking to my neck. A devil's walking stick scratched me deeply enough to make me bleed. I paused by a big clump of the plumy bushes that only seem to grow big out in the sun—Gran would have had a name for them, but I didn't—and I heard a deer moving around inside the dense growth. *At least Bellenos left me one,* I thought, and told myself I was being ridiculous. We had plenty of deer. Plenty.

To my relief, the portal was still in the little clearing where I'd last seen it, but it looked smaller. Not that it's easy to define the size of a patch of shimmery air—but last time it had been large enough to admit a very small human body. Now, that wouldn't be possible without taking a chainsaw to the body beforehand.

Either the portal was shrinking naturally, or Niall had decided a size reduction would prevent me from popping anything else unauthorized into Faery. I knelt before the patch of wavery air, which hovered about knee-high just above the blackberry vines and the grasses. I popped the letter into the quavering patch, and it vanished.

Though I held my breath in anticipation, nothing happened. I didn't hear the snarling of last time, but I found the silence kind of depressing. I don't know what I'd expected, but I'd half hoped I'd get some signal. Maybe a chime? Or the sound of a gong? A recording saying, *We've received your message and will attempt to deliver it?* That would have been nice.

I relaxed and smiled, amused at my own silliness. Hoisting myself up, I made my difficult way back through the woods. I could hardly wait to strip off my sweaty, dirty clothes and get into my shower. As I emerged from the shadow of the trees and into the waning afternoon, I saw that would have to be a pleasure delayed.

In my absence I'd acquired some visitors. Three people I didn't know, all looking to be in their midforties, were standing by a car as if they'd been on the point of getting into it to drive away. If only I'd stayed by the portal a few more minutes! The little group was oddly assorted. The man standing by the driver's door had coppery brown hair and a short beard, and he was wearing gold-rimmed glasses. He wore khakis and a pale blue oxford cloth shirt with the sleeves rolled up, practically a summertime white-collar work uniform. The other man was a real contrast. His jeans were stained, and his T-shirt said he liked pussies, with an oh-so-clever drawing of a Persian cat. Subtle, huh? I caught a whiff of otherness coming from him; he wasn't really human, but I didn't want to get any closer to investigate what his true nature might be.

His female companion was wearing a low-cut T shirt, dark green with gold studs as a decoration, and white shorts. Her bare legs were heavily tattooed.

"Afternoon," I said, not even trying to sound welcoming. I could hear trouble coming from their brains. Wait. Didn't the sleazy couple look just a little familiar?

"Hello," said the woman, an olive-skinned brunette with raccoon eye makeup. She took a drag on her cigarette. "You Sookie Stackhouse?"

"I am. And you are?"

"We're the Rowes. I'm Georgene and this is Oscar. This man," and she pointed at the driver, "is Harp Powell."

"I'm sorry?" I said. "Do I know you?"

"Kym's parents," the woman said.

I was even sorrier I'd come back to the house.

Call me ungracious, but I wasn't going to ask them in. They hadn't called ahead, they had no reason to talk to me, and above all else—I had been down this road before with the Pelts.

"I'm sorry for your loss," I said. "But I'm not sure why you've come here."

"You talked to our girl before she died," Oscar Rowe said. "We just wanted to know what was on her mind."

Though they didn't realize it, they'd come to the right place to find out. Knowing what was on people's minds was my specialty. But I wasn't getting good brain readings from either of them. Instead of grief and regret, I was getting avid curiosity . . . an emotion more suited to people who slow down to goggle at road accidents than to grieving parents.

I turned slightly to look at their companion. "And you, Mr. Powell? What's your role here?" I'd been aware of his intense observation.

"I'm thinking of doing a book about Kym's life," Harp Powell said. "And her death."

I could add that up in my head: lurid past, pretty girl, died outside a vampire's house during a party with interesting guests. It wouldn't be a biography of the desperate, emotionally disturbed Kym I'd met so briefly. Harp Powell was thinking of writing a true-crime novel with pictures in the middle: Kym as a cute youngster, Kym in high school, Kym as a stripper, and maybe Kym as a corpse. Bringing the Rowes with him was a smart move. Who could turn down distraught parents? But I knew Georgene and Oscar weren't anywhere close to devastated. The Rowes were more curious than bereaved.

"How long had it been since you saw her?" I asked Kym's mother.

"Well, she was a grown-up girl. She left home after she graduated from high school," Georgene said reasonably. She had stepped toward the house as if she were waiting for me to open the back door. She dropped her cigarette on the gravel and ground it out with her platform sandal.

"So, five years? Six?" I crossed my arms over my chest and looked at each of them in turn.

"It had been a while," conceded Oscar Rowe. "Kym had her own living to make; we couldn't support her. She had to get out and hustle like the rest of us." He gave me a look that was supposed to say he knew I'd had to get out and hustle, too—we were all working people, here. All in the same boat.

"I don't have anything to say about your daughter. I didn't even talk to her directly. I saw her for maybe five minutes."

"Is it true your boyfriend was taking blood from her?" Harp Powell asked.

"You can ask him that. But you'll have to go after dark, and he may not be too glad to see you." I smiled.

"Is it true that you live here with two male strippers?" Powell persisted. "Kym was a stripper," he added, as if that would somehow soften me up.

"Who I live with is none of your business. You can leave now," I said, still smiling, I hoped very unpleasantly. "Or I'll call the sheriff, and he'll be here pretty quick." With that, I went inside and shut and locked the door. No point in standing out there listening to questions I wouldn't answer.

The light on my phone was blinking. I turned the sound very low and pressed the button to play it. "Sister," said Bellenos, "no one here will admit to giving any blood to the girl who was killed, or giving blood to anyone at all. Either there's another fairy somewhere, or someone here is lying. I don't like either prospect." I hit the Delete button.

I heard knocking at the back door, and I moved to where I couldn't be seen.

Harp Powell knocked a few more times and slid his card under the porch door, but I didn't answer.

They drove off after a couple of minutes. Though I was relieved to watch them go, the encounter left me depressed and shaken. Seen from the outside, did my life truly seem so tawdry?

I lived with *one* male stripper. I *did* date a vampire. He *had* taken blood from Kym Rowe, right in front of me.

Maybe Harp Powell had just wanted answers to his sensational questions. Maybe he would have reported my answers in a fair and balanced way. Maybe he had just been trying to get a rise out of me. And maybe I was feeling extra fragile. But his strategy worked, though not until too late to directly benefit him. I felt bad about myself. I felt like talking to someone about how my life looked—as opposed to how it felt to be inside it, living it. I wanted to justify my decisions.

But Tara had just had her babies, Amelia and I had some big issues to settle, and Pam knew more about what I faced than I myself knew. Jason loved me, but I had to admit my brother was not too swift mentally. Sam was probably preoccupied with his romance with Jannalynn. I didn't think I knew anyone else well enough to spill my inner fears.

I felt too restless to settle down to any pastime: too fidgety to read or watch TV, too impatient to do housework. After a quick shower, I climbed in the car and drove to Clarice. Though the day was ending, the hospital parking lot was unshaded. I knew the car would be an oven when I emerged.

I stopped at the little gift shop and bought some pink-and-blue carnations to give to the new mother. After I got off the elevator at the second floor (there were only two) I paused at the glass-fronted nursery to peer in at the newborns. There were seven infants rolled up to the window. Two of the clear plastic bins, side by side, were labeled with cards reading "Baby du Rone."

My heart skipped a beat. One of Tara's babies wore a pink cap, the other a blue. They were so little: scrunch-faced, red, their faces beginning to stretch as they yawned. Tears started in my eyes. I had not ever imagined being so bowled over by the sight of them. As I patted my cheeks with a tissue, I was happy that I chanced to be the only visitor looking at the new arrivals. I looked and looked, amazed that my friends had created life between them.

After a few minutes, I ducked in to see an exhausted Tara. JB was sitting by the bed, dazed with happiness. "My mom and dad just left," JB said. "They're going to open a savings account for the kids tomorrow." He shook his head, obviously considering that a bizarre reaction, but I gave the du Rone grandparents high marks. Tara had a new look to her, a gravity and thoughtfulness she'd been lacking. She was a mother now.

I gave them both a hug and told them how beautiful the babies were, listened to Tara's childbirth story, and then the nurses wheeled in the babies to breastfeed, so I scooted out.

Not only was night closing in, thunder was rolling through the sky as I stepped out the hospital doors. I hurried over to my car, opening the door to flush out the worst of the heat. When I could bear to, I got inside and buckled up. I went through the drive-through at Taco Bell to order a quesadilla. I hadn't known how hungry I was until the smell filled the car. I couldn't wait until I got home. I ate most of it during the drive.

Maybe if I turned on the TV and simply vegetated the rest of the evening, I might feel like a worthy human being by morning.

I didn't get to carry out my program.

Bubba was waiting at my back door when I pulled up. The much-needed rain had begun to descend on my way home, but he didn't seem to mind getting wet. I hadn't seen the vampire since he'd sung at Fangtasia the night we'd killed Victor; I was startled to see him now. I gathered my food trash, got my keys ready, and sprinted over to the screen door, my key ready. "Come on in!" I called. He was right behind me as I unlocked the kitchen door and stepped inside.

"I come to tell you something," he said without a preamble.

He sounded so serious that I tossed my empty food bag and my purse onto the table and whirled around to face him.

"What's wrong?" I asked, trying not to sound as anxious as I felt. If I lost control, it would only agitate the vampire, who had not had a very successful transition from human life to living death.

"She is coming to visit you," he said, taking my hand. His was cold and wet from the rain. The sensation was unpleasant, but I couldn't pull away. Bless his heart.

As gently as I could, I said, "Who's coming, Bubba?"

"Me," said a slightly accented voice from the darkness. The back door was still open, and I could see through the screen porch door. Since she was backlit by the security light, I could just perceive the outline of a woman standing in the pounding rain. The noise of it almost drowned out her voice. "I have come to talk. I'm Freyda."

I was so completely off guard that I simply couldn't make myself speak.

Bubba stood facing out into the darkness, standing right under the light in my bright kitchen, his dark hair drenched, his jowly face determined. I was touched to my core, and I was terrified for him.

"I don't mean you harm, upon my word," she called. She turned her head slightly, and I could see her in profile. Straight nose, tight chin, high forehead.

"Why would I believe you?" I asked.

"Because Eric would hate me if I harmed you." She stepped up to the screen door. I could see her in the light, now. I thought, simply, *Damn.*

Freyda was at least five foot ten. Even soaking wet, she was beautiful. I thought her hair would be a light brown when it was dry, and she had broad shoulders, lean hips, and cheekbones that could slice bread. She was wearing a tank top with nothing underneath, and a pair of shorts, which I found just weird. Legs that pale shouldn't be sticking out of shorts.

"I need a promise that you won't harm Bubba, either," I said slowly, still not sure what I should do.

"I so promise." She nodded. I wouldn't necessarily believe her, but she was close enough to the house that the magical wards Bellenos had laid would have flared if she'd meant me harm. At least, Bellenos had told me so.

To my amazement—if I could be any more amazed—Bubba pulled a cell phone out of his pocket and hit a number on speed dial. I could hear a voice answer. Bubba described our situation, and I heard

Pam's voice say, "All right. Whatever happens, we know who's responsible. Be smart."

"So we got a safety net," Bubba told me, and I patted his arm.

"Good thinking," I said. "All right, Miss Freyda. Come on in."

She stepped out of the downpour and dripped on my back porch. There were folded towels in the laundry basket on top of the dryer. She pulled one off the stack to dry her face and rub her dripping hair. I moved aside to let her enter the kitchen, and she took another towel and brought it with her. I didn't want our wet selves dripping all over my living room, so I gestured to the chairs around the table. "Please have a seat," I said, not letting my eyes leave her for a moment. "Do you want a drink?"

"You mean synthetic blood," she said after a slight hesitation. "Yes, that would be nice. A sociable gesture."

"I'm all about the gestures. Bubba, you, too?"

"Yes, ma'am, I reckon so," he said.

So I heated two bottles, got two matching glasses from the cabinet in case they were particular, and set these items before the vampires, who had settled at the table: Bubba with his back to the door, Freyda with her back to the sink. I took the end opposite Bubba, so I was sitting to the queen's left. I waited in silence while the vampires took polite sips of their drinks. Neither one used a glass.

"You understand the situation," Freyda said.

I was relieved she wasn't going to pussyfoot around. And she didn't sound angry or jealous. She sounded matter-of-fact. I felt something cold creep into my heart. "I believe so," I said, wanting to be crystal clear. "I'm not sure why you want to talk to me about it."

She didn't comment. She seemed to be waiting for me to spell it out.

"Eric's maker was in negotiations with you when he died, and those negotiations involved you taking Eric as a husband," I said.

"Since I'm a queen and he's not a king, he'd be my consort," she said.

I'd read a biography of Queen Victoria (and rented the movie), so I understood the term. I tried to think very hard before I said anything. "Okay," I said, and paused, getting all my conversational ducks in a row. "You know that Eric loves me, that he married me according to you-all's rules, and that I love him." Just getting the groundwork laid.

She nodded, looking at me thoughtfully. Her eyes were large, tilted up a little, and dark brown. "I've heard that you have many hidden attributes. And of course, I see some that are not so hidden." She smiled slightly. "I'm not trying to insult you. It's a fact that you are a pretty human."

Okeydokey. There was obviously another shoe to drop . . . and Freyda tossed it right at me. "But you must see that I am beautiful, too," she told me. "And I am also rich. And though I've been a vampire only a hundred and fifty years, I've already become a queen. So I'm powerful. Unless I misread Eric . . . and I've known many men, *many* . . . he likes all those—attributes—very much."

I nodded to show I was giving due weight to her words. "I know I'm not rich and powerful," I said. Impossible to deny. "But he does love me."

"I am sure he thinks so," she said, still with that eerie calm. "And perhaps it's even true. But he won't forgo what I have to offer, regardless of what he may feel."

I made myself think before I responded. Inhale. Exhale. "You seem certain the prospect of power will trump the love." I said the words with my own calm, but inside I was trying not to panic.

"Yes, I'm certain." She let the edge of her surprise show. How could I ever doubt that she was right? I glanced at our silent companion. Sadness was weighing down Bubba's pale face as he looked at me. Bubba, too, thought she was right.

"Then why did you bother to come here to meet me, Freyda?" I said, struggling to maintain my control. In my lap, below the table, my hands were clenched together painfully.

"I wanted to know what he loved," she said. She examined me so closely that it was like getting an MRI. "I am pleased that he likes looks and intelligence. I am fairly sure that you are what you seem on the surface. You aren't arrogant or conniving."

"Are you?" I was beginning to lose control.

"As a queen, I can seem arrogant," she said. "And as a queen, occasionally I have to be conniving. I came up from nothing. The strongest vampires do, I have observed. I intend to hold on to my kingdom, Sookie Stackhouse. A strong consort would double my chances." Freyda picked up her glass of TrueBlood and took a swallow. She put it down with such delicacy that I didn't hear it touch the table. "I have seen Eric at this or that event for years. He's bold. He's intelligent. He's adapted to the modern world. And I hear he's amazing in bed. Is that true?"

When it became apparent that Hell would freeze over before I would talk about Eric in bed, Freyda smiled faintly and continued. "When Appius Livius Ocella came through Oklahoma with his bumboy, I took the opportunity to open a discussion with him. Despite Eric's fine points, I observed that he also likes to give the appearance of being independent."

"He *is* independent."

"He's been content to be sheriff for a long time. Therefore, he enjoys being a big fish in a small pond. It's an illusion of independence, but one he seems to hold dear. I decided it would be well to have some hold over him to induce him to consider my offer seriously. So I made a bargain with Appius Livius Ocella. He didn't live to enjoy his half."

Ocella's death didn't distress Freyda one little bit. At least we had one thing in common besides an Eric appreciation club.

She had certainly studied Eric. She had him pegged.

I wanted—desperately—to know if she'd already talked to Eric tonight. Eric had told me before that Freyda had been calling him weekly, but he'd given the impression that he'd been aloof in those conversations. Had they actually been negotiating one on one, long distance? Had they been meeting secretly? If I asked Freyda about this, she would know that Eric hadn't confided in me. I would expose the weakness in our relationship, and she would certainly pounce on it and hammer in a wedge to widen it. *Damn* Eric for being so reluctant to discuss the whole thing with me. Now I was at a real disadvantage.

"Is there anything else you want to tell me? You've accomplished what you came for, I guess. You've seen me and gotten my measure." I regarded her steadily. "I'm not sure what you want from me tonight."

"Pam is fond of you," she said, not answering me directly. "This one, too." She jerked her head at Bubba. "I don't know why, and I want to know."

"She's kind," Bubba said immediately. "She smells good. She has good manners. And she's a good fighter, too."

I smiled at the addled vampire. "Thank you, Bubba. You're a good friend to me."

Freyda eyed the famous face as if she were mining secrets from it. She turned her gaze back to me. "Bill Compton still likes you despite the fact that you've rejected him," Freyda said quietly. "Even Thalia says you're tolerable. Bill and Eric have both been your lovers. There must be something to you besides the fairy blood. Frankly, I can barely detect your fairy heritage."

"Most vamps don't get that until someone points it out to them," I agreed.

She rose, taking me by surprise. I got up, too. The Queen of Oklahoma went to the back door. Just as I was sure this excruciating interview was at an end and she was on her way out, Freyda turned. "Is it true you killed Lorena Ball?" she asked, her voice cool and indifferent.

"Yeah." My eyes didn't leave her. Now we were on very, very delicate ground. "Did you have anything to do with the death of Kym Rowe?"

"I don't even know who that is," Freyda said. "But I'll find out. Did you also kill Bruno, Victor's second?"

I didn't say anything. I returned her look.

She shook her head, as if she could hardly believe it. "And a shape-shifter or two?" she asked.

In Debbie Pelt's case, I'd used a shotgun. Not the same thing as hand-to-hand combat. I lifted one shoulder slightly, which she could take as she chose.

"What about fairies?" she said, smiling slightly, apparently at how ridiculous a question she was asking me.

"Yeah," I said without elaborating. "Right outside this house, as a matter of fact."

Her rich brown eyes narrowed. Clearly, Freyda was having second thoughts about something. I hoped those thoughts weren't about whether to let me live, but I was pretty sure she was considering how much of a threat I represented. If she did me in right now, she would have the luxury of apologizing to Eric after the fact. Warning bells were clanging too loudly for me to ignore.

I'm about to ruin my reputation for good manners, I thought. "Freyda, I rescind your invitation," I said. Then Freyda was gone, the screen door slamming shut behind her. She vanished into the pelting rain and darkness as quickly as she'd arrived. I might have seen a shadow crossing the beam of the security light; that was all.

Freyda might not have intended to harm me when she arrived, but I was pretty sure my wards would clang if she tried to cross them now.

I started shivering and couldn't stop. Though the rain had lowered the temperature a bit, it was still a June night in Louisiana; but I shivered and shook until I had to sit down again. Bubba was as spooked as I was. He sat down at the table, but he fidgeted and kept looking out the windows until I thought I would snap at him. He speed-dialed Pam again and said, "Freyda's gone. Miss Sookie is okay."

Eventually, Bubba gulped down the rest of the synthetic blood. He put his bottle by the sink and washed Freyda's out, as if he could remove her visit that way. Still standing, he turned to me with sad eyes. "Is Eric going to leave here with that woman? Would Mr. Bill have to go with him?" Bill was a great favorite of Bubba's.

I looked up at the deficient vampire. The vacancy of his face detracted a bit from his looks, but he had a genuine sweetness that never failed to touch me. I put my arms around him, and we hugged.

"I don't think Bill is part of the deal," I said. "I'm pretty sure he'll stay right where he is. She just wants Eric."

I'd loved two vampires. Bill had broken my heart. Maybe Eric was on the way to doing that same thing.

"Will Eric go with her to Oklahoma? Who would be sheriff? Whose girlfriend would you be then?"

"I don't know if he'll go or not," I said. "I'm not going to worry about who would take his place. I don't have to be anyone's girlfriend. I do okay by myself."

I only hoped I was telling Bubba the truth.

Chapter 9

An hour after Bubba left, and just after I'd finally gone to sleep, my phone rang.

"Are you all right?" Eric's voice sounded strange; hoarse, almost.

"Yes," I said. "She was very rational."

"She . . . that's what she told me. And Bubba told Pam you were all right."

So he'd talked to Freyda, presumably in person. And he'd taken Bubba's secondhand word that I was fine; so therefore, he hadn't been as quick to call me as he would have been if there'd been doubt in his mind. A lot of information conveyed in two short sentences.

"No," I agreed. "No violence." I'd lain alone in the darkness, my eyes wide open, for a long time. I'd been sure Eric would arrive at any moment, desperate to make sure I hadn't been hurt.

I was controlling myself with my last bit of self-respect.

"She won't win," Eric said. He sounded confident, passionate—everything I might have hoped would be reassuring.

"You're sure?" I asked.

"Yes, my lover. I'm sure."

"But you're not here," I observed, and I hung up very gently.

He didn't call back.

I slept between three and six, I think, and woke up to a summer day that mocked me by being beautiful. The downpour had washed everything, cooled the air, and renewed the green of the grass and the trees. The delicate pink of the old crepe myrtle was unfurling. The cannas would be open soon.

I felt like Hell hungover.

While the coffeepot did its work, I slumped at the kitchen table, my head in my hands. I remembered—too vividly—sliding into a dark depression when I understood that Bill, my first-ever boyfriend and lover, had left me.

This was not quite as bad; that had been the first time, this was the second. I'd had other kinds of losses during the same time period. Loved ones, friends, acquaintances had been mown down by the Grim Reaper. So I was no stranger to loss and to change, and these experiences had taught me something.

But today was bad enough, and I could think of nothing to look forward to.

Somehow I had to pull out of this state of unhappiness. I couldn't struggle through many days like this.

Seeing my little cousin Hunter would make me happy. Smiling in anticipation, I had already put my hand on the phone to call his dad before I realized what a criminal mistake inviting Hunter over would be. The child was a telepath like me, and he would read my misery like a book . . . a terrible situation for Hunter.

I tried to think of another good thing to anticipate. Tara would be coming home from the hospital today, and I should cook a meal for her. I tried to summon the energy to plan that, but I came up with nothing. Okay, save that for later. I cast around for other pleasant ideas, but nothing took a grip on my black mood to loosen its hold on me.

When I'd exhausted my fund of self-pity by brooding on my untenable situation with Eric, I thought I should focus on the death that had precipitated the current crisis, at least in part. I checked the news on the computer, but no arrest had been made in Kym Rowe's murder. Detective Ambroselli said, "The police are not close to an arrest, but we're pursuing several leads. Meanwhile, if anyone saw anything in the Clearwater Cove area that night, please call our hotline." So, it would be interesting to hear if Bill and Heidi had found out anything, and it would be interesting—maybe—to ask the writer, Harp Powell, why he was going around with the Rowes. I'd had the feeling he was a cut or two above what he seemed to be doing—making a quick buck off the murder of a young, self-destructive stripper.

It felt good to have a couple of projects in mind, and I clutched them to me as I went through my morning ritual. The lockers for the employee area were supposed to come today on the truck. That would be fun. If you had a very limited idea of fun.

I goaded and prodded myself into preparation and went in the back door of Merlotte's full of grim determination. As I tied on my apron, I felt my mouth curve up in my worst smile, the one that sent out "I'm crazy" signals all over the place. It had been a long time since I'd worn that particular smile.

I made a round of my tables and realized Sam wasn't behind the bar, *again*. Another man who *wasn't there when I needed him*. Maybe he and Jannalynn the Terrible had gone to Arkansas to get a marriage license. I stopped dead in my tracks, the smile turning into a scowl. Pivoting on my heel, I shot out the back door of Merlotte's. Sam's truck wasn't at his trailer. In the middle of the employee parking lot I clapped my cell phone to my ear after punching my speed dial.

After two rings, Sam answered.

"Where are you?" I snarled. If I was here being unhappy, Sam should be here, too. Weren't we sort-of partners?

"I took another day off," he said, now clued in about my mood. He was only pretending to be casual.

"Seriously, Sam, where are you?"

"Yeah, you sound pretty damn serious," he said, now borderline angry himself.

"Did you get married?" The thought of Sam being on his honeymoon with Jannalynn—having fun while Eric made me miserable—was simply intolerable. I've had moments when I recognized that my reactions to current events were out of the stratosphere (most often when I was in the grip of my monthly woes), and usually that realization was enough for me to rein in the inappropriateness.

But not today.

"Sookie, why would you think that?" Sam sounded genuinely bewildered.

"She told Alcide she was going to ask you. She told him she wanted me to help her surprise you . . . but I wouldn't do it."

Sam was silent for a moment, perhaps struggling through all those pronouns.

"I'm standing outside her house," he said finally. "Jannalynn volunteered us to help Brenda get Splendide back in order after the break-in. I did think I'd get back to Bon Temps sooner than I am. But I'm not married. And I don't have any plans to get that way."

I started crying. I put my hand over the phone so he couldn't hear me.

"Sookie, what's really wrong?" Sam's voice said.

"I can't tell you standing out here in the parking lot, and anyway, it makes me sound like the most pitiful person." I couldn't manage to get myself under control. When I thought of Freyda's cool surface, I was disgusted with my own irrational display. "I'm sorry, Sam. Sorry I called you. I'll see you when you get home. Forget this whole conversation, okay?"

"Sookie? Listen, just shut up for a minute."

I did.

"Look, my friend, we're gonna be all right," he said. "We'll talk, and everything will look better."

"Maybe not," I said. But even to my own ears, I sounded reasonable and much more like my better self.

"Then we'll deal with that," he said.

"Okay."

"Sookie, is there any reason you can think of that someone might want to tear apart the pieces of furniture you sold to Brenda? I mean, her partner, Donald, said he'd found a secret drawer, but all that was in it was an old pattern and he'd handed that to you. Did you know anything about that furniture that might give any kind of hint why anyone would break it up?"

"No," I lied. "It was just an old Butterick pattern, I think. I bet Jason or I stuck it in there when we were little 'cause we thought that would be funny. I don't even remember Gran showing it to us. You'll have to tell me all about the break-in when you come back. Drive careful."

We hung up. I shook myself, feeling my personality settling back into place on my shoulders. It was like an emotional tornado had subsided into a dust devil. I wiped my face with my apron before marching back into the bar, my cell phone in my pocket like a talisman. Everyone was eyeing me sideways. I must have startled the customers with my abrupt exit. I did a little courtesy tour around to all my tables, just to let people know I had returned to my right mind. I worked through the rest of my shift without descending to the previous level of Hell I'd inhabited.

Kennedy was singing behind the bar, still happy since Danny had revealed his big secret job hunt to her. I didn't feel like talking about vampire stuff at all, so I just rolled with her good mood.

By the time the delivery truck pulled up to the back door, I was borderline normal myself. The lockers fit right in the space I'd cleared for them, I'd already bought padlocks for everyone on the staff, and since Sam wasn't there, I got the pleasure of allotting everyone a locker and explaining that though Sam and I wouldn't go in the lockers unless there was a crisis, we would be keeping a key to each one. Since the ladies had trusted Sam all these years with their purses, they shouldn't have any problem trusting him with a change of clothes or a hairbrush. Everyone was pleased and even a little excited, because a change in the workplace can mean a lot.

Sam's truck was parked in front of his trailer when my shift was over, so I felt free to take off. Sam and I needed to talk, but not this evening.

I stopped by the grocery store on the way home to buy the ingredients for Tara's homecoming meal. I'd left a message on JB's cell phone to tell him I was bringing something over, and just as insurance I'd left a message on their landline, too.

I started cooking in my cool and empty house. I was doing my level best not to think about anything but food preparation. I'd decided to keep it simple and basic. I made a hamburger-and-sausage meatloaf, a pasta salad, and a carrot casserole for Tara and JB. The blackberries at the store had been too tempting to resist, and I made a blackberry cobbler. As long as I was cooking, I made duplicates of everything for Dermot and me. Two birds with one stone, I thought proudly.

At the little house on Magnolia Street, a smiling JB met me at the door to help me carry in the food. While I went into the kitchen to turn on the stove to warm the meatloaf and casserole a little, the proud father returned to the small, small nursery. I tiptoed in to find Tara and JB staring down at the two cribs holding these amazing tiny beings. I joined them in the admiration gallery.

Before I could even ask, Tara said, "Sara Sookie du Rone and Robert Thornton du Rone."

And I felt the bottom fall out of my heart. "You named her Sookie?"

"It's her middle name. There's only one Sookie, that's you. We'll call her Sara. But we wanted her to have your name as part of her identity."

I simply refused to cry anymore, but I admit I had to blot my eyes. JB patted my shoulder and went to get the ringing phone before it disturbed the sleepers. Tara and I hugged. The babies continued to snooze, so we sneaked out and eased into the living room. We could hardly find a seat because of the flower arrangements and baby gifts cluttering the room—in fact, the whole house. Tara was very, very happy. So was JB. It permeated their home. I hoped it was catching.

"Look what your cousin gave us a couple of weeks ago," Tara said. She lifted a brightly colored box that contained (the print said) a baby gym. The concept confused me, but Tara said it was an arched toy you laid the baby under, and the baby could bat at the bright things with little hands. She showed me the picture.

"Awww," I said. "Claude gave you that?" I simply couldn't imagine Claude selecting a gift, wrapping it, and bringing it by this house. He genuinely liked babies—though not to eat, as Bellenos might suggest. Bellenos surely wouldn't really think of . . . I just couldn't go there.

She nodded. "I guess I just send the thank-you note to your address?"

Or pop it through a hole in the air in the woods. "Sure, that'll be fine."

"Sookie, is everything okay with you?" Tara said suddenly. "You don't seem quite yourself."

The last thing in the world I'd do is intrude on her happiness with my problems. And I could tell from her brain that she really didn't want to hear bad news; but she'd asked anyway, and that counted for a lot. "I'm good," I said. "I couldn't sleep last night, is all."

"Oh, did that big Viking keep you awake?" Tara gave me an elaborately sly look, and we both laughed, though it was hard for me to make it sound genuine.

Their supper should be warm by now, and they needed some privacy. They'd been lucky to bring twins home from the hospital this early. I was sure Tara ought to rest. So I said my good-byes, told Tara I'd stop by in a couple of days to pick up my dishes, and hugged JB on my way out, resolutely blocking out the memory of how he'd looked in his G-string.

Sara Sookie. Someone was named after me.

I smiled all the way home.

Dermot was there when I pulled up, and it was a real delight to know I wouldn't be alone that night. Supper was ready. All we had to do was get it out of the still-warm oven.

I told Dermot I'd "sent" the letter Bellenos had suggested, and he was so excited that he wanted to go out to the portal then and there to see if there'd been an answer. I persuaded him to wait until the next day, but he was fidgety for a good twenty minutes.

Nonetheless, Dermot was the kind of guest you want to have; he complimented the food, and he helped do the dishes. By the time we cleared away, the night outside was humming with the noise of the insects.

"I'm going to finish caulking the attic windows," Dermot said, still humming with energy.

Though before he'd begun work on the attic room he'd never caulked anything in his life, he'd watched a demonstration online and he was ready to work.

"You rock, Dermot," I said.

He grinned at me. He was really sticking to the attic renovation, despite what I felt was an increasingly weak chance that Claude would return to claim his bedroom. After he went upstairs, I cracked the kitchen window over the sink so I'd have a little breeze while I scrubbed the sink with some Bon Ami.

A mockingbird had perched outside in a photinia at the corner of the house. The stupid bird was singing to itself loud enough to wake the dead. I wished I had a slingshot.

Just as I thought that, I thought I heard a voice outside calling, "Sookie!"

I went out on the back porch. Sure enough, Bill was waiting in the backyard. "I can smell the fairy from here," he said. "I know I can't come in. Can you step out?"

"Hold on a minute." I rinsed out the sink, dried my hands on the dish towel, and shut the window to keep in the air-conditioning. Then, hoping my hair still looked decent, I went outside.

Bill had been having some vampire downtime. He was standing silent in the darkness, lost in his thoughts. When he heard me approach, he stepped out into the bright security light, looking both intent and focused. It was easy to see that Bill had a list of things to tell me. "I'll start with the lesser things first," he said, rather stiffly. "I don't know if you've spared a moment to wonder about my efforts to find out who killed the young woman, but I assure you I'm trying to find out. She died while I was patrolling, and I won't be easy until I understand why it happened."

Taken aback, I could only nod slightly. "I don't know why you thought I . . . oh, Eric. Well, never mind. Please tell me what you've discovered. Would you like to sit?"

We both sat in the lawn chairs. "Heidi and I went over Eric's backyard with great attention," Bill said. "You know it slopes down to a brick wall, the outer perimeter of the gated community."

"Right." I hadn't spent more than ten minutes total in Eric's backyard, but I knew its contours. "There's a gate in the brick wall."

"Yes, for the yard crew." Bill said this like having a yard crew was an exotic indulgence, like having a bunch of peacocks. "It's *easier* for the yard crew to gather all the yard debris and carry it out the back, rather than go uphill to the curb." His tone made it plain what he thought of people who liked to have a job made easier for them.

"It isn't kept locked?" I was startled at the idea that it might have been swinging open.

"Normally, yes. And normally, Mustapha is responsible for unlocking it for the yard crew on the day they're expected, and he's also responsible for locking it after they're done. But the lock was missing."

"A werewolf or vampire could have snapped it," I said. "So Mustapha's not necessarily guilty of opening the gate, anyway." He'd done something wrong, though. You don't vanish unless you've done something wrong. "What did you smell? Anything?"

"Even Heidi could not say for certain who'd been there," Bill said. "Many humans, sweaty humans . . . the yard workers. A dash of fairy, but that could have been a very faint trace of the vial around the girl's neck. And a stronger trace of twoey. That could have been from the girl herself." He leaned back and looked up into the night sky . . . the only sky he'd seen in more than a hundred and thirty years.

"What do you think happened?" I asked him, after we'd been quiet for a few calm moments. I'd been looking up, along with Bill. Though Bon Temps was close, it only cast a faint glow upward, especially this late. I could see the stars, vast and cold and distant. I shivered.

"Look, Sookie," he said, and held out something small. I took it and held it up to my nose to try to make it out in the patchy light.

"It's true, then," I said. It was a rubber stopper, the kind that would close a small vial. "Where did you find it?"

"In the living room. It rolled under the dining table and landed right by a chair leg. I think the woman Kym took out the stopper when she knew she was going to see Eric face-to-face," he said. "She dropped it while she drank the blood. She tucked the vial down into her bra in case the lingering scent would attract him further. And when I found her on the lawn, I could smell that she was two-natured. That would have added to her . . . allure."

"The dad's two-natured, a Were, I think. The Rowes showed up here at my house yesterday with a reporter, to try to make something quotable happen."

Bill wanted to hear all about it. "You have the reporter's card?" he asked when I'd finished.

I went into the house and found it on the kitchen counter. Now that I took a moment to look at it, I discovered that Harp Powell was based in Terre Sauvage, a small town that lay north of the interstate between Bon Temps and Shreveport. "Huh," I said, handing it to Bill, "I assumed he was based in Shreveport or Baton Rouge or Monroe."

Bill said, "I met this man at Fangtasia. He's been published by a small regional press. He's written several books."

Bill sounded quite respectful; he had great admiration for the written word.

"What was he doing at Fangtasia?" I asked, diverted.

"He interviewed me and Maxwell Lee, since we're both native Louisianans. He was hoping to do a collection of Louisiana vampires' histories. He wanted to listen to our recollections of the times we grew up in, the historical events we'd witnessed. He thought that would be interesting."

"So, a ripoff of Christina Sobol?" I tried not to sound sarcastic. Sobol's *Dead History I* had been on all the best-seller lists a couple of years before. Amazon had sent me a notice to tell me that *Dead History II* would be out in a month. These books, as you may have guessed, were vampires' reminiscences about the times they'd lived in. Harp Powell was doing a regional twist on a national best seller.

Bill nodded. "I'm trying to remember if he asked questions about Eric. I believe that he wanted Eric's phone number in case he needed to get in touch with him. . . . I didn't give it to him, of course, but he could have discovered Eric's address online." Bill was one of the computer-savvy vampires.

"Okay, so he could have found out where Eric lives, but why would a writer have any reason to send Kym Rowe into the house, or to murder her afterward?"

"I don't have the slightest idea," Bill said. "But we can surely go ask him. I'm trying to think of some other avenue of investigation, one that doesn't lead back to someone in Eric's house."

"I'm not saying that Harp Powell isn't fishy, showing up with Kym's parents. But it seems more likely that he's just riding the publicity train. To me, it appears a lot more likely that Mustapha let Kym Rowe in so she could find Eric and offer herself. I just don't know why. Why did someone prep her and send her in to do that? Why did they get Mustapha to delay my arrival? I guess so that she'd have time to hook Eric . . . but then, why have me come in? Mustapha could have told me that the meeting had been canceled or that I should go to Fangtasia instead . . . a hundred different things."

"His role in this is a mystery," Bill said, shrugging. "She was obviously bait for Eric, designed to arouse his lust." Bill looked at me and blinked. "His bloodlust," he added hastily. "But she must have had some piece of information, if only the name of who hired her to do this. When you argued with Eric and he sent the girl away, someone went after her and seized her head and twisted." Bill made a very graphic motion with his hands. No stranger to the seizing and twisting, he.

"Disregarding why she was killed," I said, "why was she sent there in the first place? Getting me mad at Eric doesn't seem to be much of a reason."

Bill looked down at his hands. "There are a couple of theories that fit the few facts we're sure of," he said slowly. "And these theories are what I'll tell Eric. The first is that Eric himself or Pam or Mustapha followed the Rowe woman out of the house and killed her out of sheer anger at the trouble she'd caused. Perhaps—if the killer was Eric—he wanted to erase the memory of the offense he'd committed against you."

I stiffened. This was nothing I hadn't thought of myself, but hearing it out loud made it seem more likely.

"The other theory . . . well, that's more complex." Bill shifted his gaze to the dark woods. "Since a Were let the girl in, I have to assume she was part of some Were plot. I should suspect Alcide, since he's the packleader. But I don't believe that Alcide would plan such a convoluted method of discrediting Eric. Alcide's a relatively straightforward man and an intelligent one . . . at least in some respects. Evidently, women are a huge blind spot for him." Bill raised an eyebrow.

That was a pretty good evaluation of Alcide's character. "But what Were would do this without Alcide's say-so?" I said.

"Mustapha is a lone wolf." Bill shrugged. Obvious.

"But Mustapha didn't bring Kym Rowe to the house," I argued. "You said the scent trail didn't tell you that. "

"He must have known she was coming. Sookie, I know you like the man in some measure, but he knew about this in advance. Maybe he didn't know why she was coming to the house—but he knew if he let her in unchallenged, everyone in the house would assume she'd been invited. And he knew the girl wasn't there to scrub toilets or sing for the company. She was there to get Eric to drink from her. Since Mustapha was the one who called you and told you to come later, his purpose *must* have been to make sure you were not there to prevent Eric from being interested in her."

"But the only result was that I got mad at Eric. Bill, who cares that much about my love life?" Bill gave me a very direct look, and I could feel myself turning red.

But instead of making a personal reference, Bill said, "You had a visitor last night who cares very deeply."

I tried not to flinch too obviously. "You know she came to the house?"

"We all know about her presence in Area Five, Sookie. All of us who are sworn to Eric. It's hard to cover up the visit of a queen, especially one as well-known as Freyda. It's even harder to remain ignorant of exactly where she is. She went to the casino to confer with Felipe directly after she left your house, and Felipe summoned Eric there. He took Thalia with him—not Pam. Thalia said it was a very tense meeting."

That explained the delay in Eric's calling me . . . but it didn't make me feel any better. "What makes Freyda so well-known?" I bypassed all the obvious conversational openings that Bill's little speech presented to lock in on what was most interesting to me. I was all too aware that Bill could see how desperate I was to know more about her, and I just didn't care.

Bill kindly looked down at his hands as he told me, "She's beautiful, of course. Ambitious. Young. She's not content to sit on her throne and let things hum along. By the way, she had to fight for that throne. She killed her predecessor, and he didn't make it easy. Freyda has worked hard to extend the business dealings of Oklahoma. The only thing slowing her progress is her lack of a strong and loyal second. If she acquires the strong vampire she needs to serve as her right hand, she'll always have to watch her back against that vampire's ambition. If she marries this right hand, he can't succeed her. His loyalty will be assured, because his fate is bound to hers."

I pondered this for a few minutes, while Bill sat in silence. Vampires are great at that. I caught his eyes on my face. I got the impression that Bill felt sorry for me. A worm of panic twisted in my stomach.

"Freyda's strong, active, and determined," I said. "Like Eric. And you say she needs a good fighter, a good second. Like Eric."

"Yes, like Eric," he said deliberately. "Freyda would be a great match for him. Practically speaking, he'd escape from the political situation created by his murder of Victor. The king's going to have to do something to Eric. Felipe really can't afford to be perceived as ignoring Victor's death."

"Why not?"

He looked at me blankly.

"Felipe let Victor get away with whatever the hell Victor wanted to do," I said. "Why shouldn't he be perceived that way?"

"He doesn't want to lose the loyalty of the vampires who serve him," Bill said.

"That's ridiculous!" I thought steam would come out of my ears. "You can't have it all different ways!"

"But he'll try. I don't think you're really angry about Felipe. You're really angry about the hard practicality of Eric marrying Freyda." I winced, but Bill continued ruthlessly. "You have to admit that her character is much like Eric's and that they'd make a good team."

"Eric's *my* team," I said. "He loves me. He wants to stay here." I realized that I was, so to speak, batting with another hand now. I'd been just as sure the night before that Eric would leave, that he loved power more than he loved me.

"But . . . Sookie, you must see . . . staying might be the death of him."

I could read a mixture of pity and tough love in Bill's attitude. "Bill, are you sure you're able to judge that?"

"I hope that I have your best interests in my heart, Sookie." He paused, as if considering whether he should go on. "I know you'll suspect everything I say about this situation—because I love you, and I don't love Eric. But truly, I want your happiness, above almost everything else."

Almost everything else. I found myself wondering what came ahead of that. His own survival?

I heard the screen door bang, and Dermot hurried out to his car.

"Got to get to the club," he called.

"Drive careful," I called back. He was gone before I could say anything more. I turned back to Bill, who was staring at the spot where Dermot had stood, a wistful expression on his face. No wonder Dermot had hurried; he'd surely known a vampire was in the backyard and that his scent would be attractive. "Let's get back to the Kym Rowe issue," I said, to get Bill's attention. "What can I do to help you find out who killed her?"

"The first person we'd want to talk to is Mustapha, and he's vanished. Tell me exactly what he said when he was here."

"Which time? When he was here before the night of the party, or when he was here after the party?"

"Tell me about both visits."

I related the first conversation to Bill, though there was surprisingly little to tell. Mustapha'd been here. He'd relayed Pam's warning, which I hadn't understood until I'd met Freyda. He'd warned me about Jannalynn. The second time he was here, he'd been worried about Warren.

"You've told Eric this?" he asked.

I snorted. "We're not exactly having lengthy heart-to-hearts these days. My conversation with Freyda was longer than any talk I've had with Eric."

Wisely, Bill didn't comment. He recapped. "So Mustapha comes to your house, though he's been missing ever since the girl died. He tells you that he wants to talk to Alcide, but he's afraid to call him or approach him directly since Jannalynn might be around to intercept him."

I thought that was a fair summary. "Yes, and I've passed that message along to Alcide," I said. "Plus, what's most important to Mustapha, his friend Warren is missing. I think someone abducted Warren, and they're holding him in return for Mustapha's good behavior."

"Then finding Warren would be a good thing," Bill said, and I winced when I heard his voice. I'd screwed up.

"I get that it was dumb for me not to have mentioned this first of all," I said. "I'm sorry."

"Tell me about this Warren."

"You haven't ever seen him?"

Bill shrugged. "No. Why would I?"

"He's a shooter. He was stationed outside Fangtasia the night we killed Victor."

"So that was Warren. Skinny little guy, big eyes, long hair?"

"Sounds right."

"What are he and Mustapha to each other?"

It was my turn to shrug. "I have no idea. They were in prison together, I think."

"Mustapha was in prison?"

I nodded. "Yeah, his real name is KeShawn Johnson. I got that out of his head."

Bill look puzzled. "But . . . do you remember the vampire who decapitated Wybert at the beginning of the brawl at Sophie-Anne's monastery?"

"I'll never forget that. Thin, dreadlocks?"

"His name was Ra Shawn."

We were just swapping expressions. It was my turn to do Puzzled. "No, I don't recollect that at all. Oh . . . wait, yeah. Andre told me his name."

"You don't think it's an interesting coincidence? Ra Shawn and KeShawn? Both black? Both supernaturals?"

"But one's a werewolf, and the other was a vampire. Ra Shawn could have been born hundreds of years ago. I guess they *could* be related."

"I think that's just possible." Bill was giving me a long-suffering look.

"The database," I suggested, and he pulled a little bunch of keys from his pocket. There was a black rectangle attached to the key ring.

"I have it right here," he said, and I was amazed all over again at Bill's plunge into the modern world.

"And that would be a what?" I asked.

"This is a jump drive." Bill looked quizzical.

"Oh, sure." I'd had enough of feeling dumb for the evening. We went inside so Bill could use my computer. Bill carried over a chair for me and then took his seat in the rolling chair directly in front of the screen.

He inserted the little stick into a slot I hadn't even realized was on the side of my computer. After a couple of minutes, he had *The Vampire Directory* on the screen.

"Wow." I looked at the opening, some very dramatic graphics. A pair of Gothic gates hung closed, a giant lock on them. The background music was dark and atmospheric. I hadn't paid any attention when I'd used a stolen copy of the database before, because I'd been so conscious of my guilt. Now I could appreciate the graveyard humor in Bill's presentation. A written introduction appeared superimposed on the gates in many different languages. After you selected the language you wanted, a solemn voice read the introduction out loud. Bill skipped through all that. He touched a few keys, and the Gothic gates creaked open to show all our options. As Bill explained, you could sort the vampires in different ways. You could look for vampires in Yugoslavia, for example, or you could look for female vampires in the St. Louis area. Or all vampires more than a thousand years old in Myanmar.

"I can't believe you did all this," I said admiringly. "It's so cool."

"It was a lot of work," he said absently, "and I had a lot of help."

"How many languages is it available in?"

"So far, thirty."

"This must have made money hand over fist, Bill. I hope you got some of it yourself." I hoped it wasn't pouring into the bank account of Felipe de Castro. Who so didn't deserve it.

"I've made some change from it," Bill said, smiling.

That was a good expression to see on Bill's face. He didn't wear it often enough.

In a jiffy, he'd called up the entry for Ra Shawn. The vampire had been about thirty at the time of his human death, but he'd been a vampire for (maybe) a hundred years at the time of his second death. Ra Shawn's background was hazy, but he'd first been noticed in Haiti, Bill's sources had told him. The dreadlocked Ra Shawn had long been a cult figure in the black supernatural community. He had been the cool and deadly black vampire, hired by kings, gangsters, and political figures as a fighter.

"Well," I said, "Maybe Mustapha's—KeShawn's—parents were into supernatural African culture. After prison, maybe he became a Blade clone because he wanted a more current model."

"Everybody needs a hero," Bill agreed, and I opened my mouth to ask him who his had been. Robert E. Lee?

"What are you two doing?" Eric asked, and I jumped and gave a little yip of surprise. Even Bill twitched.

"It's only polite to let me know you're coming into my house," I said, because he'd really scared me and I was angry in consequence.

"It's only polite," Eric said mockingly, imitating my voice in a very irritating way. "I think it's 'only polite' that my wife should let me know when she's entertaining a male visitor, furthermore one that has shared her bed."

I took a deep breath, hoping it would help me calm down. "You're acting like an asshole," I said, so maybe the deep breath hadn't helped so very much. "I have never cheated on you, and I have trusted you never to cheat on me. Maybe I should rethink that, since you don't seem to have much faith in me."

Eric looked taken aback. "I have never fucked another woman since I took you to wife," he said haughtily.

I couldn't help but realize that left a lot of territory uncovered—but now was not the time to ask detailed questions.

Bill was sitting like a statue. I spared a second to appreciate his predicament. Eric was so plainly in a very bad mood, anything Bill said was going to be taken in evidence against him.

A diversion was in order, though I felt a flash of resentment that

I had to defuse the situation. "Why are you so mad, anyway?" I said. "Something go wrong at Fangtasia?"

Eric's face relaxed just a fraction. "Nothing is right," he said. "Felipe and his companions are still in town. He may still bring charges against me for killing Victor. At the same time, you can tell he's *delighted* we killed Victor. He and Freyda have just had a long talk in private. Mustapha is still missing. The police have been by Fangtasia to question me again. They wanted me to permit *cadaver dogs* to go over my property. I had to say yes, but it makes me furious. How stupid would I be to bury someone on my own property? They've searched the house again. T-Rex and his women came into the bar tonight, and he acted as though he were my best friend. The women used drugs in the bathroom. Thalia rousted them a little too energetically and broke Cherie's nose. I'll have to pay for her hospital visit, though she did promise not to relate what had happened in return for our not telling the police she's a drug user."

"My goodness," I said gently. "And then you walk in your girlfriend's house to find her *looking at a computer screen* with another man. You *have* had a terrible night, poor fella."

Bill raised an eyebrow to let me know I was troweling it on too thick.

I ignored him. "If I'd seen you around, or had a conversation with you that lasted longer than thirty seconds, I'd have told you that Mustapha had come by here," I said in a sweet voice. "And I'd have told you what he said."

"Tell me now," Eric said, in a much more neutral voice. "If you please."

Okay, he'd made an effort. So once again, I related the account of

Mustapha's visit, his warning about Jannalynn, and his concern for Warren's safety.

"So Bill and Heidi need to scent this Jannalynn, and then we'll know if she was the one who led the girl to my house, who sent her up to Mustapha. We'll know why he was involved with this plan if we can find him—or his friend Warren—and they'll tell us what we can do to get them out of the picture. Sookie, would Sam call this woman, if you asked him to do so?"

My mouth fell open. "That would be terrible of me, to ask him to bring her in, to betray her. I won't do it."

"But you can see that would be best for all of us," Eric said. "Bill or Heidi goes up to her, shakes her hand—then they will have her scent, and we'll know. Sam doesn't need to do anything beyond that. We'll take care of everything else."

"What would that 'everything else' be?"

"What do you think?" Bill asked impatiently. "She has information we need to learn, and she seems to be a key part of the plot to implicate Eric in a murder. This woman is a murderer herself, most likely. We need to make her talk."

"The same way the Weres made you talk in Mississippi, Bill?" I snapped.

"Why do you care if something happens to the bitch?" Eric said, his blond eyebrows rising in query.

"I don't," I said instantly. "I can't stand her."

"Then what's your issue?"

And I had no answer.

"It's because we were talking about involving Sam," Bill told Eric. "That's the stumbling block."

Suddenly they were on the same side, and that side was not mine.

"You're sweet on him?" Eric said. He couldn't have been more surprised if I'd said I had a crush on Terry's Catahoula.

"He's my boss," I said. "We've been friends for years. Of course I'm fond of him. And he's nuts about that furry bitch, for whatever reason. So that's my issue, as you put it."

"Hmmm," Eric said, his eyes examining my face with a sharp intensity. I didn't like it when he sounded thoughtful. "Then I'll have to call Alcide and make the request for Jannalynn's scent official."

Did I do as they requested, which would in some way be a betrayal of Sam? Or did I let Eric call Alcide, which would officially involve the Long Tooth pack? You couldn't call a packmaster unofficially. But I couldn't lie to Sam. My back stiffened.

"All right," I said. "Call Alcide." Eric pulled out his cell phone, giving me a very grim look as he did so. I could see a war starting, another war. More deaths. More loss. "Wait," I said. "I'll talk to Sam. I'll go into town to talk to him. Right now."

I didn't even know if Sam was home, but I walked out of the house and neither vampire tried to stop me. I'd never left two vampires alone in the house before, and I could only hope it would be intact when I returned.

Chapter 10

When I began driving back into town, I realized how tired I was. I thought very seriously about turning back, but when I contemplated facing Bill and Eric again, I kept driving north.

That was how I came to see Bellenos and our Hooligans waitress bounding across the road after a deer. I braked desperately, and my car slid sideways. I knew I'd end up in the ditch. I shrieked as the car slewed and the woods rushed up to meet me. Then, abruptly, my car's motion stopped—not by hitting anything, but by being nose down in the steep ditch. The headlights lit up the weeds, still whipping, bugs flying up from the impact. I turned off the engine and sat gasping.

My poor car was nose down at a steep angle. The rain had had twenty-four hours to soak into the previously parched soil, so the ditch was fairly dry, which was a real blessing. Bellenos and the blonde appeared, working their way around the car to get to my door. Bellenos was carrying a spear, and his companion appeared to have two curved bladed weapons of some kind. Not exactly swords; really long knives, as thin at the point as needles.

I tried to open the door, but my muscles wouldn't obey my command. I realized I was crying. I had a sharp flash of memory: Claudine waking me when I fell asleep at the wheel on this same road. Bellenos's lithe body moved across the headlights, and then he was by my door and wrenching it open.

"Sister!" he said, and turned to his companion. "Cut this strap, Gift."

A knife passed right by my face in the next second, and the seat belt was severed. Oh, *damn*. Evidently, they didn't understand buckles.

Gift bent down, and in the next instant I was out of the car and she was carrying me away.

"We didn't mean to frighten you," she murmured. "I'm sorry, my sister."

She laid me down as easily as if I'd been an infant, and she and Bellenos squatted by me. I concluded, with no great certainty, that they weren't going to kill and eat me. When I could speak, I said, "What were you out here doing?"

"Hunting," Bellenos said, as if he suspected my head were addled. "You saw the deer?"

"Yes. Do you realize you're not on my land anymore?" My voice was very unsteady, but there was nothing I could do about it.

"I see no fence, no boundaries. Freedom is good," he said.

And the blonde nodded enthusiastically. "It's so good to run," she said. "It's so good to be out of a human building."

The thing was . . . they seemed so *happy*. Though I knew absolutely

I should read them the riot act, I found myself feeling not only profoundly sorry for the two fae, but frightened of—and for—them. This was a very uncomfortable mix of emotions. "I'm real glad you're having a good time," I wheezed. They both beamed at me. "How did you come to be named Gift?" I just couldn't think of anything else to say.

"It's Aelfgifu," she said, smiling. "Elf-gift. But Gift is easier for human mouths." Speaking of mouths, Aelfgifu's teeth were not as ferocious as Bellenos's. In fact, they were quite small. But since she was leaning over me, I could see longer, sharper, thinner teeth folded against the roof of her mouth.

Fangs. Not vampire fangs, but snake fangs. Jesus Christ, Shepherd of Judea. Coupled with the pupil-less eyes, she was really scary.

"Is this the way you do in Faery?" I asked weakly. "Hunt in the woods?"

They both smiled. "Oh, yes, no fences or boundaries there," Aelfgifu said longingly. "Though the woods are not as deep as they once were."

"I don't want to . . . to chide you," I said, wondering if I could sit up. They both stared at me, their eyes unreadable, their heads canted at inhuman angles. "But regular people really shouldn't see you without your human disguises. And even if you could make other people perceive you as human . . . regular human couples don't chase deer in the middle of the night. With sharp weapons." Even around Bon Temps, where hunting is practically a religion.

"You see us as we really are," Bellenos said. I could tell he hadn't known that before. Maybe I'd given away a powerful bit of knowledge by revealing that.

"Yeah."

"You have powerful magic," Gift said respectfully. "That makes you our sister. When you first came to Hooligans, we weren't sure about you. Are you on our side?"

Bellenos's hand shot across me, and he gripped Aelfgifu's shoulder. Their eyes met. In the weird light and shadows cast by the headlights, her eyes looked just as black as his.

"I don't know what side that is," I said, to break the moment up. It seemed to work, because she laughed and slid an arm underneath me, and I sat up. "You're not hurt," she said. "Dermot will be pleased. He loves you."

Bellenos put an arm around me, too, so our little trio was suddenly positioned in an uncomfortably intimate little scene there on the deserted road. Bellenos's teeth were awfully close to my flesh. Sure, I was used to Eric biting, but he didn't rip off flesh and eat it.

"You're shaking, Sister," Aelfgifu observed. "You can't be cold on a hot night like tonight! Is it the shock of your little accident?"

"You can't be frightened of us?" Bellenos sounded mocking.

"You turkey," I said. "Of course I'm scared of you. If you'd spent a while with Lochlan and Neave, you'd be scared, too."

"We're not like them," Aelfgifu said in a much more subdued voice. "And we're sorry, Sister. There are quite a few of us who endured their attentions. Not all lived to tell others about it. You're very fortunate."

"Did you have the magic then?" Bellenos asked.

This was the second time the elf had referred to my having magic. I was very curious to know why he said that, but at the same time, I hated to expose my total ignorance.

"Could I drive you two back to Monroe?" I asked, staving off Bellenos's question.

"I couldn't bear to be shut up in an iron box," Gift said. "We'll run. May we come to hunt on your land tomorrow night?"

"How many of you?" I thought I should err on the side of caution, here.

They helped me to my feet, consulting with each other silently as they did so.

"Four of us," Bellenos said, trying not to sound as if he were asking me.

"That would be okay," I said. "Long as you let me explain where the boundaries are."

I got simultaneous kisses on both sides of my face. Then the two fae leaped down in the ditch, bent over to get a grip below the hood of my car, and *pushed.* The car was back up on the road in seconds. Aside from the severed seat belt, it didn't seem to be much the worse for the experience: dirty, of course, and the front fender was a little dented. Gift waved at me cheerfully as I took my place behind the wheel, and then the two were off, heading east toward Monroe . . . at least while I could see them. My car started up, thank God, and I turned around at the next driveway and headed home. My excursion was over. I was completely jangled.

As I pulled up, I could tell the vampires were still there. When I glanced at my car clock, I saw that only twenty minutes had passed since I'd left. Suddenly, I began shivering all over when I thought of the incident—the panicked deer, the swift and deadly pursuit, the faes' overly loving solicitousness. I turned off the car and got out slowly. I was going to be stiff all over the next morning, I just knew it. Of course Bill and Eric had heard me return, but neither of them came rushing out to see how I was. I reminded myself they didn't have any idea something had happened to me.

I stepped out of the car and thought I'd go flat on my face. I was having some kind of reaction to the whole bizarre incident, and

I couldn't stop replaying the running figures in my mind. They had looked so alien, so very, very . . . not-human.

And now I knew that someone suspected I had some powerful fae magic. If the fae suspected it was contained in an item, I didn't like my chances of keeping it, or of keeping my life, for that matter. Any supe would want such a thing, especially the hodgepodge of fae trapped at Hooligans. They were yearning for the homeland of Faery, no matter how they'd come to be trapped in our world. Any power they could acquire would be more than they had now. And if they had the cluviel dor . . . they could wish the doors of Faery open to them again.

"Sookie?" Eric said. "Lover, what's happened to you? Are you hurt?"

"Sookie?" Bill's voice, equally urgent.

I could only stand staring straight ahead, thinking hard about what would happen if the rogue fae opened the portals to Faery. What if humans could walk into that other country? What if all fae could come and go as they pleased? Would they accept that state of affairs, or would there be another war?

"I had a wreck," I said, belatedly realizing that Eric had picked me up and was carrying me inside. "I never got to Sam's. I had a wreck."

"That's all right, Sookie," Eric said. "Don't worry about going to Sam's. That can wait. We can make some other arrangement. At least I'm not smelling any blood," he said to Bill.

"Did you hit your head?" Bill asked. I could feel fingers working through my hair. Then those fingers stilled. "You reek of fairy."

I could see the hunger rising in his face. I glanced at Eric, whose mouth was compressed tight as a mousetrap. I was willing to bet his fangs had popped out. The entrancing Eau de Fae—it acted on vampires like catnip on cats.

"You guys need to leave," I said. "Out you go, before you both use me as a chewy toy."

"But, Sookie," Eric protested. "I want to stay with you and make love to you at length."

You couldn't get any more frank than that.

"I appreciate the enthusiasm, but with me smelling like a fairy, I'm afraid you might get a little carried away."

"Oh, no, my lover," he protested.

"Please, Eric, some self-control. You and Bill need to git."

It was my mention of self-control that did it. Neither of them would admit to a failure of the trait vampires prized so highly.

Eric went to stand at the edge of the woods. He said, "While you were gone, Thalia called me. I'd sent her to talk to the human, Colton, at his job. When she got there, they reported he hadn't come in for work. Thalia went to his trailer. A fight had taken place inside. There was a small amount of blood. Colton was gone. I think Felipe has found him." While Eric was still maintaining deniability over the death of Victor, Colton had actually been in Fangtasia the night Victor had died. He knew the truth, and he was human and, therefore, could be made to talk.

Bill took a step toward me. "It'll be okay," he said reassuringly, and even though he was a vampire, I could tell that he simply wanted to be closer.

"Okay, we'll talk about that tomorrow," I said hastily. At this point, I was sure that all I could do for Colton was pray for him. There was certainly no way to find him tonight.

Very reluctantly, and with many good-byes and hopeful requests that they be called if I felt unwell during what remained of the night, Eric and Bill went their separate ways.

After I'd locked the doors, I took a hot shower. I could already feel myself beginning to stiffen up. I had to work the next day, and I couldn't afford to hobble.

At least one small mystery was solved. I assumed that the absence of Bellenos and his friend Aelfgifu was the crisis that had called my great-uncle back to Hooligans in such a tear. While I was sorry for his tough night, I wasn't so sorry that I planned to wait up for him. I crawled into bed. I was briefly conscious of the profound gratitude I felt that this sucky day was finally, finally over . . . and then I was out.

I staggered out of my bedroom at nine the next day.

I wasn't as sore as I'd feared, which was a pleasant discovery.

No one stirred in my house. I carefully checked with my other sense, the telepathy that could locate any creature thinking in the house. No one was sleeping here, either.

What did I need to do today? I made a little list after I'd had my coffee and a Pop-Tart.

I needed to go to the grocery store because I'd promised Jason I'd make him a sweet potato casserole to serve to Michele and her mom tonight. It wasn't exactly sweet potato season, but he'd texted me to ask me specially, and Jason didn't ask me for much these days. As long as I had to go to the store to get the ingredients, I reminded myself to check with Tara. I could pick up anything she wanted from the grocery store at the same time.

Then I needed to think of a way to see Jannalynn, so Bill and Heidi could sniff her. Since Eric's vampire Palomino was visiting Hair of the Dog, if worse came to worst maybe I could get Palomino to lift something of Jannalynn's.

Asking Jannalynn if she'd stand still for a minute and let the vamp trackers check her out was never a serious option. I could imagine all too clearly how she'd react to such a proposal.

And Bill was considering visiting Harp Powell to talk about the dead girl. I didn't know if we would be able to find time tonight. I thought of Kym's parents and shuddered. As unpleasant as her life sounded, meeting Oscar and Georgene just once made her bad choices more understandable.

While I was thinking about the evening's possibilities, I recalled that the fae wanted hunting permission again for tonight. I tried not to imagine the consequences if they all fanned out into the Louisiana countryside to find entertainment. I remembered the unease I'd felt last night when Aelfgifu and Bellenos had referred to my magic; without knowing I was going to do it, I found myself in my bedroom looking into my dressing table drawer to check that the cluviel dor was safe and still camouflaged as a powder compact.

Of course, it was. I let out a deep breath of relief. When I looked into the mirror, I looked scared. So I thought of something else to worry about. Warren was missing, Immanuel was in California and presumably safe, but where was Colton, the other human who'd been in Fangtasia that bloody night? We had to assume that Felipe had him stashed somewhere. Colton wasn't a Were, he had no fae blood, and he didn't owe allegiance to any vampire. He was just an employee at a vampire-owned enterprise. No one would be looking for him, unless I called the police. Would that do any good? Would Colton thank me for drawing his abduction to the attention of the police? I couldn't decide.

Time to give myself a good shake and get into my Merlotte's outfit. In this weather I didn't mind wearing the shorts. I shaved my legs just to be sure they were smooth, admired their brownness, and moisturized lavishly. By the time I applied my makeup, collected my grocery list, and grabbed my cell phone off the charger, it was time to go. On my way to town I called Tara, who said she didn't need anything; JB's mom had gone to the store for them that morning. She sounded tired, and I could hear one of the babies crying in the background. I was able to draw a line through one item.

Since my own grocery list was so short, I stopped at the old Piggly Wiggly. I could get in and out of it faster than Wal-Mart. Though I saw Maxine Fortenberry and had to pass the time of day with her, I still emerged from the store with only one bag and plenty of time to spare.

Feeling very efficient, I was tying on my apron fifteen minutes early.

Sam was behind the bar talking to Hoyt Fortenberry, who was taking an early lunch hour. I stopped to visit for a second, told Hoyt I'd seen his mom, asked him how the wedding plans were going (he rolled his eyes), and gave Sam a pat on the back by way of apology for my emotional excesses over the telephone the day before. He smiled back at me and continued poking at Hoyt about the potholes on the street in front of the bar.

I stowed my purse in my shiny new locker. I wore the key to it on a chain around my neck. The other waitresses were delighted to have real lockers, and from the stuffed bags they carried in, I was sure the lockers were already full. Everyone wanted to keep a change of clothes, an extra umbrella, some makeup, a hairbrush . . . even D'Eriq and Antoine seemed pleased with the new system. As I passed Sam's office, I saw the coatrack inside, and on it was a jacket, a bright red jacket . . . Jannalynn's. Before I could think about what I was doing, I stepped into Sam's office, stole the jacket, and retreated to stuff it inside my locker.

I'd found a quick and easy solution to the problem of getting Jannalynn's scent to the noses of Bill and Heidi. I even persuaded myself that Sam wouldn't mind, if I were to tell him; but I didn't test that idea by asking permission to take the jacket.

I'm not used to feeling underhanded, and I have to confess that for an hour or two I kept away from Sam. That was unexpectedly easy, since the bar was really busy. The association of local insurance agents came in for their monthly lunch together, and since it was so hot, they were almighty thirsty. The EMT team on duty parked the ambulance outside and ordered their food. Jason and his road crew came in, and so did a bunch of nurses from the blood bank truck, parked on the town square today.

Though I was working hard, the idea of bags of blood reminded me of Eric. Like all roads leading to Rome, all my thoughts seemed to come back to the certain prospect of misery to come. As I stood staring into the kitchen, waiting for a basket of French fried pickles for the insurance agents, my heart felt as if it were beating way too fast. I revisited the single disturbing scenario, over and over. Eric would choose her. He would leave me.

What weighed on me with incredible heaviness was the idea of using the love gift given by Fintan to my grandmother, the cluviel dor. If I understood its properties correctly, a wish on behalf of someone I loved would surely be granted. This fairy object, which Amelia had heard was no longer made in the fae world, might come with a penalty for its use. I had no idea if there would be a price to pay, much less how steep that price would be. But if I used it to keep Eric . . .

"Sookie?" Antoine said, sounding anxious. "Hey, girl, you hearing me? Here's your pickles. For the third time."

"Thanks," I said, picking up the red plastic basket and hurrying to the table. I smiled all around, put the basket neatly in the middle, and checked to see if anyone needed a drink refill. They all did, so I went to get the pitcher of sweet tea, while taking one glass with me to refill with Coke.

Then Jason asked for more mayonnaise for his hamburger, and Jane Bodehouse wanted a bowl of pretzels to go with her lunch (Bud Light).

By the time the noon crowd thinned out, I was feeling a little more normal. I reminded Jason I was making his sweet potato casserole and that he should come by tonight to pick it up.

"Sook, thanks," he said with his charming smile. "Her mom is gonna love it, and so will Michele. I really appreciate you taking the time to do this. I can grill meat, but I ain't no kitchen chef."

I worked the rest of the shift on automatic. I had a little conversation with Sam about whether to change insurance companies for the bar or whether Sam should insure his trailer separately. The State Farm agent had spoken to Sam at lunchtime.

Finally it was time to go, but I had to fiddle around until the storage room was empty and I could open the locker to remove the borrowed jacket. ("Borrowed" sounded much better than "stolen.") I'd found an empty Wal-Mart bag, and I stuffed the jacket into it, though my hands were clumsy because I was trying to hurry. Just as I tied the plastic handles together and opened the back door, I saw Sam go into his office; but he didn't come out again to yell, "Where's my honey's jacket?"

I drove home and unloaded the bag of groceries and the bag containing Jannalynn's jacket. I felt as if I'd lifted the collection plate from the church. I took off my uniform and put on some denim shorts and a camo tank top Jason had given me for my birthday the year before.

I left a message on Bill's answering machine before I began cooking. I put a big pot of water on the stove so it could reach the boiling point. As I peeled the sweet potatoes and cut them into chunks for cooking, I turned on the radio. It provided background noise, at least until the Shreveport news came on. In the wake of Kym Rowe's murder, anti-vamp sentiment was escalating. Someone had thrown a bucket of white paint across the façade of Fangtasia. There was nothing I could do about that, so I pushed that worry to the back of my mind. The vamps could more than take care of themselves, unless things got much, much worse.

After I'd eased the sweet potatoes into the boiling water and turned the heat down to simmer, I checked my e-mail. Tara had sent some pictures of the babies. Cute. I'd gotten a chain letter from Maxine (which I deleted without reading), and I'd gotten a message from Michele. She had a short list of three wedding dates she and Jason were considering, and she wanted to know if all three were clear for me. I smiled, looked at my empty calendar, and had just sent my reply when I heard a car pull up.

My schedule for the evening was full, so I wasn't very pleased at having an uninvited guest. I was even more astonished when I looked out the living room window to see that my caller was Donald Callaway, Brenda Hesterman's partner in Splendide. I'd wondered if I'd hear from them after Sam told me about the break-in, but I hadn't ever imagined I'd get a personal visit. Surely a phone call or an e-mail would have been sufficient to handle any issues that had resulted from the destruction of the furniture I'd sold to them?

Donald, standing by his car, looked as crisp as he had the morning he'd spent examining the contents of my attic: creased khakis, seersucker shirt, polished loafers. His salt-and-pepper hair and mustache were freshly trimmed, and he radiated a sort of middle-aged tan fitness. Golfer, maybe. He seemed to be having some difficulty.

I opened the door, worried about the simmering sweet potatoes, which should be nearly done.

"Hey, Mr. Callaway," I called. "What are you doing way out here?" And why didn't he approach?

"Can I come in for a second?" he asked.

"Okay," I said, and he started forward. "But I'm afraid I don't have a lot of time."

He was just a little surprised that I wasn't more cordial. I got a waft of wrongness. I dropped all my shields and looked inside his brain.

He was on the porch now, and I said, "Stop right there."

He looked at me with apparent surprise.

"What have you done?" I asked. "You've screwed me over somehow. You might as well tell me."

His eyes widened. "Are you human?"

"I'm human with extras. Spill it, Mr. Callaway."

He was almost frightened, but he was becoming angry, too. That was a bad combination. "I need that thing that was in the secret compartment."

Revelation. "You opened it first, before you showed it to me." It was my turn to be astonished.

"If I'd had any idea what that thing was, I'd never have told you," he said, regret weighing down his voice. "As it was, I thought it was worthless, and I thought I might as well boost my reputation for honesty."

"But you're not honest, are you?" I glided through his thoughts, my head tilted on one side. "You're a twisty bastard." The wards around the house had been trying to keep him out, but like an idiot, I'd invited him in.

He had the gall to be offended.

"Come on now, just trying to turn a buck and keep our business afloat in a bad economy." He thought he could tell me this, and I'd accept it? I checked him out quickly but thoroughly. I didn't think he had a gun, but he had a knife in a sheath clipped to his belt, just like many men who had to open boxes every day. It wasn't a big knife—but any knife was pretty damn frightening.

"Sookie," he continued, "I came out here tonight to do you a favor. I don't think you know that you have a valuable little item. Interest in this item is heating up, and word's getting around. You might find it a tad dangerous to keep it in your house. I'll be glad to put it in the safe at my office. I did some research on your behalf, and what you think may just be a pretty thing your grandma left in the desk is something a few people do want for their private collection."

Not only had he opened the secret compartment and glanced at the contents before he'd called me to come look, he'd at least scanned the letter. The letter my grandmother had written *to me.* Thank God he hadn't had a chance to read it carefully. He was completely ignorant about me.

Something inside me caught fire. I was mad. Really mad.

"Come in," I said calmly. "We'll talk about it."

He was surprised, but relieved.

I smiled at him.

I turned and walked back to the kitchen. There were lots of weapons in the kitchen.

Callaway followed me, his loafers making little *thwacks* on the boards of the floor.

It would be very opportune if Jason arrived right now for his sweet potato casserole, or if Dermot came home for supper, but I wasn't going to count on their help.

"So you did open the bag? You looked at it?" I said over my shoulder. "I don't know why Gran left me an old powder compact, but it is kind of pretty. Gran was sort of a crackpot; a sweet old lady, but real imaginative."

"So often our elderly relatives love things that don't really have much intrinsic value," the antiques dealer said. "In your case, your grandmother left you an item that is of interest only to a few specialized collectors."

"Really? What is it? She called it something crazy." I was still leading the way. I smiled to myself. I was pretty sure it wasn't a very pleasant smile.

He didn't hesitate. "It's a turn-of-the-century Valentine's Day present," he said. "Made out of soapstone. If you can open it, there's a little compartment for a lock of the hair of the person giving it."

"Really? I couldn't open it. You know how?" I was sure that only the intention to use it could open the cluviel dor.

"Yes, I'm pretty sure I can open it," he said, and he believed that—but he'd never tried. He hadn't had time that day, had had only a quick glance at the cluviel dor and at the letter. He assumed that he'd be able to open the round object because he'd never been thwarted when he'd tried to open similar antique items before.

"That would be real interesting," I said. "And how many people are gonna bid on this old thing? How much money you think I could make?"

"At least two people are involved," he said. "But that's all you need, to make a little profit. Maybe you'd make as much as a thousand, though I have to take my cut."

"Why should I give you any? Why shouldn't I contact them myself?"

He sat at the kitchen table uninvited, while I went to the stove to check the sweet potatoes. They were done. All the other ingredients—butter, eggs, sugar, molasses, allspice, nutmeg, and vanilla—were arranged in a row on the counter, ready for me to measure. The oven had preheated.

He was taken aback by my question, but he rallied. "Why, you don't want to deal with these people, young lady. They're pretty rough people. You want to let me do that. So it's only fair that I get a little recompense for my trouble."

"What if I don't want to let you 'do that'?" I turned off the heat, but the water kept bubbling. With a slotted spoon, I scooped out the sweet potato chunks and put them in a bowl. Steam rose from them, making the kitchen even warmer, despite the air conditioner rumbling away. I was monitoring his thoughts closely, as I should have done the day he'd been here working.

"Then I'll just take it," he said.

I turned to face him. He had some Mace *and* a knife. I heard the front door open and shut, very quietly. Callaway didn't hear it; he didn't know this house like I did.

"I won't give it up," I said flatly, my voice louder than it needed to be. "And you can't find it."

"I'm an antiques dealer," he said with absolute assurance. "I'm very good at finding old things."

I didn't know if a friend had entered or another foe. Truth be told, I had little faith in the wards. The silence and stealth the newcomer employed could indicate either one. I did know I wasn't going to give up the cluviel dor. And I knew for sure I wasn't going to stand passively and let this asshole hurt me. I twisted, gripped the handle of the pot of hot water, and pivoted smoothly, flinging the water directly into Donald Callaway's face.

A lot of things happened then, in very rapid succession. Callaway screamed and dropped the knife and the Mace, clapping his hands to his face while water flew everywhere. The demon lawyer, Desmond Cataliades, charged into the room. He bellowed like a maddened bull when he saw Donald Callaway on the floor (the dealer was doing a little of his own bellowing). The demon leaped onto the prone dealer, gripped his head, and twisted, and all the noise stopped abruptly.

"Shepherd of Judea," I said. I pulled out a chair and sat in it to forestall falling down on the wet floor with the body.

Mr. Cataliades picked himself up, dusted his hands together, and beamed at me. "Miss Stackhouse, how nice to see you," he said. "And how clever of you to distract him. I'm not yet returned to full strength."

"I take it you know who this is," I said, trying not to look at the inert figure of Donald Callaway.

"I do. And I've been looking for a chance to shut his mouth forever."

The bowl of sweet potatoes was still letting off steam.

"I can't pretend to regret he's dead," I said. "But this whole incident is kind of shocking, and it's taking me a minute to collect myself. In fact, I've been through a lot of shocking stuff lately. But what else is new? Sorry, I'm babbling."

"I can quite understand that. Shall I tell you what I've been doing?"

"Yes, please. Have a seat and talk to me." It would give me a chance to recover.

The demon sat opposite me and smiled in a cordial way. "When last you saw me, you were giving a baby shower, I believe? And the hellhounds were pursuing me. Do you mind if I impose on you for a glass of ice water?"

"Not at all," I said, and rose to fetch it. I had to step over the body.

"Thank you, my dear." The lawyer finished the glass in one long swallow. I refilled it. I was glad to return to my seat.

"You look kind of beat up," I observed, for I'd watched him as he drank. Mr. Cataliades was usually very well turned out in expensive suits that could not hide his round figure but at least made him look prosperous. The suit he had on had certainly looked much better when he'd bought it. Now it was marred with snags and holes and frayed spots, and spotted with stains. His once-polished brogans could not be salvaged. Even his socks were in tatters. The tonsure of dark hair was full of debris, leaves and twigs. Could it be he hadn't had a chance to change clothes since I'd last seen him sitting here in this kitchen, taking a time-out from his pursuit by four-legged streaks of darkness?

"Yes," he said, looking down at his condition. " 'Kind of beat up' is a gentle way to put it. Those streaks of darkness were hellhounds." It was no shock to me that he could read my mind; my own telepathy had been a birth present from Mr. Cataliades. He'd always been very good at concealing his own gift, never betraying by so much as a glance that he could read human minds. But I'd figured he must have it, if he could give it away. "The hellhounds pursued me for a very long time, and I had no idea why. I could not fathom what I had done to offend their master." He shook his head. "Now, of course, I know."

I waited for him to tell me what he'd done, but he wasn't ready for that.

"Finally, I became far enough ahead of the hounds to take time to arrange an ambush. By then, Diantha had been able to find me to join in the surprise I'd planned for them. We had . . . quite a struggle with the hounds." He was silent for a moment. I looked at the stains on his clothing and took a deep breath.

"Please tell me Diantha isn't dead," I said. His niece Diantha was one of the most unusual creatures I'd ever met, and that was saying something, considering whom I could enter in my address book.

"We prevailed," he said simply. "But it cost us, of course. I had to lie hidden in the woods for many days until I was able to travel again. Diantha recovered more quickly since her wounds were slighter, and she brought me food and began gathering information. We needed to understand before we could begin to dig ourselves out of trouble."

"Uh-huh," I said, wondering where this was going to lead. "You want to share that information with me? I'm pretty sure that this guy didn't understand my gran's letter." I nodded my head at the body.

"He may not have understood the context, and he didn't believe in fairies, but he did see the phrase 'cluviel dor,'" Mr. Cataliades said.

"But how come he knew it was valuable? He definitely didn't know what it can do, because he didn't understand the reality of fairies."

"I learned from my sponsor, Bertine, that Callaway Googled the term 'cluviel dor.' He found one reference in a fragment of text from an old Irish folk tale," Mr. Cataliades said.

This Bertine must be Mr. Cataliades's godmother, in effect, the same way Mr. Cataliades (my grandfather's best friend) was mine. I wondered briefly what Bertine looked like, where she lived. But Mr. Cataliades was still talking.

"Computers are another reason to deplore this age, when no one has to really travel to learn important things from other cultures." He shook his head, and a fragment of leaf floated to the floor and landed on the corpse. "And I'll tell you more about my sponsor when we have some leisure. You might like her."

I suspected Mr. Cataliades also had flashes of foreseeing.

"Fortunately for us, Callaway came to Bertine's attention when he persisted in his research. Of course, it was unfortunate for him." Mr. Cataliades spared a downward glance at the inert Donald. "Callaway tracked down a supposed expert in fairy lore, someone who could tell him what little is known about this legendary fairy artifact; namely, the fact that none exist on this earth anymore. Unfortunately, this expert—who was Bertine, as you have no doubt surmised—did not understand the importance of keeping silent. Since dear Bertine didn't believe that there were any cluviel dors left in either world, she felt free to talk about them. Therefore, she was ignorant of the wrong she committed when she told Callaway that a cluviel dor could be made in almost any form or shape. Callaway had never suspected the item he'd held was an actual fae artifact until he talked to Bertine. He imagined scholars and folklorists would give a pretty penny to possess such a thing."

"When he showed me the drawer, I didn't get that he'd already opened it," I said quietly. "How could that be?"

"Were you shielding?"

"I'm sure I was." I did it without thinking, to protect myself. Of course, I couldn't maintain such a level of blocking all day, every day. And of course, it protected your brain only like wearing earmuffs affected your hearing; a *lot* of stuff still filtered in, especially from a strong broadcaster. But apparently Donald had been preoccupied that day, and I had been so excited at the contents of the drawer I hadn't realized he was seeing the Butterick pattern envelope and the velvet bag for the second time. He hadn't believed he'd found anything valuable or notable: a confusing letter from an old woman about having children and getting a present, and a bag containing an old toiletry item, maybe a powder compact. It was when he'd thought the find over later and Googled the odd phrase that he'd begun to wonder if those items might be valuable.

"I need to give you lessons, child, as I should have done before. Isn't it nice that we're finally getting to know one another? I regret that it takes a huge crisis to impel me to make this offer."

I nodded faintly. I was glad to learn something about my telepathy from my sponsor, but it was kind of daunting to think of Desmond Cataliades becoming part of my everyday life. Of course, he knew what I was thinking, so I said hurriedly, "Please tell me what happened next."

"When Diantha thought of questioning Bertine, Bertine realized what she had done. Far from giving a human a useless bit of information about old fairy lore, she had revealed a secret. She came to me while I was recuperating, and I finally understood why I'd been pursued."

"Because . . ." I tried to arrange my thoughts. "Because you'd kept secret the existence of a cluviel dor?"

"Yes. My friendship with Fintan, whose name your grandmother mentioned in the letter, was no secret. Stupid Callaway Googled Fintan, too, and though he didn't find out anything about the real Fintan, the conjunction of the two searches sent out an alarm that eventually reached . . . the wrong ears. The fact that Fintan was your grandfather is no secret, either, since Niall found you and chose to honor you with his love and protection. It would not take much to put these snippets together."

"This is the only cluviel dor left in the world?" Awesome.

"Unless one lies lost and forgotten in the land of the fae. And believe me, there are plenty who search every day for such a thing."

"Can I give it away?"

"You'll need it if you're attacked. And you will be attacked," Mr. Cataliades said, matter-of-factly. "You can use it for yourself, you know; loving yourself is a legitimate trigger of its magic. Giving it to someone else would seal their death warrant. I don't think you'd want that, though my knowledge of you is inadequate."

Gee. A lot of swell news.

"I wish Adele had used it herself, to save her own life or the life of one of her children, to take the burden from you. I can only suppose that she didn't believe in its power."

"Probably not," I agreed. And if she had, she almost certainly felt that using it would not be a Christian act. "So, who's after the cluviel dor? I guess you know, by now?"

"I'm not sure that knowledge would be good for you," he said.

"How come you can read my mind, but I can't read yours?" I asked, tired of being transparent. Now I knew how other people must feel when I plucked a thought or two from their brains. Mr. Cataliades was a master at this, while I was very much a novice. He seemed to hear everything, and it didn't seem to bother him. Before I'd learned to shield, the world had been a babble of talk inside my head. Now that I could block those thoughts for the most part, life was easier, but it was frustrating when I actually wanted to hear: I seldom got a full thought or understood its context. It was surprisingly deflating to realize that it wasn't how much I heard that was amazing, it was how much I missed.

"Well, I am mostly a demon," he said apologetically. "And you're mostly only human."

"Do you know Barry?" I asked, and even Mr. Cataliades looked a little surprised.

"Yes," he said, after a perceptible hesitation. "The young man who can also read minds. I saw him in Rhodes, before and after the explosion."

"If I came to be telepathic because of your—well, essentially, your baby shower present—how come Barry is telepathic?"

Mr. Cataliades pulled himself straight and looked anywhere but at me. "Barry is my great-great-grandson."

"So, you're much older than you look."

This was taken as a compliment. "Yes, my young friend, I am. I don't neglect the boy, you know. He doesn't really know me, and of course he doesn't know his heritage, but I've kept him out of a lot of trouble. Not the same thing as having a fairy godmother as you had, but I've done my best."

"Of course," I said, because it hadn't been my intent to accuse Mr. Cataliades of ignoring his own kin. I'd just been curious. Time to change the subject, before I told him that my own fairy godmother had gotten killed defending me. "Are you gonna tell me who's after the cluviel dor?"

He looked profoundly sorry for me. There was a lot of that going around. "Let's get rid of this body first, shall we?" he said. "Do you have any disposal suggestions?"

I so seldom had to dispose of a human body myself, I was at a loss. Fairies turned into dust, and vampires flaked away. Demons had to be burned. Humans were very troublesome.

Mr. Cataliades, picking up on that thought, turned away with a small smile. "I hear Diantha coming," he remarked. "Maybe she'll have a plan."

Sure enough, the skinny girl glided into the room from the back door. I hadn't even heard her enter or detected her brain. She was wearing an eye-shattering combination: a very short yellow-and-black striped skirt over royal blue leggings, and a black leotard. Her black ankle boots were laced up with broad white laces. Today, her hair was bright pink. "Sookieyoudoingokay?" she asked.

It took me a second to translate, and then I nodded. "We got to get rid of this," I said, pointing to the body, which was absolutely obvious in a kitchen the size of mine.

"Thatshutsonedoor," she said to her uncle.

He nodded gravely. "I suppose the best way to proceed is to load him into the trunk of his car," Mr. Cataliades said. "Diantha, do you think you could assume his appearance?"

Diantha made a disgusted face but quickly bent to Donald Callaway's face and stared into it. She plucked a hair from his head, closed her eyes. Her lips moved, and the air had that magic feel I'd noticed when my friend Amelia had performed one of her spells.

In a moment, to my shock, Donald Callaway was standing in front of us staring down at his own body.

It was Diantha, completely transformed. She was even wearing Callaway's clothes, or at least that was the way she appeared to my eyes.

"Fuckthisshit," Callaway said, and I knew Diantha was in charge. But it was beyond strange to see Mr. Cataliades and Donald Callaway carrying out Callaway's body to his car, unlocked with the keys extracted from the corpse's pocket.

I followed them out, watching carefully to make sure nothing fell or leaked from the body.

"Diantha, drive to the airport in Shreveport and park the car there. Call a cab to pick you up, and have it drop you off at . . . at the police station. From there, find a good place to change back, so they'll lose the trail."

She nodded with a jerk and climbed into the car.

"Diantha can keep his appearance all the way to Shreveport?" I said, as she turned the car around with a grind of the wheel. She (he) waved gaily as she took off like a rocket. I hoped she made it back to Shreveport without getting a ticket.

"She won't get a ticket," Mr. Cataliades answered my thought.

But here came Jason in his pickup.

"Oh, hell," I said. "His sweet potatoes aren't ready."

"I need say good-bye, anyway," Mr. Cataliades said. "I know there are some things I haven't told you, but I must go now. I may have taken care of the hellhounds, but yours aren't my only secrets."

"But . . ."

I might as well not have spoken. With the startling speed he'd shown when the hellhounds were chasing him, my "sponsor" disappeared into the woods.

"Hey, Sis!" Jason bounded out of his truck. "Did you just have a visitor? I passed a car. You got my sweet potatoes ready?"

"Ah, not quite," I said. "That was a drop-in I didn't expect, a guy wanting to sell me life insurance. You come in and sit, and they'll be ready in about forty-five minutes." That was an exaggeration, but I wanted Jason to stay. I was scared to be alone. That was not a familiar feeling, or one I liked.

Jason was willing enough to come in and gossip with me while I stood at the kitchen counter adding ingredients to the sweet potatoes, mashing them, pouring them over the prepared crust, and putting the dish in the oven.

"How come there's water everywhere?" Jason said, getting up from the chair to mop it off with a dry dish towel.

"I dropped a pitcher," I said, and that was the end of Jason's curiosity. We talked about the suggested wedding dates, the du Rone babies, Hoyt and Holly's marriage and Hoyt's idea that they have a double ceremony (I was sure Holly and Michele would nix that), and the big reconciliation between Danny and Kennedy, who had been spotted kissing passionately in public at the Sonic.

As I was pulling the casserole out of the oven and preparing to add the final layer, Jason said, "Hey, I guess you heard that all our old furniture got busted up? That stuff the antiques dealer took? What was her name, Brenda? I hope you got money up front. It wasn't on consignment or nothing, right?"

I'd frozen after lifting out the dish halfway, but I made myself continue with my task. It helped that Dermot came in then, and since he and Jason looked so much alike, Jason got the biggest kick out of telling Dermot how good he was looking, every single time he saw our great-uncle.

"No, I already got cash for that stuff," I said, when the mutual admiration society had had its moment. And I got the distinct impression from Jason's head that he'd already forgotten that he'd asked me.

By the time I'd finished my work and sent Jason on his way with the hot dish, Dermot had volunteered to fix hamburgers for our supper. Cooking was something else that he was interested in now, thanks to the Food Network and Bravo. While Dermot was frying the burgers and getting out anything we might want to put on the buns, I looked around the kitchen very carefully to make sure there weren't any traces of the incident.

Oh, come on, I said to myself. *Donald Callaway's murder. "Incident," my round, rosy ass.* It turned out to be a good thing I checked, because under the kitchen table I spied a pair of dark glasses that must have fallen out of Callaway's shirt pocket. Dermot didn't comment when I straightened and slid them into a drawer.

"I don't guess you've heard from Claude or Niall," I said.

"No. Maybe Niall has killed Claude, or maybe now that Claude is in Faery, he just doesn't care anymore about those of us left here," Dermot said, sounding simply philosophical.

I really couldn't argue with him that those scenarios were impossible, because I knew enough about fairies and enough about Claude to know that they were actually likely. "Are some of the guys coming to run out in the woods tonight?" I said. "I guess Bellenos and Gift told you about last night."

"Those two won't be here tonight," Dermot said, rather grimly. "I am making them work tonight as punishment. They hate cleaning the bathrooms and kitchen, so that's their duty after the club closes. They may come tomorrow night if they behave themselves. I'm sorry about your car, Niece."

All the fae were calling me Sister now, and Dermot almost always called me Niece. There were a lot worse names they could have chosen, but all this familial terminology felt awfully intimate. "The car's running okay," I said, though I'd have to get the bumper fixed sooner or later. Probably later. The seat belt had to be replaced pronto. And I was a little taken aback that Dermot was punishing the sharp-toothed elf and his running buddy as he would little children, giving them the unpopular cleanup duty. But out loud I said, "At least they were able to get the car out of the ditch. I'm only worried they'll get spotted on someone else's land or that they'll run into Bill."

"He loves you," Dermot said, turning over the hamburgers in the skillet.

"Yeah, I know." I got out two plates and a bowl of mixed fruit. "There's nothing I can do about it but be his friend, though. I used to love him back, and I gotta say there are moments when I feel the old attraction, but I'm not in love with Bill. Not anymore."

"You love the blond one?" Dermot had been sure about Bill, but he didn't sound so sure about Eric.

"Yes." But I no longer felt the surge of love and lust and excitement I'd had before the past few weeks. I hoped I might feel all that again, but I was so emotionally battered that I'd gone a little numb. It was a curious feeling—as if my hand were asleep, but I expected it would be all pins and needles at any second. "I love him," I said, but even to my own ears I didn't sound happy about it.

Chapter 11

You may wonder why I was willing to eat in the kitchen where I'd just witnessed a violent death. The fact is, Donald Callaway's demise was not the worst thing that had happened in my kitchen—not by a long shot. Maybe that was another thing I was getting numb to.

Just before our food was ready, when Dermot's back was turned, I slid open the drawer and extricated the dead man's sunglasses, sliding them into my apron pocket. I admit, I can't say my legs were too steady when I excused myself to go to the bathroom. When I was safely shut inside, I put my hands over my face and sat on the edge of the tub to take a few deep breaths. I got up, dropping Donald Callaway's dark glasses onto the bath mat. I stomped on them three times, quickly. Without stopping to think, I held the bath mat over the waste can in a funnel shape and shook it gently until all the pieces were safely at the bottom of the plastic bag acting as a liner.

After supper, I planned to take the bag out to the big garbage can that we had to wheel out to the road every Friday.

When I heard Dermot calling me, I washed my hands and my face and left the bathroom, making myself stand straight. As I passed through my bedroom, I slipped the cluviel dor into my pocket, where the sunglasses had been. I couldn't leave it alone in my room. Not anymore.

The hamburgers were good, and I managed to eat mine and some fruit salad, too. Dermot and I were quiet together, which suited me fine. As we did the dishes, Dermot told me shyly that he had a date and would be going out after he showered.

"Oh my gosh!" I grinned at him. "Who's the lucky girl?"

"Linda Tonnesen."

"The doctor!"

"Yes," he said a little doubtfully. "I think that's what she said she did. Treats human ailments?"

"Oh, that's a big deal, really, Dermot," I said. "Doctors get a lot of respect in our society. I guess as far as she knows, you're human?"

He flushed. "Yes, she thinks I'm a *very* attractive human. I met her at the bar three nights ago."

It would be pretty stupid for me to comment further. He was handsome, sweet natured, and strong. What more could a woman want?

Besides, considering the confused state of my own love life, I could hardly pass out dating tips.

I told Dermot I'd finish the dishes so he could go get ready for his date, and by the time I was ensconced on the living room couch with a book, he came downstairs in navy slacks and a pale blue striped shirt with a button-down collar. He looked amazing, and I told him so. He grinned at me.

"I hope she'll think so," he said. "I love the way she smells."

That was a very fairy compliment. Linda Tonnesen was a smart woman with a great sense of humor, but she was not what humans thought of as conventionally pretty. Her smell had scored her big points with Dermot. I'd have to remember that.

By the time Dermot left, dark had fallen. I got the bag containing Jannalynn's jacket and went out the back door, on my way to Bill's house. I felt a little better after I'd dropped the other little bag, the one containing the smashed dark glasses, into the garbage bin. I turned on my flashlight and strode to the woods. There was a little path; Bill came over often, probably far more often than I knew.

Just before I reached the cleared ground of the old cemetery, I heard a sound to my left. I stopped in my tracks. "Bill?" I said.

"Sookie," he answered, and then he was right in front of me. He had his own little plastic sack looped over his left hand. We were all carrying bags around tonight.

"I brought Jannalynn's jacket," I said. "For you and Heidi."

"You stole her jacket?" He sounded amused.

"If that were the worst thing I'd done today, I'd be a happy woman."

Bill let that pass, though I could almost feel him peering at me. Vampire eyesight is excellent, of course. He took my arm and we walked a few feet to get into the cemetery grounds. Even though there weren't many lights there, there were a few, and I could see (faintly) that Bill was excited about something.

He opened my bag, put it to his face, and inhaled. "No, that's not a scent I picked up at the gate in the backyard. Of course, considering all the scents around there and the length of time before we were able to investigate, that can't be a definite no." He handed it back.

I felt almost disappointed. Jannalynn made me so antsy that I would have liked to find her guilty of something, but I chided myself for being uncharitable. I should be glad Sam was dating an innocent woman. And I was. Right?

"You look unhappy," Bill said. We were walking back to his house, and I'd tucked the plastic bag under my arm. I'd been thinking of how I'd return Jannalynn's jacket to Sam's office. I'd have to do it soon.

"I *am* unhappy," I said. Then, because I didn't want to explain my every inner qualm, I told Bill, "I listened to the news on the radio while I was cutting up sweet potatoes. That girl Kym, the police are trying to blame her murder on a vampire because she died in Eric's front yard. Someone vandalized Fangtasia, threw white paint all over the exterior. Are Felipe and his crew still here? Why don't they go home?"

Bill put his arm around me. "Calm down," he said, his voice hard.

I was so surprised that I actually held my breath for a moment.

"Breathe," he commanded. "Slowly. Thoughtfully."

"What are you, Zen Master Fang?"

"Sookie." When he used that voice, he meant business. So I took a deep breath, let it out. Again. Again.

"Okay, I'm better," I said.

"Listen," Bill said, and I raised my eyes to his. He was looking excited again. He shook his own bag. "We've had all eyes open to try to track down Colton . . . or find his body. Very early this past morning, Palomino called from her job at the Trifecta. She's seen Colton. Felipe does have him. We've got a plan to get him out. Cobbled together, but I think it might work. If we can accomplish that, maybe we'll also discover where they're keeping Warren. If we find Warren and broadcast his whereabouts, Mustapha will come forward to tell what he knows. When Mustapha tells us who suborned him by holding Warren hostage, then we'll know who killed Kym. When we tell the police, the heat will be off Eric. Then we can solve the problem of that asshole Appius's posthumous betrothal of Eric to Freyda. Felipe and his 'posse' will go back to Nevada. Eric will have his sheriff's job, or a new title, but Felipe will not fire him or kill him."

"That's a hell of lot of dominoes, Bill. Colton to Warren to Mustapha to Kym's murderer to the police to Appius to Freyda to Eric. Anyway, isn't it too late? We're doomed. Colton's probably already told him everything."

"He can't have. Colton was grieving so hard over Audrina that I wiped his memory of her death. So he doesn't remember all of what happened that night, by any means."

"You didn't tell Eric that, did you?"

Bill shrugged. "I didn't need his permission. It doesn't matter now, anyway. Felipe won't have Colton after tonight." He brandished the bag he'd brought.

"Why?"

"Because you and I are going to kidnap him back."

"And do what with him?" Colton was a pretty nice guy, and he hadn't had what anyone would think was an easy life. I didn't want to rescue him from Felipe only to find that Bill planned to remove Colton as a witness in a very final way.

"I have it all planned. But we have to act quickly. I've texted Harp to tell him we have to reschedule. I think this is more important than asking him questions about Kym's parents."

I had to agree.

"Say we get Colton out," I said, as we hustled toward Bill's car.

"What about Immanuel? Can they track him in Los Angeles?" Immanuel the hairdresser, also human, had been there that night, since Victor's cruelty had led to his sister's death.

"He got work on the set of a television show. Ironically, it's about vampires and most of the shooting takes place at night. Two members of the crew are actually vampires. I put Immanuel under the care of one of them. He'll be guarded."

"How'd you arrange that?"

"Coincidence. It happens," Bill said. "And you're the other human, but you can't be glamoured. So if we can just get Colton away and find Warren . . ."

"Since Warren never came into Fangtasia the night we killed Victor," I said, "I don't believe his abduction has anything to do with Victor's death. I think Warren was snatched just to force Mustapha to let Kym Rowe in the back door of Eric's house." I had enough lightbulbs popping over my head to illuminate an operating room. "What do you think?"

"I think we have a lot of questions," Bill said. "Now let's go find out some answers."

Our first stop was my house, where I left Jannalynn's jacket and opened the bag Bill had brought.

"Good God," I said in disgust. "I got to wear that?"

"Part of the plan," Bill said, though he was smiling.

I stomped into my room and pulled on the blue "flirty" skirt, which began well below my navel and ended about two inches below my happy place. The "blouse"—and it was a blouse in name only—was white with red trim and tied between my breasts. It was just like a bra with sleeves. I put on white Nikes with red trim, which was the best match I had on my shoe rack. There sure wasn't any pocket in this outfit, so I stuck the cluviel dor in my shoulder bag. While I was preparing for this secret mission, I put my phone on vibrate so it couldn't ring at an awkward moment. I looked in the bathroom mirror. I was as ready as I'd ever be.

I felt ridiculously self-conscious when I came into the living room wearing the abbreviated outfit.

"You look just right," Bill said soberly, and I caught the corner of his mouth twitching. I had to laugh.

"I hope Sam doesn't decide we ought to dress this way at Merlotte's," I said.

"You would have a full house every night," Bill said.

"Not unless I lost some weight." My glance in the mirror had reminded me that my stomach was not exactly concave.

"You look mouthwatering," Bill said, and to make his point his fangs came down. He tactfully closed his mouth.

"Oh, well." I tried to accept this as an impersonal tribute, though I don't think any woman minds knowing she looks good, as long as the admiration isn't expressed in an offensive way and doesn't come from a disgusting source. "We better get going."

The Trifecta, a hotel/casino on the east side of Shreveport, was the closest thing the town had to "glamorous." At night it glowed silver with so many lights I was sure you could see it from the moon. Since the lot was full, we were forced to park outside the fenced employee parking area. But the gate was open and unguarded at the moment, so we simply walked through the lot and right up to the very prosaic beige metal door that was the employee entrance.

There was a keypad outside. Though I felt dismayed, Bill didn't seem worried. He looked down at his watch and then knocked on the door. There were some faint beeps inside, and Palomino swung the door open. She was balancing a room service tray on one hand. Laden as it was, that was an impressive achievement.

The young vampire was wearing the same outfit I was, and she looked mouthwatering in it. But at the moment, her appearance was the last thing on her mind. "Get in!" she snapped, and Bill and I entered the grungy back corridor. If you got to enter the Trifecta as a guest, it was glittery and gleaming and full of the constant machine noise and the frantic human yearning for pleasure that fills all casinos. But that wasn't for us, not tonight.

Wordlessly, Palomino set off at a fast clip. I noticed that she was able to balance the tray perfectly, no matter how much her speed picked up. I scurried after the two vampires along the beige-painted corridors, marred with scratches and chips. Everyone back here was in a hurry to get where they needed to be, either at a work station or out the back door to go somewhere more pleasant. They were saving their smiles for people they cared about. I saw a half-remembered face among the grim horde, and after I passed I recalled that she was one of the Long Tooth pack. She didn't let on by a twitch or a smile that she knew who I was.

Palomino strode ahead of us, her light-brown skin looking warm even though she'd been dead for years, her pale hair bouncing over a depressingly tight butt. We hustled onto a huge elevator. Instead of being lined with mirrors and shiny rails, this one was padded. The staff elevator was obviously used for bringing up palettes of food and other heavy items.

"I hate this fucking job," Palomino said as she jabbed a button. She glared at Bill.

"It's only for a little while," he said, and from his voice I could tell he'd told her the same thing many times before. "And then you can quit. You can quit dating the Were, too."

She was mollified and even managed to smile. "He's on the fifth floor, in 507," she said. "I walked all over this damn hotel tracking him, but since they didn't station guards outside the room, I couldn't pinpoint it until last night when I took in the room service tray."

"You've done a good job. Eric will be grateful," Bill said.

Her smile glowed even brighter. "Good! That's what I was hoping! Now Rubio and Parker may get a chance to show their skills." The two vampires were her nestmates. They were not great fighters. I hoped they *did* have other skills.

"I'll present that to Eric in the most urgent terms," Bill promised.

The staff elevator stopped, and Palomino handed the tray to me. I had to use both my hands. Lots of food and three drinks weighed it down. She pressed the Doors Closed button and began to talk very quickly.

"Keep your head turned away, and they'll think you're me," she said.

"No one would think that," I said, but after a second I could sort of see it.

Palomino was naturally brown, and I was very tan. Palomino's hair was paler than mine, but mine was as abundant and long. We were much the same height and build, and we were wearing identical outfits.

"I'm going to go be conspicuous out front," she said. "Give me three minutes to get within sight of the security cameras. I'll meet you at the back door ten minutes after that. Now, get off the elevator so I can go."

We got off. Bill held the tray for me while I took my hair out of its ponytail and shook my head from side to side to increase my resemblance to the vampire.

"As long as you had her here, why couldn't she have done this?" I hissed.

"This way she can be visibly elsewhere," Bill said. "If Felipe suspected her complicity, he could have her killed. He can't do that to you. You're Eric's wife. But that's a worst-case scenario. We'll pull the trick off." He pulled a khaki fishing hat out of his back pocket and pulled it over his head. I forbore to comment on the way he looked.

"What trick?" I asked, instead.

"Well, it is a sort of conjuring trick," he said. "Now you see him. Now you don't. Remember, there are two guards in there with him. They'll open the door, and your job is to make sure it stays open. I'll come in and do the rest."

"You couldn't just break the door down?"

"And have security here in two minutes? I don't think that would be a good plan."

"I'm not sure this is, either. But *okay*."

I marched down the hall and knocked on the door of 507 with the knuckles of my left hand, managing this by kind of wedging the tray into the corner formed by the door and its frame. I smiled big at the peephole and took a deep breath to let my chest do its thing. I sensed the appreciation through the door. I counted the heads inside the room: three, as Bill had told me.

The tray was not getting any lighter, and I was conscious of a definite relief when the door opened. I could hear Bill's footsteps coming up behind me.

"All right, come on in," said a bored voice.

Of course, both of the guards were human. They would have to be on duty during the day, too.

"Where you want this?" I asked.

"Over there on the coffee table'll be fine." He was very tall, pretty heavy, with very short gray hair. I smiled at him and bore the laden tray over to the low table. I squatted and slid it into place. The other guard was with Colton in the bathroom, waiting until I left to emerge; I read that right from his brain.

The room door was still open, but the guard was standing close to it. After a second's anxious search I spotted the plastic folder containing the check and handed it to the hulk without getting closer to him. He made a little face but moved nearer, his hand extended, the door he'd released beginning to swing shut. But in slid Bill, moving smoothly and silently at the man's back. While I kept my eyes fixed on the folder, Bill reached up and around to hit the man in the temple. The guard dropped like a sack of wet oatmeal.

I grabbed a napkin from the tray and wiped my fingerprints off the tray and the folder while Bill shut the room door.

"Dewey?" said the man in the bathroom. "She gone yet?"

"Uh-huh," Bill said, deepening his voice.

The second guard must have sensed something was up, because he had a gun in his hand when he opened the bathroom door. He might have been prepared with weaponry, but he wasn't mentally prepared, because at the sight of two strangers he froze, his eyes widening. It was just for a second, but that was all it took for Bill to leap onto him and sock him in the same place he'd hit the hulk. I kicked the gun under the couch when it fell from the guard's hand.

Bill hurried to pull the unconscious man out of the way while

I darted into the bathroom to untie Colton. It was like we'd done this a dozen times! I confess I felt pretty proud at the way it was going.

I looked Colton over while I began working on the duct tape across his mouth. He was not in great shape. Colton had worked for Felipe in Reno and then followed Victor to Louisiana, where he'd been employed at Vampire's Kiss. His apparent devotion hadn't stemmed from affection but from a thirst for vengeance; Colton's mother had died as a result of Victor's teaching a lesson to Colton's half brother. Carelessly, Victor had never dug deep enough to get the connection, and as a result, Colton had been a great help to the Shreveport plan to eradicate Victor. His lover Audrina had taken part in the fight and paid for her devotion with her life. I hadn't seen Colton since that night, but I'd known he'd stayed in the area and even kept his job at Vampire's Kiss.

Colton's gray eyes were full of tears after I yanked the duct tape off. His first words were a stream of profanity.

"Bill, we need a handcuff key," I said, and as Bill began rummaging in the guards' pockets to track it down, I cut the tape around Colton's ankles. Bill threw the key to me, and I unlocked the cuffs. Once I tossed them aside, Colton didn't know what he wanted to do first: rub his wrists or massage his stinging face. Instead, he flung his arms around me and said, "God bless you."

I was startled and touched. I said, "This was Bill's plan, and now we've got to skedaddle before anyone comes looking. Those guys will come to eventually." Bill had reused the handcuffs on the hulk and was using Second Guard's own belt to secure his arms. The roll of duct tape they'd used on Colton was also heavily deployed.

"See how you like that, motherfuckers," Colton said, with some satisfaction. He stood up and we went to the door. "Thanks, Mr. Compton."

"My pleasure," Bill said drily.

Colton seemed to take in my scanty outfit for the first time, and his gray eyes widened. "Wow," he said, one hand on the doorknob. "When Palomino brought in the food last night, I caught a glimpse of her. I hoped she recognized me and would do something for me, but I never expected this." He looked at me again before forcing his eyes away. "Wow," he said, and swallowed.

"If you've finished ogling Eric's woman, it's time to get out of here," Bill said. If his voice had been dry before, it was toast now.

"Just don't let anyone see me," Colton said. "And after I get out of this town, I never want to talk to another vampire in my life."

"Though we've risked our lives to rescue you," Bill said.

"Time to work out the philosophy later," I said, and they both nodded. In a second, we were on the move. I had a napkin in my hand, and I used it when I shut the door of 507 behind us. We went down the hall in single file and reached the staff elevator, passing only one couple on our journey. They were completely wrapped up in each other and didn't do more than stop groping for a moment in reaction to our presence. The staff elevator came quickly, and we stepped on to join a middle-aged woman who was carrying some dry cleaning in a plastic bag. She nodded to us and kept her eyes on the floor indicator. We had to go up with her before we could go down, and my palms started sweating with anxiety. She was ignoring Colton's disheveled condition with a deliberate air. She didn't want to know, which was great. It was a relief when she stepped off.

When we began our descent, I was terrified someone would be waiting for us on the fifth floor; the door would open, and we'd be confronted with the two men we'd left bound. But that didn't happen. We got down to the second floor, and the doors whooshed open. There were several other workers there: another room service server with a rolling cart, a bellman, and a woman in a black suit. She was very well groomed and wearing high heels, too, so she was definitely higher up on the food chain.

She was the only one who paid us any attention when they all crowded on. "Server," she said sharply. "Where's your name tag?" Palomino had worn one on the upper slope of her right breast, so I clapped my hand to the place mine should have been. "Sorry, it must have fallen off," I said apologetically.

"Get another one right away," she said, and I looked at her tag. "M. Norman," it said. I was sure I wouldn't get a surname. Mine would say "Candi" or "Brandi" or "Sandi."

"Yes, ma'am," I said, since now was not a time to start a class war.

M. Norman's gaze went to Colton's handsome face, admittedly marred by the removal of the duct tape and admittedly a little bruised. I could see a little crease between her brows as she tried to figure out what could have happened to him and if she should ask any questions. But her tailored shoulders lifted in a tiny shrug. She'd exerted her authority sufficiently for one night.

When the elevator stopped at the ground level, we got out of it like we owned the hotel. We rounded a corner, and there was the back door, Palomino walking toward it ahead of us. She glanced over her shoulder and looked faintly gratified to see us coming. She tapped the code into the keypad by the door, and then she opened it. We strode by her into the parking lot. Palomino, on the way to her red car, looked curiously at the street beyond the fenced lot for a moment, as if she sensed something strange. I didn't have time to check it out as we walked briskly between the parked employee cars and out the gap in the fence.

We were almost to Bill's car when the Weres caught up with us. There were four of them. I only recognized one; I'd seen him at Alcide's house. He was a gaunt-faced, long-haired, bearded guy named Van.

Vamps and Weres just don't mix, generally speaking, so I stepped ahead of Bill and did my best to manage to smile. "Van, good to see you tonight," I said, struggling to sound sincere when every nerve in my body was screaming at me to get the hell out of the vicinity. "You gonna let us get on our way?"

Van, who was several inches taller than me, looked down at my face. He wasn't thinking about my body, which was a nice change, but he was thinking about . . . making some kind of choice. It's very hard to read Were thoughts, but that much I could discern.

"Miss Stackhouse," he said, and nodded. His dark hair swung forward and back with the motion. "We been looking for you."

"How come?" I might as well get this settled. If we were going to fight, I needed to know why I was going to get beat up. I sure didn't want that.

"Alcide's found Warren."

"Oh, good!" I was really pleased. I smiled up at Van. Now Mustapha could come in from the cold, tell us what he'd seen, and all would be well.

"Thing is, what we found is a dead body, and we ain't sure it's really him," Van said. When my face fell, he added, "I'm real sorry, but Alcide wants you to have a look at him and tell us it's Warren for sure."

So much for a happy ending.

Chapter 12

"You-all were headed somewhere?" Van asked.

"We were taking this one to the airport," Bill said, nodding at Colton. This was news to me and to Colton, but it was good news. There really was a plan to get Colton away from the reach of Felipe.

"Why don't you two continue on, then," Van said reasonably. He didn't ask any further questions or demand to know Colton's identity, which was a relief. "I can take Sookie to the body, she'll check the identity, and I'll get her home. Or we can meet up somewhere."

"At Alcide's?" Bill asked.

"Sure."

"Sookie, you okay with that?"

"Yeah, all right," I said. "Let me get my purse out of your car."

Bill clicked his car open and I reached inside to get my purse, which held a change of clothes. I definitely wanted to find a couple of minutes of privacy to put on something a little less revealing.

I felt uneasy without knowing exactly why. We'd recovered Colton, and if he could get the hell out of town, he'd probably be safe. If Colton couldn't tell the little he remembered about that evening at Fangtasia, Eric would be safer, and therefore I would be safer—and so would all of the Shreveport vamps. I ought to be feeling happier. I slung my bag over my shoulder, glad that I had the cluviel dor with me.

"You're okay with these wolves?" Bill asked in a very low voice as Colton got into Bill's car and buckled his seat belt.

"Uh-huh," I said, though I wasn't so sure. But I shook myself and called myself paranoid. "These are Alcide's wolves, and he's my friend. But just in case, call him when you're on your way, would you?"

"Go with me," Bill said suddenly. "They can identify Warren by smell, maybe. Mustapha could definitely do that, when he resurfaces."

"Nah, it's okay. Get Colton to the airport," I said. "Get him out of town."

Bill looked at me searchingly, then nodded in a jerky way. I watched as Bill and Colton drove off.

Now that I was alone with the werewolves, I felt even odder.

"Van," I said, "Where did you find Warren?"

The other three crowded around: a woman in her thirties with a pixie haircut, an airman from the Air Force base in Bossier City, and a girl in her teens with very generous curves. The teenager was in the first throes of experiencing her power as a Were, almost drunk with her newfound ability; it dominated her brain. The other two meant business. And that was all I could get of their thoughts. We were walking north on the street to a gray Camaro, which seemed to belong to Airman.

"I'll show you. It's a little ways east of town. Since Mustapha wasn't a pack member, we never met Warren."

"Okay," I said doubtfully. And I thought of making some excuse not to get in the car, because my uneasiness was mounting like a drumroll. We were alone on a dark street, and I realized they had boxed me in. I had no real reason to doubt that Van was telling me the truth—but I had an instinct that was telling me this situation stank. I wished instinct had spoken up more clearly a few minutes ago when I'd had Bill at my side. I got in the car, and the Weres crowded in. We buckled up, and in a second we were driving in the direction of the interstate.

Curiously, I almost didn't want to discover that my suspicion was valid. I was tired of crises, tired of deceit, tired of life-or-death situations. I felt like a stone being skipped across a pond, longing only to sink to the anonymous bottom.

Well, that was stupid. I gave myself a mental shake. Not time to long for things I couldn't have at the moment. Time to be alert and ready for action. "Do you really have Warren?" I asked Van. He was sitting to my right in the backseat of the Camaro. The plump teenager was crowded in to my left. She didn't smell particularly good.

"Nope," he said. "Ain't ever seen him, that I know of."

"Then why are you doing this?" I might as well know, though I already felt sadly sure this was going to end poorly.

"Alcide asked that black bugger Mustapha to join the pack," Van said. "He ain't asked us."

So they were all rogues. "But I saw you at the last pack meeting."

"Yeah, I was going through rush, like they do in fraternities," Van said, deeply sarcastic. "But I didn't make the cut. Guess I got *black-balled*."

"I thought he had to let you in," I said. "I mean, I didn't know the packleader got to pick and choose."

"Alcide is a little too selective," said the airman, who was driving. He turned a little so I could see his profile as he spoke. "He doesn't want anyone with a serious criminal record in his pack."

Alarm bells sounded then in my brain, way too late. Mustapha had been in prison, though I didn't know the charge . . . yet Alcide had been willing to accept him into the pack. What had these rogues done that had been so bad that a wolf pack wouldn't have them?

The girl beside me tittered. The woman in the passenger's side of the front seat cast her a dark look, and the girl stuck out her tongue like a ten-year-old.

"You got a police record?" I asked the plump girl.

Plump gave me a sly look. She had straight brown hair that fell to her shoulders. Her bangs were almost in her eyes. She'd stuffed herself into a striped tube top and blue jeans. She was wearing flip-flops. "I got a juvenile record," she said proudly. "I set my house on fire. My mama got out just in time. My daddy and the boys didn't."

And I got what her daddy had been doing to her, just a single line of memory from her, and I was almost glad he hadn't made it out. But the brothers? Little boys? I didn't think she was too happy her mom had made it out, either.

"So Alcide wouldn't admit any of you?"

"No," said Van. "But when there's a changeover, and the pack has a new leader, we'll be in. We'll have security."

"What's going to happen to Alcide?"

"We're gonna overthrow his ass," said Airman.

"He's a good man," I said quietly.

"He's a douche," said Plump.

During this charming conversation the woman in the front seat had not spoken, and though I couldn't read her thoughts, I could read the ambiguity and regret that were making it hard for her to sit still. I sensed she was on the cusp of a decision, and I feared to say something that would tip her over to the wrong side.

"So where are you taking me?" I said, and Van put his arm around me.

"Me and Johnny might appreciate a little alone time with you," Van said, his free hand lodging itself under my skirt. "You looking so fine and all."

"I wonder what *you* were in jail for," I said. "Gee, let me guess."

The woman looked back at me, and our eyes met. "You going to put up with that?" she asked Plump. Thus goaded, Plump grabbed Van's wrist and pulled his hand away from my crotch.

"You said you wouldn't do this again," she growled, and I mean growled. "I'm your woman now. No more."

"Course you're mine, but that doesn't mean I don't want to cleanse my palate with a little country-fried steak," Van said.

"Charming," I said, which was unfortunate, because Van punched me and I saw bright lights for a second. You don't want to get hit by a werewolf. Really.

I had to keep from gagging from the pain, but I resolved that if I threw up I was going to do it all over Van.

He grabbed my hand and squeezed it, squeezed it until I could feel the bones rubbing together. This time, I had to cry out, and he liked that. I could feel the pleasure radiating out from him.

Help, I thought. *Can anyone hear me?*

No answer. I wondered where Mr. Cataliades was. I wondered where his great-great-grandson, whom I'd always called Barry Bellboy, was. Too far away in Texas to hear my mental voice . . .

I wondered if I'd see tomorrow. I had planned on it being a happy day for me, a special day.

At least Van seemed to be taking Plump's hostility seriously now, and he quit hurting me. Dealing out pain to me excited her jealousy just as much as him feeling me up. Unhealthy. Not that it was my problem, not that it would make any difference after we got wherever we were going. I'd picked up on a stray thought or two. I was beginning to get the bigger picture. It had a big skull and crossbones right in the middle.

The traffic was fairly heavy, but I knew what would happen to me if I signaled another car. I knew, too, what would happen to the people in that car. Not a single police car in the stream of traffic . . . not a one. We were on the interstate going east, back toward Bon Temps. There were a dozen exits, and when we left the interstate, none of them would have this much traffic. Once we got into the woods, I'd be doomed.

Well, I had to do *something.*

Just as a motorcycle began passing the car, I attacked Van. He'd been thinking about something entirely different, something involving the plump girl, so my sudden twist and lunge was a huge shock. I tried to grasp his neck, but my fingers wouldn't meet around it, and I had a hank of his hair bundled into my grip. He yelled and his hands shot up to grip mine. I dug my thumbs in ferociously, and Airman turned to glance back. Glass shattered and as I closed my eyes I saw a fine mist of red. Someone had shot Airman in the shoulder.

We were at a level spot on the interstate, thank God. As we abruptly swerved off the pavement, the quiet woman in the front seat reached over and switched the car off. *Remarkable presence of mind,* I thought in a daze, and we began gliding to a stop. Plump was screaming, Van was beating the shit out of me, and there was blood all over everything. The smell triggered the wolf in them, and they began to change. If I didn't get out of the car, I was going to get bitten, and then I'd qualify to be a pack member myself.

As I struggled with Van in a vain attempt to reach the door handle, that door flew open and a black-gloved hand reached in to grab mine. I seized it like a drowning man seizes a rope, and just like a rope, that hand hauled me out of deep trouble. I barely managed to grab my bag with my free hand.

"Let's get out of here," Mustapha said, and I jumped on the back of his Harley behind him, my bag slung over my shoulder and mashed between us to keep it secure. Though I was still trying to grasp what had just happened, my wiser self was telling me to think later, get the hell out of there now. Mustapha lost no time. Just as we zipped across the grassy median to head back into Shreveport, I watched a car pull up to offer help to the apparent wreck.

"No, they'll get hurt!" I yelled.

"It's Long Tooth wolves. You stay on." And off we took. After that, I concentrated on clinging to Mustapha as we rocketed through the night. After my initial gush of relief, it was frustrating not to be able to ask any of the fifty questions racing through my mind. I wasn't totally surprised when we pulled up in the circular driveway in front of Alcide's house. I had to exert a conscious effort to unclench my muscles so I could dismount. Mustapha took off his helmet and gave me a thorough look. I nodded to let him know I was okay. My hand would hurt from the squeeze Van had given it, and I was covered with dots of blood, but it wasn't mine. I looked down at my watch. Bill had had time to deposit Colton at the airport, but he should be driving here. The whole thing had happened that quickly.

"What you doing wearing prostitute clothes?" Mustapha asked severely, and hustled me over to the front door.

Alcide opened the door himself, and if he was bowled over with surprise, he did a good job of hiding it.

"Damn, Sookie, whose blood?" he said, and waved us in.

"Rogue werewolf," I said. I reeked.

"No cars coming, so I had to take action then," Mustapha explained. "I shot Laidlaw. He was driving. The pack's taking care of the others."

"Tell me," Alcide said, bending down to look me in the eyes. He nodded, satisfied with what he saw. I opened my mouth. "In as few words as possible," he added.

Apparently, time was of the essence.

"Palomino found where Felipe was keeping a guy hostage, a guy we needed to rescue. Discreetly. I kind of resemble her, so to leave her cover intact, I pretended to be her wearing this *waitress outfit*." I glared at Mustapha. *"That the casinos picked out,"* I added, to make myself clear. Alcide gave me a little shake to speed me up.

"Okay! So Bill and I came out with the hostage and we were gonna drive off, when this group of four Weres comes up, and the leader, Van—whom I'd seen here, by the way, so I thought he was okay—Van tells us you sent them to get me and I need to come with them, because they've found Warren's body and they want me to verify that it's really Warren."

Alcide turned his back and shook his head from side to side. Mustapha looked down at the floor, his face a map of complex emotions.

"So Bill headed to the—away, with the hostage, and I got in the car with Van and them, and I realized pretty quick that they were rogues because you wouldn't have 'em. That Van . . ." And then I just didn't want to talk about him anymore.

"He hit you, huh?" Alcide said, turning back to eye my face. There was a moment of fraught silence. "He rape you?"

"Didn't have time," I said, glad to get that out of the way. "I don't know where they were taking me, but Mustapha shot the driver and got me out of the car, and here I am. So. Thank you, Mustapha."

He bobbed his head, still involved in his own thoughts, his own worry for his friend.

"Was there a woman with them, kind of quiet, about thirty?"

"Pixie haircut?"

Both the men looked blank. "Real short hair, light brown, tall woman?"

Alcide nodded vigorously. "Yes, that's her! She okay?"

"Yeah. She was sitting in the passenger front. Who is she?"

"She's my undercover," Alcide said.

"You have undercover agents?"

"Yeah, of course. Her name's Kandace. Kandace Moffett."

"Can you please explain all this?" I hated to sound stupid. Telepaths get used to knowing stuff, I guess.

"I'll give you the *Reader's Digest* version," he said, to my surprise. "But come in the bathroom and wash yourself off while I fill you in. Mustapha, man, I owe you."

"I know," Mustapha said. "Just help me find Warren. That's all I need."

Alcide hustled me into a bathroom right off the entrance hall. It was all granite countertops and pure white towels, and I felt like the nastiest thing the cat had ever drug in. Alcide didn't necessarily mind the blood, because that's not a Were hang-up, but I sure did. I turned on the shower and stepped under it after shucking my shoes, which were the cleanest things I was wearing. When Alcide's back was turned,

I stepped out of the waitress outfit and let it fall to the floor of the shower. I grabbed a washcloth, soaped it up, and began scrubbing. Alcide resolutely kept his eyes turned away.

"Start talking," I reminded him, and he did.

"After I talked to you about Jannalynn, I began to think about her pretty seriously," he said. "The more I took her recent actions apart, the more I thought I should look deeper. I figured out that Jannalynn was not telling me the truth about a few things. I wondered if maybe she was skimming off the top at Hair of the Dog." He shrugged. "Sometimes when she was supposed to be around, she was out of touch. I thought maybe her romance with Sam was going over the top, but when she'd tell me one thing about them, you didn't seem to know anything about it. And Sam's your partner, so you'd know, I figured."

So he'd called me to talk about Sam and Jannalynn's "wedding plans," at least in part to hear my reaction; of course, I'd been completely shocked.

"I saw her one time when she didn't see me. She was at a bar way across town, instead of at the Hair. And she was with the rogues I had turned down. I knew she was planning something. I'd had them all over at social evenings at the house, talked to 'em. The only one worth anything was Kandace, and she wasn't sure she wanted to be in a pack. Didn't like the power struggles. I got to respect that, but I thought she'd be an asset."

I thought maybe he'd also liked Kandace's assets, but that was his business.

"So I called up Kandace, and I asked her to meet me alone. Without me even bringing it up, she volunteered to tell me what was going on, because it troubled her."

Alcide clearly wanted me to give Kandace a virtual pat on the back, so I said, "She must be a good person."

He smiled, gratified. "Kandace said Jannalynn wanted to challenge me, defeat me, but first she wanted to get a good toehold in the pack by socking away some money, enlisting pack members to her side, getting some of her own muscle. Her proposal to these rogues was that they could come into the pack if they'd do her bidding; then when she beat me, she'd let them have full benefits."

I wondered if that included health and dental, but I wasn't going to go down a side path while he was still in a sharing mood. I hung up the washcloth and poured a dollop of shampoo into my hands. I began to scrub my scalp and hair. "Go on," I said, by way of encouragement.

"So," he said. "I got a guy she didn't know to follow Jannalynn. He saw her meeting with your buddy Claude. There's just no good reason for that."

I stopped rinsing the shampoo from my hair. "What . . . why? Why was she meeting with Claude, of all people?"

"I have no idea," Alcide said.

"So all we have to do is find Jannalynn and ask her a lot of questions," I said. "And find Warren. And hope that Claude comes back from Faery, so I can question him. And get Felipe and his vamps to leave us alone, here in Shreveport. And get that Freyda out of here."

Alcide looked at me, wondered whether to speak, and decided on full disclosure. "Is it true, Sookie? Palomino told Roy that Eric's engaged to a vampire from Oklahoma?"

"I can't talk about it," I said. "Or I'll get real upset, Alcide, and you just don't want that tonight. I owe Palomino a solid favor for getting us in to rescue . . . a guy, but she shouldn't be telling vampire business around town."

"You owe her more of a solid than you know," he said. "She saw you being grabbed, and she called me. Right before Bill did. That was smart, Sook, getting him to call. It was all I could do to get him to continue on his way and check back in later. I promised him I'd keep you safe."

"So you called Mustapha? You've known where he was all along?"

"No, but after I got your phone messages, I called him. As you'd advised, when Jannalynn wasn't around. He'd run down his last lead on Warren, and he had to talk to someone. I still don't know where he's been hiding."

"But it's thanks to you that he found me in time."

"Both our efforts and some guessing, too. He knows those rogues. He figured they'd head back to their house outside Fillmore. Van does bad stuff to women, and he'd want to have some time with you before he handed you over to Jannalynn. The follow-up car was his idea, too."

"Oh my God." I felt sick, wondered if I was going to throw up. No. I got hold of myself.

After a little rinsing, I was as clean as I was going to get. Alcide left the bathroom so I could change into my more modest shorts and T-shirt. It was really interesting how much difference a few covered inches could make in your self-respect. Now that I felt more like myself, I could begin to think some more.

I came out of the bathroom. Alcide was having a beer, and Mustapha was drinking a Coca-Cola. I accepted one, too, and the cold sweetness tasted wonderful going down.

"So what are you going to do with the rogues, for right now?" I asked.

"I'm going to stow them in a reinforced shed my dad built," Alcide said. Jackson, his dad, had owned a farm outside Shreveport where the pack could run at the full moon.

"So you have a special place to stow people," I said. "I'm sure

Jannalynn has a special place, too. You been thinking about where that might be?"

"Jannalynn's from Shreveport," Alcide said. "So, yeah, I've been thinking. She lives in the apartment above Hair of the Dog, so that's out. No place there; besides, we'd have heard Warren if he'd been stashed there, or we'd have smelled him."

"If he was alive," I said, very quietly.

"If he wasn't, definitely we'd have smelled him," Alcide said, and Mustapha nodded, his face expressionless.

"So where does she have of her own, a place she could be fairly sure no one else would go?"

"Her mom and dad retired to Florida last year," Alcide said. "But they sold their house. Our computer guy who works at the tax assessor's office couldn't find anything else in Jannalynn's name."

"You sure that house sold? In this market?"

"That's what she told me. And the sign was down, last time I went by," Alcide said.

Mustapha stirred. "It's on a big lot, and it's pretty far out of Shreveport," he said. "I was out that way once, driving with Jannalynn, when the pack was courting me. She said she used to ride dirt bikes out there. They had horses, too."

"Anyone can take down a sign," I said.

Alcide got a call just then and talked to the pack members who'd secured my abductors. They were on their way to Alcide's farm. "You don't have to be too civil," Alcide said into the phone, and I could hear the laughter that came from the other end of the line.

I'd been struck by another thought, and as we went out to Alcide's car, I said, "I guess growing up as a full-blooded Were in Shreveport,

Jannalynn would be pretty much bound to know all the others around her age. Even the kids who weren't full-blood."

Alcide and Mustapha shrugged, almost in unison. "We did," they said, and then smiled at each other, though their growing tension made that hard to do.

"Kym Rowe was half-Were and not much older than Jannalynn," I observed. "Her folks came out to my house. Her dad's Oscar, a full Were." Mustapha stopped in his tracks, his head bowed. "Mustapha, was it Jannalynn who made you let Kym into Eric's house?"

"Yeah," he said, and Alcide stopped and turned to him. His face was hard and accusing. Mustapha said to both of us, "She told me she had Warren. She told me I had to let this Rowe girl into the house. That was all I had to do."

"So it was her plan," I said carefully. "*Her* plan. To get Eric to drink from this girl?"

"No, it was not her plan," Mustapha said clearly. "She was hired to find a Were girl willing to carry it out, but it was the plan of this dude named Claude. I've seen him at your place. Your cousin?"

Chapter 13

I was shocked. I was more than shocked.

And the first coherent thought I had was, *If Dermot was in on this, it'll break my heart. Or I'll break his neck.*

In our long drive through the night to Jannalynn's parents' former place, I had more time than I needed to think, or maybe not enough. I was scrambling for some solid foothold, some sure thing. "Why?" I said out loud. "Why?"

"I sure don't know," Mustapha said. "The day I came to your house on the run, it was everything I could do to sit at the table with that Dermot and not try to choke it out of him."

"Why didn't you?"

"Because I didn't know if he was in on it. That Dermot, he's always nice, and he seems to have a lot of love for you. I just couldn't see him stabbing you in the back like that. Or taking Warren, either, though I could see he might think that wasn't so bad—not knowing Warren, hardly knowing me."

I had to assume it had been Claude's blood that had made Kym so irresistible to Eric.

"Dammit," I said, and leaned forward to bury my face in my hands. I was glad to be sitting in the backseat where neither of them could see my face.

"Sookie, we'll figure all this out," Alcide said. He sounded very confident and strong. "We'll get this all taken care of. We'll clear Eric with the police."

From which I understood he was scared I'd start crying. I could sort of sympathize with that, and, anyway, first things first. I was kind of beyond crying. I'd already shed enough tears.

Glancing out the window, I saw we were now in a suburban area where the lots were at least four acres; maybe this had been out in the country once upon a time, until Shreveport had grown.

"It's right around here," Mustapha said, and when we saw a white fence bordering the road, he said, "This is it. I remember the fence."

There was a horse gate across the driveway, and I hopped out to move it because I just wanted to get out of the car. They drove through and I followed them. It was completely dark out here, no streetlights. There was a security light in the front yard, but that was it. No lights on in the ranch-style house or in the freestanding garage a few feet behind it, where the driveway terminated. A dilapidated swing set rusted in the front yard. I pictured little Jannalynn playing on it, and found myself picturing a swing hitting her in the head.

I grimly erased that image and joined the two men who'd gotten out of the car to stand uncertainly in the noisy night. The crickets and all the other myriad bugs of Louisiana were having a concert in the woods that bordered the property. I heard a dog bark, far away.

"Now we break in," Alcide said, and I said, "Wait."

"But—" Mustapha began.

"Be quiet," I said, finally feeling that there was something I could do rather than get swept into events as they passed me by. I sent out my other sense, the one that had shaped my life, the one given me at my birth by the demon Mr. Cataliades. I searched and searched, looking for the signature of a mind, and just when I was going to give up, I felt a faint flicker of thought. "There is someone," I said very quietly. "There is someone."

"Where?" Mustapha asked eagerly.

"In the attic over the garage," I said, and it was like I'd fired off the starting gun. Werewolves are creatures of action, after all.

There were outside stairs on the side of the garage, which I hadn't seen. The sharper eyes of Alcide and Mustapha had, and up they swarmed. Mustapha, catching a scent he recognized, threw back his head and howled. It made my hair stand up. I moved to the foot of the steps, and though I still couldn't see much, I could make out the two figures on the landing above beginning a furious motion. It accompanied a rhythmic thud. I realized the two men were throwing themselves against a door. There was a *ka-BANG* that had to be the door flying back, and then a light came on.

Mustapha howled again, and I feared that Warren was dead.

I just couldn't stand it; the death of the little blond sharpshooter with his pale freckled skin and his missing teeth was somehow more than I could bear tonight. I sank to my knees.

"Sookie," Alcide said urgently.

I looked up. Mustapha was coming down the stairs, a body in his arms. Alcide was right in front of me.

"He's alive," Alcide said. "But he's been up there without air-conditioning or ventilation or food or water for God knows how long. I guess the bitch couldn't be bothered. We got to get him some help."

"Vampire blood?" I suggested, but very quietly.

"I think Mustapha might consider that now," Alcide said, and I knew that Warren must be very bad.

I called Bill. "Sookie, where are you?" he yelled. "I've been calling! What happened?"

I glanced at the screen. I did have a lot of missed calls. "I had the phone on vibrate," I said. "I'll tell you everything, but I want to ask you a favor first. Are you still in Shreveport?"

"Yes, I'm back outside the Trifecta, trying to pick up the trail of those dogs!"

"Hey, listen, chill. It's been a real bad night. I need you now, my friend."

"Anything."

"Meet me at Alcide's. You can save a life."

"I'm on my way."

On our way back into Shreveport, Mustapha took my place in the backseat with Warren's head on his lap. When I proposed that Bill give Warren a drink to help him live, Mustapha said, "If it can bring him back, I'll do it. He may hate me later. Hell, I may hate myself. But we got to save him."

Our drive back into Alcide's neighborhood was shorter than our drive out because we knew our way now, but we grudged every stop-light or slow driver ahead of us, and Mustapha's urgency pounded at me. Warren's brain signature became weaker, flickered, resumed.

Sure enough, Bill was standing waiting at Alcide's, and I leaped out of the car and pulled Bill around to the backseat. When the door opened and he saw Warren, recognition flared in his eyes. Of course, Bill knew Mustapha, and he remembered Warren the shooter. I hoped it hadn't occurred to Bill that it might be a good thing if he died, since he was yet another witness who could testify—at least in a limited way—to what had happened the night we'd killed Victor.

"He wasn't in the club," I said, grabbing Bill's wrist, as Mustapha gently lifted Warren's head so he could vacate the car to leave room for Bill.

And Bill looked at me, a huge question on his face.

"Feed him," I said. Without another word, Bill knelt by the car, bit his own wrist, and held the bleeding wrist over Warren's parched mouth.

I don't know if Warren would have done it if he hadn't been so thirsty. At first, Bill's blood trickling into the slack mouth seemed to raise no reaction. But then something sparked in Warren, and he began to consciously drink. I could see his throat moving.

"Enough," I said, after a minute. I could sense Warren's brain firing back up. "Now, take him to the hospital, and they'll do all the right stuff for him."

"But they'll know." Alcide was scowling at me, and so was Mustapha. "They'll question him about who took him." Bill, standing and holding his wrist, looked only mildly interested.

"You don't want the police to arrest Jannalynn?" That seemed like the best of all possible worlds to me.

"She'd kill them if they tried," Alcide said, but I knew from the conflict flowing from his head that he wasn't voicing his real concern.

"You want to punish her," I said, in as neutral a voice as I could manage.

"Course he does," Mustapha said. "She's pack. She's his to punish."

"I do want to ask her some questions," I said. It seemed like the right time to get that out in the open. Otherwise, Jannalynn might end up dead before I'd had a chance to extract information.

"What about Sam?" Bill said, out of the blue.

"What about him?" Alcide asked after a moment.

"He's not gonna be happy," I muttered. "They weren't ever as close as she told you they were, but after all . . ."

"She's his woman," Mustapha said, shrugging. He looked down at Warren. Just then Warren's eyes fluttered open. He saw Mustapha and smiled. "I knew you'd find me," he said. "I knew you'd come."

It was touching, it was awkward, and I was totally confused.

"So it was Claude," I said out loud. "I just can't believe it. Why would he want Eric to drink from a borderline whore like Kym? Why would he give her his own blood to drink?" I was beyond mincing words, or being charitable.

"Claude could tell you why," Bill said grimly. "Where is he now?"

"Niall came to get him. I haven't seen Claude in days."

"And he left Dermot here?"

"Yeah, he left Dermot in charge of all the stray supes at Hooligans," I said.

"I'd heard everyone there was some form of fae," Bill said, confirming my belief that supes gossiped just like humans did. "Did Claude give you a time for his return?"

"No. Niall took him to Faery to investigate who actually put a curse on Dermot. Claude said it was Murry, but Murry's dead. I killed him, in my backyard." I sure had everyone's attention now. It seemed that all the separate parts of my life were finally colliding. My personal highway was jammed with fairies, werewolves, vampires, and humans.

"So it was pretty convenient for Claude to name Murry as the bad guy," Bill said, and that kind of hung in the air for a minute before everything came crashing down.

"Claude," I said. "It was Claude all along." I felt numb.

After a little while, we were all sorted out. Since no one knew where Jannalynn was, Mustapha and Warren were invited to spend the night at Alcide's, and Mustapha accepted for them both since Warren was still not talking much. Apparently, he wasn't going to go to the hospital, which I had to accept. At least he was getting a bottle of Gatorade. Mustapha let him have it in little sips.

Bill and I got in his car, and Mustapha thanked Bill for coming to Warren's aid. He didn't like telling Bill he owed him a favor, but he did it.

Alcide was already on the phone as we pulled out of the driveway, and I was sure he was checking on his pack members who'd locked up the rogues. I would put money on his main interest being Kandace. I didn't know if she'd go into lockup with the rogues or if she'd abandon the pretense of being a rebel. At the moment, I could only be glad that wasn't my problem.

I was glad Bill was driving. I had too many thoughts crowding my head. I wished there were a way to warn Niall what a snake he was nurturing in his bosom. And as long as I was getting biblical, I'd never in my life been so glad I'd said no to someone when they'd wanted to have sex with me.

"Why would Claude have done such a thing?"

I didn't realize I'd said it out loud until Bill answered.

"Sookie, I don't know. I can't even guess. He doesn't hate Eric, or at least I can't think of any reason why he should. He might be envious you have such a handsome lover, but that's hardly sufficient reason . . ."

I wasn't about to tell Bill that Claude had told me he occasionally bedded a real woman. Eric would surely have been more in Claude's natural ballpark.

"Okay, let's think," I said. "Why would he try to make trouble in such a devious way? He could have set fire to my house." (Though that had already been done.) "He could try to shoot me." (Ditto.) "He could abduct me and torture me." (Likewise.) "If his goal was to make trouble for Eric, there were at least twenty more direct ways to cause it."

"Yes," Bill said. "But a direct way would have led straight back to him. It's the indirectness of it, the slyness of it, that convinces me that Claude wanted to stay in your good graces, stay close to you."

"It's not out of love. I can tell you that."

"Is there something I don't know about, Sookie? Some reason Claude would want your company, want to live in your house and stay close to you?" After a moment of silence, Bill hurried to add, "Not that any sane male wouldn't want to, even someone like Claude who likes other men."

"Why, yes, Bill," I said, "And it's funny you should bring that up. As a matter of fact, there *is* such a reason."

Though I clammed up then because I didn't need to spread the word any wider, I was fuming. I might as well get "I HAVE A CLUVIEL DOR" tattooed on my forehead. *Thanks, Grandfather Fintan, for the great gift.* And while I was at it, *Thanks, Sponsor Cataliades, for the telepathy.* And *also* while I was angry at people in my past—*Thanks, Gran, for (a) having an affair with a fairy and (b) not using the cluviel dor while you had the chance and, therefore, sticking me with it.*

I had to talk myself down a little bit after that internal explosion of rage, all the more powerful because it was silent.

I took a deep breath and let it out, as Bill had advised me to do earlier in the evening. The procedure did let off some steam and gave me the control necessary to clap some discipline onto my thoughts. One of the things I really like about Bill is that he didn't pester me with questions while I was working through all this. He just drove.

"I can't talk about it now," I said. "I'm sorry."

"Can you tell me if you've heard from Niall or Claude since they left?"

"No, I haven't. I put a letter through . . . that is, I sent them a letter because Dermot's having a hard time controlling the remaining fae. I'm sure you know they're getting restless."

"They are not alone," Bill said darkly.

"And you're referring to what?" I was too tired and upset to make any guesses.

"All our guests are still here—Felipe, Horst, Angie," he said. "It's like having a visit from a king in the eighteenth century. You could be poor after such an honor. And they've bonded mightily with the stupid wrestler—T-Rex. Felipe even talks of asking him if he wants to be brought over. Felipe thinks he would make a popular spokesman for the pro-vampire movement."

"Is Freyda still here, too?" I was humiliated that I had to ask Bill to know the answer, but I wanted to know the answer so badly that I would accept the humiliation.

"Yes. She's spending as much time with Eric as he'll permit her."

"I didn't get the impression that she was in the habit of waiting for permission."

"You're absolutely right. I can't decide if Eric is genuinely trying to discourage her or if he's driving up his price."

I felt like Bill had slapped me.

He said instantly, "Sweetheart, I'm so sorry. I should have kept my mouth shut." He sounded genuinely contrite, but I didn't trust anyone anymore.

"You really think Eric's capable of that?"

"Sookie, you *know* Eric's capable of that, and much more." Bill shrugged. "I won't be less than honest with you. And I won't sugarcoat this situation. From my point of view, Eric's involvement with Freyda is a wonderful thing. But for your sake, I hope Eric is so deeply devoted to you that he's determined to drive Freyda to a more amenable mate."

"He loves me." I sounded like a terrified child telling her father that she *really, really* wasn't afraid of the dark. I despised that in myself.

"Yes, he does," Bill agreed readily.

That conversation was clearly over, and it was one we wouldn't have again.

I had a fantasy that when we got to my house, Eric would be sitting on the back steps waiting for me. He would have ditched all his Nevada company. He would be waiting to assure me that he had sent Freyda packing, that he'd told her how much he loved me, that he never wanted to leave me no matter how much power and wealth she offered him. He would be shooting a final bird at his maker, Appius Livius Ocella. All the vampires in his sheriffdom would be happy about his decision because they liked me so much.

As long as I was having a fantasy, I decided to build on it. In the daylight, Claude would return to my house with Niall. Niall would say that he had brainwashed Claude, and that Claude was now an agreeable person who regretted any of his past deeds that had offended others. They both embraced Dermot as an equal and took him back to Faery with them, along with all the other fae at Hooligans. I could be sure they would be happy forever, since it was a fairy tale.

Then I mentally married off Jason and Michele and gave them

three little boys. I married off Terry and Jimmie and gave their Catahoulas many litters. I named Alcide packmaster for life and threw in a happy marriage to Kandace and a resultant daughter. I gave the du Rone twins full scholarships to Tulane, and for Sam . . . I simply couldn't think of the best gift for Sam. Of course, the bar would prosper, but with his tendency to fall for women on the supernatural side . . . well, the bar would prosper. Quinn would live happily ever after with his tigress, Tijgerin, and she would be able to rehabilitate the unpleasant Frannie, who would become a nurse.

I was probably skipping a few people. Oh, yeah, Holly and Hoyt. They'd have a girl and a boy, and Holly's son by her first marriage would love his stepdad and his new siblings. Hoyt's lifelong friendship with my brother would never come between the couple again, because my brother would never drag Hoyt into trouble. Again.

India would find some fine young woman, and the state of Louisiana would pass a bill to enable them to get married legally. No one would ever, ever make lesbian jokes or misquote scripture at them . . . as long as I was fantasizing.

"Bill, what's your favorite fantasy?" I asked. Weirdly enough, I felt much better after designing all these happy endings.

Bill glanced over at me quizzically. We were almost to my house. "My favorite fantasy? You come down into my daytime resting place stark naked," he said, and I could see the gleam of his teeth as he smiled. "Oh, wait," Bill said. "That's already happened."

"There's gotta be more to it," I said. Then I could have bitten off my tongue.

"Oh, there is." His eyes told me exactly what happened after that.

"And that's your fantasy? That I come into your house naked and have sex with you?"

"After that, you tell me that you have sent Eric on his way, that you want to be mine forever, and that to share my life you will permit me to make you a vampire like me."

The silence now was thick, and the fun had drained out of the fantasy.

Then Bill added, "You know what I'd say when you told me this? I'd tell you I would never do such a thing. Because I love you."

And this, ladies and gentlemen, concluded our evening's entertainment.

Chapter 14

When I woke up in my own bed, the sun was glaring outside. I did not have to work today; getting to skip on your special day was a Merlotte's rule. Last night had been an incredible night, all in all. I'd rescued two hostages, helped to get a bunch of bad rogue Weres off the streets, and begun unraveling a conspiracy. Hard to top that!

I'd also been kidnapped and bitterly disillusioned.

I wanted to look good because my spirits were so low. When I was getting dressed to run errands and to go to an appointment I'd made days before, I put on my makeup and brushed my hair up into a ponytail that cascaded down from the crown of my head. While I was cleaning out my purse in the process of finding a pair of earrings, my hand closed around the cluviel dor. I pulled it out and gazed down at it, the pale green soothing any anxiety I had about the day to come.

I rubbed it between my hands and enjoyed the warmth and the smoothness.

I wondered (for the fiftieth time) if I needed any special spell to activate its magic. On the whole, I figured not. My grandmother would have passed such a spell along to me, though as a staunch Christian she disapproved of magic. But she wouldn't have neglected some element I might find necessary for my protection.

I should put it back into my makeup drawer with the usual light camouflage. But I didn't. After a brief debate, I slid the round object into my skirt pocket. I understood, finally, that having it was no good if it was inaccessible. Leaving it in the drawer was equivalent to having an unloaded gun when burglars broke into your house.

From now on, the cluviel dor went where I went.

If Eric . . . if he decided to leave with Freyda, would I use it? According to Mr. Cataliades, since I loved Eric, if I made a wish for him, it would be granted. I tried to picture myself saying, "Eric must not choose to go with Freyda."

On the other hand . . . if he decided to go with the queen, he loved me less than he loved the possibilities in his future with her. Would I want to stay with someone on those terms?

A lot of bad things could happen today, but I was going to keep my fingers crossed that they wouldn't. I just wanted one happy day.

As I was getting up from the dressing table, I had second thoughts about leaving the cluviel dor in my pocket. Was it really safe to carry such an irreplaceable object around with me? Apparently all the fae collected at Hooligans could tell there was something special about me despite my minimal dash of fairy blood. That special thing must be my proximity to, or ownership of, the cluviel dor. I shouldn't underestimate how much they'd want it if they knew I had it, not with their terrible desire to be back in the world they loved. I hesitated, pondered again replacing it in the drawer.

But then I thought, *Unloaded gun.* And I popped it from my pocket into my purse, which latched shut and was therefore more secure.

I heard a car pull up outside. I looked out the living room windows to see that my caller was Detective Cara Ambroselli. I shrugged. I wasn't going to let anything bother me today.

She came in with a sidekick, a young guy whose name I couldn't remember. He had short brown hair, brown eyes, undistinguished clothes, and he wasn't tall or very thin or very muscular or very anything. Even his thoughts were fairly neutral. He was nuts about Ambroselli, that was something about him I could empathize with. And Ambroselli simply thought of him as her adjutant.

"This is Jay Osborn," Detective Ambroselli said. "You're all dressed up today."

"I have an appointment this morning," I said. "I can only give you a few minutes." I waved my hand at the couch, and I sat opposite them.

Osborn was looking around the room, recognizing the age of the house, of its furnishings. Ambroselli was concentrating on me.

"T-Rex is quite a fan of yours," she said.

It was lucky I'd been warned ahead of time. "That's pretty weird," I said. "I just met him the night Kym Rowe got killed. And I have a boyfriend." Theoretically.

"He's called me to see if I'd give up your phone number."

"I guess that says it all, that he doesn't have it." I shrugged.

Then we went over the evening at Eric's again, from beginning to end. But just when I thought we'd wound up, Ambroselli decided to throw in one last question.

"Were you late that night because you wanted to make a big entrance?"

I blinked. "Huh?"

"Coming in late to get T-Rex's attention?" She was asking questions at random. She didn't believe this.

"If I'd wanted to get his attention, I guess I would have come earlier to spend as much time with him as I could," I said. "The ladies he was with were good-looking women, and I don't know why he'd be specially interested in me."

"Maybe your vampire boyfriend wanted T-Rex to be his friend. Couldn't hurt to have a popular guy like a wrestler on your side, in public opinion."

"I don't think I'm the strongest bribe Eric could come up with," I said. I laughed.

Ambroselli was at an impasse in the case. She was hoping that by going from witness to witness and scattering half-truths and asking questions she might stir up some fact that she could use. Though I could sort of sympathize with her, she was wasting my time.

"T-Rex hasn't called me, and I don't expect him to," I said, after a moment. "If you'll excuse me, I have to leave myself."

Ambroselli and Osborn stood and slowly took their departure, trying to look as though they'd learned something significant.

When I got to Bon Temps, I dropped by to pick up my dishes from Tara's house. The twins were asleep. Tara was slumped on the couch, almost dozing herself. I was glad I'd knocked very quietly. I think she would have thrown the pans at my head if I'd woken up Sara and Rob.

"Where's JB?" I whispered.

"He went to get some more diapers," she whispered back.

"How's the breastfeeding going?"

"I feel like Elsie the cow," she said. "I don't know why I even button my blouse."

"Is it hard? To get them to nurse?"

"About as hard as getting a vampire to bite you," she said.

I grinned. It was nice to hear that Tara could joke about something that had once made her crazy.

"By the way," Tara said as I turned to go, "Is there something weird going on at Hooligans?"

"What do you mean?" I jerked around, very much on the alert.

"Maybe that answers my question," she said. "That was quite a reaction, Sookie."

I had no idea how to answer her. I said, "Has JB had any trouble there?"

"No, he loves everybody on the strip team," she said. "We finally had a good talk about it. You know, and I know, that he loves to be admired, bless his heart. And there's a lot to admire about JB."

I nodded. He was lovely. Not bright; never that. But lovely.

"But he thinks there's something wrong?"

"He's noticed some strange things," she said carefully. "None of the other guys could ever meet him for lunch, and they could never tell him what their day job was, and they seemed to pretty much live at the club."

I didn't know what to tell her. "I wonder how JB got hired," I said, to fill in until I could think of a good way to warn her off Hooligans. I was sure the du Rones still needed extra money, though the twins had been able to leave the hospital at the regular time.

"How he got hired? He'd heard about Ladies Only night from the women at the gym, and they all told him he was built well enough to perform," Tara said rather proudly. "So one day he went over to Hooligans on his lunch hour." One of the babies started fussing, and Tara darted into their tiny room to emerge with Sara. Or Robbie. "If one starts crying, the other one will," she whispered. She jiggled the baby gently, humming to the child. It was as if she'd been a mother for years, instead of a few days. When the little head rested on her chest, she murmured, "Anyway, your cousin Claude said since JB'd helped you recover from your ordeal—did he mean your car wreck?—that he'd give JB a job. Also . . ." She met my eyes briefly. "Remember, I met Claude when I was pregnant? He was the one who told me I'd have twins that day in the park? He told JB he understood a father has to provide for his children."

It hadn't been a car wreck I needed to recover from, but torture, of course. JB had helped me with physical therapy for weeks; I did remember telling Claude about that. Ha! Claude's kindness to JB was a good thing to hear, especially at this point in time. But I knew what my cousin really was, and I knew he was scheming some terrible thing.

I left the little house after running a finger over the soft, soft baby cheek. "You're so lucky," I whispered to Tara.

"I tell myself that every day," she said. "Every day." In my friend's head, I could see the kaleidoscope of miserable scenes that had composed her childhood: her alcoholic parents, the parade of drug users through her home, her own determination to rise above the shack, rise above the degradation and squalor. This small, neat house, these beautiful babies, a sober husband—this was heaven to Tara.

"Take care of yourself, Sookie," she said, looking at me with some anxiety. She hadn't been my friend this long for nothing.

"You just watch out for those young'uns. Don't you worry about me. I'm doing okay." I gave my friend the most convincing smile

I could summon, and I let myself out of the house very quietly, easing the door shut.

I went to the drive-through at the bank to use the ATM, and then I drove to the newly opened law offices of Beth Osiecki and Jarrell Hilburn. There were those who would argue that Bon Temps was overburdened with lawyers, but all of them seemed to be busy and thriving, and since Sid Matt Lancaster, who'd had a huge practice, had recently passed away, all his clients needed new representation.

Why'd I picked the new kids on the block?

For that very reason: They were new, and I didn't know them, and they didn't know me. I wanted to start with a clean slate. I'd seen Hilburn before, for my transaction with Sam. Today I was seeing Osiecki, who specialized in estate planning. And since she was new, she'd agreed to see me on a Saturday.

A girl barely out of her teens was sitting at the receptionist's desk in the tiny anteroom of the storefront office. Osiecki and Hilburn had rented the first floor of an old building right off the square. The electrical system would need overhauling, I was sure, but they'd painted and brought in good secondhand office furniture. Some potted plants made everything look a little nicer, and there wasn't any canned music playing, which was a huge plus. The girl, who didn't even have a name plaque, beamed at me and checked her appointment book, which had large white spaces.

"You must be Ms. Stackhouse," she said.

"Yes. I have an appointment with Ms. Osiecki?" I sounded out the name.

"Oh-seek-ee," she said very quietly, presumably so the owner of the name wouldn't hear her correction.

I nodded, to show I'd gotten it now.

"I'll see if she's ready," the girl said, leaping to her feet and making her way to the little corridor leading to the rest of the space. There was a door on the left and a door on the right, and after that the area seemed to widen into a common space. I could glimpse a big table and a bookcase full of heavy books, the kind of books I would never pick up to read.

I heard a brisk knock and a murmur, and then the teenager was back. "Ms. Osiecki will see you now," she said, with an expansive sweep of her hand.

I went back to talk to Ms. Osiecki after taking a deep breath.

A woman of about thirty stood up from her broad desk. She had well-cut short red-streaked brown hair, blue eyes, and brown glasses. She was wearing a nice white blouse and a wildly flowered skirt and high-heeled sandals. She was smiling.

"I'm Beth Osiecki," she said, in case I'd gotten lost between the reception area and her office.

"Sookie Stackhouse," I said, shaking the outstretched hand.

She glanced down at the pad, and I could see she was going over the notes she'd scribbled the day before when I'd called her. She looked over at the big Scenic Louisiana poster by her desk. "Well," she said, shooting me a quizzical look. "It really is a special day for you, isn't it? It's your birthday, and you're going to make your will."

I felt a little strange after I left the lawyers' office. I guess there's nothing to make you think about your own demise like making your will. It's also a literally do-or-die moment. When your will is read, it will be the last time people will hear your voice: the last expression of your will and your wishes, the last statement from your heart. It had been a strangely revelatory hour.

Beth Osiecki was going to put everything in legalese, and I had to come in day after tomorrow and sign it. Just in case, I told her, I'd like to sign a list of the points I'd made. The list was in my own handwriting. I asked her if that would make it legal.

"Sure," she'd said. She'd smiled. I could tell that she was adding to her meager store of "strange client" stories, and that was okay with me.

When I left Beth Osiecki's office, I was pretty proud of myself. I'd made a will.

I couldn't quite figure out what to do next. It was three in the afternoon. I'd had a late breakfast, and a full lunch was out of the question. I didn't need to go to the library; I had several library books I hadn't read yet. I could go home and sunbathe, which was always a pleasant pastime, but then I'd sweat all over my good makeup and my clean hair. I was in danger of doing that now, standing here on the sidewalk. The sun was glaring down ferociously. I figured it was at least a hundred degrees. My cell phone rang as I hesitated to touch the handle of my car door.

"Hello?" I fished a tissue out of my purse and used it to cover my fingers as I opened the door. The heat rolled out.

"Sookie? How are you?"

"Quinn?" I couldn't believe it. "I'm so glad to hear from you."

"Happy birthday," he said.

I could feel my lips curve up in an involuntary smile. "You remembered!" I said. "Thanks!" I was absurdly pleased. I hadn't exactly thought Tara would be thinking about my birthday, since she'd just brought twins home from the hospital, but maybe I'd been a tiny bit flattened when she hadn't mentioned it this morning.

"Hey, a birthday is an important day," the weretiger said. I hadn't seen him since Sam's brother's wedding. It was good to hear his deep voice.

"How are you?" I hesitated for a moment before adding, "How's Tijgerin?" The last time I'd seen Quinn, he'd just met the beautiful and single and one-of-the-last-of-her-kind weretigress. I don't think I have to draw you a picture.

"I'm . . . ah . . . going to be a father."

Wow. "Way to go!" I said. "So you guys have moved in together? Where are you living?"

"That's not exactly the way we do it, Sookie."

"Um. Okay. What's the tiger procedure?"

"Tiger men don't bring up their young. Only the tiger mom."

"Gosh, that seems kind of old-fashioned." And kind of wrong.

"To me, too. But Tij's real traditional. She says that when she has the baby, she'll go into hiding until he's weaned. Her mom told her that if it's a boy I might see him as a threat." I couldn't read Quinn's mind over the phone, but he sounded plenty exasperated and not a little resentful.

As far as I knew—and I'd done a little reading on tigers when I was Quinn's girlfriend—only males who were not the actual dads were apt to kill tiger cubs. But since this was totally none of my business, I choked back the indignation I felt on Quinn's behalf. At least, I tried to.

So she'd used him to get pregnant with a weretiger baby and now she didn't want to see him anymore?

I told myself sternly, *Not my battle.* (Werewolves were much more modern in their thinking. Even werepanthers!)

Since my silence had lasted too long, I leaped in with both feet.

"Well, I'm so happy that you'll have a cub, since there aren't many of you-all left. I guess your mama and your sister are excited?"

"Uh . . . well, my mom is pretty sick. She brightened up a lot when I told her, but it was just temporary. She's back in that nursing home. Frannie found a guy, and she took off with him last month. I'm not really sure where she is."

"Quinn, that's so tough. I'm really sorry."

"But I'm raining on your birthday, and I didn't mean to. I really did call you to tell you to have a great day, Sookie. No one deserves it more." He hesitated, and I could tell there were more words that he wanted to say. "Maybe you could call me sometime?" he asked. "Tell me what you ended up doing to celebrate?"

I tried to do some concentrated thinking in a very short time, but I just wasn't up to figuring out all the cracks and crevices in this tentative overture. "Maybe," I said. "I hope I do something worth talking about. So far, all I've done is make my will."

There was a long moment of silence. "You're kidding," he said.

"You know I'm not."

There was a serious silence.

"You need me to come?"

"Oh, gosh, no," I said, putting a smile in my voice. "I've got the house, the car, a little money saved up. It just seemed like time." I hoped I wasn't lying. "Well, I gotta go, Quinn. I'm so glad you called. It made the day special for me." I snapped the phone shut and dropped it into my purse.

I got in the slightly less-hot car and tried to think of somewhere fun to go, something fun to do. I'd picked up the newspaper and checked my mailbox on my way to town, and hadn't pulled out anything but my auto insurance bill and a Wal-Mart ad leaflet.

I decided I was just hungry enough to treat myself to something special. I went to Dairy Queen and got an Oreo Blizzard. I ate it inside since it was way too hot to sit in the car. I said hello to a couple of people and had a brief chat with India, who came in with one of her little nieces in tow.

My cell phone rang again. Sam. "Sook," he said, "can you come by the bar? We're short a case of Heineken and two of Michelob, and I need to know what happened." He sounded pretty snappish. Damn.

"It's my day off."

"Hey, you pretty much bought into the business. You gotta pull your share of the weight."

I mouthed a very bad word at the phone. "Okay," I said, sounding just as irritated as I felt. "I'm coming. But I'm not staying."

I strode through the employee entrance as if I were on my way into a bullfight ring. The *hell* we were short three cases of beer. "Sam," I called, "you in your office?"

"Yeah, come here," he called back. "I think I found the problem."

I flung open his office door and everybody in the world shrieked in my face. "Oh my God!" I said, shocked to the core.

After a throbbing moment, I understood that I was having a surprise birthday party.

JB was there, and Terry and his girlfriend, Jimmie. Sam, Hoyt and Holly, Jason and Michele, Halleigh Bellefleur, Danny and Kennedy. Even Jane Bodehouse.

"Tara had to stay with the babies," JB said, handing me a little package.

Terry said, "We thought about giving you a puppy, but Jimmie said we better check with you first." Jimmie winked at me over his shoulder.

Sam held me so tight I thought I'd quit breathing, and I thumped him on his shoulder. "You creep," I said in his ear. "Missing cases of beer! I like that!"

"You should have heard your voice," he said, laughing. "Jannalynn said to tell you she was sorry she couldn't make it. She had to open at Hair of the Dog."

Sure, I believed she was really unhappy at not being here. I turned away so Sam wouldn't see my face.

Halleigh apologized for Andy's absence, too; he was on duty. Danny and Kennedy gave me a kind of group hug, and Jane Bodehouse gave me a highly alcoholic kiss on the cheek. Michele held my hand for a moment and said, "I hope you have a wonderful year this year. Will you be my bridesmaid?" I grinned wide enough to split my face and told her I'd be proud to stand up with her. Jason wrapped one arm around me and handed me a beribboned box.

"I didn't expect presents. I'm too old for a present party," I protested.

"Never too old for presents," Sam said.

My eyes were so full of tears I had a hard time unwrapping Jason's gift. He'd given me a bracelet my grandmother used to wear, a little gold chain with pearls set at intervals. I was shocked to see it. "Where was this?" I asked.

"I was cleaning the pie-crust table I got out of the attic, and it was pushed way in the back of that shallow drawer, caught on a splinter," he said. "All I could think of was Gran, and I knew you'd wear it."

I let the tears run out, then. "That's the sweetest thing," I said. "The nicest thing you've ever done."

"Here," said Jane, as eagerly as a child. She put a little gift bag in my hand. I smiled and dug my hand in. Jane had given me five "get a free car wash" coupons from the place her son worked. I was able to thank her sincerely. "I'll use every one," I promised her.

Hoyt and Holly had gotten me a bottle of wine, Danny and Kennedy had gotten me an electric knife sharpener, and JB and Tara had regifted me with one of the five slow cookers they'd gotten when they got married. I was glad to get it.

Sam handed me a heavy envelope. "You open that later," he said gruffly. I gave him a narrow-eyed look. "All right," I said. "If that's what you want."

"Yeah," he said. "It's what I want."

Halleigh had made her version of Caroline Bellefleur's chocolate cake, and I cut it so everyone could have a piece, Dairy Queen Blizzard be damned. It was marvelous. "I think that's better than Miss Caroline's," I said, which was close to heresy in Bon Temps.

"I put a pinch of cinnamon in," she whispered.

After the party I went out the front to get birthday hugs from India, now on duty, and Danielle, who was working in my place.

Halleigh wanted me to come over to her house to see the nursery, which was completely ready for its expected occupant. I was so glad to be with a happy person who had no agenda. The visit was a real treat.

After that, I had a quick supper with my grandmother's friend. Maxine, Hoyt's mom, had been a couple of decades younger than Gran, but they'd been tight. Maxine was so happy about Hoyt's wedding that I was feeling really cheerful after this visit; plus, Maxine had told me some funny stories about Gran. It was nice to remember that side of Gran, the familiar side, instead of thinking of her affair with Fintan. Dang, that had knocked me for a loop. Thanks to Maxine, I had a nice hour remembering the Gran I'd always thought I knew.

It grew dark as I drove home. Today was so much better than

yesterday. I couldn't believe how lucky I was to have such good friends. The warm night seemed benevolent instead of scorching. I had a good time singing along with the radio since there was no one to hear my awful voice.

I'd hoped to at least get some phone messages from my vampire friends—of course, I'd been hoping to hear from Eric most of all. But my cell phone didn't chirp on the drive back to my place. I stopped briefly at the end of the driveway to collect my local newspaper, and then I drove up to the house.

It wasn't a total surprise—but it was a total relief—to find that they were waiting for me. Pam's car was parked at the back of the house, and Bill, Eric, and Pam were sitting in lawn chairs in my backyard. Pam was wearing a low-cut flowered T-shirt and white cropped pants as a nod to the season—not that the temperature made any difference to her. Her high cork sandals were a great finishing touch.

"Hi, you-all!" I said, gathering all my gifts up out of the backseat. I gave Pam a special nod to acknowledge her ensemble. "What's up at Fangtasia?"

"We came to wish you a happy day," Eric said. "And I suppose, as usual, Bill will want to express his undying love that surpasses my love, as he'll tell you—and Pam will want to say something sarcastic and nearly painful, while reminding you that she loves you, too."

Bill and Pam looked decidedly miffed at Eric's preemptive strike, but I wasn't going to let anything dim my mood.

"And what about you, Eric?" I asked on counterattack. "Are you going to tell me that you love me just as much as Bill, but in a practical way, while finding some way to subtly threaten me and simultaneously remind me that you may be leaving with Freyda?" I bared my teeth at him in a ferocious smile as I trotted by the trio on my way up my back steps. I unlocked the screen door, crossed the porch, unlocked the kitchen door, and went inside with my armful.

After dumping the presents on the kitchen table, I stepped back out onto the porch and opened the screen door. "Any of you have anything new to say?" I looked from one to the other. "Or shall I just consider all this as said?" Pam was looking away to hide her grin.

"Just that he was right," Bill said, smiling openly. "I do love you more than Eric does. Have a great night, Sookie. Here is a gift for you." He held out a little box with a bow on it, and I extended my arm to take it.

"Thank you, Mr. Compton," I said, returning his smile, and he strode off into the woods. At the edge, he turned to blow me a kiss.

Pam said, "Sookie, I brought you something, too. I never thought I'd want to spend time with a human, but you're more tolerable than most. I hope no one hurts you on your birthday." As birthday wishes went, that kind of sucked, but it was genuine Pam. I stepped down off the porch to give her a hug. She returned it, which made me smile. You never knew with Pam. Her touch was cold and she smelled of vampire. I was very fond of her. She produced a small box, highly decorated, and pressed it into my hand.

She stepped back and looked from me to Eric. "I'll leave you two to whatever talk you want to have," she said, her voice neutral. Eric was her maker, and there was a limit to the verbal abuse she could deal out. In a moment she was gone.

"Won't you give me a hug, too?" Eric looked down at me, one eyebrow hiked up.

"Before I start giving out hugs to you I need to know what our situation is," I said. I sat down on the back steps, setting my presents carefully to the side. Eric sat down, too.

I wasn't happy anymore, of course, but I was much calmer than I'd thought I'd be when I'd realized we had to have this conversation. "I think you owe it to me to level with me," I began. "For weeks, it seems like we haven't really been a couple, though you still tell everyone I'm your wife. Lately, that's just meant we have sex. I know it's a tradition that guys don't like relationship talks. I don't think I do, either. But we have to have one."

"Let's go inside."

"No. That might end up with us in bed. Before we do that again, we need to have an understanding between us."

"I love you." The security light glinted off his blond hair and was swallowed in his all-black getup. He'd dressed for a funeral tonight.

"I love you, too, Eric. But that's not what we're talking about, is it?"

Eric looked away. "I think not," he said reluctantly. "Sookie . . . it's not just a straightforward decision, you over Freyda. If it were only one woman over another . . . it's you I love. That's a given, not a choice at all. But it's not that simple."

"It's not that simple?" I repeated. I felt too many things to select one emotion, to say, *That's the way I feel; I'm in dread.* Or *I'm angry.* Or *I'm numb with fear.* I had all those feelings, and more. Since I couldn't bear to look at Eric's face any more than he could bear to look at mine, I looked up at the starlit sky. After another moment's silence, I said, "But it is, isn't it. That simple."

The night swelled with magic; not the beneficent kind of love-magic that sweeps couples away, but the kind of magic that rips and tears, the enchantment that creeps out of the woods and pounces.

"My maker gave this to me as his last order," Eric said.

"I would never have believed you'd try this argument," I said. " 'I'm just obeying orders.' Come on! You can't hide behind Appius's wishes, Eric. He's *gone*."

"He signed a contract, and it's legally binding," Eric said, still keeping his composure.

"You're giving yourself an excuse for doing something painful and wrong," I said.

"I'm locked into it," he said, his expression savage.

I looked down at my feet for a minute. I was wearing my happy sandals again, high-heeled and with little flowers on the strap across my toes. They looked ridiculously frivolous, appropriate for a single woman's twenty-eighth birthday. They weren't kiss-your-lover-good-bye shoes.

"Eric, you're a strong vampire," I said. I took his cool hand. "You've always been the boldest, baddest guy around. If your maker were alive, I'd believe you couldn't help this. But I watched Appius die, right here in my yard. So here's my bottom line; here's what I really believe. I think you could get out of this if you hated Freyda. But you don't. She's beautiful. She's rich. She's powerful. She needs you to watch her back, and the reward will be lots of the stuff you love." I took a deep, shuddering breath. "All I got is me. And I guess that's not enough." I waited, praying to hear a rebuttal. I looked up at him. I saw no shame. I saw no weakness. I saw instead a laserlike intensity in his blue eyes, so like my own.

He said, "Sookie, if I turn down this opportunity, Felipe will punish both of us. Our lives will not be worth living."

"Then we'll leave," I said quietly. "We'll go somewhere else. You'll work for some other king or queen. I'll find a job."

But even as I spoke the words, I knew he would not opt for this.

In fact, I found myself wondering if I would have said it if I'd believed there was any chance he'd say yes. On the whole, I thought I would, though it would have meant leaving everything I found dear.

"If only there were some way to prevent this," Eric said. "But I don't know of any way, and I can't tear you away from your life."

I didn't know whether my heart was ripped in two, whether I felt anguish or relief. I'd been sure he'd say that.

But he didn't say anything else.

He was waiting for me to speak.

The apprehension was so strong in me that I felt my eyebrows draw together in a question. "What?" I asked. *"What?"* I couldn't imagine where he wanted me to go in this terrible conversation.

Eric seemed almost angry, as if I weren't picking up my cue.

I continued to be bewildered; he continued to try to force some statement from me.

When he was sure I genuinely didn't have a clue, Eric said, "You could stop this if you chose." Each word came clear and distinct.

"How?" I dropped his hands, spread my own to show my ignorance. "Tell me how." I rummaged through my mind as fast as I could, trying frantically to understand what Eric could mean.

"You say you love me," he said angrily. "You could stop this."

He turned to walk away.

"Just *tell me how*," I asked, hearing and hating the desperation in my voice. "Goddammit, just TELL ME HOW."

He cast a look over his shoulder. I hadn't seen that expression on his face since we'd met, when he'd regarded me as just another disposable human.

And then he was in the air. And then he was lost in the night sky.

I stood staring up for a minute or two. Maybe I expected blazing letters to appear in the sky to explain his words. Maybe I thought Bill would pop out of the woods like a deus ex machina to tell me what Eric had been so sure I would understand.

I went back into the house and automatically locked the door behind me. I stood in the middle of the kitchen, cudgeling my tired brain into activity.

Okay, I said. *Let's figure this out. Eric said I could stop him from leaving with Freyda.* "But it can't be just that I love him, because I told him that, and he knows it," I whispered. "So, it's not how I feel, it's some act I need to perform."

What act? How could I prevent their marriage?

I could kill Freyda; however, not only would that be a horrible thing to do, since she'd done nothing more than desire the man I loved, but any attempt to kill the powerful vampire would be simply suicidal.

And killing Eric would hardly produce a happy ending, and that was the only other way I could imagine stopping him.

I guess I could go to Felipe and beg him to keep Eric, I thought. Though Eric had said Felipe would punish both of us if Eric remained in Louisiana, disobliging Freyda, I seriously considered how I would go about appealing to the king. What response would he have? He knew I'd saved his life once upon a time, but though he'd made me big promises, he hadn't exactly come through with them. No, Felipe would laugh when I went down on my knees. And then he'd tell me he thought he ought to honor Appius's wishes and let Appius's child make such an advantageous match.

In return, I was sure Felipe would be favored in any subsequent dealings between Oklahoma and Nevada or Arkansas or Louisiana.

All in all, I really couldn't see any chance at all that Felipe would agree to let Eric remain in Shreveport. Eric's worth as a sheriff couldn't equal the huge plus of having him at Freyda's side, murmuring things into Freyda's ear.

Okay, begging Felipe was out. I can't say I wasn't relieved.

I was still poking at my brain, trying to get it to spit out an idea, while I showered and put on my nightshirt. Eric had been so sure I could stop the Freyda-Felipe deal. How? It was like Eric thought I had a magic wish, something tucked up my sleeve.

Oh.

I froze, one arm through an armhole, the rest of the nightshirt bunched around my neck. I didn't breathe for a long moment.

Eric knew about the cluviel dor.

Chapter 15

I sat up all night.

My brain ran through the same old paces like a chipmunk in a cage. I always ended with the same conclusion.

Eric was trying to get me to admit I had the cluviel dor. What would have happened if I'd understood him last night, if I'd admitted it? Would he have taken it from me? I didn't know if he simply sought it for himself, or if Freyda would barter the cluviel dor in return for Eric's services, or if Eric simply wanted me to use it to stop him from going to Oklahoma.

And here's what happens when you have too much time to think: I actually considered the idea that Eric might have engineered this whole episode with Freyda to get me to reveal the location of the cluviel dor. That was a sickening possibility. If I hadn't experienced past betrayals, such an idea would never have crossed my mind. Even though I had accepted the world as it was, it made me sad that I was sure such a long-term and planned deception was possible.

Every new thought seemed to be worse than the previous one.

I lay in the dark watching the clock change.

I tried to think of things I could do, something besides lie in this bed. I could run across the cemetery to talk to Bill, who was surely up. That was a terrible idea, and I discarded it the first ten times it occurred to me. The eleventh time, I actually got out of bed and walked to the back door before I made myself turn away. I knew if I went over to talk to Bill right now, something might happen that I would surely regret—and that wasn't fair to me or Eric. Not until I knew for sure.

(I really knew for sure.)

I opened my purse and took the cluviel dor into my hand. Its warm, smooth surface relieved my pain, calmed me. I didn't know if I could trust this feeling or not, but it was far preferable to my previous misery. I heard Dermot come in and walk very quietly through the house. I couldn't bear the idea of explaining the situation, so I didn't let him know I was awake.

When he was safely upstairs, I moved into my dark living room and waited for the dawn. I fell asleep just as the night was lightening gradually into day. I slept sitting up on the couch until I woke four hours later, a cramp in my neck and stiffness in all my joints. I got up, feeling like I imagined an old woman felt first thing in the morning. I unlocked the front door and stepped out onto the porch. I heard birds singing, and the heat of the day was well advanced. Life was trudging onward.

Since I couldn't think what else to do, I went into the kitchen and started a pot of coffee. At least I didn't have to go to work today, since Merlotte's was closed on Sunday.

The night before, I had tossed our weekly local newspaper on the table unread, so while I sipped the coffee I took off the rubber band and spread it out. It was only a few pages, a little tube compared to the Shreveport daily paper, which I also read. Often the Bon Temps paper had news that was more interesting, though. That was the case today. *Bear in Local Woods?* read the headline. I skimmed the article hastily, and my heart sank, if there were any lower depths to hold it.

Two deer carcasses found by local men had led to some excited speculation. *"Some large predator did this," said Terry Bellefleur, who happened upon one of the killing sites while training his dog. "It didn't exactly look like a bear or panther kill, but this deer was killed by something big."*

Dammit. I'd warned Bellenos to stick to my woods.

"Oh, I didn't have quite enough to worry about," I said, rising to pour some more coffee. "I needed something else."

"What are you worried about?" Claude asked.

I screamed, and my coffee mug went flying.

When I could speak, I said, "You. Do. Not. Do. That. To. Me." He must have come in through the unlocked front door. He had keys, anyway, but I would have heard them in the lock and had some warning.

"Cousin, I'm sorry," he said contritely, but I could see the amusement in his eyes.

Oh, shit. Where had I put the cluviel dor?

I'd left it on the coffee table in the living room. It took every bit of self-control I had not to break and run for the living room.

"Claude," I said, "things haven't been going well while you were gone." I struggled to make my voice level. "Some of your fae workers have been taking little vacations." I pointed to the paper. "I guess Dermot spent the night at Hooligans. You should read this." If he hadn't come through the backyard, he might not have seen Dermot's car.

Claude poured himself a cup of coffee and obediently pulled out a chair.

His actions weren't threatening, but I was looking at the man who'd sent Kym Rowe to her death; for all I knew, he was the one who'd killed her when she hadn't gotten Eric to do the job. Claude's sudden reappearance—without Niall—would have been enough to raise the hair on my arms even if I hadn't known about his collusion with Jannalynn.

Why had Claude returned by himself? There was something in his face that hadn't been there before. I was willing him to sit down, willing him to give me the time to walk into the living room and retrieve the magical object.

"Where is Niall?" I asked, picking up my mug, which (amazingly) hadn't broken. After I put it by the sink, I got a wad of paper towels to mop up the spilled coffee.

"Still in Faery," Claude said, ostensibly concentrating on the paper. "Oh, did you like your friend's act at Hooligans? Your human friend?"

"JB. Well, his wife and I were sure surprised. Him being the only human, and her not knowing he was doing it and all."

"He needed a job, and I remembered the pretty lady who was with child," Claude said. "See, I did a good thing. I'm not so bad."

"I never said you were."

"You look at me, though, from time to time, as if you can't understand why I get to breathe the same air you do."

I was genuinely staggered. "Claude, I'm so sorry if I've ever given the impression I thought you were worthless. Certainly I don't feel that way." Or did I? No, I didn't. I thought he was selfish and charmless and maybe guilty of murder, but that was different.

"You don't want to have sex with me. If you had more fae blood, you certainly would want it."

"But I don't. You're gay. I'm in love with someone else. I don't believe in having sex with relatives. We've had this conversation before. I really, really don't want to have it again."

The feeling of wrongness and badness kept growing; especially after my experience with the rogue Weres, I knew better than to ignore it. I also knew Claude was stronger than I was, and I assumed he had skills I'd never seen.

"Okay," he said. "You're trying to let me know that my kith and kin are hunting at night? Is that the point of giving me this newspaper?"

"Yes, Claude. That's the point. Dermot's about been nuts, trying to keep them in line. Did Niall get the letter I sent?"

"I don't know," Claude said.

I was bewildered. "I thought you went back with Niall to investigate who'd cast the crazy spell on Dermot," I said. "He's been spending lots of nights at the club and trying real hard to keep things running." I was frightened for myself, of course, but I was frightened for Dermot, too. I hoped Dermot was awake by now; Claude wouldn't take my word for it that Dermot wasn't there. He'd go up to check.

"So what have you been doing in Faery? Did you ever find out who cast the spell?"

"Niall and I have had some disagreements," Claude said, his beautiful dark eyes flashing up to meet mine. "I'm sorry to say that Niall believes it was me who cursed Dermot."

I was left with no response, since I was by now pretty sure myself that Claude was the culprit. "I think that's awful," I said, with absolute sincerity. He could take it as he chose. "I'm gonna go open the shades in the living room. Have some more coffee. I think I've got some Toaster Strudels in the freezer if you're hungry." I walked down the hall to the living room, trying not to hurry, trying to make my footsteps regular and nonchalant. I even went directly to one of the front windows and raised the blind. "It's gonna be a pretty day," I called, turned, and in one gesture swept up the cluviel dor and put it in my nightshirt pocket. Dermot was halfway down the stairs.

He said, "Did I hear Claude's voice?" and made as if to hurry past me. Apparently, he hadn't even looked at what I'd picked up, which was a relief—but not at the top of my list of problems just at the moment.

"Yes, he's home," I said, in what I hoped was a natural voice, but I gripped Dermot's arm as he went by me. I looked at him with as much warning as I could pack into my eyes.

Dermot's blue eyes, so like Jason's, widened in shock. There was no gesture I could make that would clearly translate as "I think he wants to do something awful to us! He killed Kym Rowe for some reason I can't fathom, and I think he cursed you!" but at least Dermot understood that caution was called for.

"I told him you weren't here," I whispered. He nodded.

"Claude," he called. "Where have you been? Sookie didn't hear me come in last night, she says. The other fae are champing at the bit to hear your news." He started toward the kitchen.

But he met Claude coming into the living room. I didn't think Claude had witnessed our silent colloquy, but at this point I wouldn't put money on anything good. Yesterday had been my good day, apparently, even though it had ended as badly as I thought it could have. I'd been wrong! Claude could have returned last night. Yep, that would have been worse.

"Dermot," said Claude. His voice was so cold it stopped Dermot dead. I went on and opened the other blind.

"What's wrong? Why have you returned without Father?" Dermot said.

"Grandfather has issues he must deal with," Claude snarled. "In Faery."

"What did you do?" Dermot asked. He was brave. I was trying to unobtrusively creep into my room to retrieve my cell phone. I didn't know whom I would call; I didn't know who could deal with a fairy. "What did you do, Claude?"

"I thought that when I went back with him, I would find support for our program," Claude said.

Uh-oh. I didn't like the sound of that. I took two more steps to my left. Hooligans! I'd call the fae at Hooligans! Wait. Unless they were backing Claude in whatever the hell his program was. Shit. What should I do? Dermot wasn't armed. He was wearing sleep pants and no shirt.

My shotgun was in the closet by the front door. Maybe the closet should be my goal, instead of the cell phone. Did I have Hooligans on speed dial? How long would it take the police to get out here if I hit 911? Would Claude kill them?

"And you didn't?" Dermot said. "I'm not sure what program you mean, Claude?"

"You naïve simpleton," Claude said scathingly. "How hard have you worked at ignoring what was going on all around you, so you could stay with us?"

Claude was just being mean now. If I'd had any sleep, I wouldn't have snapped then, but I hadn't, and I did. "Claude Crane, you are just being an A-number-one asshole," I exploded. "And you shut up right now!"

I'd succeeded in startling Claude, and he turned his gaze on me for just a second, but Dermot took advantage of that second to hit Claude as hard as he could, which proved to be plenty hard. Claude lurched to his right, and Dermot kept punching. Of course, the element of surprise was gone after the first blow. Claude had another skill besides stripping. He could fight dirty.

The two launched into it, two beautiful men doing something so ugly I could hardly bear to watch.

The heaviest thing around was a lamp that had belonged to my great-grandmother. With a flash of reluctance I picked it up. I proposed to bash Claude's head in, if I got the opportunity.

But then my back door flew open and Bellenos bounded through my kitchen and down the hall. He had a true sword in his hand, instead of his deer-hunting spear. Gift was with him, long knives in both her hands. Three more of the Monroe fae were with them: two of the strippers, the fairy "policeman" and the part demon who'd worn leather when he'd come onstage. The curvy ticket taker followed. She hadn't bothered with looking human today.

"Help Dermot!" I yelled, hoping that was what they'd come to do. To my overwhelming relief, they whooped with excitement and threw themselves into the brawl. There was a lot of unnecessary punching and biting, but when they were sure Claude was subdued, they all began laughing. Even Dermot.

At least I was able to put the lamp back on the table.

"Would someone tell me what's going on?" I asked. I felt (as usual with the supes) two steps behind the crowd, and no telepath enjoys feeling that way. I was going to have to hang around with humans for a long time to make up for this sad ignorance.

"My dearest sister," Bellenos said. He smiled that disconcerting smile at me. He looked especially toothy today, and since there was blood between some of those teeth, the effect was not reassuring.

"Hi, y'all," was the best I could do, but they all grinned back, and Gift gave Dermot an enthusiastic kiss. Her extra eyelid flickered down and up again, almost too fast for me to note.

In the meantime, Claude was lying on the floor in a panting, bloody bundle. There was still plenty of fight in him, from the glares he was throwing around, but he was so clearly outnumbered that it seemed he'd given up . . . at least temporarily. The ticket taker was sitting on his legs, and the two strippers were each pinning one arm.

Gift came to sit by me; I'd collapsed on the couch. She put her arm around me. "Claude was trying to incite us to rebel against Niall," she said kindly. "Sister, I'm surprised he didn't try to test your loyalty, too."

"Well, he wouldn't have gotten very far!" I said. "I would have thrown him out in a New York minute!"

"Then see, that was intelligent of you, Claude," said Bellenos, bending over to speak to Claude face-to-face. "One of the few intelligent things you did." Claude glared at him.

Dermot shook his handsome head. "All this time I thought I must try to emulate Claude, because he had been so successful out here in the human world. But I realized that when he thought people were pleased with him, he didn't perceive that it was only because he is beautiful. Much more often, when he talked to people, they came to regard him with dislike. I couldn't believe it, but he'd done well in spite of himself, not because of his own talents."

"He does like children," I said weakly. "And he's nice to pregnant women."

"Yes, that's true," the policeman stripper said. "By the way, you can just call me Dirk, my stripping name. Siobhan is sitting on Claude's legs. And this is Harley. I'm sure you remember Harley."

"Oh, yeah, who could forget Harley?" I said. Even under the circumstances, I had a gratifying flashback of how Harley's straight black hair and coppery red body had looked under the lights at Hooligans. Harley tried to bow from a crouching position, which isn't easy, and Siobhan grinned at me. "So . . . Claude really was locked out of Faery, along with you-all? That wasn't a lie?"

"No, not a lie," said Dermot sadly. "My father hated me because he thought I'd always worked against him. But I was cursed. I thought he'd done the cursing, but I see now it must have been Claude all along. Claude, you betrayed me and then kept me trotting behind you like a dog."

Claude began to speak in another language, and then the fae moved with an unbelievable speed. Gift yanked off her bra top, and Harley stuffed it in Claude's mouth. It would have been petty of me to take any notice of Gift's bare chest, so I rose above it.

"That was a secret fairy language?" I hated to ask, but I just wanted to know. My days of ignorance were over.

Dirk nodded. "We speak to each other that way; it's what we have in common: full fairy, demon, angel, all the half-breeds."

"Dermot, did you and Claude really come here because of my fairy blood?" I asked Dermot. Claude's mouth was otherwise occupied.

"Yes," Dermot said uncertainly. "Though Claude said there was something here that attracted him, and he spent hours when you were gone searching your house. When he couldn't find what he wanted here, he thought perhaps it was in the furniture you sold. He went to that shop and broke in to examine all the furniture again."

I felt a little bubble of rage float to the top of my brain. "Though

I was nice enough to let him live with me. He searched my house. Went through my stuff. While I was gone."

Dermot nodded. From the guilty glance he gave me, I was pretty damn sure Claude had enlisted my great-uncle in his search.

"What was he looking for?" Harley asked curiously.

"He sensed a fairy object in Sookie's house, a fairy influence."

They all looked at me, simultaneously, with sharp attention.

"Gran—you-all know my fairy blood comes from my grandmother and Fintan, right?" They all nodded and blinked. I was sure glad I hadn't been trying to keep that a secret. "Gran was friends with Mr. Cataliades, through Fintan." They nodded again, more slowly. "He left something here, but when he stopped by a few days ago, he picked it up."

They appeared to accept that pretty well. At least no one leaped up to say, "You liar, you have it in your pocket!"

Claude thrashed on the floor. Clearly, he wanted to put in his two cents' worth, and I was glad the bra was in his mouth.

"If I'm getting to ask questions . . ." I said, waiting for Bellenos to interrupt, to tell me my time was up. But that didn't happen.

"Claude, I know you tried to sabotage me and Eric. But I don't know why."

Dirk raised interrogative eyebrows. Did I want him to remove the gag?

"Maybe you can just let me know if I get something right," I suggested, hoping that the gag stayed in. "Did you go to Jannalynn for help because you wanted to enlist a shifter of some kind?"

Glaring at me, Claude nodded.

"Who's that?" Dermot whispered, as if the air would answer him.

"Jannalynn Hopper is the second of the Long Tooth pack in

Shreveport," I said. "She's been dating my boss, Sam Merlotte. But she hates me, which is a long story for some other time, though it's pretty boring. Anyway, I knew she'd love to do me a bad turn if she could. And the young woman who got murdered in Eric's front yard turned out to be a half-Were with a death wish and severe financial problems, ripe for a desperate plan, I figure. Claude, you gave her some of your blood to make her alluring to Eric, I think?"

The fae all looked absolutely aghast. I couldn't have said anything more abhorrent to them. "You gave your sacred blood to a mongrel?" hissed Gift, and kicked Claude heartily.

Claude closed his eyes and nodded.

Maybe he wanted them to kill him on the spot. Kym Rowe hadn't been the only person to develop a wish to die.

"So I get how you did it . . . but why? Why did you want Eric to lose control? What benefit to you?"

"Oh, I know that one!" Dermot said brightly.

I sighed. "Maybe you would explain."

"Claude told me several times that if we could get Niall to return to your side, we could attack him here in the human world, where he wouldn't be surrounded by his supporters," Dermot said. "But I ignored his scheming. I was sure Niall wouldn't return and couldn't return, because he was firm in his resolution to stay in Faery. But Claude argued that Niall loves you so much that if something happened to you, he'd come to your side. So he tried to ruin Eric, thinking that at best you and Eric would fight and Eric would hurt you. Or you'd be arrested for murdering him, and you'd need your great-grandfather. At the very least, you would throw Eric aside and your misery would bring Niall running."

"I was pretty miserable," I said slowly. "And I was even more miserable last night."

"And here I am," said a voice I recognized. "I've come in response to your letter, which opened my eyes to many things."

He was glowing. My great-grandfather hadn't troubled with his human appearance, either. The white-blond hair floated in the air around him. His face was radiant, his eyes like fairy lights on a white tree.

The little cluster of fae in my living room fell to their knees.

He put his arms around me, and I felt his incredible beauty, his terrifying magic, and his crazy devotion.

There was nothing human about him.

He put his mouth right by my ear. "I know you have it," he said.

Suddenly we were standing in my bedroom instead of in the living room. "You gonna take it?" I asked, in the smallest possible voice. Those were fae in the living room. They might hear.

"Don't even show it to me," he said. "It was from my son to his loved one. He intended it for a human. It should stay in human hands."

"But you really, really want it."

"I do, and I have very poor impulse control."

"Okay. No looks." Danger. I was trying to relax, but it's not easy loving and being loved by a powerful prince who has no human frame of reference; furthermore, one whose great age has kind of unhinged him. Just a little bit. From time to time. "What will happen to the fae in my living room?"

"I will take them with me," Niall said. "I have taken care of a lot of things while Claude was with me. I never let him know what I already understood about him. I know what happened to Dermot. I have forgiven Dermot."

Okay, that was good.

"Will you close Faery? For good?"

"Soon," he whispered, his lips again uncomfortably close to my ear. "You have not asked yet who told your lover that you have the . . . object."

"That would be a good thing for me to learn."

"You need to know." His arms grew uncomfortably tight around me. I made myself relax against him.

"It was me," Niall said, almost inaudibly.

I jerked back as if he'd pinched my butt. *"What?"*

The brilliant eyes bored into mine. "You had to know," he said. "You had to know what would happen if he believed you had power."

"Please tell me you didn't engineer the whole Appius thing?" That would be more than I could bear.

"No. Eric is unfortunate in that people feel the need to take him down a peg, including his own maker. The Roman wanted to keep control over so vital a being even after his own death, which became far more likely once he turned the child. So unstable. Appius Livius Ocella made mistakes in his whole long existence. Perhaps changing Eric was his finest hour. He created the perfect vampire. Eric's only flaw is you."

"But . . ." I couldn't think of what I'd been about to say.

"Of course, that's not how *I* perceive it, dearest. You are the one right impulse Eric has had in five hundred years or more. Well, Pam is all right. Even Eric's other living child does not rival her maker."

"Thanks," I said numbly, the words not sinking in at all. "So you knew Appius?"

"We met. He was a stinking Roman asshole."

"True."

"I was glad when he died. Out in your front yard, wasn't it?"

"Ah. Yes."

"The ground around your house has become soaked with blood. It will add to its magic and fertility."

"What happens now?" I said, because I simply couldn't think of what else to say.

He lifted me and carried me out of the bedroom like I was a baby. It didn't feel like the times when Eric had carried me, which had had a definitely carnal edge. This was incredibly tender and (like a lot of things about my great-grandfather) incredibly creepy.

He put me on the couch as carefully as if I were an egg. "This is what happens next," he told me. He turned to the other fae, still on their knees. Claude had stopped thrashing and was looking up at Niall with resignation. For the moment, Niall ignored his grandson.

"Do you all want to go home?" he asked the others.

"Yes, Prince," said Dirk. "Please, with our kindred waiting at Claude's club? If we may? If you will."

Dermot said, "With your blessing, I'll stay here, Father."

For a moment they all looked at Dermot incredulously, as if he'd just announced he was going to birth a kangaroo.

Niall folded Dermot to him. I could see Dermot's face, and it was ecstatic, frightened, everything I had felt in Niall's embrace. Niall said, "You won't be a fairy anymore. The American fae are all leaving. Choose."

The conflict on Dermot's face was painful to see. "Sookie," he said, "who can finish your upstairs work?"

"I'll hire Terry Bellefleur," I said. "He won't be as good as you, Dermot."

"No television," Dermot said. "I'll miss HGTV." Then he smiled. "But I can't live without my essence, and I am your son, Niall."

Niall beamed down at Dermot, which was what Dermot had wanted his whole life.

I got up because I couldn't stand to have him leave without a hug. I even started crying, which I hadn't expected. They all kissed me, even Bellenos, though I felt his teeth scrape lightly on my cheek, and I felt his chest move in a silent chuckle.

Niall made some mysterious signs over my head and closed his eyes, just like a priest giving a blessing. I felt something change in the house, the land.

And then they were gone. Even Claude.

I was stupefied. I was willing to bet that over at Hooligans, the bar stood empty, the doors locked.

The fae were gone from America. Their departure point? Bon Temps, Louisiana. The woods behind my house.

Chapter 16

As you can imagine, it wasn't easy to go on and have a normal day after that.

I hadn't slept all night, and the traumas had just kept on coming.

But after I showered and straightened up the living room, which had suffered a bit during the fight, I found myself sitting at the kitchen table trying to absorb everything: last night, this morning.

It was taking a lot of energy to do that. About halfway through setting my mental house in order, I had to think about something else. Luckily, there was something right in front of me that would serve.

Among the presents I'd tossed to the table last night was Pam's little box, Bill's box, and Sam's envelope, which I'd never examined. Pam had given me perfume, and I liked the smell of it very much. Bill had given me a necklace with a cameo pendant. The likeness on it was my gran's. "Oh, Bill," I said, "you did great!" Nothing could top such a gift, I thought, as I reached for Sam's envelope. I figured he'd picked a fancy birthday card—with, maybe, a gift certificate enclosed.

Sam had officially made me a partner in the bar. I legally owned a third of Merlotte's.

I put my head on the table and swore. In a happy way.

This past twenty-four hours had been my personal trail of tears. No more!

I picked myself up out of that chair, slapped on about a ton of makeup and a sundress, and put a smile on my face. It was time to rejoin the land of the living, the everyday world. I didn't want to learn one more secret or suffer one more betrayal.

I was due to meet Kennedy for breakfast at LaLaurie's, which (she'd told me) served a great Sunday brunch. I didn't think I'd ever eaten a meal and called it "brunch." Today I did, and it was really excellent. White tablecloths and cloth napkins, too! Kennedy was wearing a pretty sundress, too, and her hair was in full pageant mode. The hickey on her neck was not quite covered by her makeup.

Kennedy was in an excellent mood, and she confided in me way more than I wanted to know about the wonderfulness that now lay between Danny and her. Danny was even now running errands for Bill Compton since he didn't have to work at the lumberyard, which was closed on Sunday. It was going to work out. He'd be making a living wage. When their finances stabilized, maybe they would move in together. "Maybe," she emphasized, but I wasn't fooled. Their cohabitation was a done deal.

I thought of my happy fantasies of the night before; had it really just been the night before? I tried to remember all the happy endings

I'd imagined for everyone, and I tried to recollect if I'd included Danny and Kennedy in the roundup.

After I left LaLaurie's, full and happy, I knew I couldn't wait any longer to thank Sam for his amazing gift. His truck was parked in front of his trailer. His carefully watered hedge and yard were flourishing despite the heat. Not many men would try to keep a yard around their double-wide if it was parked behind a bar. I'd always tried to let Sam's house be his house. I could count on my fingers the times I'd knocked on his door.

Today was one of them.

When he answered the door, my smile faded away. I could tell something was mighty wrong.

Then I realized that he knew what Jannalynn had done.

He looked at me bleakly. "I don't know what to say to you," he said. "This is the second time I've been with a woman who tried to do you harm."

It actually took me a second to remember who the other one had been. "Callisto? Oh, Sam, that was a while ago, and she was hardly a woman. She didn't mean any of it personal. Jannalynn, well, she definitely did. But she's an ambitious young woman; she's trying . . ." My voice trailed off. *She's trying to take over the pack from her packmaster, to whom she swore loyalty. She's trying to make sure my boyfriend gets arrested for murder. She conspired with a fairy to pay Kym Rowe to go to her death. She kidnapped Warren. She left him to die. She was trying to kill me, one way or another.*

"Okay," I said, conceding defeat. "You fucked up with Jannalynn."

He blinked at me. His reddish-blond hair was standing up like porcupine quills all over his head. He tilted his head to one side as if he wasn't sure I was quite in focus.

His mouth quirked up in an unwilling grin. I grinned back. Then we both laughed. Not a lot, but enough to clear the air.

"Where is she?" I asked. "Do you know what happened night before last?"

"Tell me," he said, standing aside so I could come in.

Sam had heard a sketchy version from a pack member who'd become a friend of his, a young man who worked for Jannalynn at Hair of the Dog. "You didn't tell me what you suspected about her," Sam said. He left that sitting there between us.

"Sam, let me tell you about what's happened the last couple of days, and you'll understand, I promise," I said, and with a certain amount of editing, I told him.

"Good God, Sookie," he said. "You really know how to have a birthday, huh?"

"The best part of my birthday was my present from you," I said, and I took his hand.

Sam turned red. "Aw, Sook. You earned it. You deserve it. And look, I didn't make you *equal* partner, did I?"

"Trying to make your gift look like less won't work for me," I said. I kissed him on the cheek and got up, to make the moment lighten so Sam would be more comfortable. "I got to get home," I said, though I couldn't imagine what for.

"See you tomorrow."

It would be a lot sooner than that.

I felt curiously blank on the drive home to my empty house.

For what seemed like forever, my spare time had been taken up by Eric. We were making plans to meet, or we were together, or we were talking on the telephone. Now that it seemed our relationship was unraveling, I had no idea what to expect from our next meeting. If we had a next meeting. But I couldn't imagine how I would fill the hole in my life left by his absence. Now that I knew who'd tried to get Eric into trouble, I knew that his involvement with me had led to this moment. He'd never have been targeted by Claude, by Jannalynn, if it hadn't been for me, and that was such a reversal on the usual situation—I'd been the object of so many schemes because Eric was my lover—that I couldn't quite wrap my head around it. I wondered how much Eric knew of what had transpired, but I couldn't bring myself to call him to tell about it all.

He had known I had the cluviel dor, and he had expected me to use it to get him out of the arrangement Appius had made with Freyda.

And maybe I would have done that. Maybe I still would. It seemed the obvious choice, the most apparent thing to do with the magic. But it also seemed to me that Eric was expecting me to magically get him out of a situation that he should defeat by his own efforts. He should love me enough to simply refuse Freyda. It was like he wanted the decision out of his hands.

That was an idea I didn't want to have. But you can't erase a thought; once you've had it, it's there to stay.

I would love to feel an absolute conviction that yanking that cluviel dor out of my pocket and wishing with all my heart that Eric would stay with me was the right thing to do.

I poked at that thought. I prodded that thought. But it just didn't feel right to me.

I took a much-needed nap. When I got up, though I wasn't really all that hungry, I microwaved a dish of lasagna and picked at it as I thought. No one at the bar had heard news of any more mysterious deer deaths, and now I was sure there never would be. I wondered about Hooligans, presumably now sitting empty, but it wasn't anything to do with me anymore. Oh, gosh, the guys were sure to have left some stuff upstairs. Maybe this evening I'd pack it up. Not that there was any address to forward it to.

Okay, maybe I'd take the clothes to Goodwill.

I watched television for a while—an old black-and-white movie about a man and a woman who loved one another but had to overcome all sorts of things to be together, a cooking show, a couple of episodes of *Jeopardy*. (I couldn't get any answers right.) My only phone call was from a fund-raising organization. I turned them down.

They were disappointed in me, I could tell.

When the phone rang again, I picked it up without bothering to turn down the sound on the TV.

"Sookie?" said a familiar voice.

I pressed the Off button on the remote. "Alcide, how is Warren?"

"He's much better. I think he's gonna be fine. Listen, I need you and Sam to come to the old farm tonight."

"Your dad's place?"

"Yeah. Your presence was requested."

"By whom?"

"By Jannalynn."

"You found her?"

"Yeah."

"But Sam, too? She wants Sam?"

"Yeah. She deceived him, too. He has a right to be there."

"Did you call him?"

"He's on his way to pick you up."

"Do I have to?" I said.

"You whining, Sookie?"

"Yeah, I guess I am, Alcide. I'm mighty tired, and more bad stuff has happened than you know."

"I can't take any more than I have on my plate. Just come. If it makes you want to attend this little soiree more, your honey's gonna be there."

"Eric?"

"Yeah. The King of Cold himself."

Fear and longing rippled along my skin. "Okay," I said. "I'll come."

By the time I heard Sam's truck in the driveway, the lack of sleep I'd experienced the night before was hitting me in a major way. I'd spent the minutes I'd waited by refreshing my memory about the route to Alcide's family place, and I'd written the directions out. When Sam knocked on the door, I stuck the paper in my purse. We were going to be walking around a farm at night; I'd want to leave my purse in the car. I made certain the cluviel dor was still in my pocket and I felt the now-familiar curved shape.

Sam's face was grim and hard, and it felt wrong to see him that way.

We didn't talk on the way to the farm.

I had to turn on Sam's overhead light from time to time to read my directions, but I was able to steer us right. I think the preoccupation with actually getting there helped keep us from worrying too much about what we'd see when we arrived.

We found a mess of cars parked higgledy-piggledy in the front yard of the old farmhouse. To call it "remote" was to be kind. Though there was more cleared land around it than there had ever been at my place, it was even more private. No one lived here full time any longer. Alcide's dad's dad had owned the farm, and Jackson Herveaux had kept it after he'd gone into construction so he'd have a place to run at the full moon. The pack had used it often. The front of the house was dark, but I could hear voices around the back. Sam and I trudged through the high weeds. We didn't say a word to each other.

We might as well have walked into another country.

The meadow behind the house was mowed and smooth. There were lights up. I could see from posts that normally there was a volleyball net set up across a sand court. A few yards away, there was a pool that looked new. I even spotted a baseball diamond farther back. A Weber grill was under the covered patio. Clearly, this was where the pack came to relax and have fellowship.

I saw the tall and quiet Kandace first. She smiled at me and pointed to Alcide, who stood out among his people as much as Niall did among his. Tonight Alcide looked like a king. A king in jeans and a T-shirt, a barefoot king. And he looked dangerous. The power gathered around him. The air was humming with the magic of the pack.

Good. We needed more tension.

Eric shone like the moon; he was pale and commanding, and there was a large empty space around him. He was alone. He held out his hand to me, and I took it, to a flare of dismay from the twoeys.

"You know, about Jannalynn and Claude?" I looked up at him.

"Yes, I know. Niall sent me a message."

"He's gone. They've all gone."

"He told me I would not hear from him again."

I nodded and gulped. No more crying. "So what's going to happen tonight?"

"I don't know what we're here to see," he said. "An execution? A duel? With the wolves, I can't predict."

Sam was standing by himself, just under the awning over the patio. Alcide went up to him and spoke, and Sam shrugged, then nodded. He stepped out to stand by Alcide.

I looked around at the faces of the pack members. They were all restless because of the night and because of the promise of violence in the air. There was going to be bleeding tonight.

Alcide raised an arm, and four figures were led from the back of the house. Their hands were bound. Van, Plump, the bandaged Airman (Laidlaw, Mustapha had called him), and Jannalynn. I didn't know where they'd caught up with her, but her face was bruised. She'd put up a fight, which was no surprise at all.

Then I saw Mustapha. He'd blended with the darkness. He was magnificently nude. Warren was in the shadows behind him, huddled in a folding lawn chair. He was too far away for me to get a good look at him.

Mustapha had a sword. *Too many of those in my life these days,* I thought, feeling Eric's cold hand tightening on mine.

"We are here to judge tonight," Alcide said. "We've had to judge members all too often lately. The pack has been full of dissension and disloyalty. Tonight I require all of you to renew your oaths, and tonight I say that the penalty for breaking them is death."

The werewolves drew in breath sharply, collectively, like a single quiet scream. I looked around. Werewolfism manifests itself along with puberty, so none of the faces were younger than early teens, but that was young enough to make their presence shocking.

"After the judgments are rendered tonight, anyone who likes can challenge me on this spot," Alcide said. His face was savage. "No candidate has announced against me, but if anyone would like to win here and now, without a ceremony, you're welcome to try single combat. Prepare yourself to fight to the death."

Everyone was frozen in place now. This was not at all like the packmaster challenge I'd seen before, the one in which Alcide's father had died. That had been a formal, ceremonial contest. Alcide himself had succeeded to the position when his father's challenger, Patrick Furnan, had died fighting side by side with Alcide against a common enemy. Packmaster by acclamation, I guess you'd term it. Tonight Alcide was throwing down the gauntlet to every wolf present. It was a big gamble.

"Now for judgment," Alcide said, when he had looked into the face of every pack member.

The prisoners were pushed forward to land on their knees in the sand of the volleyball court. Roy, the Were who was dating Palomino, seemed to be in charge of the miscreants.

"The three rogues I had turned down for admission into the pack acted against us," Alcide said in a voice that carried across the yard. "They abducted Warren, the friend of Mustapha, who in turn is a friend—though not a member—of this pack. If he hadn't been found in time, Warren would have died."

Everyone moved in unison, turning to stare at the people on their knees.

"The three rogues were incited by Jannalynn Hopper, not only a pack member, but also my enforcer. Jannalynn couldn't subdue her pride and ambition. She couldn't wait until she was strong enough to challenge me openly. Instead she started a campaign of undermining me. She looked for power in the wrong places. She even accepted money from a fairy in return for finding a half-bitch who would try to get Eric Northman arrested for murder. When Eric was too smart to act the way she thought he would, Jannalynn stole into his yard and murdered Kym Rowe herself, so Kym wouldn't tell the police who'd hired her. Some of you remember running with Oscar, Kym's father. He's joined us tonight."

Kym's father, Oscar, was skulking behind Alcide. He looked oddly out of place, and I wondered how long it had been since he'd come to a pack meeting. What regrets did Oscar have now about his daughter's life and death? If he was any kind of father, any kind of human being, he had to be thinking about how she'd lost her job, how she'd needed money so badly that she'd agreed to be bait for a vampire. He had to be wondering if he could've helped her out.

But maybe I was just projecting. I had to keep my mind in the here and now.

"Jannalynn was willing to sacrifice Were blood to serve her own interests and those of the *fae*?" Roy said. I was pretty sure Alcide had prepped him to ask that.

"She was. She admits it. She has written a confession and mailed it to the Shreveport police station. Now we're going to ensure it's taken seriously."

Alcide dialed a number. His cell was on speakerphone. "Detective Ambroselli," said a recognizable voice.

Alcide held the phone in front of Jannalynn. Her eyes closed for a moment as she was readying herself to step off a cliff. The Were said, "Detective, this is Jannalynn Hopper."

"Uh-huh? Wait, you're the bartender at Hair of the Dog, right?"

"Yeah. I have a confession to make."

"Then come on in, and we'll sit down," Ambroselli said cautiously.

"I can't do that. I'm about to vanish. And I've mailed you a letter. But I wanted to tell you, so you can hear it's my voice. Are you recording this?"

"Yeah, I am now," Ambroselli said. I could hear a lot of movement on her end.

"I killed Kym Rowe. I came up on her when she was leaving Eric Northman's house, and I snapped her neck. I'm a werewolf. We're pretty strong."

"Why'd you do that?" Ambroselli asked. I could hear someone muttering to her, and I guessed she was getting advice from the other detectives around her.

For a moment, Jannalynn's face looked blank. She hadn't thought of a motive, at least not a simple one. Then she said, "Kym stole my wallet from my purse, and when I tracked her down and made her give it back, she disrespected me. I . . . have a bad temper, and she said some stuff that made me sick. I lost it. I have to go now. But I don't want anyone else blamed for something I did."

And Alcide hung up. "We'll hope that will clear Eric. That's our responsibility," he said, and nodded at Eric, who nodded back.

Jannalynn made her face hard and looked around, but I noticed she didn't actually meet anyone's eyes. Even mine.

"How'd she get these sleazeballs to help her?" Roy asked, jerking his head at the kneeling prisoners. He'd definitely been prepped.

"She promised them membership in the pack when she became packleader," Alcide told the Weres. "Van is a convicted rapist. Coco burned her own family, father and two brothers, in their home. Laidlaw, though not convicted in a human court, was thrown out of his own pack in West Virginia for attacking a human child during his moon time. This is why I had turned them down for the Long Tooth pack. But Jannalynn would admit these people to run with us. And they did her bidding."

There was a long silence. Neither Van, nor Plump (Coco), nor Laidlaw denied the charges against them. They didn't try to justify themselves, which was pretty damn impressive.

"What do you think we should do with the rogues?" Roy asked when the silence had lasted long enough.

"What crimes did they commit *here*?" asked a young woman just past her teens.

"They abducted Warren and imprisoned him at Jannalynn's family home. They didn't feed him and left him in an attic room without air-conditioning or any means of relief from the heat. He almost died as a result. They abducted Sookie and were taking her to their own place, and we can only imagine what they would have done with her there. Those actions were at the behest of Jannalynn."

"And she held out the promise of admission to the pack upon your death." The young woman sounded like she was thinking hard. "Those are bad things to do, but in fact Warren lived, and Sookie was rescued by the pack. Jannalynn won't be your successor, and they won't join the pack."

"This is all true," Alcide said.

"So they acted about like you'd expect rogues to act," the young woman persisted.

"Yes. Not lone wolves," Alcide explained for the benefit of the youngest Weres present. "But rogues, who've been turned down for pack membership, maybe by more than one pack."

"And what about Kandace?" the young woman said, pointing to the short-haired rogue.

"Kandace told us what was happening because she didn't want to be a part of it," Alcide said. "So we're going to put her membership to the vote in a month. After people have time to get to know her."

There was a general round of nodding, kind of guarded. Kandace might have told on the other rogues because it was the right thing to do, or she might be a natural snitch. Getting to talk to her on an individual basis was the best course.

"I think we should let these rogues go," called an older man. "Blackball them from ever being a pack member anywhere. Put out the word."

Van closed his eyes. I couldn't tell if he was feeling relief or misery. Coco was crying; Laidlaw spat on the ground. Not smooth when people were deciding your life or death.

In the end, they were released. It was unceremonious. Roy untied them and said, "Git."

Eric looked away to hide his appalled reaction to such a lack of ritual. Laidlaw took off toward the east, running awkwardly because of his bandaged shoulder. Coco and Van went north. In a moment they were out of sight, and that was the end of the rogues, as far as the Long Tooth pack went.

Jannalynn remained. Responding to a gesture from Alcide, Roy untied her hands and she stood to her unimpressive height, rubbing her wrists and stretching.

Mustapha stood to face her on the sanded volleyball area.

"I will kill you," he said in his deep voice. He was not even wearing the dark glasses.

"Try, jungle bunny," Jannalynn said, and held out her hand. She got a sword, too, handed to her by Roy. I was a little surprised; execution seemed more in order than the right to fight. But nobody had asked me.

She was trying to make Mustapha angrier with her insult, but the epithet didn't have any effect on him whatsoever. Some of the pack looked disgusted. The rest looked . . . like people waiting for a sporting event to begin. I looked up at Eric, who seemed interested, nothing more. Suddenly, I felt like punching him. This woman had talked a desperate stripper into drinking fairy blood and seducing a vampire, both dangerous processes with unknown outcomes. Kym might have been reckless enough to risk her own death, but that didn't make Jannalynn's scheming any less pernicious, or the pain I'd felt as a result any more bearable.

I thought she deserved to die for what she'd done to Sam alone. His face was rigid with the effort of holding in his feelings. My heart hurt for him.

The two combatants circled each other for a moment, and suddenly Jannalynn executed one of her flying leaps, hoping to come down on top of Mustapha. The lone wolf pivoted, and his sword blocked hers. She went spinning to the ground, but she was up in a second and back on the attack. Mustapha had told me he wasn't sure he could win a fight with Jannalynn, and for a few seconds she had the advantage. Not only did she hack away at him—this wasn't fencing, not like Robin Hood—but she shrieked, she screamed, she did everything she could to confuse and distract her opponent.

I noticed that she was working gradually closer to the edge of the sand. Closer to Alcide and Sam.

She might be a Were, but some intents were so strong I couldn't miss them.

"She's after you," I yelled in warning, and just as the words left my mouth Jannalynn leaped, spun, and came down on Alcide, who leaped aside at the last fraction of a second.

She got Sam.

He crumpled to the ground as his blood spurted. Jannalynn paused in shock at having cut her lover, and in that moment Mustapha grabbed her by the hair, threw her to the sand, and beheaded her. I'd seen beheadings before, but they're pretty spectacularly horrible.

I didn't even remember Jannalynn's until much later, because I was launching myself across the intervening space to crouch by Sam, who was bleeding out into the grass by the patio. I heard someone screaming and knew it was me. Alcide crouched down by me and reached out to touch Sam, but I shoved him away. Sam's eyes were wide and desperate. He knew the severity of his wound.

I started to call for Eric, so he could give Sam his blood, but as I put my hand to Sam's neck, Sam's pulse stopped. His eyes closed.

And everything else in the world did, too.

In my universe, everything fell silent. I didn't hear the chaos around me. I didn't hear a voice calling my name. I shoved Alcide away for a second time. My course was perfectly clear. I reached in my right pocket, pulled out the cluviel dor, and put it on Sam's chest. The creamy green glowed. The band of gold radiated light.

Amelia had always told me that will and intent are everything in magic, and I had plenty of both.

"Sam. Live." I hardly recognized my own voice. I didn't have spells, but I had the will. I had to believe that. I pressed the cluviel dor to Sam's heart, and I put my left hand over the terrible wound in his neck. *"Live,"* I said again, hearing only my own voice and the silence in Sam's body.

And the cluviel dor opened at its gold seam, revealing a hollow interior, and the concentrated magic inside it flew out and poured into Sam. It was clear and shining and otherworldly. It flowed through my fingers and into Sam's neck, and it vanished into the terrible wound. It filled Sam's body, which began to glow. The cluviel dor, now empty of magic, slipped from my right hand, which rested still on Sam's chest. I felt movement with my left hand, so I pulled it away from the gash and watched.

It was like watching a film run in reverse. The severed vessels and tendons inside Sam's neck began to knit. I held my breath, afraid even to blink or move. After a long moment, or several long moments, I could feel Sam's heart begin to beat under my fingers.

"Thanks, Fintan," I whispered. "Thanks, Gran."

After a small eternity, Sam's eyes opened. "I was dead," he said.

I nodded. I couldn't talk to save my soul.

"What . . . how'd you do that?"

"Tell you later."

"You . . . you can *do* that?" He was dazed.

"Not again," I warned him. "That's it. You got to stay alive from now on."

"Okay," he said weakly. "I promise."

Eric left while I was with Sam. He left without speaking to me.

When I got Sam to stand, we had to walk past Jannalynn's body. Sam looked at the corpse of the woman he'd dated for months, and his face was blank. He had a lot to process.

I didn't give a shit about the rest of the Were evening. I figured no one was going to challenge Alcide on the spot, and if they did, I wasn't going to stick around to watch another fight. I also figured if Mustapha wanted to join the pack, no one was going to vote against that, either. Not tonight. I didn't even worry about the effect of tonight's spectacle on the smaller teenage Weres. They had their own world to live in, and they had to learn its rules and ways pretty damn quick.

I drove, because I figured a guy who'd just died and come back probably should be left to think about the experience. Sam's truck wasn't hard to operate, but between driving an unfamiliar vehicle and remembering the way to get back to the county road to go home, I was pretty preoccupied.

"Where'd Eric go?" Sam asked.

"I don't know. He left in hurry. Without speaking." I shrugged.

"Kind of abrupt."

"Yeah," I said briefly. I figured his was the voice I'd heard yelling, before I'd focused on Sam. The silence hung around and got awkward.

"Okay," I said. "You heard about Freyda. I figure he's going to go with her."

"Oh?" It was clear Sam didn't know what reaction to give me.

"Oh," I said firmly. "So he knew I had this thing. This magic thing that I used on you. And I guess he thought it was kind of a test of my love."

"He expected you to use it to save him from this marriage," Sam said slowly.

"Yeah. Evidently." And I sighed. "And I kind of expected him to tell her to go to Hell. I guess I thought of it as a test of *his* love."

"What do you think he'll do?"

"He's proud," I said, and I just felt tired. "I can't worry about it right now. The most I can hope for is that Felipe and his crew leave for home and we get some peace."

"And Claude and Dermot are gone, to Faery."

"Yep, their own land."

"They'll come back?"

"Nope. That was the idea, anyway. I guess JB is out of a job, unless the new management of Hooligans wants him. I don't know what'll happen to the club now."

"So everything has changed in the past few days?"

I laughed, just a little. I thought of seeing JB strip, looking at the wet chair in Tara's shop, the faces of the babies. I'd talked to Mr. Cataliades. I'd seen Niall again. I'd bid good-bye to Dermot. I'd loathed King Felipe. I'd had sex with Eric. Donald Callaway had died. Warren had lived. Jannalynn had died. Sam had died. *And* lived. I'd worried and worried and worried about the cluviel dor—which, I realized, I didn't have to worry about, ever again.

I was relieved when Sam agreed to spend the night in the spare bedroom across the hall. He and I were both exhausted for different reasons. He was still pretty shaky, and I helped him into the house. When he sat on the bed, I knelt before him to take off his shoes.

I brought him a glass of water for the bedside table.

I moved toward the door, walking as quietly as I could.

"Sookie," Sam said. I turned and smiled at him, though he wasn't looking at me. His eyes were shut and his voice was already slow and thick with sleep. "You have to tell me what the cluviel dor is all about. How you made it work."

That was going to be a delicate conversation. "Sure, Sam," I said, very quietly. "Another day."